SUPERCOIL

ROBERT ARI

U.S.A.

Cover and Interior Design by The Book Cover Whisperer
ProfessionalBookCoverDesign.com

ISBN: 978-1-7338182-0-9

FIRST EDITION

OPERATION DESERT STORM,
IN THE IRAQI DESERT, 230 MILES SOUTHEAST OF BAGHDAD,
JANUARY 1991

Looming apparition-like in the desert heat, the Great Ziggurat of Ur had kept watch long since its magnificent city, the birthplace of Abraham, crumbled and disappeared beneath the Sumerian sands. During the temple's four-thousand years of dereliction, it had witnessed countless invaders in their march through history, the Persians, Alexander, the Arabs and the Ottomans. Now the flames of war advanced again within sight of the temple's desolate terraces: of four flying shadows racing northward, into Iraq.

From beneath the transparent canopy of his F-16's cockpit, Black Squadron commander Jack McDermott gazed intently at the distant ancient monument. No doubt, he thought, the people of the Ziggurat had believed their power to be eternal.

"It sure feels strange flying a Falcon again," Lebrun, his wingman, declared in earnest, immediately recalling McDermott to the present.

"Just like riding a bike, Two," McDermott replied. Though some pilots had to grapple with readjusting to conventional planes after flying stealth for long periods, he remained confident of his elite crew, on this critical classified mission.

The target they were fast approaching was a secret Iraqi site believed to have launched a recent sneak SCUD missile strike on a U.S. base, killing two dozen American soldiers. Their mission was to neutralize this once-presumed dormant site before more deadly volleys were sprung. Lebrun's comment, however, revived McDermott's own curiosity on why their squadron were assigned the conventional F-16 "Falcon", instead of the stealthy F-117, against such heavily defended target.

"Re-check your instruments and mission profiles," McDermott commanded.

Wordless acknowledgments came as Morse-like clicks from the wingmen's transmitters. Following his own orders, McDermott began scanning the various data on his HUD, the head-up display embedded in the canopy directly in front.

Strapped to his left leg in fighter jock fashion and illuminated faintly under panel lights was a clipboard containing mission characteristics and target maps, which he knew by heart.

The target lay inside an embankment designed as a spade, of sandy walls over ten stories high. The brute-force defensive layout was to thwart ground-hugging aircraft, by forcing the invaders to pop-up over 100 feet, which would distort their aim and expose them to anti-aircraft guns placed atop the ramparts at regular close intervals. An access strip followed an axial path inside the sandy diamond, then exited from under the walls to continue for a six-mile stretch to a military airbase.

Positioned at the embankment's four pinnacles were surface-to-air missile batteries. Owing to their longer range and guidance capabilities, these quad of SAM sites posed the most serious threat to his squadron and would have to be neutralized first. The anti-aircraft guns could then be taken out at closer range.

Satisfied with his final preparations, McDermott checked his HUD's readout.

"Coming up on the Squat Eye," he announced, referring to the seventy-miles outermost range of Iraqi air defense early warning radar, with a "Low Blow" missile guider then taking over at thirty miles out from base. The two radars operated in tandem to track intruders, especially the fighter types like his Falcon.

"Roger that," Lebrun replied. "Proceeding to engage."

McDermott watched Lebrun wave a right-hand salute before banking starboard and breaking away. Afterburners engaged, the F-16, in full military thrust, dashed outward in a wide-arc path, closing in on the SAM site at near the speed of sound.

"Radar warning," Lebrun messaged, as his Falcon entered the lethal field of the Low Blow. But the hostile radar's emissions had also divulged its own location. In seconds, its coordinates were pinpointed by the F-16's onboard computer and programmed into a High-speed Anti-Radar Missile under the craft's left wing.

Almost simultaneously, the HARM blasted off its pylon railing and streaked toward the radar source, its computer no longer needing guidance from the Falcon.

One minute later, McDermott saw the Low Blow's radar signal abruptly vanish from his head-up display. But there were three more sites to neutralize, and a single SAM unit packed enough firepower to obliterate his squadron many times over.

With his remaining wingman, Todd Severson, they held on course toward the center of the diamond, while the fourth Falcon, flown by Jimmy Franke, broke formation as planned, speeding westward to knock outs the remaining SAM sites.

Seconds after the strong overlapping radar signatures of all SAM sites were washed away in rapid succession, McDermott beheld the huge sand walls of the Iraqi complex appear on the horizon, leaping towards him at 400 miles per hour. From where the forward SAM site had once been, a plume of smoke billowed into the desert sky, flanked by two shorter stacks, the handiwork of Lebrun and Franke.

As a stream of sharp warning beeps filtered into his helmet, McDermott's gaze shot back to the hitherto uncluttered aerial radar screen: it now revealed five triangular shapes marked red for hostile. They were, to his surprise, a pair of Iraqi MiG-25 "Foxbat" flying in support of three elite—and, in this theater, rare—MiG-

29 "Fulcrum" C. Their sudden two o'clock appearance in a still-gaining posture meant they had just taken off from the nearby airbase.

"Stay in tight formation," he commanded Severson while resisting the urge to engage. "Descend to minimum NOE altitude and maintain course."

The two planes dropped to the lowest safe altitude, of 40 feet above deck, flying at "nap-of-the-earth" and activating the Ground Proximity Warning System only when the altimeter indicated less than 35 feet. At such a low altitude, they would be largely lost to Iraqi radars as ground clutter although they ran the all-too-real risk of becoming a sprawling field of hot metal on the desert floor.

Element leader Lebrun, now flying far ahead of McDermott's pack and without a wingman, was first to come into contact with the Iraqi squadron, which had appeared on his head-up display at about the same time he made visual contact.

Lebrun mulled the eerie swiftness of the Iraqi response in taking to the sky less than two minutes after the destruction of SAM sites. Their pilots, he thought, must have been in their planes already, lying in wait. He made a mental note to report this curious observation upon return, then shifted his attention back to survival.

The quintuplet Iraqi formation had broken into deployments for aerial combat. Two MiG-29s maintained a westerly course, while the third Fulcrum and its pair of supporting Foxbats turned southwards, heading directly for Lebrun, less than 10 miles away. Their dual-pronged dispersion pattern suggested pursuit of only him and Franke. McDermott and Severson remained undetected, for now, and it was up to Lebrun to ensure the MiGs wouldn't spot or engage the trailing attack duo.

At that instant the MISSILE WARNING shrilled in Lebrun's helmet as each forward Foxbat let loose an air-to-air R-73 missile.

In a classic evasive response, Lebrun gunned his engines and rolled his F-16 into a tight descending left turn while ejecting an expanding stream of intensely hot flares from its tail. The pursuing R-73 heat-seeker was respectable but not well-suited for close combat, as only five miles now separated the fast-approaching adversaries. At less than a mile from target, the Soviet-made missiles' thermal trackers became immersed in a mist of bright-heat particles, each registering ten times hotter than an F-16 engine. Confusedly, the missiles detonated.

The ensuing blistering haze persisted for only a few seconds before it burned itself out, but not quickly enough for the forward Foxbat, which had closely followed the path of its own missile. Flying straight into the floating inferno, its air intakes inhaled a half-dozen flares, which ignited the jet fuel all the way to the main tank. The explosion disintegrated the Foxbat in midair.

The aft Foxbat barely escaped the fate of its companion by veering clear of the floating flares at the last second, but by then Lebrun had deftly completed his turn to six o'clock, directly behind his former pursuer and within a few hundred yards. At such close range, he fired his Vulcan three-barrel cannon, riddling the Foxbat with fifteen rounds of 20mm bullets and sending it crashing to the desert.

Peering out at the smoke-filled sky, Lebrun had no visual sign of the third MiG, and his scope was now being jammed. The deadly Fulcrum had vanished.

McDermott witnessed the destruction of the Foxbats on his radar before it, too, blanched with jamming, presumably by the remaining MiGs. No matter, as the sandy diamond was finally in sight.

Ignoring the safety system's protests to a dangerously low altitude, McDermott accelerated his Falcon to near Mach One for a mad dash to the target before easing the throttle upon reaching the 100-foot high embankment, which nearly filled his canopy's view. At this speed, he would have only a split second to react before becoming a permanent fixture in the side of the imposing bulwark.

He yanked the joystick at the precise instant beyond which was certain death and called on the entire 29,000 lbs. of thrust in his Pratt & Whitney engine for a brief after-burner burst. The Falcon whisked steeply up, to a near vertical turn, then shot skyward like a missile, the g-forces kneading him into his seat like putty.

Soon as he cleared the wall, he cut power to the straining turbofan engine, applied his aerial brakes, an act that nearly brought him to a midair halt, and sank the plane's nose just as it dropped back on the other side of the wall.

Glimpsing left, he saw that Severson had successfully followed suit. Their bold low-altitude maneuver had prevented the anti-aircraft batteries from firing at them during the approach or while inside the fortress, for the guns' barrels could not be brought to aim at below their elevated horizon.

The duo steadied their plunging Falcons barely 35 feet above ground, then lit up the TARGET TERRAIN sign on their target-acquisition-and-detection-sight displays. The onboard computer swiftly tallied the live visual sensor data to the presorted surveillance satellite images for an exact match. Together, the Falcons roared along the center road, each plane's targeting computer picking up what it had been seeking to destroy: a section of the eight openings lined with reinforced concrete, leading to an ammunition depot interred under the sandy embankments.

McDermott selected the quad of silos to the right, knowing Severson were to select those to the left. His TARGET ACQUIRED display flashing, he sequentially launched two pairs of specially made 1,000-lb Air-to-Ground laser-guided missiles and felt a mild heave as avionics adjusted engine lift power to reflect the Falcon's now lighter weight.

He had little time, however, to behold the ensued explosive spectacle of their missiles hitting their preprogrammed aim, as he spotted six mobile SCUD launchers directly ahead. They appeared ready for firing, with a phalanx of Iraqi missile officers scurrying toward the control-station trailers.

McDermott swore into his oxygen mask. Flying at NOE he could not target the missiles without raising an inferno directly in their own flight paths. He would have to make another pass, from a higher altitude.

But at that instant the MISSILE WARNING system shrilled again. His gaze swiveled back up the canopy bubble, to see a sole Fulcrum swooping from behind at his four o'clock. A wisp of smoke trailed the hurtling missile it had launched from its right-wing pylon. Had Lebrun been present, he would have recognized the MiG-29 as one that had evaded him earlier. With a locked-on missile in close chase, McDermott had to take immediate evasive action to avert certain death.

Gunning his engines to full throttle, he sent the Falcon lurching forward, rolling slightly to the right, then swiftly peeling up from the belly of the artificial canyon. The result was to suddenly replace his plane with an air pocket in the pursuer's missile guidance system. The R-40 missile was thrice faster but with its stubby tail fins not as maneuverable as the F-16. And it could not pull out of its steep dive in time to avoid ground contact at nearly Mach Three. The impact sent a geyser of sand into the air.

Realizing that Severson was a sitting duck within the sandy enclosure, McDermott broke off his planned exit run and rolled left, climbing to over-fly Severson as the Fulcrum now switched its pursuit to him.

Snaking an aerial scissoring path to evade the MiG's lethal 30mm GSh-30-1 cannons, McDermott piloted his ascending F-16 to clear the mammoth perimeter wall. But once in the open, the MiG also accelerated, finally closing on its prey.

Again, the MISSILE LOCK warning appeared. But before McDermott could apply countermeasures, the Fulcrum burst into myriad blazing shards of metal.

Franke had appeared as if on cue, gaining an angle of zero directly behind the plane and connecting a Sparrow-7 to the MiG's tail pipe before it could fire again.

"That bandit's fangs got sunk in the floorboard," McDermott said.

"You're still way ahead on the count, Captain," the wingman replied.

"Let's hope that was the *last* count. See anything else?"

"Nothing, my scope is still jammed for medium and long range."

"Mine too," McDermott said. "We're almost done here. I'll take one more pass. Break off ground engagements and regroup at the rendezvous point."

"Yes sir," Franke said and banked south with Severson following his new lead.

As McDermott checked his scope in preparation for his last pass, the short-range jamming abruptly resumed. Resorting to a visual scan of the skies, he spotted the electronically undetectable source of the mysterious jamming: a pair of menacing shadows partly eclipsing the sun in their lethal swoop toward his lone F-16.

The remaining two Fulcrums.

Operating from the nearby base, the MiGs must have been fully fueled and loaded with a comprehensive array of interceptor air-to-air missiles. McDermott's F-16, though more versatile, was fitted primarily in ground-attack mode for this mission, packed with mostly air-to-ground missiles for use on the silos. He now would have to mainly rely on his short-range machine gun cannons.

Setting the Falcon's pitch to high-alpha, he realigned the rear stabilizers for a near 90-degree angle of attack, then gunned the afterburners. Throwing the full force of the engine into ascent, he shot the beast straight up in a classic muscle climb zoom, seemingly aiming for a head-on collision with his pursuers.

In mere seconds, the lonely low-flying F-16 seemed to have been transformed into a manned SAM closing on the Fulcrums at over 600 mph. Slim contrail pairs formed behind its wingtips, then fell off gracefully like tumbling ribbons.

Almost instantly, he saw the MiGs let loose a brace of deadly R-40TD air-to-air missiles his way. With full visuals and in a headlong sprint, McDermott needed no instruments to warn him of the approaching danger. But instead of veering away he maintained course and increased speed to near supersonic. The added thrust came like a knock-out punch, but he held on as the pressure of the sharp climb rapidly mounted, sending the vertical-speed indicator gauge off the chart and nearly immobilizing him. Even inhaling of a breath had become a grueling task.

Yet as the missiles drew so close that most pilots would have spiraled into a fatal panic, McDermott's calm situational awareness remained extraordinarily keen. Waiting until the missiles had drawn so close that for an instant, he could clearly perceive details of the Iraqi Air Force enamel painted on the Soviet-built hunters, he jerked his plane out of the collision path.

Flashing past its sleek ventral by mere inches, the R-40TD heat-seekers failed to outmaneuver the F-16. McDermott, knowing full well that this time the missiles did have turning room to re-approach from behind, ejected a half-dozen heat flares, on whose intensely hot signatures the pursuers' trackers locked and detonated.

The two Fulcrums, however, still loomed as the main large objects in view. The MISSILE READY sign flashed on the attack screen, and McDermott launched his only two air-to-air missiles, one locked onto each MiG. At such close range, the far more sophisticated AMRAAMs allowed no time for the lead Fulcrum to evade or counter. One missile sailed into the left air-intake of the dual engine fighter, quickly reducing it to an expanding field of glowing debris.

But the second AMRAAM failed to connect with the trailing Fulcrum, which had veered so to position the lead MiG in the intercept line of both missiles. The explosion of the forward Fulcrum blinded the aft AMRAAM's guidance systems, and tossed it end-over-end like a flicked toothpick, to detonate far from its target.

Now, with no air-to-air missiles left and too distant to fire cannons at a fully loaded MiG, McDermott was down to his last option.

Decelerating in vertical speed to zero, he engaged fly-by-wire and air-braking to deftly pitch the F-16 through the horizon, in a nose-first swoop towards earth. The precisely executed maneuver, the aerial equivalent of a full back somersault, plunged him into a precipitous headlong dive at 20,000 feet.

The Fulcrum pursued in an equally steep dive, now practically in the F-16's control zone, directly behind at six o'clock, the optimal firing position, and closing fast to coming within weapon's range for a lethal serving of 30mm MiG gunfire.

McDermott trained one eye on the altimeter, whose digits, fast rolling toward zero in the straight descend, appeared to have gone haywire . . . 15,000 feet . . . 12,000. . . 9,000. . . Outside the canopy, the desert landscape was welling up at a frightful pace. The tremendous g-forces, accumulated by the mad dives, were taking their toll, as he knew they were surely doing to his pursuer. His blood was being forced down to his body's lower regions and away from his brain, his vision was narrowing, and he was on his way to "g-loc," or total black out.

As the g-forces mounted past eight times normal gravity, he felt the loc coming on. Darkness caved his vision, reducing it to a slender line.

On the verge of passing out, he implemented a final trick, learned in flight school. He tightened his powerful leg muscles, constricting them like a pair of pythons coiling about their prey, and squeezing the blood out of the lower extremities and forcing it up toward his brain.

The ploy restored his vision and mental faculties. A glance at the g-register showed it pass 9-Gs, but he was just getting warmed up, and this time he needed neither guns nor missiles to dispense with his pursuer.

Tugging at the control stick, McDermott sharply leveled out of the dive, at just 300 yards above deck. The same did not happen to the fast-closing Fulcrum. With its pilot blacked-out, the MiG-29 plunged head-on into the desert at nearly top speed, leaving a deep crater filled with twisted, charred metal.

Freed from the MiGs, he quickly rolled towards the embankment, switched his F-16 out of air combat "Dogfight Mode" and readied for ground attack.

Activating the bomb-damage-assessment camera for a live recording of the destruction from his first pass, he dipped the F-16 just slightly into the fortress' lozenge courtyard, low enough to get an accurate cannon fix. He saw the scrambling Iraqi missile crew who had taken full advantage of the respite granted by the Fulcrums' intervention by raising the SCUDs to upright launch position. Another thirty seconds and they would all be airborne, wreaking lethal havoc.

Time was running out.

Sequentially targeting the tail end of each mobile SCUD unit at its booster fuel reservoir, McDermott fired a salvo of machine gun bullets followed by a brace of AGM-65 Maverick air-to-ground missiles as he made a second pass. The aerial fusillade rained on the SCUDs like a fiery maelstrom. Their booster fuel ignited and obliterated the transport trucks, and the crew.

Gaining altitude to clear the southern defensive rampart, McDermott gunned down the last of the Iraqi anti-aircraft artillery on the way out. Now he was finally in the open, his scope operating free of walled interferences.

Yet not all was clear, as his attention was drawn to the left, at the distant eastern air-strip. Its concrete runway gleamed brightly under the midday desert sun though not as intensely as the three sleek elongated figures that were fast converging at its center. Even from this considerable distance, their highly swept-back wings gave them away to McDermott's keen eyes as a trio of MiG-25 model PD, the Foxbat's newer cousin tailored as a dedicated long-range interceptor, the F-14's Soviet counterpart. The Iraqis were planning on giving chase to the returning invaders.

The PDs, rolling in a triangular precision formation, were quickly gaining speed for take-off, when from above an oblong object descended gracefully in a shallow arc to impact the gleaming tarmac less than twenty feet astern of the planes. A dazzling red fireball erupted, then leapt far forward with the immense velocity imparted by its momentum, rapidly expanding to cloak the trio in a fiery blanket. Seconds later, three explosions burst out of the Napalm's infernal cover.

It was Lebrun again. He not only had destroyed three MiGs with one precision-dropped Napalm bomb but had put the airstrip out of commission for the duration of their return flight, ensuring them a safer trip home.

McDermott's sight followed the sleek growing shape of the F-16, till it swung about to pair up with his own. They had survived again, their mission completed.

"Let's go home, Lebrun," he said.

Gunning their blazing afterburners, the duo accelerated to supersonic speed toward their rendezvous with Severson and Franke, and the safety of allied airbase.

Behind them, from the carcass of the Iraqi fortress, smoke columns soared into the sky before bending flat by the high winds that blew incessantly southwards. The looming distorted pillars of black appeared as the tentacles of a dying beast.

McDermott's duo soon caught up to the other at the rendezvous point. The quad ensemble synchronized cruising velocities, reverting to a tight wedge formation at ground-hugging NOE altitude, as they flew toward the friendly Saudi border.

They had completed the mission unharmed, but McDermott was uneasy. He had seen no large explosions from the alleged munitions stockpiles in the silos. They must have been empty. And the only explosions from the SCUDs were of their detonated fuel tanks, not payloads. So why had the Iraqis frantically tried to launch the SCUDs, and in a near suicidal act, sacrificed their precious Fulcrums?

McDermott activated the satellite link to his forward base, then transmitted a summary report on the success of his attack, the lack of evidence for extensive stores of weapons, and no loss to his squadron. It was relayed on a specially encrypted channel that only Major Gorik, his commander, could decipher.

While awaiting acknowledgement, he lifted his target chart, beneath which he had taped a picture of his wife, from their honeymoon, five years prior. He had carried that portrait on all his missions since, as a talisman and added incentive to return alive, to a future life that was inching closer with each passing day. He had sworn to her that this was his last mission. Her memories, however, were dancing with the sensation that something about the events of the last hours did not add up, when the base operator's voice thundered over the satellite link. The words chilled but did not surprise McDermott. "Unit Triple Zero One. We're detecting enemy activity in your return route alpha. Divert to route beta at once. V-base out."

Like a flipped switch, McDermott's mind regained the present, as he tuned the transponder to squadron frequency. "All Elements," he announced, "alpha route unsafe, maneuver to beta route immediately. Set speed to 400 knots to conserve fuel. Radio silence absent emergencies. We're not home yet, so stay alert. One, out." As he banked west, he saw others follow in perfect unison.

The beta route was twice as long as the primary one, on a westerly approach, mostly within Iraqi airspace. Twelve minutes later, they were still over Iraq, with nothing to see but sand. The HUD readout of their ground-hugging flight remained benign, showing only faraway friendlies returning from deep-penetration missions.

At his squadron's current speed, he reckoned no more than six minutes before entering the safety of Saudi airspace. He tried to calm himself by rationalizing away growing prescient feelings of unease, as he sensed a clear, phantom danger.

Then he *saw* what he had *felt* well before his scope registered the fact. The source of the danger was Franke's F-16, flying in the far-left echelon. McDermott immediately broke the radio silence. "Three!" he said sharply, "I'm picking up a signal from underside your cockpit area. Is your radar jammer malfunctioning?"

"Negative," Franke replied. "My scope is—" milliseconds after McDermott saw a missile slam into the fuselage directly beneath his wingman's cockpit, taking the pilot into the void.

McDermott could not dwell on the horrid event, as MISSILE WARNING was now flashing on his own HUD. His gaze dropped to the desert floor, just in time to catch the glistening off a pewter-colored missile-tip soaring skyward. At such close range, the supersonic interceptor zipped past his view frame instantaneously. Immediately to McDermott's starboard, Severson's plane exploded.

Lebrun broke formation, and McDermott rolled his F-16 left as another missile thundered past them. He expected to be next, almost wanted to be next. But he had to try to save Lebrun. He flew out of NOE, to gain altitude for a commanding aerial view of the field, only to be struck by a wall of painful disbelief as he witnessed Lebrun's plane disintegrate. Before him, his friends' planes plunged to earth in three separate paths of smoke and flame.

But there was no time to lament. Outlined by an unmarked camouflage against the bright desert was a sole standing figure holding a shoulder launcher of light surface-to-air missiles. So close had Lebrun's plane been to the figure that the skein plume of a recently fired missile seemed to connect the launcher to its target.

McDermott trained his Vulcan gun cannon on the figure and fired continuous salvos. The powerful swatting blows from the 20mm bullets caught the man squarely in the chest with full force, hurtling him like a cardboard cutout for yards.

To his surprise, the MISSILE WARNING shrill, once again filtered through his helmet. For a moment the deafening blare fused seamlessly with his anguish, and his thoughts stalled as his eyes raced blindly across the defense panels. In his extremity, he reached under the target map for glimpse of his wife's picture, her memory had an instantaneous power, and he pulled out of climb and set for evasive maneuvers as death closed in at Mach Three.

He briefly steadied the F-16 atop the ascend arch before plunging into a steep dive to parry the oncoming missile. The intense heat source of the plane's engine was to be lost to the projectile, causing it to spin out aimlessly till its fuel ran out.

For the first time in his life, the maneuver failed. The missile simply pivoted in midair with a sharp vertiginous turn and resumed course, closing fast on its target.

Ten seconds to impact.

Engaging the infrared counter-measure system, McDermott jettisoned a trail of floating incandescent orbs which would be mistaken for the plane's exhaust by the missile's super-cooled IR sensor. He released the orbs in precisely timed sets of three to multiply the decoy's heat signature. Simultaneously, he cut off power to the engine and let the Falcon drop like a pointed rock in another tight turn.

Yet the missile ignored the dispersed pods' staggering heat sources and remained locked on his plane. With the desert floor once more on the rise, he relit the engine and broke out of the dive at cherubs three with less than 300 feet of sky remaining under the trough. The missile plunged, at first seemingly headed for a ground burst, but then recovered and zoomed up, straight for him.

He suddenly realized why all his IR and radar countermeasures proved useless: the missile was not targeting his engine, but his cockpit! That was why Severson's plane was bulls-eyed in the canopy's underside, just as with the others. But what lay there that the missile could possibly track? No time for answers. The missile was almost upon him, aiming for a direct high-explosive cockpit impact.

With no chance to eject safely clear of an exploding plane, McDermott resorted to a desperate wager. Invoking his superb situational awareness to free his mind of hysteria, he dared to wait a split second before gunning the engines forward, then slamming down the fighter's underbelly against the missile in its final approach.

The missile impacted at once, exploding against the aft underside with a deafening impact, jolting the plane as if rear-ended by a five-ton truck.

His gamble had paid off in saving his life, but the burst crippled the plane nonetheless, tearing into the fuselage and shredding the fly-by-wire mechanisms vital to aeronautic stability and control. The Falcon was spewing debris all over the desert, jettisoning a white cloud of gases and hydraulic fluids like a comet. Without power, all the critical avionics were dying; and as the sole engine failed it was turning his F-16 into a nightmarish proverbial "lawn dart."

He had to eject; no other option remained. Tearing the top target sheet from his leg-strap so that it would be destroyed with the rest of the plane, he discovered in a swift reassessing glance out of the canopy, his dangerously low altitude.

The plane was standard equipped with a zero/zero ejector seat that functioned successfully even when the plane was parked, a precaution meant to save a pilot's life, such as in a fire outbreak while refueling on the tarmac, which made conventional dismount impossible. But whether it could save his life during a near-ground ejection while hurtling 350 mph was another story. If the fast descend did not kill him, the forward speed of his ground impact surely would. The effect would be no different than a head-on collision with a race car going at top speed.

He had to gain altitude.

He steadied the joystick to climb for two more seconds before the fly-by-wire completely failed. The maneuver had gained him only a few hundred vertical feet, still an unsafe ejection altitude for punch out at this speed, but he had no choice. Releasing the joystick, he grabbed the manual ejector handle and pulled with both hands. For a millisecond that felt like eternity, nothing happened. Then the canopy blew away, followed by his seat blasting out into the air.

The hulk of his discarded F-16 swished beneath, frightfully close, the raised tail fin barely missing his neck. At that speed it would have been akin to a two-ton guillotine, tossing his severed head for miles like a punted football. The plane's trailing turbulence caught him next in a dizzying maelstrom that added to his excess momentum. He had become disoriented by the spin, the ground was nearing, his forward velocity could still outrun a Ferrari, and his chute not opened.

Luckily, the pilot seat had not yet detached, and the extra down-weight was helping to stabilize him in the wild gyration. When he had gauged the last possible moment, he released the seat and pulled at the parachute cord. The camouflaged sheet shot up from his back sack, dragging countless white cords with it. He was yanked upwards but was still going forward way too fast.

A boom reverberated from the desert floor. He saw the exploding remnant of his Falcon spewing a thick plume of smoke. Nearby, a military armored personnel carrier—whether friend or foe, he could not tell—was trailing dust. They must have seen his chute and be coming for him, and he had no firearms for defense.

Rhythmically pulling the maneuvering cords, he created a slithering, elongated path to the ground, as he essayed to further slow his descent. The desert still rushed near as he steadily brought his speed to just under thirty-five miles per hour. With one last glimpse ahead, he saw the armored car fast closing on his landing site.

Right before reaching the ground, he put his knees together and rolled into the sand, just as during training when jumping out of a speeding vehicle. But on those occasions no parachute had trailed him. Its cords quickly wrapped around his body as he rolled, restraining his arms and legs. He was hurtling toward an outcropping of rock, but was unable to use his entangled hands, as his head smashed against it.

The last things McDermott heard before darkness enclosed him were the sharp snapping of his neck bones, rapidly approaching footsteps, and cries to which he could not respond.

THE WESTERN TEST RANGE, OVER THE PACIFIC OCEAN NORTHWEST OF SANTA BARBARA, CALIFORNIA MANY YEARS LATER...

Cruising silently against the backdrop of a starry and serene oceanic night, the enormous craft appeared innocuously civilian from most angles. The near-total lack of emitted light save for the faintly reflected glow of a crescent moon imparted to the plane a pale spectral aura. A passenger vessel by contrast would have its fuselage riddled with scores of brightly lit windows, as astral pinpricks. Otherwise, with the exception of a peculiar protrusion on its nose, the plane might have been easily mistaken for one of the myriad commercial leviathans plying the Pacific.

But the craft was oddly off course, flying in an area not frequented by airlines en route to the nearby Los Angeles International Airport. Even more intriguing was the craft's anomalous flight pattern: for the last few hours it had been immured in a wide-arced "figure 8." No plane arriving from Asia would have had sufficient fuel reserves to maintain such curious pattern for so long.

From behind the flight deck's expansive slanted panes, Brigadier General Victor McCane, supreme commander of Operation Sure-Fire, stared into the cockpit, where the dim glow of several navigational instrument panels faintly silhouetted his pilot, copilot, and navigator. They were operating under lights-out conditions for the duration of the test exercise. As if possessing night vision, the crew expertly performed their complex tasks in the near dark.

McCane couldn't tolerate the lack of light or the seemingly interminable wait.

This was the first official testing of the Theater Missile Defense System, or TMD, designed to shoot down a wide variety of enemy missiles, from short-range SCUD to medium-range Valoris. The most sophisticated defensive system in existence, it fully integrated an elaborate space network of launch reconnaissance satellites with ground-based command and control units. But the system had yet to demonstrate its effectiveness under live battle conditions.

If all went well with this test run, a bright future awaited the program, and McCane almost surely would join the most elite level of command. If the test failed, all bets were off.

A voice from the command center indicated all-ready.

"On my way," said McCane. He rushed down the Boeing 747-400's spiral staircase from the upper cockpit level to join the crew on the main full deck. Entering the command center, he squinted: the windowless center was not subject to the cockpit's light-restricting safeguards.

An enormous shielding ahead of the wing attachment completely walled off the command center from nearly two-thirds of the bird's aft portion, save for a small airlock "emergencies only" service chamber. To the front, a similar occlusion by the spiral staircase barred passage to double-decker plane's nose portion directly beneath the cockpit. Overhead, a slender but heavily insulated shaft resembling a support beam ran a direct course between the two bulkheads. The command center, despite accommodating four rows of electronic consoles manned by the highly trained battle management staff, appeared to McCane as if interposed between the two vital organs of a whale.

Leaning against an aft wall by one of the radar scopes was a large man. The sight of Colonel Erwin Gorik, commander of the Black Squadron and currently of the ABL-phase of Operation Sure-Fire, always instilled a sense of unease in McCane.
    "Welcome, General," Gorik said, coming to a slack attention.
    "What's the situation?"
    "All ground units report ready. On your command."
    "Send the launch signal."

WHITE SANDS MISSILE RANGE, NEW MEXICO

The White Sands Missile Test Range, in the Tularosa Basin 250 miles south of Santa Fe, was a near-perfect proving ground. Almost every state-of-the-art missile type in the United States' arsenal, dating back to the 1940s captured German V-2 rockets, had been test fired there. At roughly 100 by 40 miles and surrounded by soaring mountain ranges, the test range occupied a zone larger than the Los Angeles metropolitan area. Yet Colonel Jenkins, commander of the land-based phase of Operation Sure-Fire, knew that White Sands, a thousand miles from the Western Test Range, was far from the ideal launch site of latest Valoris medium-range missiles, as part of the initial testing of the much vaunted TMD shield.
    Jenkins was to oversee the launch of seven Valoris missiles at a designated target 850 miles northwest of their base, about halfway to the Western Test Range.
    "Crap!" he said, almost directly into the launch operator's ear. Using precision-guided surface-to-air intercept missiles, the TMD system was designed primarily to defend against short- and medium-range theater ballistic missiles. These were advanced versions of the legendary Patriot Missiles first used in the 1991 Gulf War, to great effect. But unlike their less-accurate predecessor, which required a launch in volleys to intercept just one target, –TDM's newer Patriot IIs could be launched in singular fashion. Advancements in integrating direct satellite tracking to instant ground cueing had enabled an unprecedented high degree of accuracy in

target acquisition, thus attaining the hitherto elusive perfect efficiency ratio of one missile to one kill in countless prior field tests.

The Patriots II would have rendered a superb performance, but for one problem: the deployment configuration specified a target just outside their maximum effective range. By Jenkins's correct calculations, the Patriots II would completely consume their rocket fuel within a few miles from the seven targets.

"Launch request detected," said the young man, flinching slightly. "Request verified and acknowledged. Standing by for launch approval, sir!"

Jenkins grunted and then took a deep breath. "Issue the launch code."

"Launching missiles. Repeat. Launching missiles."

In the distance where the silo doors had silently opened onto the desert night, there appeared a half-dozen points of flickering light, far-off bonfires whose flames were veiled from view. The missiles were not fitted with their traditionally intended multimegaton nuclear warheads aimed at the inhabited world, but such prospects gave Jenkins shivers nonetheless.

In rapid succession, seven sleek cone-topped cylindrical metal bodies leapt free of their concrete pens, entering the desert night in unison, with a thunderous roar. The blinding flash of the booster rockets immediately followed, as if a salvo of small rising suns had brought a transient, eerie dawn to the remote outpost.

ABOARD THE ABL

"Satellite surveillance detects seven discrete launches in close time proximity," the radar aide announced. "They are coming from the White Sands, sir."

"Right on time," said McCane. "Alert our Ground Unit Two and alter course for interception." The aid promptly entered a series of prestored destination coordinates into the navicomputer, for use by the pilots upstairs.

The whine from the port engines increased insistently, followed by a slight leveling of the deck as the ABL banked right. Breaking free of its interminable double-looped path, the aerial behemoth set out directly for the distant horizon, toward the California coast.

THE PATRIOT II MISSILE BATTERY UNIT, THE NEVADA DESERT, 300 MILES NORTHWEST OF LAS VEGAS

Major Vaughn Adams drank coffee in the command chair of his Patriot II missile battery mobile command unit at Ground Unit Two, somewhere in the designated "intercept zone," a 100-square-mile stretch of desert. His mind had been replaying a recent argument with Gorik, when Johnson, the radar operator, cleared his throat.

"Sir, satellite readout indicates all the TBMs' trajectory as slightly off course."

The major carefully put his Styrofoam cup down and approached the console. "Unlikely."

"They'll miss the zone's perimeter by fifteen miles. See, sir?"

Adams did see.

"Contact Central Command, Johnson. Request guidance."

Johnson spoke briefly into his headset while keying his console. Suddenly, Adams saw the display data change, to a trajectory that now placed the TBMs within range of the Patriots. Without any acknowledgment of this change, the console instructed them to maintain TBMs tracking and to fire when within range.

On Adams's orders, Johnson retransmitted his message.

"Sir," Johnson stammered when the same response reappeared. "Command does not acknowledge a problem. We are instructed to follow our initial orders."

The temperature seemed to have jumped ten degrees in the cluttered cabin.

"Establish direct uplink to the reconnaissance satellite! Compare the two data."

"But sir, that's against orders."

"So was activating the tracking gear ahead of time," said Adams. "It's my job to do everything I must to track incoming missiles. Establish uplink *now*!"

The operator punched a series of buttons. "Uplink established. Data incoming."

Adams stooped over the display. Data briefly flickered on the console, and then the uplink was severed. But in that instant, he and Johnson were able to confirm the first set of data had reappeared and that the TBMs were shockingly off course.

ABOARD THE ABL

"That son of a bitch contacted the satellite," Gorik said quietly. "Why didn't the corrected data get transmitted?"

"He began tracking earlier than we had programmed our computer to initiate data adjustments," said the aide. "I immediately severed his satellite link."

"I will deal with him soon enough," Gorik grumbled. "Message Major Adams: any more violations and he will be relieved of his command."

"Yes sir," the aide replied meekly.

Furious, Gorik's eyes darted across the cramped compartment, seeking focus on something to soothe his growing rage. He let out a serpentine hiss.

Ten minutes remained to intercept.

En route, the ABL had steadily increased its altitude, climbing to 40,000 feet, far above the inland cloud cover blanketing most of western and central California.

As the target area neared with each passing moment, McCane was becoming increasingly distracted, and kept shifting focus to the emergency door of the command unit's aft partition.

Behind that rear wall stood the world's most powerful airborne laser, to which the plane owed its nickname, capable of outputting sufficient energy to shoot down scores of incoming missiles, despite their tremendous speed. He considered a successful field deployment's impact on the military to be as far-reaching as the H-bomb's advent. The rest of the ABL functioned as ancillary to laser's operations, with emphasis on laser-beam control and firing systems, tasked to track, point and fire the laser with the requisite accuracy and strength to shoot-down the targets. The intricacies of such secondary systems were a marvel unto themselves but had paled in comparison to the seeming miracle of an airborne weapons-class laser.

The battle-management staff, shielded from lethal exposure to the reactions within the laser chamber by the massive aft wall, provided the necessary human component. This Boeing 747-400, the largest of its kind in the world, especially fitted with four of the world's highest-thrust turbofan engines, was the aerial platform on which the tremendous weight of the laser and all its peripheral equipment and personnel had been lifted into the heavens.

An astounding feat by any measure, the ABL transcended sheer military applications. Its career-advancing potential was foremost in McCane's mind.

"We're in position now, sir," the navigator announced.

"Resume circular flight pattern over current position," Gorik answered.

"Roger."

McCane recalled yet again that he was in a terrifying position. Knowing little on how to manage such a project, he had placed it in Gorik's hands. If Gorik failed, McCane would take the blame, in a career-obliterating flash.

THE PATRIOT II MISSILE BATTERY UNIT

Johnson felt his forehead contorting into deep furrows as Adams ranted on about Gorik. Yet he knew that after the usual song and dance, his superior would follow instructions. Orders were orders.

"This new data is crap, we will waste seven missiles! Johnson, I want visual confirmation of this clusterfuck! Use your infra-reds and lock onto the Patriots when they approach. Get going!"

Johnson grabbed his goggles and hurried outside. Relieved to escape the windowless metallic post, he scrambled up a nearby hillock for a vantage point on the intercept zone, then put on his IR goggles. In their passive mode, the goggles merely detected radiated heat in the form of invisible infrared beams, then visually translated them into a bright red-bathed image, in this case dissolving the black night into a crimson day.

Johnson could thermally spot objects miles away and even see indication of hotter items encased within cooler ones, like the emanating white infrared glow of the engine under his Jeep's hood. The stifling heat of the mobile command post made it the second whitest spot on his scope.

But he quickly shifted focus to his task, as he glanced at his watch. Its reverse timer, set to a countdown upon the TBMs launch, had almost reached zero. He perused the eastern horizon. And then, as if on cue, appeared several fast-moving brilliant light points: the TBM boosters registering as white-hot blots on his infrared. There were no associated sounds, for the Mach 7 supersonic missiles were approaching faster than their own boosters' propagated rumble.

The TBM's false silence, however, did not fool the radar-driven Patriots II. Sensing the oncoming threat as if by magic, each interceptor missile swiveled in its railed launcher, locked onto a TBM, and blasted into the night sky with a thunderous roar.

Johnson's vigilant sight tracked the path set by the bright soaring plume of each booster rocket, a seemingly erratic pyrotechnical streak which rapidly steadied on a deadly collision course.

ABOARD THE ABL

"Ground Unit Two is launching Patriots," a battle crew member announced, then paused briefly before an update: "all Patriots have been launched to engage the TBMs. Interception in six seconds and counting."

"Can we shoot down all fourteen in six seconds?" McCane asked.

Ignoring his superior's question, Gorik set the automated intercept sequence to engage in three seconds.

The TBM trajectories had been placed deliberately beyond the range of the Patriots to preclude any chance of real interception, so that the destruction of either missile would be attributed unmistakably to the ABL. "Tracking system has verified the targets," the crew member stated. "Firing the primary laser."

A slight vibration ensued on the deck, and the lights flickered slightly. McCane could almost sense the enormous quantity of energy slip behind the aft safety bulkhead, as the now fully powered weapons-class laser unleashed its deadly load via the connector shaft overhead, into the plane's forward beam-control compartment, to align automatically with their targets. From its elongated "laser turret" nose cone housing a rotating 1.5-meter beam-director telescope that focused a laser on target, the awesome lasing power of the ABL sliced out through the sky.

It appeared on the screen as a single massive surge but in fact constituted 14 separate bursts of alternating intensity, all fired inside the merest fraction of a second. Each burst followed the tracking paths delineated by the initial search beam to a TBM or its Patriot interceptor. Traveling at the speed of light, the bursts covered the 250-mile distance to their targets in less than two-thousandth of a second, blasting holes through each missile's metal body directly above the fuel tank and causing the still-unused booster fuel to ignite.

After consecutively executed interceptions, the targeting scope on the battle engagement radar registered a vacant sky. The entire sequence, from the first laser release to the final target's destruction, had taken less than five seconds.

"All targets successfully destroyed," the crew member announced. "Repeat, all targets destroyed."

McCane was unaware that throughout the sequence his expression had remained frozen in disbelief.

THE PATRIOT II MISSLE BATTERY UNIT

Johnson gazed wild-eyed at the silent heavens as if approached by a ghost in the night. His mind could not reconcile the events with what he had expected. Seven intercepting Patriot missiles and their target TBMs, had been destroyed by a series of strange beams, which appeared as long needles of light lashing the horizon.

Though invisible to the naked eye, the beams' blazing hot infrared signatures had registered as ultrafine straight white lines on his scope. They had followed a definite pattern and had struck intermittently.

Johnson set to head back toward the command post, still in deep thought. He reckoned the beams had crossed the over 100 miles from behind the far horizon in a millisecond. He had seen brilliant trails left by shooting stars before, but none were so close to the earth, or left so long a streak or . . . *shot down fourteen missiles with pinpoint accuracy.* As the significance of the event began to set in, he found his pace quickening to a trot and then a run.

TANARIS MILITARY AIRBASE,
IN THE PAINTED DESERT OF ARIZONA,
500 MILES NORTHEAST OF PHOENIX

Tanaris airbase was the headquarters of the Black Squadron, an elite unit born during the height of the Vietnam War. The Squadron was tasked to carry out vital clandestine operations behind enemy lines in any tactical environment, whenever called upon, in peacetime or in war. Far more than a superb batch of fliers piloting top-secret airplanes that officially never existed, the Squadron consisted of men whose virtuosity exceeded that of the most agile and seasoned special-op forces, counterintelligence agents, and electronic warfare experts.

Headed by Colonel Erwin Gorik since 1982, the Squadron, had racked up success after success. Now, decades later, Gorik was the unchallenged commander of the Airborne Laser Weapon program, and Tanaris was the program's assembly grounds. It was from Tanaris that the ABL had set out for the Western Test Range.

This testing was for Gorik far more than just another success. It was a major step towards the fulfillment of a dream conceived decades before, in the aftermath of the Iraq War. The SCUD-attack calamity that had claimed the lives of more than two dozen U.S. soldiers in Saudi Arabia had officially been attributed to a "wholly unforeseeable" malfunction on the older Patriot's guidance computers, a malfunction that had rendered them inoperative at the most crucial moment.

That tragedy, however, had occurred at a time most propitious to Gorik's career, by paving the way for Congress to fund his new antimissile defense system.

Gorik braced as the ABL touched down. With a soft thud and muffled breaking noises, the giant 747 connected with the unlit runway as if landing on the night air and taxied into its hangar. It was soon surrounded by scurrying ground crew rolling a mobile staircase to its sole portal. Gorik watched them as he waited for McCane to precede him out. A small army of technicians then set on a reverse up-stairs course to retrieve laser performance and other data.

It was a typically calm desert night, but Gorik's heavy footsteps tapped a sharp echo on the tarmac. "There's champagne on ice awaiting us, General," he said.

"Then I take it we didn't go over budget," McCane said, laughing.

"Two point one billion dollars. Give or take a hundred million."

"Only 2.1? We had asked for 17 billion. The Congressional Budget Committee should be getting most of their money back then."

"There is no left-over money to give back."

"Come again?"

"We built a super weapon with the rest."

"With the rest? Then what the hell was *that*, Colonel?" asked McCane, pointing towards the doors beyond which rested the ABL.

"A preview." They now stood outside a hangar 100 yards from the ABL's. Gorik pressed his palm against a biometric reader panel, and the authorization light switched to green. A cacophony of screeching metal ensued, and giant doors began to part. In a few seconds they had slid all the way back, allowing moonlight to partly illumine what appeared to be an empty, cavernous space.

"*This* is our super weapon," Gorik said pointing into the darkness. "We'll demonstrate it tomorrow." He modulated his voice to a more pious tone: "on your command of course."

EN ROUTE TO AN UNKNOWN DESTINATION

Leaving a stunned McCane by the hangar, Gorik hopped into his Jeep and drove off into the night. With hands on the steering wheel, he voice-activated a hearing-aid sized device hanging on left his ear and placed an encrypted call by uttering a single name. It was answered at once.

"We had a protocol breach," Gorik spoke without greetings. "Yes, it's *him* . . . see to it that it does not happen again . . . Yes, the usual should do."

Satisfied, the colonel ended the call, his mind already on the eventful day ahead.

THE PATRIOT II MISSILE BATTERY UNIT

Major Adams was slumped wearily in his mobile command unit's steel chair and sipping lukewarm coffee, having tired of pondering on what a startled Johnson had reported upon return.

They were still awaiting permission to leave, at now well past midnight. Adams attributed the delay to his earlier satellite-accessing infractions. Protocol mandated his superiors file reports for later disciplinary inquiries. Nothing was to get done at these late hours, so he assumed they were stringing him along to make a point.

With the unit's noisy heat-spewing instruments now shut off, he was aware of the quiet stillness of the cool desert night.

"I wonder when they'll call," mused Johnson.

At 3:12 a.m., Adams heard the distant rumblings of an approaching vehicle. Minutes later, it had stopped just outside, and left idling. Dry earth crunched under a pair of heavy boots.

In the doorway now stood an unfamiliar figure, his countenance, awash in the moonlight, bore a knife scar running along the left cheek, one that Adams reckoned had come close to blinding him. "Identify yourself, soldier," Adams said.

"You disobeyed direct orders," the stranger replied. "You compromised the security of this project. And your subordinate is implicated."

Johnson shifted apprehensively, but Adams was an old dog in this field. It was not the first time he had been reprimanded, nor would it be the last. He was about to tell the stranger to go screw himself when the man reached into his coat and pulled out a silencer-capped pistol. He swiftly shot Johnson from five feet, and the young man jolted against the wall. Before Adams could reach for his own revolver, he, too, had been shot squarely in the heart.

THE CEMETERY

The secluded burial site lay amid a forest of centuries-old trees that shrouded rows of mostly disintegrating tombstones. It was a forlorn abandoned setting, and hardly ever visited, especially not on such dreary and drizzly day.

Except someone *was* there.

Standing by a newer slab was a stout, broad-backed man wearing a dress uniform of the United States Air Force. His chest was embellished with an array of medals that spoke of unparalleled bravery in combat. With cap tucked tightly between his right arm and torso in a gesture of respect, he stood unmoving as the chilling rain pelted his body by the howling wind. He paid them no heed. They might as well have fallen on a marble statute.

He cast a deep furrowed gaze at the morbid inscription in the obsidian gravestone: *In loving memory of* . . . his mind drowned in an ocean of sullen thoughts of the one whose remains it cruelly covered. His chest heaved, heart palpitating in agony, and feeling as if his every limb was being kneaded with a pressure greater than any high-g flights maneuvers he had ever attempted.

All the stern military trainings, those cold brutal years in combat which had all but inured him to the emotions of death could not stop the rivulet of tears that now coursed their way down his chiseled face and gathered in with the drenching rain. The love for his wife, alive or slain as she now lay buried before him, proved supreme to all, to his very existence. The unbearable anguish had racked his soul and riven his mind, and in that unclear grievous stance each moment felt as days.

The wind whistled through the tree branches in a continuous plaintive dirge as he knelt, gently laying down a carefully prepared bouquet of her favorite flowers. At home he had placed a fresh stem by her picture every day for the past decade since her passing. His fingers touched the smooth contours of the lifeless slab, as countless fond memories of his beloved flashed before him. The happiness was short-lived as the thought of her loss once again gripped at his heart like a vise. He attempted to focus on the immediate future. After interminable grievous years, matters would finally be different. Circumstances had presented a long-sought opportunity to avenge her.

His eyes caught the glint off his donned medals, once a source of great pride and purpose. Now as he sullenly gazed at what lay before him, those shimmering insignias struck him as no more than a collection of worthless molded ores. One by one, he tore them off, gently placing each aside the tombstone. No purpose did they serve him now, there was nothing left to serve a purpose for.

TANARIS

From the air-conditioned comfort of the control tower, a lone McCane watched the tarmac shimmer beneath a blistering desert sun. The hot cement surface was spewing back solar energy as heat, causing the air directly above it to waver in a distorted dance, especially in the proximity of huge closed metal doors of the hangar housing Colonel Gorik's true super-weapon. McCane was reminded of standing tense aboard the ABL's cockpit the night before. Today he would try to remain relaxed even though unimaginable power was tantalizingly close.

He was angry with Gorik for hiding a program of this magnitude from him but should the colonel's even most conservative estimate of the capabilities of this weapon be true, McCane would gladly forgive the deception.

His trance was broken as Gorik entered the control room, followed by a radar operator who promptly took a seat at the radar console. "The bird is ready to fly, General," said Gorik in his usual smug tone. "Proceed," McCane nodded, and the operator picked up the receiver at the end of the direct line to the hangar.

"Y-Bird, this is control tower," said the operator. "You're cleared for take-off."

No reply came, but the hangar doors responsively parted, letting the sun's rays to pierce its cavernous dark interior. McCane followed their course and watched an immense avian object take shape, of a craft so black that it seemed to distort the rays. The plane's diamond-shaped nose was first to emerge from the hangar's confines. A dull gleam off the low-profile cockpit windows followed. Extending immediately from the cockpit were expansive wings that gave the craft the appearance of an enormous arrowhead. To McCane, the mystery plane looked like a familiar B-2 stealth bomber. But he knew that its impenetrably black surface housed unparalleled secrets.

Thunderous booms resonated, followed by the sound of jet engines building up thrust.

"A thing of beauty," Gorik said.

McCane nodded, though its appearance had struck him as hideously sinister. "Brief me again on the mission profile," he addressed the colonel.

"The Y-bird will fly to a classified off-shore Atlantic location near Florida coast, where it will refuel midair as part of the exercise, then turn tail, towards Tanaris, as its intended target. Our job is to detect and intercept the Y-bird before it can reach this base. We have placed the entire radar defense network in the southern United States on high training alert. No one knows of the bird's true nature; their task is simply to identify any bogey on their scope. The Y-bird's pilot is free to choose any route back, and to engage any Air Force 'hostiles'."

McCane's realized that his throat was quite dry. "And we are only simulating its weapon?"

"Yes sir," Gorik said. "We don't want to wipe out the entire air defenses of the southern U.S. in an exercise."

"Amen," the general muttered.

McCane watched in awe as the plane trundled its sleek dark shape to reach the runway, then rapidly gained speed under the enormous thrust of its powerful twin engines and took to the sky. Once its undercarriage had retracted into the black pool of its massive underbelly, the radar signal was lost. Even from the general's elevated vantage point, it was now difficult to perceive the ultra-sleek plane. The once ponderous vessel quickly narrowed in visibility to a thin black line slicing through the heavens, receding against the garish desert sun. And it was gone.

THE AERIAL REFUELING RENDEZVOUS POINT, OVER THE ATLANTIC OCEAN, OFF THE FLORIDA COAST, NORTHWEST OF THE BAHAMAS

"Where the hell is it?" the captain asked his boom operator. His massive KC-135 aerial had arrived at the refueling point well ahead of schedule.

"No sign of her, on any of our scopes," replied Watkins. "Three minutes to rendezvous."

"She's not going to make it," the captain said. "Proceed to the boomer pod."

Watkins hesitated at the seemingly contradictory message.

"Not gonna let those bastards claim we were tardy too!" the captain explained.

Watkins exited directly to the looming upper cargo area. The ceiling lights reflected off the floor railings installed for rapid loadings. His trek along the fuselage to the plane's tail portion ended at the boomer station "pod" which had a curious layout resembling a metallic trench dug five feet deep and dimensioned to accept a prone man. It was not unlike a crypt.

At the pod's base lay a mat, onto which Watkins laid on his stomach. He scooted a bit forward to face a further depression, which housed a large screen shielded by a cover and framed by a series of controls and gauges on its low rim.

The sophisticated gadgetry arrangements were for guiding the fuel boom. The refueling process demanded ample precision since the coupling procedure and the unloading of hundreds of gallons of high-octane fuel from one bird to another at 30,000 feet was inherently dangerous for both planes.

Watkins punched a few control buttons, and the shielding panoply slid aside to reveal the breathtaking panorama of the blanketing clouds beneath. He caught occasional glimpses, through breaks in the cloud cover, of the aquamarine Florida waters far below.

From his aft vantage point, his unaided eyes could take in 5,000 square miles. Another 5,000 miles of frontal view was displayed on his closed-circuit monitor, courtesy of the cockpit crew. And yet there was nothing, not even the slightest contrail trace or wake in the clouds.

"Boys, the Y-Bird is not in sight," he said. "Am I missing something?"

"Negative boom buddy," came the reply. "No visual or radar contact here either. Still got 30 seconds."

"There goes one more for the tardy list," Watkins said.

"Roger that. The captain says sit tight for now. Over and out."

Watkins glanced at the clock panel, and was about to enter numbers in the electronic tardy list when he felt a slight reverberation. To most it would have felt merely as the mildest turbulence, but long years of service in the boom pod had trained his ears to instantly mark the minute differences.

"Son of a bitch!" he exclaimed.

The mystery visitor emerged suddenly, from almost directly beneath the tanker, reminding Watkins of a giant manta ray surfacing from the ocean depths, a huge expansive shape so dark it had seemingly punched a jagged hole into the white matte of lower clouds. It appeared menacing, even to a friendly observer, its strange layout defying all conventional aircraft designs. A jet-black floating wing with no defined fuselage, its wide span nearly extending to beyond Watkin's framed periphery.

He quickly informed the cockpit of his sighting, then after waiting a few seconds till the two craft had attained the flight formation required for contact, he set about the refueling.

Placing his jaw on a padded chin-rest, he reached for the protruding joystick and pressed DETACH. A large, needle-shaped shaft tucked under the tanker's underbelly descended its distal end toward the plane below. The beam sported a pair of mounted ruddevators, small fins jutting out in a V-shaped formation for added aerodynamic stability during refueling. The white boom with its down-pointed tip now stood in sharp contrast to the dark plane below, giving Watkins a surreal impression of dipping an enormous quill into a pool of levitating black ink.

The time had come for the B-2 to fulfill its end of the mating ritual. From that seamless stealth mosaic, a single black tile began to flip to expose on its underside a gray fuel receptacle. It was made oversized to lessen the risk of the approaching boom nicking the surrounding stealth covering.

The flying wing configuration made it easier for the bomber to be caught in the tanker's slip stream. Cautiously moving the joystick by side-swaying his forearm to control the ruddevator fins, Watkins deftly positioned the boom above the receptacle's exact center and mated the nozzle to the bomber's fuel opening locking toggles. The nozzle's safety poppet valve now allowed fuel to flow to the bomber through a hydraulically extended tube.

The planes' matched velocities made the dark expanse appear stationary. With its outboard drag rudders set on slightly open to decelerate for attaining matching speeds, the mystery craft was so close to the tanker that the view screen cropped out the wing's extremities.

Watkins was tempted to initiate his usual pass time chat with the mystery plane's pilot via the intercom wire in the boom, which eliminated wireless eavesdropping, but remembered he was forbidden to contact this top-secret plane.

With 80,000 pounds of high-grade JP-8 fuel pouring steadily into the black bomber at the rate of 1,000 gallons per minute, Watkins used the time to take visual stock of the other plane. As part of the Black Squadron tanker crew, Watkins had viewed countless refuelings by standard B-2s. All the more reason why this one intrigued him. This plane was over 50 percent larger than its siblings but cleverly configured to the originally scaled proportions, which concealed its augmented dimensions from a distant observer. The airfoil appeared as a mere platform for the central cockpit, which bulged smoothly out of the plane's otherwise seemingly paper-thin body and was escorted on either side by huge flat-topped serrated engine air intakes, all, he well knew, for the sake of low radar visibility. The sleek design was studded with articulated control surfaces intricately placed along the entirety of its span, especially the trailing wing edges. And the central bulge protruded higher at the plane's midpoint than on a standard B-2.

On a standard B-2, the cockpit panes were laid in a horseshoe formation and partitioned by vertical breaks for added structural integrity. This B-2, however, had an extra window aft of the horseshoe's mouth: a single perfectly circular translucent piece seamlessly integrated into the plane's smooth curvatures, but tinted darker than the discrete cockpit panes, and almost indistinguishable from the black stealth covering. That explained why he had not noticed it immediately. Watkins guessed it as a canopy for shielding surveillance equipment. If there was an identical feature on the craft's underside, he would have to change his mind.

Every pass exposed more oddities and nuances to his expert eyes.

Then a brilliant flash burnt into those remarkable eyes, turning off the outside world as though he had blacked out. When he opened his eyes again, the pain was intense and he could see nothing, not even his waving hands. Then the searing sensation returned. Whatever had hit him first struck him again, this time with far greater force, pulsing through his brain at unbearable levels. His body quickly went limp and sank lifelessly into the bench seat.

Less than a minute later, in the tanker's cockpit, the fuel-transfer gauge petered to a halt after its initial mad-dash increase in digits. With fuel transfer completed, the detachment signal switched from red to green as the mothership automatically broke off its umbilical cord.

And then something else also happened.

Temperature sensor readings on the boom suddenly began to rise. No controllable source of power known to man could have produced such high release rates of energy in so focused an area in midair.

Then the boom's lower segment broke loose along a glowing hot incision line, its heat igniting the conduits now exposed residual fuel. Fire quickly raced up to the plane's main reservoir, still housing 223,000 gallons of JP-8. Within seconds, an inferno had engulfed the tanker.

An enormous aft explosion then blew its way along the plane's keel, sweeping from stern to bow and into the cabin, pulverizing the massive craft. The blast was so powerful that for a brief moment, and at close range, it seemed to match the intensity of the far-away sun.

Exposed to such brilliant ephemeral luminous source, an ominous flickering shadow was cast on the lower clouds, that of an even darker craft, receding rapidly across the ocean, to the East.

TANARIS,
THE OPERATIONS ROOM

"We must notify the president at once," McCane snapped, hoping to elicit a concerned response from Gorik, who perversely seemed perfectly composed.

Since the news of the refueling incident 12 hours prior, McCane had crashed into despondency when the rescue teams found no survivors, from either plane.

"No," Gorik's replied, unperturbed. "This is not a 'situation', yet."

"Not *yet*?" said McCane. "The mightiest weapon in the world has disappeared!"

"To an outsider, we've lost only a conventional B-2. Remember: no one knows ours even exists," Gorik said evenly.

"But the Executive Order! The B-2's disappearance also means the loss of a thermo . . ."

Gorik cut off his superior. "The E.O. is limited to *weapons*. Besides, we have no proof of foul play."

McCane fell silent, but visibly indignant.

"Please, General," said Gorik, in a suddenly soothing tone. "Before any rash moves, let us first obtain the proof that the bomber also went down in the Atlantic."

"How are we supposed to do that without compromising secrecy? This is not 1986, and we are not in Northern California." McCane was alluding to an infamous fatal incident in which an F-117 Stealth Fighter crashed into the forested Sierras and disintegrating. Due to ultra-high secrecy surrounding the then-black-classified fighter and its revolutionary stealth skin, a specially assembled team promptly cordoned off the crash site along with miles of adjacent land. For three weeks the team painstakingly scoured the grounds, collecting even the tiniest pieces of the F-117's strewn radar-absorbing material. Such a land-based undertaking would be a cakewalk, thought McCane, compared to the daunting prospects they now faced.

"We don't know how intact the plane's structure and its internal secrets may have remained," McCane explained. "And the Black Squadron has virtually no naval presence to do an underwater search. Plus no one in the Navy we can trust knows squat about stealth planes."

Gorik seemed to ponder these statements. "We will handle it covertly."

"How so?" McCane asked, feeling coddled. Gorik had been all too happy to leave his superior out of the decision-making process.

"There are tons of unconventional commercial deep-sea activities off of Florida, like crazy enterprises looking for lost gold of sunken Spanish galleons. We can unobtrusively send down a stealth expert, disguised as a civilian, to distinguish between the debris to see if any are of the B-2. We then analyze the data and submit a detailed report to the president."

McCane felt sure that Gorik's plans were designed to help his subordinate save face. "Who do you have in mind as your 'expert'?" he asked.

Gorik rubbed his chin. "Deep sea diving can be risky, and I can't lose more crew members at this point. But what about Ryson?"

"Major Ryson?"

"No. The other one . . . the lieutenant."

"You mean *Ian* Ryson? Our ex-military outside consultant?"

"Yes, and he would be perfect," Gorik said. "He was a part of the 1986 search team, but now is civilian enough to go unnoticed. Besides, he is most familiar with this plane, even if he doesn't know it actually exists," Gorik's face broke into one of his disconcerting smiles.

McCane felt a swell of appreciation for the sinister genius lurking behind those dark eyes. Once again, he was glad to have the wily colonel on his side during a dangerous time, even though Gorik was often also the cause of his problems.

"I'll set things in motion," said the general, reaching for the phone.

BRIGHTON, COLORADO, FIFTEEN MILES NORTH OF DENVER

The clanking of metal keys on a door broke the quiet of the empty one-bedroom suburban apartment. The front door was quickly unlocked, and a figure entered.

The figure did not bother to turn on any lights as he set for the kitchen refrigerator door. Squinting in the fridge's internal lights, he reached for a beer can, popped it open, and took long pulls from the aluminum container.

When the last drop of the malted amber liquid had washed down, he let out a sigh. He had felt badly in need of this infusion, after yet another interminable day at the engineering plant. He was beginning to think about his evening when the phone rang—a shrill in the dark. He hoped the call to be from Kathleen, his long-time girlfriend. No matter what hell he had gone through the day, he would at least have the pleasure of talking to her each evening.

He was disappointed, however, to see a private number on his display.

"Ian Ryson speaking," he answered.

"Lieutenant, this is Major Murray."

Ryson froze, a long pause that was noticed by Murray, who then read off his authentication code to put his mind at ease.

"Listen Ian," the voice filtered in. "The big guy wants you to report to contact locale in one point eight hours. There has been a . . . development."

Ryson's ears perked. "How dire?"

"Code Red."

"Good God!" Ryson exclaimed.

"Hurry! Study the mission's packet that my crew gave you," the major urged.

"My *mission*? What crew?" Ryson began, but the major had hung up.

Suddenly the lights in the living room clicked on as if by themselves. The lieutenant froze at the sight of three men in trench coats sitting on his sofa. They had been there all along, one had buttoned his coat halfway, and Ryson caught a glimpse of a holstered standard-issue automatic.

"At ease Lieutenant," called out one of the men, who then approached to display his clearance badge.

Ryson exhaled in relief.

"You arrived forty minutes later than usual, and we didn't want to attract unwanted attention by standing outside."

Ryson nodded. "Got a name?"

"Corporal James Dorn, from the Internal Security Unit." He saluted. "It is my duty to see that you are safely delivered to the major, and," he added, "on time."

Recalling drill exercise during his days in the Air Force, Ryson headed directly to the bedroom. He pulled out a large duffle bag from under the bed and packed it full of all essentials in under a minute. The men were already waiting outside.

"Where's the packet?" he asked.

"You'll get it on the flight over. Security reasons," Dorn explained.

"Let's go then" Ryson commanded.

ABOARD THE MILITARY TRANSPORT

Before breaching the seal on the packet provided by Corporal Dorn, Ryson had followed protocol by waiting for the small transport plane to first lift off the runway. Inside the manila envelope he found a thick wad of briefing documents beneath a military version of a cover letter.

Ryson had already surmised most of the situation. Murray's categorizing the event as Code Red meant a weapon of utmost strategic value had been lost. And as an expert on stealth technology, Ryson would be called on only if the loss involved a stealth craft, as had happened back in 1986, in the Sierras.

Except that the earlier event had been marked as Code Yellow, meaning no strong possibility of foul play, and the crash determination had been limited to the finding of holes in the aerodynamics envelope of the stealth craft. Code Red, however, denoted that foul play was suspected, and if confirmed the situation would graduate to Code Black.

Thus far, nothing above Yellow had sprung its ugly head in the history of stealth. It be his job, if possible, to bring proof that a Code Black should be averted.

Always a superb reader, in minutes Ryson had digested the packet's contents: a scattershot collection of hastily assembled pages stamped TOP SECRET, which had obviously once been a presentation to high-ranking officials, presumably in the Pentagon. The contents revealed, in relatively scant detail, specifications and schematics of a B-2 stealth bomber, which Ryson knew by heart. Except that this bomber was coated with a new generation of radar-absorbing materials.

The dossier must have originally contained over 50 pages, as evidenced by the gaps in the sequential page numbering. Curiously, his hastily redacted version contained less than 20 pages.

Before long he figured out the object of that purge: the weapons capabilities of the B-2. This struck him as odd, since although a B-2's payload capacity was justifiably classified, the types of bombs it could carry were well known. Ryson attributed the purge to the rampant secrecy paranoia surrounding the Black Projects. He glanced at his watch. They would arrive in Austin in nine minutes. Whatever questions he had would be answered soon enough.

Or so he hoped.

JEFFERSON AIR FORCE BASE,
AUSTIN, TEXAS

The camouflaged jet silently dropped landing gears and gracefully touched the tarmac at the military airbase, then taxied to a stop at the far corner of the runway.

A jointed metallic ladder unfolded beneath the fuselage's now opened main door, followed by the descending figures of Ian Ryson and a trio of escorts who made their way to the inside of a bulky communication trailer parked at the edge of tarmac. Ryson saw the trailer's cavernous interior was packed with all sorts of electronic instrumentation. There was a crew of about a dozen men.

Corporal Dorn led them to a door on the back wall displaying the placard "Unit Commander", then had only Ryson enter the office compartment.

A decorated officer sitting behind a desk promptly greeted the lieutenant.

"Major Murray, sir!" Ryson saluted his superior.

"At ease son." The major pointed to a leather chair across his desk.

Ryson took a seat, as Murray reached for his small office fridge to pull out a couple of beer cans, then tossed one to Ryson. The lieutenant greedily popped the top open and was halfway done with the contents before feeling uneasy for swilling in front of his superior officer.

"It's okay, Ian," the Major said. "I would be a little nervous too now." A moment of awkward silence followed before Murray got down to business.

"I assume after reading the packet you still have many questions."

Ryson nodded.

"This project is under tight wraps. Even *I* do not know most of its details. So get used to not having all, if any, of your questions answered. Understood?"

"Yes sir." Ryson was starting to feel butterflies again. Murray was known for not disclosing a mission's potential dangers to his men, but something else was eating at Ryson—a sensation he had been struggling against for years. "Why bring me here with such urgency?" he asked. "I assume it be weeks till the plane's parts are brought ashore for me to examine."

"It's not wise to assume so much, Ian," Murray said, then leaned closer, continuing in a fatherly tone. "*We* expect you to partake in the initial recovery."

"You must be joking!" Ryson said with trembling voice, for going underwater was one of his most powerful phobias—and one he could never confess. "One man cannot recover an entire bomber's worth of disintegrated crap. I'm a specialist in airborne stealth, I don't know squat about underwater garbage collection—"

"Relax Lieutenant," Murray said. "Your task is mainly to observe." Then he adopted a more commanding tone. "You will scour the seabed for strewn stealth materials, and we'll send in an ocean scrubber to clean the area. The only thing we want recovered is the tanker's boom."

"But the boom tells you nothing useful on the stealth craft!" Ryson exclaimed.

Murray pulled out a small tape recorder from his drawer, adjusted the volume to so low that only he and Ryson could hear, and pressed the play button.

The tape played back the last transmission made by the pilot of the ill-fated KC-

135 aerial tanker, moments before it disintegrated in flight. Ryson could hear the pilot's frantic voice referencing the tremendous temperature buildup in the boom, the resulting fire, and mention of the unknown status of the stealth craft, code named "Y-Bird." The tape ended abruptly, the pilot cut off in mid-sentence, presumably at the moment the explosion blew the plane apart, killing all aboard. A few more seconds of static followed before Murray turned the recorder off.

"You *do* remember this is a Code Red situation?" gazing intensely at Ryson.

"Yes. But why me?" Ryson asked.

"Because you're the only one who can do the search without compromising the stealth project. Hopefully, you'll find the stealth plane intact as well. Any more questions, Lieutenant?" he asked, slamming a drawer.

"Yes, one more."

The major sighed. "Shoot."

"All sections on the craft's weapons capabilities were excised from my packet."

"So?"

"Is there something down there still ticking, waiting to go off, especially if something gets too close—say a manned undersea vessel? If I didn't care for my life outside of military, I would have stayed with the Arizona group. . ." Immediately, Ryson regretted mentioning this sour memory.

Murray leaned forward, in what looked to Ryson like an unconvincing bit of stage play, and whispered. "No, the plane poses no such threat."

When Ryson did not immediately respond, Murray said, "you will report to our base near Fort Pierce, Florida and undergo training in the operation of the underwater recovery unit. You'll be ready to go in no more than three days. There are some men next door who can fill you in further."

Ryson was mulling a new protest, but Murray had already gotten up to show him the door.

"As I said, Ian, nothing for you to worry about. Just bring back the damn boom."

The door opened onto the trailer's main compartment, where the security detail was waiting. Ryson cast a resentful look at Murray and made his way to the adjacent room.

This second compartment was also a relatively large space, with a sizable middle white table, ringed by four figures poring over scores of maps and schematic diagrams. The sound of shutting doors caused the quad to look up, almost in unison, half-startled, like men coming out of a hypnotic trance.

The youngest of the group, dark-haired and evidently in his mid-twenties, was the quickest to welcome the newcomer. "You must be Ian Ryson," he said cheerily. The others only directed an interested gaze toward the lieutenant.

"Yes I am," Ryson replied. "And you are. . . "

"Arthur Tafstein" he said. "And this," pointing to the figure wearing a Navy uniform, "is Captain Donald Hadley."

"Glad you are here, son," Hadley said.

Tafstein next turned to the other figures, introducing a middle-aged man wearing thick glasses as Dr. Beckman, the aircraft crash expert, and then a much older figure in his early sixties sporting a white beard as Professor Carl Maxim, the material science guru. Both men greeted the lieutenant the same way as the Naval officer: with an air of gloom.

"Captain Hadley," Beckman explained, "is in charge of the mission's naval planning and operations, to make sure the area is secure from any unauthorized underwater sea vessels."

"You can count on it," Hadley growled.

"Professor Maxim is our Air Force affiliate expert," Beckman continued, "to tell us if a failure in the composite material of the plane was the culprit. Arthur is his assisting graduate student from the Air Force."

In no patient mood, Ryson opted for the direct approach to speed things up.

"What are your mission plans?" he asked Hadley point-blank.

"My team is already in place," Hadley started, an air of naval discipline manifesting in his tone. "We have chartered an unmarked civilian deep-sea exploration vessel, to attain our goal of maintaining anonymity.

"This ship carries a state-of-the-art underwater vessel that can be submerged from its internal bay, undetected," the naval officer further explained. "The vessel can operate just yards above the ocean floor. If any item of interest is spotted, the patrolling mothership can be positioned to retrieve it via an onboard crane. All the necessary preparations for your mission are thus done. Except for your training."

"How many crew can that vessel carry?" Ryson asked. Hadley's mention of the depth to which he would be descending had given him the shivers.

"Two."

Ryson felt relief in not going alone. "Where is the boom's tail?" he continued.

Hadley strode toward the far wall where a large physical oceanic map hung that contained the natural terrain features of the underwater area off the Florida coast, displayed on the precise multi-colored computer printed layout. Somewhere in its center was a crudely hand-drawn dotted perimeter, delineated in the shape of a slender triangle extending eastward, with a red "X" at its westerly most apex.

"The 'X' here marks the tanker's last proximate location," Hadley went on. "The dotted lines enclose the eastward extending triangular area that is the debris field, where we suspect the boom is likely to be found."

Ryson checked the map's scale and performed a quick mental calculation to arrive at a rough estimate of its expanse. The results were not encouraging.

"That's over fifty square miles of seabed, Captain. Can you narrow it down?"
Hadley cast a silencing look at Ryson, as if he had just spoiled a surprise.

"Mr. Tafstein has calculated a more precise estimate of the boom's location,"
he said, gesturing the graduate student to approach the board.

"Thank you sir," Tafstein started timidly on elaborating the debris field's
abnormal geometry. "The debris field is not circular since this explosion occurred
aboard an airborne plane travelling at two hundred mph. The boom's momentum
and trajectory then took it both downward *and* forward, to impact the seabed about
thirty miles east of the incident location."

The graduate student fell silent, as did the rest. Each man had his own stake in
the outcome of this uncertain assignment, and all hopes rested on the performance
of a man who, deep down, was the one least interested in the matter.

"Well, what are we waiting for, then?" Hadley asked, trying once again to get
things underway. "Let's go take a look!"

"There is only one problem, gentlemen," Tafstein said calmly. Ryson already
knew what was coming: he had recognized the problem when he had analyzed
where the far end of the estimated enclosure fell. "The tanker debris field," Tafstein
explained, "is at the edge of an underwater plateau which precipitates to a creviced
ravine whose depth is well beyond the safe limits of our exploration vessel."

OVER THE GULF OF MEXICO,
EN ROUTE TO FORT PIERCE AIR FORCE BASE, FLORIDA

Sheer terror. That is how his ravaged mind grappled with it—as words, as a
concept, as a feeling and an image, not as the gruesome details of an event that had
become selectively obscured by the utter force of anguish they had brought down
on his soul. His life had never been the same after the accident. Such an easy thing
to say, but a reality that was extremely difficult to grasp and accept, and even
harder to explain to others.

But sometime, he would remember, and the stage was always the same: he
would be out for a pleasant stroll, and suddenly sheer terror lay ahead, gaping in
his path, like an abyss. He would try to veer off the path, but to no avail. And in
that interminable fall into utter despair, there was nothing to grasp for. With each
descending moment some dismal memory of that day would flash before his eyes
as he continued the plunge into oblivion, *falling, falling, falling* . . .

Then, as his mind touched the extreme nadir of unbearable anguish beyond
which could only lay the depths of Hell, he would come to a bone shattering halt,
as if caught in an invisible web whose unforgiving threads nearly tore him asunder.
He knew that this was merely a prelude, however, to an even deeper plunge unless

he could find his way back to the surface.

Through sheer will he would commence the arduous, excruciating, and seemingly endless climb from that well of despair. With every bone in his body shattered, he would cling to the thorny vines within his grasp, pulling himself up until he had made it back to daylight.

There he would lie prone, gasping for air, drenched in sweat, wondering if the ground beneath might gape once more to devour him for good. He knew that he had to get up and run, to fast flee the forsaken spot. But this time something was holding him down. He struggled to break free, but his efforts were stymied, as if he were being kneaded in place by a pair of giant hands. And there were voices, far away at first, but rapidly drawing closer, getting louder. Someone repeatedly calling a name, *his* name.

"Ryson! Lieutenant! . . . Lieutenant Ryson!"

Sunlight poured into his peripheral vision as the trance faded, and at last reality registered. Directly in front, a pair of eyes focused on him, and large hands were firmly palmed around his shoulder blades. It required great effort to extract that face from memory and associate it with its proper name and owner.

"Are you alright, sir?" The man asked.

Ryson was still nonresponsive. Then it all came back to him: he was on a flight to Florida, on a mission . . . these men were the assigned security officers.

"Corporal . . . Dorn?"

The man nodded and repeated, in a tone of concern, "Are you alright, sir?"

"Er... yes," Ryson replied. Sweat was dripping from his face.

Dorn released his grip and handed Ryson a paper towel. "Can I get you anything, Lieutenant?" he asked.

"Said I'm okay, damn it!" Ryson snapped. He now realized he had never before been awakened from the recurring nightmare. It had always come to its own end. He noticed his abrupt response had taken the guards by surprise as well. Even the burly man in the distance appeared to take a step or two back toward his seat. Only Dorn held his ground although Ryson sensed the fear in him, too.

"I'm sorry to have disturbed you, sir," Dorn apologized. Ryson tried to calm his nerves first as he dried his face with the paper towel. "I guess I was dreaming," he said. "Must have been that steak and potato lunch before the flight. Tell me corporal," he inquired of Dorn, "what exactly was I doing that made you react?"

"Ah ... nothing really sir. I must have overreacted."

"I asked you a question, Corporal."

"Well," Dorn replied with reluctance, "it all sort of happened very fast. You were reviewing some documents when I saw you close your eyes. Next thing you know I noticed unusually heavy breathing, and your face was perspiring profusely." Dorn reticently paused. "And … shaking … as if from lots of pain—"

"It was just a fitful sleep," Ryson said curtly, then looked down and found his right hand clutching the report he had been reviewing. The pages were crumpled under his coiling fingers and were blotched with dripping facial sweat that had distorted the fine lettering.

Ryson was profoundly upset. An old nemesis he had nearly written off had struck again after a long absence and with full force. Worse, he had been unable to withstand it. He had been struck during a nap and had come out only with the unexpected help offered by the corporal. And it had happened in the middle of an important mission. What if the episode was to reoccur during a self-piloted flight, or his upcoming deep-sea exploration, would he survive?

He gazed out the plane's oval window, over the calm waters of the Mexican Gulf and felt something there tugging at him, like an invisible rope yanking him down, to his death.

SOMEWHERE ON THE FLORIDA COAST

"Careful! Don't pull the control stick; just nudge it!" cautioned William Markins, the unsuspecting civilian instructor hired covertly by Hadley's crew to train Ryson in navigating undersea. Fair haired and in his forties, Markins had operated underwater pods since turning sixteen, with an impeccable reputation to match.

"It might send too much power into the turbofans," Markins went on, "and kick up an obscuring seabed dust cloud. Next thing you know, boom! You've blindly hit a rock outcropping and water is gushing in. So long, sailor!"

"Noted," Ryson said with suppressed irritation. "But enough with the dismal scenarios."

The event pretty much summed up their interactions over the past three days in the tiny training pod. Markins would immediately jump on Ryson's rare rookie navigating mistakes with the most depressing possibilities he could think of. Still, Ryson had never ended up making the same error twice, but the unsettling comments kept pouring forth.

Markins, sitting in the navigator seat of the small submersible barely fit for two men, took his eyes off the instruments, and swiveled his chair to face his unnerved pupil. "Sorry, buddy," he half-apologized, "this could be a very dangerous machine in the depths. No second chances most of the time."

"I appreciate the concern," Ryson said. "But you shouldn't mentally paralyze your trainees." Ryson was claiming to be a vacationing Midwest elementary school teacher who had never gotten the chance to explore deep sea. Markins had already told him that he was mastering things in a few days that usually took others weeks.

The depth meter read fifty feet underwater, the most they could descend in their confined learning pool. But the onboard computer ran simulations that altered the outside sensor readouts to conditions encountered at nearly twenty times that depth, or roughly where Ryson had claimed he would be going. None of the dangers Markins had cautioned threatened them here. But in a few short days. . .

"Outside pressure at 900 lbs. per square inch," Ryson read the simulated data.

"Underwater turbulence?" The instructor quizzed.

"None. The sonar is also clear of any vessels in the area."

"Your instrumentations handling is phenomenal Mr. Dunaway," said Markins, addressing Ryson by his undercover name, "but remember that knowledge alone does not substitute for real-life experience, and can even cause overconfidence."

A silent moment followed before Ryson replied. "I promise to be very careful."

"Then our work here is done. Take her up to the surface if you please."

Ignoring feelings of excitement in finishing his training, and fear of what lay ahead, Ryson gently nudged the lever, buoying the pod upwards.

SECRET COMMAND LOCATION,
NEAR FORT PIERCE AIR FORCE BASE, FLORIDA

"What do you mean I have to go underwater *alone*?" Ryson protested in disbelief.

But Captain Hadley, who had flown in the day before, would not budge. "Ian, you know the regulations," he exhorted. "No civilians are to board that vessel. And the only guy on this side of the Mississippi with that high a clearance and underwater training is you."

"The success of this mission is paramount to a stupid clearance," Ryson shot back. "I'm just not sure I can operate that thing by myself."

Hadley raised a quizzical eyebrow, as he waved out a file he was holding. "According to this instructor's report, you received the highest grade of any of his crash-course students, *ever*."

"Captain, running predetermined simulation maneuvers in an enclosed training area with an instructor present is one thing. I just don't think it's wise to send one inexperienced man on this mission at where we are taking this vessel. Markins is far better trained than me."

"Yes, and he's also a civilian," Hadley quickly pointed out. "This is not some god-damn gold hunt, Lieutenant. It's a top-secret military mission . . ."

"Which now has a high risk of failure," Ryson interjected, exasperated with the talk. "Can't we get him a temporary clearance?"

"Lieutenant, I'm a Navy captain, and even *I* can't get clearance for this mission. You expect I tell Major Murray a civilian instructor is better qualified than me?"

So that's it, Ryson thought. Of course. Hadley would feel humiliated if Markins somehow got clearance to go. But what the captain didn't realize was that if Markins didn't go, there was a fair chance the recovery effort too would end up at the ocean floor, permanently. The thought didn't comfort Ryson, since he'd be left on the bottom with the rest of the detritus.

TANARIS,
THE OPERATIONS ROOM,
ONE DAY LATER

Gorik turned his attention away from the vast office windows overlooking the bustling airbase to face McCane, who had just gotten off the phone with Murray.

"Ryson is being prepped to go down," McCane said worried, his hand on the receiver. "We've lost enough men, don't want to lose more in this recovery effort."

"It might not be a bad thing for the program," said Gorik, leaning back.

McCane nodded vaguely, as usual unhappy with Gorik's failure to reassure him that his plans were noble.

If the plane was found in the ocean's depths, the analysis of the wreckage might reveal design flaws that could require years to remedy before a replacement airworthy prototype was built, a clear setback for McCane. And if the plane was not there at all, then countless other problems arose, most notably foul play notions requiring presidential involvement, which he dreaded the most of all.

McCane had to admit that the best alternative might indeed be for Ryson to find and report the bomber as intact but would still fail to survive the mission. Only then could Gorik argue that the bomber had crashed for reasons other than lack of air-worthy design and order immediate construction of a replacement. He loathed the thinking that a loss of life was acceptable collateral. It was a ghastly affair, but one about which the likes of Gorik would have no concern.

Suddenly, McCane shuddered.

ABOARD THE SEARCH VESSEL,
OFF THE FLORIDA COAST

"Mother One, this is Orbiter One, do you copy?" Ryson spoke into the headset.

"Roger, Orbiter One, we hear you loud and clear," the command center replied from deep inside the surface vessel. "Your communication link and subsystems are working perfectly. All checks out on redundancy error detection up here."

"I am ready to proceed then," Ryson confirmed.

"Orbiter One, you are cleared to submerge. Good luck, Lieutenant."

A red flashing warning light bathed the internal bay, directing all crew to leave the cavernous enclosure. Ryson observed the last of the departing technicians raise an encouraging thumbs-up in his direction, then step outside the bay.

The main access door closed with a loud metallic *clang*, followed immediately by sounds of sea water rushing into the closed compartment from the internal ducts. Ryson suppressed his apprehension in watching his small vessel get rapidly buried in the aquamarine haze. He tried not to think of live burials, however close the analogy might be, but forced himself to concentrate on the instrument readouts.

A green light lit up on the console, indicating that pressure on both sides of the internal bay had equalized. In silence, the artificial bay's large metal gate then slid aside, revealing the dark, seemingly bottomless water pit that was the Atlantic Ocean. The sight terrified Ryson with evoked nightmarish thoughts.

Taking a deep breath, he released the pod from its restraining pylon into the depths below, and exiting the portals and the protective innards of the mother ship.

The descent was uneventful: an almost direct plunge to the abyss, like a sinking rock, with Ryson monitoring the depth meter for the distance left to absolute bottom. He kept his head down, focused on the displays, hoping it might help him overcome his fear.

Despite a flawless handling of the pod's navigation, he pretended that Markins was sitting behind him and bent intently over the screen, as he had been so often during the simulations.

After nearly fifteen minutes of virtual freefalling down to 1,300 feet, the pod's proximity sensor blinked to life by the rapidly approaching ocean floor. Ryson immediately fired up the electric engines that drove the upturned propellers and brought the craft's descent rate to a dead halt just a few yards above the darkened seabed. Then for the first time since leaving the confines of the mothership, Ryson forced his eyes up, to gaze out the submersible's plexiglass canopy.

He had half-expected to be greeted by a magnificent underwater view of clear Florida waters, like those in tourist magazines. To his disappointment, however, the scenery outside the transparent shield was one of darkened emptiness. In every direction, the ocean floor appeared both anticlimactic and terrifying, as if he were standing face to face with oblivion.

The environment bore heavily on him, and, for an instant, visions from the nightmare were evoked by a brain that had descended to the dark depths against its will. Ryson suddenly found himself struggling to maintain control over his senses. If he lapsed into the nightmare now, here in the deep, it would all be over. He felt a cold sweat gathering on his forehead and frantically set to work, sending his nearly galvanized right hand flying for the light switch, flicking it to ON.

At once, the pod's powerful outside floodlights came to life, replacing oblivion with a view suffused with luminance. His mind reacted positively to the change. There was now a perception of depth in the forward scenery, which no longer resembled a confined, dark pit. His breathing grew less strained as he forced his focus back onto his assigned tasks.

He reached for the centrally located joystick, which among its other functions, served as the pod's high-tech steering wheel and accelerator. The control rod reminded him of the Hands-On Throttle and Stick used on fighter aircraft, as it proved equally responsive to his application of pressure. He gingerly nudged it.

A slight vibration followed as the craft moved slowly forward, wading through the waters and steadily gaining speed to a preset cruising velocity. Ryson punched the destination coordinates into the onboard navicomputer, all the while keeping his vision glued to the graphic display that would guide him to the downed tanker.

The journey to the debris field went smoothly, save for occasional interruptions by undercurrents that required manual engine adjustments. Still, Ryson was on high alert. The undercurrents reminded him of the notoriously unpredictable high winds he had often coped with during his flight days. At any instant, he knew, as Markins had often explained, the currents might sweep him into their turbulence without warning.

He was able to control his thoughts and kept the nightmare at bay all the way to target. Thankfully, Tafstein's estimates regarding the tanker's whereabouts were right on the money. Before long, the first inklings of what he had come for began to appear on his radar scope.

Ryson turned on the more powerful secondary search-lights, rotating them up to a leveled stance. The focused beams instantly sliced through the inky liquid, illuminating far away stationary objects that stood out in sharp contrast to their obscure surroundings. There were also occasional signs of organic life—of fish and other marine creatures that glided effortlessly about.

But of most interest was the huge structure in the distance which the beams of light now barely touched upon. From afar it resembled, in sheer size, an approaching leviathan. To Ryson, it was the unmistakable silhouette of the massive cockpit portion of a jumbo-jet, resting on the alluvial ocean floor. When seen from his head-on angle, it appeared almost intact though eerily out of place, like a ghostly spaceship. He felt a tingling of excitement seep through his cautiousness as he nudged the control stick forward and automatically reset to a new course.

As the tanker's frontal compartment grew closer, so did the evidence of destruction. The blown-out cockpit windows were the first indicators of the plane's fate: clearly, the space had exploded from within and left jagged outward protruding edges along the metallic frame.

Like a minnow trailing a whale, Ryson's pod, hovering only mere feet above the ocean floor, was dwarfed by the fuel tanker's giant decapitated head. He was approaching the structure's far end now. Immediately behind the plane's severed head lay the immense debris field, whose location Tafstein had accurately mapped. Everywhere, myriad metallic parts were strewn across the ocean floor. Their reflective aluminum surfaces, lacking the patina of marine growth, made them easy to spot in the pod's powerful search lights. It was a world of mystery, and Ryson spent the next few hours raptly scouring the field.

As an aerial-explosion accident expert, Ryson soon became convinced of the tanker's fate. The debris bore silent witness to an enormous midair explosion that had violently rent the huge plane and rained metal on the ocean from 30,000 feet. Now, more than a thousand feet below sea level, jagged and twisted aluminum pieces were all that remained of that once high-flying technological miracle.

It was what he had so far *not* seen, however, that disturbed him most: no remnant of the B-2, whose black stealth fragments would contrast sharply with the tanker's reflective aluminum make. And so far, he had not recognized a single piece of stealth debris.

But he would not give up the search. At the very least he could intelligently conjecture alternative scenarios. Perhaps the secret plane had not been blown to pieces by the force of the explosion but simply tossed out of control to some other part of the ocean miles away.

Such an occurrence was remotely possible at best, though Ryson was not sure if this was obvious to Hadley, which meant that the myopic naval captain would be all too keen to make a second underwater search at Ryson's expense. He shuddered at the prospect of having to come back to this forsaken seabed, in a far more dangerous mission, at an even greater depth.

And what about the boom? So far, he had also seen no evidence of it. As he approached the farthest eastern end of the search area, the debris accumulations were becoming increasingly sparse, and still there was no sign.

And there was grave danger here.

During his nearly five-hour long eastwardly course, the sedimentary ocean floor had appeared smooth to visual observations from the pod's window and level as a football field extending for miles. But with each occasional glance at the depth meter Ryson realized that the flat appearance of the floor was an illusion.

Despite appearing flat, the seabed was far from level and steadily descended on a fairly steep gradient, like a hillside driveway, toward the dreaded precipice of the underwater ridge. The undercurrents were steadily gaining in strength, like a river approaching a waterfall, and the turbulence, registering at more than three knots, were now buffeting his vessel vigorously. Ryson increasingly performed manual adjustments to the reverse thrusters and rudders to keep the pod at a stable speed.

Without such counter thrusts, which effectively acted as his only means of braking, he would be fatally swept away over the ledge and into the inaccessible depths.

Yet a hypothetical engine failure was not the concern foremost in his mind. What worried him most was the dwindling readings on the pod's oxygen meter. Another hour at best, and he would have to head back up to the surface. And in that case, he would definitely be forced to come down again to search for the boom.

A glimpse at the underwater map showed at least another forty-five minutes to the edge of the field at his current safe speed. He had spent more time studying the debris field than he should have and was low on oxygen and long on both travel distance and distaste for a revisit.

Deliberately disregarding the safety protocols, he lowered the reverse thrust on the engines, essentially taking his foot off the brakes, and thereby allowing the pod to gain momentum with the downhill undercurrent. The trick worked, giving the vessel a new top speed. Twenty-five minutes later, and he was making good time, now only minutes from the marked perimeter. At least he could claim to have covered the whole area even if no boom was found.

And then he saw it.

It became manifest like the huge mast of a sunken treasure ship, erected high out of the dark waters. It had not been sunk by gravity alone, but had impacted the ocean bed with great force, almost as if fired from above by a massive gun.

Ryson re-engaged the reverse thruster, slowing the pod in time to reach the boom. The towering titanium pole, now less than twenty feet away, was menacingly close. But it was the sonar readout that terrified him.

The boom had landed a mere ten yards from the edge of the dreaded precipice. Even at his current slowed pace, he could easily be swept over the ledge. The chilling realization sent a shiver down his spine as his hands quickly flew for the emergency engine controls and turned two of the engines to a downward position.

With its rotatable turbo propellers, the pod could hover above an area like a helicopter, using only two engines. In control now, Ryson supplied the other twin engines, still in reverse thrust, with maximum power in a maneuver that brought a steady, carefully slowed pace to the submersible as it cautiously approached the boom. Soon he was positioned to commence the attachment of the recovery unit to the boom. Following procedure, he activated the outside mechanical arm.

Keeping one hand on the main controls, he used the other to operate the manipulator arm. Slowly, he set the telescopic mechanical arm in motion which stretched out like a radio antenna, each segment housing a thinner one within.

The arm was fitted with a mechanical vise, which he guided toward a specific portion of the boom. The engineers had assured him that the boom's composite material of nearly solid titanium enabled it to be lifted from virtually any segment without breaking apart, but this particular spot also afforded a favorable weight distribution along the boom's length.

Within seconds, the vise clamped shut around its prey, securing the pod to the boom, and thus to the seabed. For the first time since leaving the mothership, Ryson gleefully found his virtually anchored pod in a genuine stationary position. At least for the moment he would not be dragged by the undercurrent and could tend to the task of arranging for the boom's retraction. The surface naval vessel, which was inconspicuously shadowing his pod from above, patiently awaited retrieval of its prize.

He set a dedicated reverse-timer on the panel to ten seconds and, with the press of a button, cut loose the front half of the mechanical arm from the rest and from the pod. The now disjointed recovery unit silently drifted away in a slow pivoting motion around its distal end, which was still secured to the boom. The detachable mechanical arm, specifically designed for such recovery tasks, performed the separation without a hitch.

The timer quickly raced toward zero, at when two large self-inflating sacks squeezed out of the hollowed severed arm, and grew rapidly to full size, forcing the arm's severed end to point upward. Within seconds, the two red-colored floatation units led upward, with enough pull to trigger a pressure-sensitive release mechanism of an internal reel within the arm.

Ryson's eyes followed the balloons in their graceful ascend through the dark waters, tailed only by a rapidly unwinding fine titanium wire. Just a matter of time now, no more than a few minutes at most, before the flotation units would break the surface near the recovery vessel, which was already in position to use its huge onboard crane to pull the boom up by the unbreakable connecting titanium wire.

As far as Ryson was concerned, he had accomplished his boom recovery job. A wave of elation swept over him. But in his joy and relief, he had forgotten to monitor the undercurrents' increasing turbulence, which had unexpectedly built in strength to a near torrential force.

Without warning, powerful streams hoisted the tiny pod like a jellyfish, violently flinging it against an outcropping of rocks on the seabed. Ryson, who was afforded no response time, felt a shattering impact as if running his ford Mustang into a telephone pole at 60mph.

He was thrown forward, and saw the dials and gauges rushing toward his head. Had it not been for the protection of his shoulder strap, he would have been fatally bounced around the pod's inside like a pinball.

Slowly, he regained control of his faculties. Everything had gone dark in the pod as the inside lights had flickered and then come back on for an instant only to die again for good. The impact must have damaged the external power units, or their relays feeding the pod's innards.

Unexpectedly, the external lights stayed on a bit longer—just enough time for Ryson to catch sight of the outside view. The crash had kicked up considerable seabed silt, obscuring visibility. He gathered it would be a while before the sediment settled and he could reconnoiter his position. To his surprise, the expansive dust cloud quickly disappeared, swept away by the gale force oceanic undercurrents. Then, just as the last of the outside lights died, he caught glimpse of a spectacle that shook him to the bone.

He was facing the precipice straight in the eye. His pod had crashed at its very edge and was careening dangerously to one side, only inches from a complete free-fall into its jaws, to a cold watery grave. Any moment now his life could be over.

He had to act quickly to arrange for rescue, but there was no power or time to transmit calls for help. Worse, launching a rescue unit required a manual release of the emergency lever, but to his horror he was unable to move. Arms, legs, even fingers were frozen in place, unresponsive to his will.

It took him a few seconds to comprehend what had happened. His terrified mind, riveted to nightmare visions of the dreaded precipice, had locked out all bodily movements. Now, even as his eyes roved around the darkened pod in desperation, his thoughts remained solidly focused on the yawning chasm below. He knew that if misfortunes were to plunge him to those abysmal depths, it would be neither a rapid nor painless death, but would start with the deafening grind of the pod's buckling hull kneaded under the ever-increasing water pressure until the thick spherical protective armor would crumple as tinfoil in a child's palm. His rib cage and skull would crumple next, as he endured an agony of mental writhing.

For the first time, he struggled to reason himself out of his fear, as if addressing a friend: this was an awful place to die, especially for a man of the skies, at least that's what he had once been. For many years he had increasingly regretted his decision to leave the Air Force. Now, facing death in the eye, he knew that he wanted to return to that life, if he lived through this predicament. And if he must face death, then what better way than to perish in the air, in the clouds, doing what he loved to do, and not in a pit, trapped inside a pod teetering over a watery abyss?

The conviction registered in his mind like the distant cries of approaching help heard by lost mountaineers who had abandoned all hope of rescue. He began shifting focus from the imminent danger directly ahead of him, to survival and to the future. He marked the time for an opportune mental moment, then garnered all fortitude in commanding his arms to push the emergency rescue lever into place.

He braced again for failure. Yet this time his mind responded positively, and the paralysis began to ebb.

His arms moved feebly, as if coming back to life, though he knew the sensations to be the psychological by-product of his fears. Slowly, his fingers wrapped around the lever, he began to pull, first with one arm and then with both. Finally, he threw the full body weight into the effort.

The trick worked, and the handle rotated into position for release. A moment of terrifying silence followed during which Ryson prayed that the emergency rescue unit had not been damaged by the impact. A slight shuddering ensued as the unit launched to the surface, a contraption identical to what he had used on the boom, except connected to the pod's hull.

All that the surface vessel had to do was reel him in. All he had to do was wait, but that proved excruciatingly difficult. The recovery vessel had only one crane, and, knowing Hadley, it would surely be put to recover the boom first. Ryson felt his body go limp again, and losing control of his limbs, but this time it didn't concern him. It did not matter now anyway, as there was nothing left for him to do but an infernal wait as his pod teetered at the edge of a fatal plunge.

Tilting his head back, he forced his eyes up toward the boom and the long lifeless titanium thread that reached for the surface. He seemed to discern a visible movement, an almost harmonic vibration, as the wire began straining to tautness, the result of a great upward force. Yet the boom remained obstinately unaffected. Nothing happened during the next few minutes, though he knew the pull on the wire was being systematically increased. To his relief, the huge mast finally moved, slowly at first and then gathering momentum as it began to exit out of the seabed, in one solid continuous motion. Soon, as the last impacted portion had cleared the ocean floor, the entire contraption began its swift ascent.

Ryson's eyes followed the spectacle upward. The slender, dark metal mass became consumed by the sunlit waters far above, and soon thereafter, he felt a gentle tugging on his own vessel as he was hoisted, miraculously, to the surface.

JEFFERSON AIR FORCE BASE, AUSTIN, TEXAS

"Yes Major, we have recovered the first item," Hadley's voice filtered over to Murray's desk phone. "But we could not locate the other object of interest."

"And now how did our recovery expert fare?" Murray inquired.

"A last-minute mishap put his pod out of commission, but no injuries."

"Events like that build character."

"If you survive them."

Murray placed both feet on his desk and breathed deeply. Although "the other object of interest," as Hadley had cryptically described the bomber, had not been found, perhaps the boom would tell them what had happened to it. "Any theories?"

he asked, staring at the ceiling.

"Our flown-in experts are sorting it out right now in the next room. Your person is there with them. It seems to be taking an awful long time."

"Better thorough, than miss anything. And knowing our person, I'd bet you my house that right now at least he is happy to have his feet on solid ground."

IN THE MOBILE COMMAND UNIT,
FLORIDA

Ryson was starting to think fondly of his time in the Atlantic depths. At least things had been quiet there.

After fourteen hours of nearly non-stop deliberations amongst Maxim and Beckman, the pundits still had no plausible explanation of what had brought about the explosion that sealed the fate of the tanker and the top-secret bomber.

The theories of Dr. Beckman, the aircraft crash expert, had been pitted squarely against those of Professor Maxim, the material science guru. None evidently had been willing to give an inch, and the bickering had rendered the group pensive.

"I'm of the firm opinion," Beckman repeated, "the engulfing turbulence during refueling forced the planes into a fatal cant, thus placing a tremendous strain on the connecting fuel rod, causing it to snap. The fires then ensued, as we discussed."

Ryson's exasperated gaze landed on Maxim, but the aged man seemed deep in thought. Perhaps Beckman had finally stumbled onto something worth pondering.

"Highly improbable," Maxim eventually spoke. Despite a reputation for scientific obstinacy, his years of accumulated field experience had also taught him the pragmatic value of maintaining an open mind toward the unexpected. He was suddenly face to face with a nearly incredible possibility. And his insight did more than merely confute Beckman's latest hypothesis.

"But may I present this: the severance was not due to a straining or explosion mishap, as we have been pondering. You see, this section has been *cut* loose."

There was a sudden collective gasp.

"*Cut* loose?" Even Ryson, taken aback by the bold comment, found himself enthralled with Maxim's explanation.

"Yes, gentlemen. And quite deliberately, I might add."

"What proof do you have of this?" Beckman countered.

"You both have seen how all tanker fragments were rent into shards by the explosion force, a very uneven and messy disintegration of metal."

He paused momentarily, to allow for others to imagine his depicted scene.

"But this here," he said, pointing to the severed edge of the tail pipe, "is a very smooth cut; no sharp edges of any kind. Had there been an explosion or excess strain prior to the severance, it would have ruptured the metal conduit into a million shards or jagged edges. Thus neither could have predated or caused the severance."

"My God!" Ryson exclaimed.

Beckman walked up to the display table and gazed intently at the boom from this newfound perspective. "But there's a problem, Maxim. What on earth cut it? Even in a ground hangar a deftly operated blow torch could not cut titanium so smoothly, let alone at 30,000 feet!"

All eyes were on Maxim. "I can think of only one device so powerful that it could accomplish a task of such precision," he said. "But, unfortunately, it is quite impossible for it to be the cause in this case."

"And what device might that be?" Beckman asked.

"A laser, gentlemen," Maxim stated. "And a very powerful one indeed."

TANARIS

From the bay windows of the raised operations room, General McCane gazed across the eroding landscape of the Painted Desert, abruptly-rising distant mesas behind which the setting sun had left a darkening ocher sky in its wake. McCane had often cherished the scene, but not today. Anxiety was eating at him.

The cavernous room's maid door swung open, and Gorik entered, holding an updated report he had read on the way over. He marched along the huge burnished conference table to stand next to McCane and began speaking without a salute.

"Our Florida experts' extrapolations were too accurate for comfort," Gorik commented in a tone that struck McCane as irate. "They think it was a laser."

McCane shook his head. "The B-2s carry helium-argon lasers for reconnaissance," he said, referring to the B-2s' staple terrain-following and mapping onboard lasers. "Such lasers can't generate enough power to cut anything, let alone titanium of that thickness, and in so little time!"

"Perhaps the helium-argon could not, but the COIL certainly can."

"Good God! Are you telling me our own ABL targeted that rod in mid-air?"

"No, we believe the SuperCOIL did."

Gorik's calmly stated words resonated in McCane's ears as thunder. "That's impossible! It *must* have been an accident, a weapons systems malfunction -"

"It was no accident."

The further realization struck McCane like a hammer. "But . . ."

"But nothing!" Gorik snapped. The recent turn of events had obviously taxed him beyond his limited patience. "Look, I'll spare you a quantum physics lecture on the operations of lasers at 30,000 feet. That laser was fired on purpose *and* with great skill, not an accident at all. Someone wanted to blow that tanker out of the sky and damn well succeeded."

McCane had a pretty good idea who that mysterious diabolical "someone" was. The real question was, why?

"And where's the SuperCOIL?" McCane asked, the blood rushing to his face.

"Destroyed," Gorik said. "Maybe not at the searched crash site Ryson searched, but not far away."

"What makes you think that?"

"We have no reports of its sighting anywhere. There are only certain airstrips within its maximum fuel range that are long enough to accommodate such a plane, and intelligence indicates it has not landed at any of them. And of course it cannot have remained airborne all these days."

"A suicidal act then?"

"Most likely. The pilot was the best, but not the happiest one," Gorik replied.

A dark cloud seemed to form behind his ruthless eyes as their gaze steadied to the far distance. He said nothing for a time, leaving his superior to his own thoughts. Finally, he broke the silence. "Just wanted it to be a spectacular suicide, evidently. That crazy son of a bitch!"

McCane shook his head in resignation. "This is clearly foul play now, placing us in Code Black and requiring me to notify the commander in chief ... at once."

The comment sent Gorik into a rage. "And what do you think the president will do? He'll appoint a special counsel to investigate us, and it will tear Tanaris apart."

The general massaged his jaw and frowned. "We'll recommend Ryson again. We can always hide the facts from him." He hoped that Gorik's initial gambit, which had once bought them time, might serve to conceal the truth from outsiders.

"Don't be so sure," Gorik countered. "Remember, Ryson is our outside consultant on this project even if he doesn't know what his findings were used for ultimately. If he somehow manages to piece it all together..."

"It's just suicide; you said it yourself. Nothing to hide now."

"Except for the secrecy of the project, and the way manufacturing operations of the plane were conducted. All that might be jeopardized," Gorik pressed.

"We have no other choice," McCane said, shaking his head in despair. "We cannot keep this an internal affair any longer. The President *must* be notified."

"And that could mean the end of the Black Squadron and Tanaris. And, yes, even of your role as a government puppet," Gorik retorted.

Veins suddenly bulged from McCane's forehead like the tracks of worms crawling beneath skin. "How dare you!" he cried, pounding his fist. Staring across the desk at his subordinate, he bellowed, "I am a *Brigadier* General, *Colonel*!"

But Gorik seemed unmoved by the pulling of rank theatrics. He simply straightened his uniform with apparent indifference and sauntered toward the door.

Before exiting, he stopped to turn briefly to the now bewildered man standing behind an ornate desk.

"Suit yourself," Gorik stated. His transfixing gaze of restrained fury sent shivers down his superior's spine. "Indeed, we both know who is really in charge here." He paused for an instant of heavy, oppressive silence, then walked out.

As if released from a lethal, invisible grip, McCane's knees began to quiver. He slumped in a nearby chair, his anger fizzled like a match tossed into the Arctic sea. Beads of cold sweat drenched his temples and began to stream along his pallid face. He understood Gorik's last statement all too well.

McCane owed his Brigadier General rank to being a cleverly contrived facade for Gorik's operations. Through this arrangement, McCane had gained access to Congress and to the most inner chambers of the U.S. government while Gorik and his devices remained out of official existence. Thus, even though the esteemed General was publicly extended every courtesy by the colonel, in conformity with his superior rank, they both had no illusions about who really was in charge. Despite his rapid military ascension, McCane was nothing more than a high-level page boy to Gorik, relaying messages to and from the netherworld of Black.

This arrangement provided him ample rewards, as his rank afforded him audiences with the president, the Joint Chiefs, and other high-ranking government officials. It was an unparalleled opportunity for wielding power to his own ends.

He would also be fully apprised of all developments in the Black Projects, some of whose details even the president knew not of, which satisfied McCane's own unquenchable curiosity for ultra-secret endeavors.

All would have been perfect if he not for dealings with the indispensable Gorik, whom McCane had never fully understood or trusted. Though he owed his ascent in the ranks of the military almost entirely to the colonel's scheming ways, there remained an air of immense foreboding that always seemed to engulf the colonel and with which McCane, despite his best efforts, could not fully come to terms.

The general had always managed to associate that peculiarity with the nature of Gorik's enterprise, however. It was not easy living in the Black world, much less for more than three decades, and to succeed with such amazing consistency in the face of seemingly insurmountable odds. Yet McCane had to admit that with Gorik the true costs of success should not be measured only in terms of dollars spent, but also of lives lost or ruined beyond reclamation.

In time, when McCane's own political foothold in the highest echelons of power had become established more firmly, he intended to sweep Gorik aside, replacing him with an individual more obedient to his whims, who did not evoke in him such a sinister sensation.

Until then, theirs was a purely symbiotic partnership, during which McCane hoped the fires of whatever unknown machinations Gorik resorted to would not consume those on the outside of the colonel's disturbing inner dark world.

ON THE OUTSKIRT OF BRIGHTON, COLORADO

The lone sports car's twin headlights lit up the dew-glossed back-country road that wound its way up a residential hillside. Staring intently out the windshield, Ian Ryson remained focused as he deftly maneuvered through the frequent hairpin turns. The attentive shifting of the manual transmission precisely a step ahead of the road twists evoked the thrills of those long-gone days when he flew various fighter craft during aerial maneuvers.

The intense attentiveness the drive exacted also served to purge his mind of other matters, namely that night's dinner with Kathleen, his long-time girlfriend. She was not happy with his brief recall to a life they both believed he had fled forever. Ryson had never been able to tell her the exact nature of his classified assignments, yet she had correctly gleaned them to be the source of his past torments, and the decision to leave that life behind seven years before.

Standing at five foot six, with an athletic figure and disarming smile to match, Kathleen was a beautiful and intelligent woman with whom Ryson had forged a deep, loving bond in the past four years. But he was apprehensive about the next logical step in their relationship—engagement, and he had been unable to fully communicate the reasons for his apprehension, which, he knew, she sensed keenly.

Despite his sincere protests, she could not be persuaded that marrying her was his ultimate wish. But before promising this earthly angel the rest of his life he would have to conquer the traumatic effects of the event that had changed everything for him.

He wanted their married life to be perfect, as he had once hoped for his first fiancée and himself. He did not want to shackle Kathleen to a life of his nightmares arising from an era she had not been a part of.

Throughout their candlelit dinner of sushi, they had gazed into each other's eyes and held hands. She was lovely as always, caring and witty, gently teasing him about his occasional fumbling of the chopsticks, or his quirky way of saving the salmon piece, which he liked best, for the last. Afterwards, they had slow-danced the night away.

Ryson had reassured her that his old life truly was over for good. But after dropping her off, his thoughts drifted back to his near-death experience in the underwater pod, and his self-promise to face all the hurdles he had been deterred by for so many years, if only he would live to see another day.

An undaunted will had saved him in the pod. The experience had offered him a new taste of what life once had been and could be again. He now needed to uphold that promise but did not quite know how, especially in regard to Kathleen. It was still too soon, way too soon, to know how things would unfold. There were so many questions still to answer.

Ten minutes later, he arrived at his apartment door. Reaching for his keys, he glimpsed at his wristwatch: 3:15 am, his weary mind aching for sleep. In a few seconds he stepped inside, and following his custom for the last seven years, he didn't bother to turn on any lights as he reached for a beer can in the fridge. He popped it open, lips parting in expectation of a pull from the aluminum container. But something gave him pause from that first swig. Somehow he no longer felt the need for the beer, or at least not tonight.

"The beer not cold enough, sir?" a startling voice pierced the living room darkness. Ryson dropped the can, as if having received an electric shock.

A lamp flicked on, and his gaze darted to the light source, then to a man in a trench coat who was sitting on the sofa, and felt relieved though annoyed.

"Damn it, Dorn, can't you learn to knock first?" he said.

"Sorry," said the corporal. "Didn't want to draw attention by camping outside."

"Heard that one before," Ryson threw him an irritated glance, then reached for a paper towel, and got down to wipe up the spilled beer. "So who screwed up now and needs me to fix it?"

"I don't know, sir, but you're to report to duty at once."

The statement froze Ryson in mid-action. He slowly stood up to get a clearer look at Dorn.

"On whose orders?"

Dorn was averting eye contact. "The White House, from the president."

Ryson's eyes widened with astonishment. He slowly rose to full height, and with trembling hands set the beer-soaked towels on the counter.

"Sir, in here is the full report," Dorn said, patting his briefcase. "I am to hand it to you once we are made airborne."

Ryson felt a deluge of questions washing over him but knew there could be no other answers from Dorn. Except maybe one.

"We are going to Washington D.C.?"

"No sir, to Tanaris."

Ryson involuntarily cringed. Beads of cold sweat broke out on his palms in a reflexive psychosomatic bout. For to him, and to many others before him, Tanaris, the mystery airbase located deep in the eroding badlands of Arizona desert, was an accursed place. This was news he had much rather have gone without.

EN ROUTE TO TANARIS

Once again, Ryson adhered to strict security protocols and waited for his military plane to become airborne before breaching the seal on the packet given to him.

He found inside it a blue folder bearing the great seal of the President of the United States and containing "Classified"-stamped briefings on White House letterhead signed personally by the president. The first document read as follows:

Lieutenant Ryson:

As you are aware, a stealth bomber has been lost, and pilot foul-play is strongly suspected as the primary reason.

To better assist with your designated task, a summary of this plane's capabilities is now in order: the lost B-2 represents our foremost efforts in creating a laser-capable airborne platform for destroying enemy missiles while in flight.

This airborne laser was recently tested in a modified Boeing 747-400F equipped for firing 40 laser bursts, which destroyed 14 missiles in flight during a top-secret test exercise.

The concept has been further implemented in a specially designed B-2 bomber where the combining of a shoot-down laser with a stealthy operation platform offers an invaluable combat advantage. The lost plane thus is a weapon of utmost strategic importance to the interest of the United States, and its recovery remains paramount in our efforts.

Following foul-play protocols for conducting an outside investigation of a secure military installation, I hereby assign you to Tanaris airbase to determine the causes of this malicious incident, particularly in regard to the pilot, or any other possible collusion.

My enclosed official written authorization allows you full access to all areas of Tanaris, no matter how restricted. Your Tanaris contact person, Brigadier General McCane, has guaranteed a full cooperation by all ranking officers of the airbase, including base commander Colonel Erwin Gorik, in assisting with your mission.

We hope your efforts are successful in identifying the causes of this foul play, in the interest of more thoroughly securing our top-secret endeavors in the future.

The letter continued regarding the importance of such classified missions, but Ryson did not bother to go through the mostly boiler-plated text. His heart had been beating faster ever since he read these words: a stealth bomber with weapon-grade laser. What a fantastic concept!

But soon as the initial shock passed following a few minutes of contemplation, as a man of both engineering and science he had dismissed the idea as more fiction than reality. The stealth bomber the president so proudly referred to could not have been more than a conceptual prototype.

To begin, any laser powerful enough to destroy a Theater Ballistic Missile (TBM) such as the bulky SCUD, would have to generate at least 2+ megawatts of power, enough to turn on twenty *thousand* 100-watt light bulbs.

Now it was true that neither the shooting down missiles in midflight by laser nor the use of an airborne platform to do so were of themselves novel ideas. In the early 1980s, lasers far more powerful than two megawatts were used to target and destroy orbiting satellites, objects bigger than SCUDs—and at much greater distances. Except that these weapons had all been ground-based lasers weighing hundreds of tons, well-above any airplane's lift capability.

Around the same period, weapon-grade airborne lasers were also created, a remarkable accomplishment. Except that weight restrictions had limited their power output to a mere 400 kilowatts, enough for firing a few shots to destroy small test air drones, but nothing as big and fast as a TBM.

To his knowledge, no laser with greater than one megawatt of power had ever been made airborne. Even more intriguing, was that the current laser could fire over 40 shots. Ryson reckoned the plane had to carry over a million pounds of lasing materials, and that in addition to the laser modules and anything else onboard, including the plane's massive frame.

An expert on B-2 design, Ryson knew well that none of the 20 existing B-2s were capable of such lift thrust, it was simply too heavy. The construction of an entirely new stealth bomber would thus be required, something quite impossible under the prevailing circumstances.

And so there remained the issue of stealth itself.

During the construction of the existing B-2s, more than 4,800 suppliers were contracted. But within two decades since the last B-2 had rolled off the assembly line, more than 90 percent of those suppliers had gone out of business or shifted their technical focus elsewhere. Reassembling such skilled work force would prove so prodigious that Ryson, who still operated in the Black, would have known about it through one channel or the other.

Lastly, the new stealth plane would need an entirely new design drawn from scratch, and Ryson estimated the actual cost of its assembling and test flights to go well above ten *billion* dollars, five times that of the already prohibitively expensive B-2s, which required Congressional budgetary approval and its publicity.

Something was thus glaringly flawed with the report, he concluded. At best, such a plane would be in the planning stages for years or even decades out. It could not already have been built and flown. This president, like many before him, had probably been sold a bill of goods by a wily military advisor.

Ryson tossed the report back into the briefcase, then switched off the overhead reading lights and gazed out into the moonless night beyond the window. The desolate ground below had become a dark blanket devoid of light, and a thin layer of clouds blocked out most of the stars above. There was nothing to see.

Shifting focus back to the dim cabin, he spotted Dorn reclining in his seat near the cockpit entrance, arms folded over his chest, enjoying some shut-eye. Ryson decided to follow suit. He knew he would need to have his wits about him whether the report was accurate or not.

THE OVAL OFFICE,
12 HOURS PRIOR

Outside the bullet-proof windows, a thunderstorm was busy unleashing its full fury, assailing the neatly groomed lawn and trimmed roses with salvos of large wind-blown raindrops. A dense covering of menacing black clouds made it seem much later in the day than it was.

Inside the Oval Office, the president mulled the report he had received just hours earlier. He was not seated behind the main office desk, which he had always found too formal, with its memories of televised speeches and photo ops, but comfortably at a sofa. In his front, sat a mug of steaming coffee placed on the low-lying table next to stacks of documents marked *Top Secret*.

Seated at the table's opposite edges were General William H. Norton, top dog of Air-Combat Command of the United States Air Force, and Secretary of Defense Edward Fleisler. Both had been urgently chauffeured from the Pentagon at the height of rush hour.

The president took a coffee sip and began. "Gentlemen," he said, placing the mug of scalding liquid back on its china coaster, "you have been brought with haste, so let's get down to it, then. How familiar are you with Tanaris airbase?"

"It's located in the Painted Desert of Arizona and is headed by Colonel Erwin Gorik," Fleisler replied.

"Neither the man nor the locale is very well liked," Norton added.

"What makes you say that?" the president asked.

"Tanaris has become Tonopah's 'evil' twin," said Norton, referring to the Nevada Air Force Base northwest of Las Vegas, the once-secret home to the F-117 Stealth Fighter.

"What the General is saying," Fleisler interjected, "is that the two airbases were revamped simultaneously back in the 1970s from a near-derelict post-World War II status. Their blueprints were almost identical. I just wish as much thought had gone into selecting similar commanders."

Norton added, "very few have heard of Tanaris, whereas Tonopah is now relatively well known on the outside."

"It was the Cold War," Fleisler explained. "Tanaris was to be a backup to Tonopah, and thus constructed in utmost secrecy. Tanaris's depressed cratered setting offers more protection against nearby nuclear blasts than Tonopah's wide-open expanse. In case of nuclear strike, we could fly our stealth planes there from Tonopah to organize a counter strike. That is why meticulous care was given to keeping the two bases identical so minimizing the pilots and crews readjusting and reaction time to a new setting."

"And when did the two start to diverge?" the president asked.

"When Gorik, then a second-in-command major at Tanaris, became its lead following the previous base commander's mysterious death," Norton replied. "At first, Gorik continued playing second fiddle to the Tonopah commander. But it soon became obvious that the new chief had grand plans of his own. And with the help of General McCane, he virtually hijacked Tanaris out from under our noses.

"After the Soviet Union's collapse, Tanaris's backup role status was in decline. Gorik rapidly expanded it to include a research and development facility, which rivaled Tonopah's. On its face the transformation seemed like a sound expenditure of taxpayer's money, but Gorik is secretive and, I think, a viciously territorial man. I have long been concerned that he is using the excuse of black-classified projects to virtually close his affairs to the outside, even to most inner circles of the military. It is now behind an Iron Curtain of its own as far as I am concerned."

The president's expression indicated both comprehension and skepticism.

"And the military as well as the commanders-in-chief were more than willing to look the other way so long as fantastic weapons technologies emerged from that setting without anything serious getting out of hand," Fleisler added. "We just got briefed on a new Airborne Laser platform they tested out there. Impressive stuff."

"All I know," Norton said, "is I keep losing some of my best trained Air Force pilots to that airbase as their culled recruits, and I never hear from them again. As the Secretary just pointed out, the place is ultra-secretive. I've had more luck gathering intelligence on North Korean or Chinese air forces than on Tanaris."

"When the Soviets were our chief threat, such secrecy was vital," the president said, with an edge of criticism in his voice. "But now I am not sure if this habit should continue at Tanaris, at least not under the current command."

"What are your thoughts, sir?" Norton asked.

"It appears it's time to pay our wayward colonel a visit. About five hours ago," explained the president, "I was provided with a detailed report from General McCane that one of our black-classified bombers had disappeared off the coast of Florida, and foul play is presumed."

"What kind of bomber?" Norton inquired.

"A stealth bomber."

"That's impossible!" Norton objected. "All twenty are at Whiteman Air Force Base under my personal command and visually accounted for every day."

"The craft in question is not one of the original twenty stealth bombers, General. And it's something very different from them."

"In what way?" Norton demanded.

"For now, let's just say it's of increased range and payload."

"Who authorized this ... production?" The Secretary grumbled.

There was a thunder burst, and audible on the windows was the drumming of increasingly heavy raindrops. "Technically no one did," said the president, sighing. "It was constructed under wraps, hidden even from me."

"The colonel has finally gone too far!" Norton exclaimed.

"Agreed, General," said the president. "But I am surprised about how such a relatively small R&D place like Tanaris can produce such an advanced airplane in the first place."

"It's not all that surprising," the Secretary explained. "The size of the facility isn't so much a factor, Mr. President, but the quality of people working there. You recall our own Skunk Works, a relatively small division of Lockheed. From 1940s till the mid-1990s, they were located in barely two hangars next to Burbank's civilian airport, just outside of Los Angeles proper. And yet they developed and flew nearly all the legendary planes of the last century, including the U-2, SR-71 'Blackbird', and the F-117, the world's first stealth craft. All were revolutionary designs decades ahead of their time.

"They did all of that starting from scratch, and at the height of the Cold War while up to their necks in secrecy protocols. Highly intelligent, experienced people like that can make anything, and make it fly, given enough funding and a modicum of outside support."

"I know all about Skunk Works, Mr. Secretary," the president said, a hint of annoyance creeping in his voice. "I just had never heard that Tanaris was anywhere near that caliber."

"Sir, it may be a close-second, and five times larger in size," Fleisler said. "The colonel has turned Tanaris into its own little version of the US Air Force Special Projects Office. But what I do not get is how he could do it. Projects like this mandate investitures of enormous additional operating resources. Skunk Works has corporate and government funding behind them. Money is something you cannot do without, no matter how talented your scientists are."

The president sighed again. Fleisler had pointed out a glaringly obvious sore spot, especially to a man who had spent most of his career procuring defense contracts for exotic military weapons research.

"Colonel Gorik had a massive specially earmarked budget at his disposal—fifteen billion dollars," the president explained, watching both the General's and the Secretary's faces carefully. "But it was meant for their laser project, and only research in new stealth materials and design studies for a successor to the B-2. He must have diverted funds from one project to the other. I don't know how the internal audits didn't catch it."

"Perhaps I can answer that, sir," Norton volunteered. "Both were airborne projects, so he must have simply passed on the unauthorized acquisition orders for the stealth plane, as the legitimate ones for Airborne laser 747. The payrolls for scientists, R&D etc., could have been even more easily intermingled. These things are routinely mis-named on purpose, anyway, to provide a cover for the Black projects. We got nailed in our own game. But..." Norton stopped, suddenly showing reticence.

"Go on."

"His biggest ally in all of this was our blind trust in him."

The president lowered his head. He knew well what Norton alluded to. "*Our*" was a tactful way of referring to the Commanders-in-Chief, past and present.

"I should have been more vigilant," the president admitted. "You get to serve at most eight years but have to deal with unelected officials who have been at their posts for decades. You can't just come in and rock the boat by distrusting everyone without solid reasons, especially veterans like Gorik and the Tanaris Black Squadron operations.

"My immediate predecessors spoke highly of Tanaris, and I decided to let it well enough alone. With all our international image issues, unwarranted intrusions into a well-oiled internal organization was not on my mind. I will be the first to admit that I was wrong."

"It was not your fault, Mr. President," Norton said.

"Perhaps, but it *is* my responsibility. Damn it, I am the leader of this country!" The president said, looking at the hung portrait of Harry S. Truman which reminded him that the buck stopped there. "And it gets worse," he continued. "The new bomber has been lost for a few days now, but I was not notified till this morning because Gorik resisted the idea."

"That's why I was told to put my entire southern sector on high alert to look for an unidentified simulation flight-test bogey!" cried Norton. "I guess that weasel Gorik figured since we wouldn't spot it on our radars, we wouldn't dispatch fighters for a visual."

"Correct," the president said. "And now we have not only lost a bomber," he continued, "but also our trust in the base commander in charge of our most secret and potent weapon."

"We can hope it was an error in judgment," the Secretary said. The look of disdain on Norton's face, however, indicated that he was not so ready to exonerate the colonel.

"Let's hope indeed," the president said. "But this time I'm not going to take my chances by sitting still, so I have appointed someone to visit the base and see what he can find."

"Who was your choice, sir?" Fleisler asked.

"An ex-pilot named Ian Ryson. He used to work at Tanaris, knows stealth like the back of his hand. He was the man selected by Gorik to scour the crash site."

"Can we trust an ex-Tanaris man, recommended by Gorik?" Norton cautioned.

"We have reason to believe he has no love for the place, or for Gorik, so we're satisfied that he would be unforgiving in his discoveries."

"And what would you like for us to do, Mr. President?"

"To treat this with the utmost care and provide Ryson will all the assistance he may need, as he will, no doubt, be stonewalled. I have given him your top-priority contact numbers."

"Yes sir," the two replied.

"If this story leaks to the public, you will need to create a convincing cover up."

"*If* it does" the General said half-heartedly, "I'll tell the press the bird belonged to the Air Force, not to that loose screw in Arizona. I'll phrase it suited for print."

The president smiled, relaxing at last. Blaming the Air Force for something it had nothing to do with was still the lesser of two evils from national security standpoint, which required that the secrets of Tanaris remained secret. Everyone in the room understood this. After Ryson's investigation was conducted, a more long-term solution could . . . might . . . be devised.

"Thank you, General, for seeing the greater good. Meanwhile, I would like us to scour the crash area on our own and have our intelligence on high alert all over the world. If that plane is not sitting at the bottom of an ocean trench, then I damn well need to know where it is. God help us if it has fallen into the wrong hands."

"Why not just relieve Colonel Gorik of his command?" Norton pressed.

"Because we would also have to re-man an entire organization that is fiercely loyal to him, a serious setback to our black-classified projects there. So we first need to quietly investigate this matter before blowing any whistle; if we have proof, Gorik's people should be more inclined to accept new leadership.

"Besides, relieving Gorik without solid evidence of wrongdoings would cause this matter to surface to the public," said the president, "and our new-bomber secrecy would be blown. It would also bring a serious breach of procedure to the eyes of the public. So I want for our man to dig deep to find something more with which we can persuade Gorik to step down, and quietly."

The Secretary and the General glanced at each other. The president read the exchange to mean that they knew he was thinking of next year's campaign.

"Lots of work ahead, let's get to it," the president said, concluding the meeting.

The men left the president nearly drained and pensive, for he had withheld key information from them. Gorik's real offense was not so much that of building a stealth bomber, but of one that housed an airborne laser. The ramification of such an action to the international military scene was huge, and if the weapon landed in the wrong hands it could have a devastating effect on U.S. security.

Slowly, the president took his seat behind the main desk in the Oval Office. A powerful discharge of lightning flashed across the windows, followed by a crash of thunder that violently shook the panes. Finally, the president was forced to recognize the formidable presence of a storm outside the White House.

APPROACHING TANARIS

The military-chartered plane banked slightly along its left wing into a wide arcing turn, in preparation for its final descent. Nearly 50 miles back the pilot had obtained the necessary clearance from the control tower to enter Tanaris airspace, one of the most forbidden zones in the world. Only Black Squadron members, supporting technical crew and research personnel could routinely enter this exclusive airspace.

Peering out the plane's window, Ian Ryson had impassively followed the barren expanse of the Painted Desert for the last half hour. Tucked away in a remote corner of this desert was Tanaris, out of sight and out of existence to most, and yet quite real. Now, with his craft preparing to land, he was rewarded with a bird's eye view of the elusive airbase.

Situated at the edge of an elevated mesa, Tanaris lay surrounded by upraised land forming a solid curving wall which hemmed all but its slightly fragmented southern boundaries.

On a terrain contour map, the Tanaris basin thus resembled an expansive crater with an amorphous rim, accessible via two narrow slithering canyons, one of which served as the airbase's only inroad. This natural geological shield, combined with the restricted airspace, had successfully kept curious eyes at a far distance.

The advent of the top-secret airbase, over three decades before, had however bestowed on the once pristine setting a sinister appearance. To those distant observers who from the vantage point of the elevated mesas had seen many a fast, strange dark craft egress the crater's rim in tight formations, the mystery crater might have resembled a spewing hornet nest.

Ryson gazed at the scenery with ambivalence, eyes roving the layout of the airbase he had come to know all too well through his many years of service. This, he thought, was how a recidivist must feel when returning to prison.

He knew nearly every aspect of it by heart: the most prominent features being the twin 14,000-foot parallel runways stretching north-south, and six dozen evenly-spaced identical hangars housing nearly all the Black Squadron air wings of often classified planes. A massive control tower overlooked the aerial operations in Tanaris's restricted air-traffic zone.

Ryson was barely interested in the layout, which looked just like the layout to which he had grown accustomed during his last assignment here.

Except . . .

He sat up suddenly, squinting into the northeastern sector. Nearly abutting the crater's massive rim stood a series of new and curious structures of enormous constructions, dwarfing even the largest of the old regular hangars. Ryson shifted for a better glimpse of these gigantic edifices whose finer details had remained obscured under the expansive elongated morning shade of the high north wall.

With the plane in rapid descent, Ryson was quickly losing his vantage point. But just seconds before it was lost, he saw the rays of fast-rising sun glinting off a large, white dome-shaped structure at the edge of the shadow boundary, whose strange design utterly mystified him.

EN ROUTE TO THE PENTAGON

Fierce winds whipped the rain over the men as they exited the stately front portal of the White House. General Norton pulled his uniformed hat tight to avoid it getting blown off.

"What course of action do you propose, Mr. Secretary?" he asked Fleisler.

"I will explain on our way, to the Pentagon." The Secretary gestured to the stretch limo that had just pulled to a stop in the front.

The nimble chauffer held a mostly ineffective umbrella against the rain as the two men quickly got inside, and the closing door shut out the wind's roar. The limo then peeled away from the curb, leaving the gated premises of the White House.

Norton said nothing for a while as he gazed at the rivulets of rain flowing down the tinted windows to help keep his mind off the recent events, but to no avail. The thoughts of such advanced stealth craft in the hands of malicious foreign powers bore heavy on him. If its secrets got out, it could once again destabilize the use of strategic bombers as the "third leg" of the United States' offensive nuclear triad, with the ground-based and submarine launched Inter-Continental Ballistic Missiles constituting the other two. Each leg of the triad was considered vital in precluding a successful simultaneous preemptive attack against all three "legs" to destroy the United States' ability to launch a retaliatory counter strike.

He remembered the 1970s, when this third leg had been severely threatened, by the then Soviet Union's vast improvement in its defensive radar network. It was a rude awakening that came not in the form of a direct conflict in Europe, but by foreign armies in the desolate deserts of the Middle East. In October 1973, Egypt and Syria launched a full-scale attack on Israel in what came to be known as the Yom Kippur War. To neutralize Israel's superior Air Force which had soundly defeated them in the Six Day War of 1967, Egypt and Syria had obtained a reported 30,000 of the latest radar-guided Soviet-made SAMs to provide a comprehensive coverage of the battlefield. The investment paid off handsomely. In just 18 days, 109 Israeli fighter jets were destroyed by these radar-guided weapons, an astounding average of 6 warplanes per day.

Alarmed, NATO conducted computerized simulations of a direct war with the Soviet bloc. Inferring from losses of the Israeli Air Force, regarded as equals in aircraft and piloting skills to the western air forces, but accounting for the Soviets' superior personnel training and air defense networks integration compared to Egypt and Syria, the study reached a most disconcerting conclusion: in an all-out war, NATO air forces would be devastated by the Soviet defenses in just 17 days.

Particularly vulnerable were the once dependable B-52s, the backbone of the U.S. Air Force strategic bomber fleet since 1955, whose long range and cargo capacity was considered vital for massive conventional or nuclear payloads delivery deep inside the Soviet airspace. The B-52, a huge sub-sonic plane, was now incapable of outrunning newer Soviet fighter interceptors, and its shape made it pop up on long-range radar as big as a flying barn from hundreds of miles out, allowing the Soviet defenses time to lock onto and shoot it down at closer ranges.

And using electronic countermeasures and radar jamming at most only 'blurred' the enemy radars' vision but not eliminating them. Considering the vast expanse of the Soviet Union over which a bomber would have to fly just to reach its target, such early detections would be tantamount to a death knell to its crew.

In development at the time were supersonic bombers, such as the B-1, designed to travel at speeds exceeding Mach 2 while avoiding radar detection from ground sites by flying at tree top level to hide among ground clutter and slip by the Soviet defensive net.

Norton, then a colonel, recalled his initial excitement in having been put in charge of an air-wing to be soon equipped with the new B-1s. But his joy had proven short-lived in hearing that the Soviets had developed look-down shoot-down radars which allowed their fighter jets to detect and intercept these low flying aircraft among ground clutter.

It seemed the advantage kept tilting toward the Soviets because their advancements in radar technologies far outpaced those of western anti-radar.

At this critical juncture however, had come the timely advent of stealth craft in the late 1970s. These planes, such as the F-117 and later the B-2, which could evade detection altogether by entering enemy airspace unseen and unheard, rather than jamming or suppressing its radar sites, had not only managed to miraculously save the U.S bomber force in the nick of time, but even materially contributed to the eventual demise of the Soviet Union in 1991.

Norton did not want to see his prized bomber force destabilized once again by a foreign country gaining enough insights into advanced stealth technologies to develop counter measures.

He shook his head in silence, then turned to Fleisler who struggled to type something on his cell-phone's touch screen, before finally pressing 'send' to conclude the ordeal.

"So what you have planned?" Norton asked again.

"I just texted Admiral Connelly."

Norton's face twisted. "That pompous old horse?" he shifted in his seat to face the Secretary. "After the way he publicly chastised the Air Force?"

"I know there is no love lost between you two, but right now we need him for another underwater sweep of the crash site!"

"Fine," Norton said grudgingly, focusing on the rain streaked windows. "But I swear if he gets out of line, I will kick his ass."

"That is all I can ever hope for," Fleisler replied.

TANARIS

The plane landed, promptly taxiing off the runway to an access pathway leading into the base, then heaved to in front of a huge grated, metal gate 150 feet across.

The gate was part of a comprehensive network of cordoning fences, barbed wire rolls, and guard-posts, along with hundreds of motion and thermal sensors planted about and linked to a central computerized network. In case of a security breach, the network would automatically alert scores of armed men with trained attack dogs who constantly patrolled the perimeter.

Within minutes the pilot obtained the necessary clearance for entry, and the massive gate rolled to open, revealing a cement ribbon for the plane to follow. It passed numerous hangars till it came to a complete stop in front of one of the large, newly built structures.

Soon as the whine of the engines died out, Ryson quickly descended the plane's staircase to the gray tarmac and came face to face with the figure of Brigadier General Victor D. McCane.

Ryson swiftly saluted his superior. "Ian Ryson reporting for duty, sir!"

"At ease, Lieutenant," McCane smiled, carelessly returning the gesture.

Ryson lowered his salute and cast an attentive look at his gray-haired superior. McCane's features had not changed much since they had last met some ten years ago, and neither had his deceptively disarming features: his warm smile, solid blue eyes, and trust-worthy expression. If anything, the aging general seemed rather out of place in this hub of brash hot-shot pilots and supersonic airplanes. And yet Ryson knew that without his enormous influence within the Department of Defense, most of what he now saw would never have come to pass.

"I feel honored in seeing you on the tarmac," Ryson nervously remarked.

"Anything for a presidential envoy," McCane deadpanned, then motioned toward the idling jeep a few yards away. "Shall we?"

Ryson hopped on, as the general took the wheel and set the vehicle in gear, heading toward the north-end of the base.

"No personal driver, General?" Ryson inquired.

"Best if no extraneous personnel overhear us on this ultra-important matter," McCane replied sternly. "Your very presence will occasion unwanted curiosity."

"Of course," Ryson said, then opted to cut the small talk. After all, he and McCane had never been friends.

In a few minutes, the jeep had pulled alongside a new office building, and McCane killed the engine. Ryson got off, then followed the general as they headed for the main entrance.

Preoccupied with thoughts, he had not looked up on the entire ride. As they approached the entrance, however, he gazed up at the building's towering twenty-story apex. The imposing edifice boasted a stylishly fashioned glass façade in sharp contrast to the standard gray-cemented and mostly windowless hangars, assembly facilities, and other structures at Tanaris. It was a deep and dark construction, an obsidian monolith that defied the landscape around it.

"Colonel Gorik's new headquarters?" He gently rubbed at the gathering stiffness in the nape of his upward tilted neck.

"Yes. He personally oversaw its design and construction," McCane replied, sounding more like an amusement park guide than a general.

They entered into a high vaulted ceilings foyer. Beams of muted sunlight streamed through darkened panes, casting an eerie morbid glow on the enormous mosaic emblem of the fearsome Black Squadron emblazoned on the polished marble floor. There was no hint of a warm reception. It was clear, that the edifice's intended grand design was to evoke intimidation in all outsiders who set foot in it.

Ryson sought to fend off the environs' stifling negativity, as they traversed the great hall to an elevator. They stepped inside, and it thrusted upward.

At the top floor, a wide hallway led them to an ornate conference room. It was grand, akin to a Pentagon war room, yet far more lavish. It sported marble floors, and wall-mounted gold-framed pictures, medallions, and trophies. Except for the military context, it rivaled the corporate boardrooms of a Fortune 500 company.

Judging from its size and sophistication, this room also served as a military teleconference station for off-base audiences of great importance.

"Sit," McCane pointed to a chair aside a massive V-shaped conference table.

Ryson complied, then opened his briefcase's twin locks with a clank that echoed in the empty room.

In front of all the seats were consoles and other communication gizmos. In his long career he had seen nearly every monotonously devised conference venue by the standardize-everything military. But this room clearly had been custom-designed to provide a backdrop of power for the person occupying the throne-like seat at the table's apex. There were no windows for natural ambient illumination, only projectors strategically placed in the raised ceiling to light individual wall ornaments, and to visually accentuate the prominence of the head of the table.

This whole place, Ryson concluded, was a theatrical stage geared to impress or intimidate prominent audiences communicating via the display screen, a clever stratagem considering those who funded the operations at Tanaris like the Pentagon and the president almost never visited.

Ryson turned to McCane but found the general had walked to the highchair. He stood next to it, as if in reverence, staring intently at a side door at the far end of the conference room.

It was from that door that Colonel Gorik ultimately emerged; his broad shoulders and strongly built stature made the portal look rather small. Clad in a dark military uniform bearing the insignia of the Black Squadron, he briskly paced with heavy boots to the highchair.

McCane saluted the colonel first despite his own higher rank. Ryson observed this curious behavior with apprehension, and his legs felt weak, the nightmares of his past besetting him. He had hoped to not have to face Gorik so soon.

Ryson forced himself up to face the superior officer. The colonel had a stone-cold countenance, high cheekbones, piercing dark eyes, and serpentine grin. A primal chill reverberated down Ryson's spine and tingled painfully.

Gorik kept his gaze trained on the lieutenant till Ryson's eyes reflexively rolled down to stare at his briefcase.

"You may be seated."

Ryson's knees bent, as if under hypnosis, as his body slid back into the chair. The colonel expectedly took the main chair, with McCane standing at his side.

"So you are back in Tanaris, Lieutenant," Gorik observed with a predatory stare. "And under much different circumstances than your last visit."

Ryson summoned the courage to look at Gorik. "It is at the request of the president," he said sheepishly.

"The *president*," Gorik repeated. "Of course you did know that it was *us* who asked for you, didn't you?"

"I suspected so. But I'd just as soon have been left alone," Ryson replied, then immediately regretted speaking his mind.

But Gorik seemed to have liked the response, "I get the feeling you're not too thrilled about this mission?"

"Frankly sir, no, not in particular," Ryson replied, now a bit more at ease. At least his abdominal muscles had relaxed.

"Do you know why you are *really* here Lieutenant?" Gorik snapped.

Ryson was puzzled. Gorik obviously had something else in mind besides the lost B-2.

"As you are fully aware," Gorik went on, "a weapon of extreme strategic importance has been lost, possibly due to pilot's foul play. But I'm afraid you will find that your little trip here has been largely, if not completely, unnecessary."

Ryson raised an eyebrow. "Why?"

"We have conducted our own thorough internal investigation, as is mandated in these cases," the colonel continued.

"What did you find, sir?"

"Some rather disturbing news on this particular pilot. Take a look." Gorik remotely had one of the small monitors embedded in the table in front of Ryson flicker to life. A standard identification card photo filled the screen, of a fair-haired officer dressed in a flight suit.

"This is the man in question," Gorik went on. "Major Jonathan Evertt. He is, or was, one of our best pilots. Unfortunately, no one suspected him of, shall we say, a serious character flaw."

"Character flaw?"

"Yes. Apparently, he secretly operated under the influence, from time to time." Ryson's eyes widened.

"We found trace amounts of hallucinogenic substances in his belongings. Small dosages to not show up on our periodic drug tests, or he knew how to timely purge it from his system."

Ryson cast a closer look at the picture. Nothing in that face hinted at any substance abuse problems. Then again, some faces were unrevealing.

"And you believe this may have caused the crash?"

"Correct. We think he relapsed following the long flight to Florida and panicked during the refueling. Perhaps the spectacle of the tanker's large body hovering so close evoked collision fears. Reflexively, he tried to break off the procedure and dislodged the boom while it still dispensed fuel, thus setting fire to both craft. We are still uncertain on the exact details."

Ryson, though not convinced, was in no place to refute Gorik's theory to his face without obtaining some solid evidence of his own.

"You will find all the needed proof in these documents." Gorik produced a folder from his briefcase, sliding it to Ryson. "So you see, your visit here serves no real purpose."

"Then knowing this, why did the president still pick me?"

"He will not listen to us under the protocols," Gorik said, "until an independent body, such as you, has concluded its investigation." He paused dramatically. "I am sure once you reach the same conclusions, the president will then agree the whole program should not be jeopardized because of an unfortunate and isolated mishap."

"Mishap?" Ryson asked, pretending to study the dossier to avoid Gorik's intense gaze. "We need tighter drug testing measures then. I will recommend some following my investigation. First I need to talk to a few people."

Gorik appeared irritated, but Ryson felt his own unease was not gripping him as strongly now; somewhere he'd found an unexpected inner strength where none had existed for a long while. He peeked back at the highchair. Gorik's eyes were still trained on him.

"Lieutenant, internally we consider this a closed case. If you have to interrupt others to ask questions in complying with your investigative duties, do so but only if you absolutely must. Your stay here should not last one minute more than absolutely necessary. Is that clear?"

Ryson was taken aback by the extent of Gorik's audacity, despite being no stranger to the colonel's hubris. But this time it had gone too far. Gorik had attempted to countermand the president's direct order. Surely this could not be tolerated, at least not by McCane, who reported directly to the president. He eyed McCane to elicit some support, but the general had remained perfectly still and silent throughout the whole process, like a cadet at boot camp.

McCane had receded into the background and might as well have been one of Gorik's many ornaments in the conference hall. He had no idea how much truth the ominous analogy bore. An awkward long silence followed.

Gorik took this as a sign that his orders would be complied with, like all he issued at Tanaris. "Anything else?" he asked, eager to put this behind him. Ryson was not so ready to oblige.

"If that B-2 isn't one of the existing twenty, where it came from?" Ryson asked.

Gorik's eyes narrowed. The question stung as it was not related to the pilot. He perched in the highchair, placed his elbows flat on the table, and cast a pointed intimidating look at Ryson, who sunk back into his chair.

"Lieutenant, let me remind you that your task here is to investigate the pilot and his foul play, not the planes or anything else at this facility. The President expects you to conduct a quick and effective investigation and prepare your report in a few days. I trust you will not waste your time with matters not pertinent to the case."

"I will do my best not to," Ryson replied.

"Good," Gorik hissed. "Now, I am assigning you some help."

Just then, the side door re-opened and a dark muscular figure marched to Gorik's side.

Ryson recognized the new man was a pilot. The stature, and his march revealed a military aviation background. A deep scar traversed his left cheek and under the left eye, an embossed vein brimming with scar tissue. The injury had come dangerously close to blinding him to end his aviation career. It was a curiously uncharacteristic wound for a fighter pilot since it was a clean, deadly knife incision that hinted at hand-to-hand combat.

The scar only enhanced the predatory eyes, making Gorik appear gentle in comparison. This beast was ready to pounce on command. Whatever "assistance" Gorik referred to was merely watchdog duty.

"Lieutenant, this is Major Kessler, commander of Alpha Squadron."

Ryson's eyes bulged. He had heard about Kessler, only a captain when Ryson had been here before. He'd never come face-to-face with the man and wished he wasn't now.

Kessler's reputation as a brutal and merciless field commander was second only to Gorik's. Anything Gorik wanted done, Kessler tackled and succeeded time and again; no surprise he was now the commander of the elite Alpha Squadron.

The Alpha squadron was once comprised of the most righteously devoted ace pilots, and poster boys for what young pilots aspired to be. Ryson recalled the stories fondly told of their previous commander, Captain McDermott, and his squadron entourage who at times had stood up even to Gorik, back when Kessler's gang of thugs were mere cross-base rivals in the Beta Squadron. And then a tragic event in the Gulf War had changed all that, and the very fabric of things at Tanaris. Ryson had no time to dwell on that dark past, as Gorik continued.

"Major, this is Lieutenant Ryson. You will be assisting him with his investigative efforts."

Kessler nodded but kept those falcon-like eyes trained on Ryson.

Ryson's rage welled. He welcomed the sensation, tapping into an alternate source of power dormant for seven long years.

"Colonel, I appreciate the Major's help." His tone was resolute. "But the president ordered me to do this impartially, and *alone*."

Gorik glared, but his voice was calm. "Very well, but should you require assistance, the Major will always be a phone call away—perhaps even closer."

This reply was deceptively downplayed. "Thank you, sir. I would like to get started right away with your permission."

"Be my guest," Gorik pointed at the main door and motioned to McCane. "The General will take you through the security clearance procedures."

Ryson shut the dossier in the briefcase and headed out, the general on his heels. They exited the conference room, the doors shut, and their footsteps receded.

Kessler broke the silence. "What if he finds out the truth?"

"We planned this far too well for that," Gorik reassured.

"He is not intimidated for long," Kessler cautioned. "You sensed it just now. We aren't dealing with the same weakling from years back. We can only keep him on the ropes for so long."

"No worries. Time is still our ally."

"What are you are getting at?"

"He hates Tanaris—too many horrid memories. After a few days he'll wish he wasn't here. He won't get past the cover-up. He will corroborate our conclusions, with a few minor variations and convince the president. Then we can focus on replacing our stealth bomber."

Kessler mulled it over, unconvinced. "But what if he really does find out?"

Gorik's reply lacked all compassion. "Then he does not get out alive."

Kessler's vile face broke into a grin. It wasn't the first time his master had green lit him to commit murder. Kessler had always strived to match the colonel's ruthlessness zeal. It affirmed his belief in his commanding officer and in himself.

Gorik dismissed Kessler with a side nod. "Shadow Ryson."

Before Kessler exited, Gorik spoke again. "Major, the objective is to ensure a continued way of life for our Tanaris endeavors. I have a new pilot in mind for the replacement B-2—you."

Kessler's head swiveled back, and he saluted his master before striding out.

Outside the building, Ryson took a long deep breath of the fresh desert air, exhaling slowly to calm his nerves.

"Gorik is not an easy man to get along with, especially in these trying times," McCane consoled, but looking as if in a trance of someone who had bet the house on an unfamiliar game.

"All things considered I would rather be somewhere else," Ryson said, pointing back to the lofty tower, which struck him as dark spear arrogantly piercing the sky.

"The sooner you conclude your investigation, the sooner you'll return home."

Ryson nodded as they headed for the jeep. McCane took the driver's seat and revved the engine. Gears grinding, the jeep set off with an awkward lurch toward the security installation. They cleared the command tower's long shadow. Ryson felt Gorik's grip on his mind release in the desert sun. He exhaled and leaned back in his seat, the warm winds brushing his pallid face.

THE SECURITY STATION

"Here is your all-access black badge," the brawny Security man handed a black plastic card to Ryson, who clipped it on his shirt pocket then followed McCane out. The building was designated maximum security, requiring High-level clearance, which Ryson found most peculiar.

"It is so no one can intrude on your work," McCane volunteered an explanation.

"Very thoughtful." Ryson didn't buy the bogus rationale, knowing an ultra-secure office location meant anyone visiting his office would be identified, and thus discouraged from providing any revealing information.

This is not going to be easy, Ryson thought.

RYSON'S OFFICE

After McCane departed, Ryson entered his assigned office, a windowless white-walled enclosure, decorated with a standard-issue green metal desk and chair, and not unlike an interrogation room. The sole amenities were a personal computer, and phone. His disdain became a longing for the outdoors, away from the airbase. But he was not about to give in so easily.

He sat down to examine his files. Their contained information was suspiciously brief, a dozen sheaved documents on the life of Major Jonathan Evertt in reverse chronological order.

Evertt had graduated with honors from the U.S. Air Force Academy outside of Colorado Springs. Ryson skimmed through the list of recommendations. He had trained on the venerable B-52, then assigned to the supersonic B-1 bomber, and ultimately recruited to join the elite B-2 stealth bombers. Six year ago, after fifteen years of impeccable service, Evertt supposedly died when a military transport plane crashed over the Pacific Ocean during a routine training exercise. No bodies were ever recovered.

Ryson was mildly amused by this last official entry, a Black Squadron ruse employed when recruiting their most elite pilots. The entire operation had been carefully staged. Evertt and other recruits had boarded a retirement-slated transport plane rigged for mechanical failure, then parachuted out minutes before its planned fatal ocean plunge. They were scooped up by a Black Squadron rescue helicopter, brought straight to Tanaris and issued new identities.

They were living new lives now and forbidden from making contact with anyone from their past. This was the high price of flying the most sophisticated and futuristic aircraft in the world. The recruiting criteria went beyond aviation skill, including a complete psycho-analysis report on a recruit's adaptability to a new way of life, which Ryson read with interest. Yet each passing page piqued Ryson's curiosity but for the wrong reasons.

There was little evidence of any drug use by Evertt, who rarely drank alcohol and never smoked. The report described a health nut, who spent countless hours training for the Black Squadron's various physically demanding tasks. Had he turned to drugs for reasons such as constant job stress, or living an isolated secret life with little contact with the outside world?

Ryson leaned back in the chair, invoking a squeaking protest from the rusty contraption, then looked up at the white-washed ceiling. He could just feel something wasn't right with this report. The facts too neatly fit the puzzle.

From his years playing detective during recovery efforts, he knew nothing came simple in investigations. This one was just suspiciously easy, as if someone had hoisted a trophy fish to be snagged, leaving the truth buried in the muddy waters.

With eyes closed, he raised his left heel, rhythmically rocking the chair. He had many options to pursue, though the only way to determine the truth was to verify the accounts of the report by those who knew the man.

Ryson then spent hours searching the central network computer, crosschecking Evertt's files against other Tanaris pilots. But no associated records could be found. Evertt had not been part of any team, and had no squadron flying buddies, a strange occurrence even for a place like Tanaris.

It seemed no one knew him at all. Log entries indicated he resided in a small rural city 50 miles from Tanaris, and flown in by helicopter. That fact was most curious. To protect their cover, no one with classified status was allowed to live off base. Still, odds were no one in that town would recognize him from his past.

Someone had taken great pains to separate Evertt from other black-classified personnel. Eventually, Ryson narrowed his search to Evertt's commute chopper pilot, the flight engineer who would have instructed Evertt on the operation of the bomber, and a few technical personnel.

He printed the short list and maps of each person's whereabouts at Tanaris.
Time to get down to business.

INVESTIGATIVE MEETINGS

The door tag read "Sergeant Wilson". But he was rarely there. Anyone who worked with the venerable aircraft engineer knew he preferred the cavernous hangars where he cultivated new deeply classified planes and cherished the control tower's panoramic views of his powerful birds taking flight.

For the past few days however, he had shunned those favored spots, and hidden in his office. His most prized possession had taken off and not returned. He feared the worst.

Six years of his best work had vanished without a trace. He mourned as he sipped an Irish coffee, thanks to his trusty whiskey flask. He looked up to see a man standing in the doorway.

"You must be Ian Ryson," Wilson said.

"Yes Sergeant." Ryson had called Wilson from his Jeep earlier. The two men had never met. "I am here about Jonathan Evertt."

Wilson's head tilted back. "The name don't ring a bell."

"He was the pilot of the disappeared stealth bomber," Ryson stated, annoyed.

Wilson's deep green eyes popped open. "His name was Evertt?" he asked in a bewildered tone. "No one ever told me that."

"Then what did you address him as?" Ryson was getting really irritated.

"We never spoke face to face," Wilson explained. "He was always already in the cockpit, and we communicated by voice altered intercom. I was instructed to address him only as 'pilot'."

Ryson realized that Wilson was not putting him on.

"Strict orders, directly from the top boss," Wilson explained. "Gorik was very adamant, and laid some curious procedures in place, even before this—Evertt—guy got here. The pilot was not to be seen or directly talked to. It took some getting used to but worked just fine for six years. Six years!" Wilson grimaced and he took another sip from his coffee.

"Were any changes made to the plane or its systems in the past week that you could not clearly communicate to him?" Ryson pressed on.

"No. Plus, he would have sensed it."

"Come again?"

"Look, this may sound really weird, but this pilot had an uncanny way of knowing any changes made to the plane once he manned the cockpit, even before I told him about it. It gave me the shivers. Sometimes I wondered if I was really talking to a pilot, or to the plane itself."

Ryson cast a puzzled gaze at Wilson for his bizarre count.

"Did you ever observe him in flight, or analyze the flight recorder data?"

"Sure, many times."

"Any flying behaviors that placed the plane in danger?"

Wilson cracked a wide grin. "This airbase is full of hot-shot pilots, all pushing the envelope by placing the plane in 'danger'."

"Sergeant, I was a pilot myself here. We both know the difference between hot-dogging and involuntary recklessness."

"*Involuntary* recklessness?"

"Yes, like flying under the influence."

Wilson jumped out of his chair and slammed down his near-empty mug hard enough to splash coffee. He leaned forward, hands on the table's front edge and stared at Ryson.

"Absolutely not! This man was the best damn bomber pilot I ever knew. Whatever he did, however dangerous it may have looked, he was always in control. The flight data recorder proved that every time. I've never seen anyone maneuver a bomber with such precision and finesse, dives and tight turns like you would not believe. That plane was definitely not designed for that kind of acrobatics, but he made it do it anyway."

Ryson cocked his head and fell silent. Wilson seized at it to turn the tables.

"Lieutenant, what happened out there? No one is telling me a damn thing."

"Refueling mishap," Ryson said, then took a step back from the desk.

The Sergeant stood upright, shaking his head. "That pilot was way too good to let a refueling accident take him down."

"It happens to the best of them."

Wilson let out a sigh. "That is bull crap, and you know it." He flopped back on the chair and reached for his mug, reverting to a somber mood.

Ryson had no answers for that. It was tough to argue logic with an emotional and inebriated person. Time to wrap things up. He thanked the Sergeant, who barely nodded, and headed for the jeep parked outside.

His next destination was a heli-pad by the service hangar that had housed Evertt's ill-fated B-2. A Huey helicopter sat atop the circular "H" landing zone, with one of its access panels behind the cockpit open, and a person's lower body protruding from the edge.

Ryson parked on the bright yellow perimeter line and approached the unsuspecting man. Metallic clanks interspersed with curse words echoed from the Huey's innards.

"Captain Maines?" Ryson bellowed from a distance.

"That I am," the man yelled back. "I don't recognize the voice."

"Lieutenant Ian Ryson. May I have a word?"

"Not now; got to repair these hydraulic oil pumps."

"It is very urgent."

"Says who?"

"Colonel Gorik."

As if zapped, the man's head popped out, nearly bumping against the propped-up panel as he extracted himself from the Huey's innards, revealing a lanky character in a helicopter pilot uniform. He wiped his grease-smudged palms on rag before approaching Ryson.

"Albert Maines at your service," he extended a hand, which Ryson shook back.

"Captain, you were tasked with flying a Major Evertt to and from base, right?"

"Call me Albert. I fly lots of people," Maines looked skywards, rubbing his jowl. "But the name don't ring a bell."

"You shuttled him daily from a small city fifty miles of here."

Maines eyes popped wide open, as if a long mystery in his life was about to get solved. "You know *that* man?" he asked excitedly, then turned concerned. "Last time I flew him in, but not out; that never happened before. Anything wrong?"

"Not at liberty to discuss that, Albert. Tell me how he looked."

"That depends on what you mean by 'looked'."

Ryson rolled his eyes, "Christ, can't I get a straight answer from anyone?"

Taken aback by the outburst, Maines raised hands to his chest with open palms.

"Never saw his face," he explained. "He was always in his flight suit, his helmet on with the visor shut. Talking to him was forbidden, so it made for very uncomfortable short flights. I'm an ex-bomber pilot, done eighteen-hour sorties, but none as interminable as those taxi flights."

Ryson pursed his lips. He asked a few more questions about the mysterious pilot's physical characteristics, all of which matched Evertt's description in the file, without shedding any light on his personality. But Ryson sensed there was more to him than Maines let on.

"Albert. Listen to me. You are not telling me everything. I am here on the direct order of the President of the United States, and I do not report to Colonel Gorik or anyone at Tanaris. You can tell me the truth."

Maines pondered, then shook his head. "I am sorry, got nothing else."

Ryson gazed at Maines, still unconvinced, and thanked him for his time before heading back to the Jeep. Maines watched him go. Ryson had started the engine when Maines's oversized head poked through the side window.

"Jesus, Albert!"

The captain cautiously scanned the area before ducking his head back in.

"Lieutenant, may I have a word with you, off the record?" he said in a subdued tone, like a boy about to confess at Sunday school.

"Okay, what's on your mind?"

"Not now, but we will talk again before long."

Ryson raised an eyebrow, but Maines was already walking back, then disappeared behind the Huey.

Ryson reached for his cell phone and as he drove summoned the remaining personnel on his short list. Over the next few hours, he interviewed everyone from the electronics expert, to the systems specialist, and their stories were all the same. None had ever seen Evertt's uncovered face.

He then headed back to his quarters, feeling more despondent than ever.

OFFICERS' QUARTERS

Ryson's quarters were situated far from the regular Tanaris personnel buildings. The distant accommodations were meager, as a cheap motel room. Someone did not want this guest to feel too welcome during his visit.

Ryson splashed cold water on his face from the bathroom sink and changed into jeans and T-shirt. The television was tempting, but he opted for the files in the briefcase and began reprocessing its data in light of the information he had gathered today.

After few hours of careful study, he was convinced that independently determining anything conclusive on the destruction of the tanker or the B-2 was next to impossible. Just signing off on the investigation seemed very appealing and would be easier on all involved who mattered to him. He had a serious girlfriend waiting. He'd spent years distancing himself from military life. He would be free to leave this desolate outpost with the stroke of a pen if he verified the files as true, or at least inconclusive.

No one would fault him for that—except himself.

It dawned on him that he had unfairly blamed himself for many past events and could not burden his conscience with more regret: of quitting before exploring every possible option.

He pushed the file aside, and pondered its discussion with Wilson, who had described a man of great aviation skill and technical knowledge. But was this man Jonathan Evertt?

As a science person, Ryson cherished logical deductions. Determining how the B-2 had crashed due to aviation phenomenon lined up nicely with his forte but uncovering the human emotional motives did not. Perhaps the answer lay not in the people's subjective corroborations, but in the immutable laws of physics. Could he solve this riddle with a purely scientific approach?

Ryson had a strong hunch that the mystery behind the B-2's fate went far beyond Gorik's assertions that the B-2 pilot's tanker-disengagement errors had caused the fuel boom's severing. Under such circumstances, the boom would have shattered into jagged ends; yet the recovered artifact had been precisely cut, by a laser, as Maxim had deduced.

In the end, it all boiled down to one question: did such a powerful laser indeed exist? He had to know the answer to that question. And this time he knew just the right man to ask.

AT THE TECHNICAL OPERATIONS HEADQUARTERS, TANARIS

Jeffery O'Neil, the Chief Engineer and operations head of black-classified projects at Tanaris, reclined in his office chair. Ignoring the technical schematics cluttering his desk, he tried to find his place in the half-read newspaper story.

In his mid-sixties, he felt age creeping up on him, and often now he dreamt of his long-ago life as a top-notch but free-spirited aerodynamics designer for an outside defense contractor. Then three decades ago he had been called to this mysterious locale by a charismatic man whom he had since come to fear and loathe, a man named Gorik.

Gorik had offered O'Neil a chance to build the most sophisticated fighters and bombers in the world, backed by billions of dollars in defense spending, and the aviation's brightest technical minds at his unfettered disposal. The offer proved too tempting, and soon O'Neil was realizing the aerial visions of his unscrupulous Tanaris superior. Twenty years had passed quickly, but not without their troubles.

Gorik proved to be demanding and meddlesome, and even O'Neil was not immune to his reign of terror. O'Neil's engineering team overcame inhuman pressures to deliver stunning accomplishments which lead to Gorik's rapid ascendance but did little for those he commanded.

And Gorik always manipulated O'Neil, utilizing the old carrot and stick, leaving O'Neil resigned to having no real alternative than spending his remaining days at this base.

Hidden behind his newspaper, he grumbled at the ongoing civilian report on a crashed air tanker which had mysteriously suffered mechanical failure off the Florida coast, but the Air Force had vehemently denied the story.

There was another interrupting knock on the open door. O'Neil cursed quietly.

"What do you want *now*, Dorfman?" he bellowed from behind the printed page at his pesky new hire.

"Just a moment of your time, old bastard."

O'Neil froze halfway through turning the page. The voice was definitely not Dorfman's, but of an all too familiar echo he had not heard in years.

"Ian!" O'Neil exclaimed, setting the paper aside. He sprang from his seat and warmly welcomed Ryson, then gestured him to sit in an expensive office chair.

The two men quietly studied each other for a bit. An uncharacteristic gleeful smile creased O'Neil stern face at the sight of his longtime friend and former employee. Ryson wondered if this was how prisoners felt during visits.

"Nice new office you've got here, Jeff," he said, looking about.

"You can have it."

Ryson ignored the disgruntled remark. O'Neil was the most powerful technical operations man at Tanaris, a man Ryson both respected and pitied, and he was sure the chief engineer felt the same toward him though for entirely different reasons. That dreadful day in Ryson's past, the event that had ended it all for him here, hung silently between them.

At the recall of old times, O'Neil reverted to his business self. He tossed the paper into Ryson's lap. "So is this article what brings you here, Ian?" he asked, in his usual incisive tone.

Some things never change, Ryson thought, *not even after twenty years*.

"Perhaps. You head the laser division now. They must have been in a hurry to get something out to have put you in charge."

"You have no idea," O'Neil said, taking a long sip of his coffee.

"So you really put a multi-megawatts class laser in a stealth bomber?"

O'Neil suddenly choked, some of the dark liquid escaping his lips and running down his chin. "How the hell?" His eyes bulged, then reached for a tissue and dabbed his chin dry.

Amused, Ryson watched his old mentor collect himself. "It's all top secret," O'Neil reverted to a calmer tone, "you know that."

"See this black badge?" Ryson tapped on the obsidian colored plastic pinned to his shirt, "I have a direct mandate that compels anyone at Tanaris to cooperate."

O'Neil looked on curiously as Ryson produced the Presidential authorization.

After quickly reading it, O'Neil raised an eyebrow. "Impressive," he remarked. "You left as my direct report, but now back as a Presidential investigative officer. What have you gotten yourself into, Ian?" he asked in concerned paternal tone.

"It's more like *drafted* into. All things being equal, I'd rather be home."

O'Neil nodded.

"But I have a task to perform," Ryson continued. "Now tell me about this laser."

"It has nothing to do with your determining of mechanical failures on a tanker."

"Maybe I'm not here for what you think I'm here for."

O'Neil smiled, being reminded of their good old days. But business was business.

"This can land me in hot water," he half-pleaded. "Does the colonel approve?"

"My Presidential authority supersedes Gorik's tactical base command," Ryson said. "Now tell me about this laser."

O'Neil rubbed his chin. "Is this your direct order for me to fully cooperate?"

"Yes," Ryson replied.

Rather than being intimidated, O'Neil felt excited, as a child who had unlatched the cookie cabinet. "To disclose everything I know with impunity?" he continued mischievously.

"Yes. I would go on record."

O'Neil stood with the alacrity of a twenty-year old, quickly downed the dregs of his coffee, and grabbed his car keys. "Let's get going then!"

MOSCOW, RUSSIA

Grumbling under his vodka-laced breath, Ivan Leonid Trostov awoke as the predawn sky brightened. He had gone to bed three hours before, only to be awakened involuntarily by a force of habit he wished he'd left behind. Bleary eyed, the retired Soviet Air Force general got up, put on his brocade slippers, and shuffled to the kitchen.

He passed through his spacious opulent living room, now in chaos following the previous night's party. Remnants of white powdered substances smeared the glass tables, and expensive empty vodka bottles were strewn about, along with a number of feminine undergarments, left behind by their hired owners.

Though Trostov had scarcely partaken, his socio-politically influential client-guests had fully enjoyed that successful evening, which could only translate to later lucrative deals, the likes of which had made every luxury around him possible.

Reaching for the coffee-maker pot, he poured a generous serving of the imported Colombian brew into a fine china cup and added a bit of cream. He savored the aroma for a few seconds before downing the contents like a shot of hot liquor. Within a minute, his eyes popped wide open, and he became sharply aware of his surroundings.

A subdued buzzing sound filled the kitchen. Like an alert tiger, Trostov's head swiftly turned to his cell-phone on the marble counter. He answered it.

"Da?"

A voice spoke in Russian, "Your antique crystal shipment came in last night."

The news washed away Trostov's residual mental fatigue more effectively than any massive dosage of caffeine could have.

"All the pieces are intact?"

"Evidently."

"Excellent," Trostov said, then hung up.

He took a deep breath, as if a huge burden had been lifted from his shoulders. Ever since becoming aware of their existence years ago, he had actively pursued these rare items. Now his efforts would bear him the greatest fruit of all.

"I have it!" the eccentric millionaire, soon to be billionaire, muttered.

EN ROUTE TO THE ITF COMPLEX, TANARIS

"Where we headed, boss?" Ian Ryson asked, as their Jeep hurtled toward the distant cluster of large buildings at the airbase's south end.

"Upfront," O'Neil's index finger pointed, "the ITF complex."

"The *what* complex?"

"I-T-F," O'Neil repeated over the howl of wind sweeping through their open-top vehicle. "Integrated Test Force; it houses our entire airborne laser research."

"Must be new. When I was here last, this was just desert."

O'Neil cast a quick glance at Ryson.

"Actually, it was built eight years ago." Shifting the Jeep's transmission to a higher gear, he sent the engine's rumble to a new pitch. "Maybe you should have visited us since," he continued amiably.

O'Neil's wistfulness would have been missed, Ryson thought, by anyone else. O'Neil was not a man who would befriend his employees easily, but Ryson's unique sharp wit had impressed him into making a rare exception. In Ryson he saw a younger version of himself, the man he once had been.

Then Ryson had abruptly left Tanaris, undergoing prolonged psychiatric treatments that took him back to the civilian world. With the passage of time, Ryson drifted out of O'Neil's memories, and the two had lost touch. Their relationship was not the only collateral damage from the ordeal.

"I'm sorry, old buddy," Ryson said, gazing into the distance.

"This place it is not easy to want to come back to," O'Neil said understandingly.

With the Jeep approaching closer, the shimmering blurred outlines of ITF buildings began to take more sharply defined form. The closest structure was an elongated hangar viewed broadside, behind which rose a huge dome. Ryson would not be able to guess its purpose.

Added to the mix was a parked passenger plane behind the hangar's wall, with only its nose and the tail visibly protruding from each end. Judging by the plane's bulbous cockpit, Ryson would probably assume it was a 747, but curiously one without a dorsal fin. The configuration of the complex was an enigma—a strange, eerie sight, even for a place like Tanaris.

O'Neil volunteered an explanation.

"The ITF complex has six buildings. The closest one is the System Integration Laboratory. SIL is where we do the ground-based laser testing. The dome structure you see is behind it."

Ryson seemed to be still reprocessing the scene based on O'Neil's input, when they pulled up to a double gate. It was the only entry point across the series of twelve-foot-high chain-link fences that surrounded the ITF complex.

As the Jeep passed through the security gates, heading straight for the heart of O'Neil's eight years of top-secret research, he looked at Ryson. A wave of excitement had swept over the lieutenant's countenance, like a medieval acolyte following a grand old wizard to his magic den.

THE AIR-COMBAT COMMAND,
LANGLEY AIR FORCE BASE, VIRGINIA
100 MILES SOUTHEAST OF WASHINGTON DC

A young private appeared at General Norton's office. Norton waved the subordinate in, who saluted, delivered a sizeable parcel he had carried laboriously in both hands, then exited.

Norton was content to be back on his home turf of Langley Air Force Base in Hampton, Virginia, situated on a verdant peninsula jutting into the Chesapeake Bay, with a single 10,000-foot runway as its center axis. The visually unassuming set-up belied the importance of this facility as the headquarters of the all-powerful Air Combat Command, the post-Cold War successor to the renowned Strategic Air Command, which was primarily tasked with delivering nuclear weapons inside the Soviet Union in a full-scale war.

ACC boasted an impressive aerial arsenal, spread nationwide, including the Whiteman Air Force Base in Missouri from which all twenty remaining B-2 bombers operated.

Norton, a proud ex-fighter jock, ran all complex assignments with the same precision as his F-15 on final approach to a target. This recent task, however, was different from all that had come before, and he was forbidden to share much about it with those around him.

He pulled out the package's paper-heavy contents, a compilation of all the aerial activities registered on the southern sector's alerted radar stations over a 5-hour period, when the stealth craft had flown eastwards to the Florida coast.

Eager to identify the black-classified craft, Norton had ordered key bases to full alert hours before schedule so to pre-spot the bogey as it headed east, identify the aircraft's type, and alert what to search for when the real hunt began on its return westerly path. He was cheating and knew it, but the temptation to teach the arrogant

Gorik a lesson in humility had been too great to resist.

But Norton had deliberately not been informed that he hunted a stealth craft. So far as he had known, all stealth planes on that day were accounted for by his direct orders.

When the news arrived of the test's "cancellation" minutes before the chase was to have begun, he assumed no plane had flown out. Now he was very interested in verifying whether the outbound aircraft had indeed evaded his net undetected.

Despite his rank, as a trained former radar officer, Norton enjoyed this type of sleuthing, as an opportunity to hone his hands-on skills.

He pored over the documents, page after page, looking at registered radar activities. It included all kinds, even flight of large feathered birds, but nothing that could not be attributed to something known. That is until he examined the site closest to the refueling tanker.

The details here were amazingly clear. One minute the massive tanker was a prominent blip on the screen, the next it had broken into several large segments that loosely held formation until they crashed into the ocean. Prior to the accident, only the extended boom could be seen on the tracking radar, as if the tanker had been dumping fuel into thin air, except that no fuel droplets were picked up on the radar until after the boom was severed.

If that bomber had not registered on radar when it most definitely should have been there, what chance did he have of knowing it had flown undetected over any of the other sites?

Disconcerted, Norton slammed the report shut and slid it to the edge of his smoothly polished desk. He took off his reading glasses and massaged the sinuses underneath with his index fingers. It seemed the damn thing really was as stealthy as the president had indicated, and as a seasoned Air Force general he did not like its implications.

AT THE ITF COMPLEX, TANARIS

O'Neil parked by the SIL's midsection and they walked close to the hangar's high wall for a respite from the blistering sun. Ryson's pace quickened as he drew closer to the long structure's end, anticipating a full view of the 747 parked behind it.

He turned the corner, then stood flabbergasted. The massive jumbo jet was in full view—only it was not stationed behind the hangar, but actually went straight through the sidewall!

The entire forward section of the plane's double-decker cockpit popped right out of the SIL's exterior front wall, as if a mounted hunting trophy in a lodge, complete with a darkened rim around the contact areas. The mundane analogy helped Ryson overcome his astonishment.

"I see it's Boeing hunting season again."

O'Neil smiled. "It's not mounted, the building is just a partial cover."

Ryson gazed at the surreal scene, as if a wingless fuselage had pulled into a covered bridge a tad too short to fully shelter it. But this was no ordinary hangar; the five-story high structure lacked a traditional giant sliding front door, was only three times the width of the 747 fuselage it housed and capped with a shallow angled sloping roof.

The plane itself was painted a dull gray, in sharp contrast to the hangar's white-washed finish. Its cockpit windshields were sheathed with thick black plastic covering. As he focused on the craft, an inexplicable feeling of unease swept over him that dampened his initial excitement to gloom. He ignored the troublesome sensation for now and focused on his fact-finding.

"Where did this 747 come from?" he asked with some concern.

"Airplane junkyard. We found a viable derelict, chopped off its wings and rear dorsal, then hauled the remaining airframe to this specially made laboratory."

"A plane without wings or rear dorsal?"

"They're not needed for our testing purposes, Ian. We're only interested in the fuselage where the laser systems are housed on a real plane."

Ryson took in the whole view, still unable to completely shake off his gloom.

"Lasers are complex systems," O'Neil elaborated, "they have many subparts which need to be properly integrated and the kinks worked out. The SIL is where we construct, install, and ground test the laser on a 747 before implementing it on an actual flying platform. Make sense?"

"It sure does," Ryson nodded.

"Let me show you how it all works. Follow me."

The two entered the SIL through a service door. The semi-illuminated interior of the 7,000-square-foot structure was a long corridor, with the looming pipe-like airframe of the 747 running its course to the far end.

The air here was much cooler, to Ryson's relief. Instruments, crates, and machinery of all kinds littered the scene. But curiously the place had the aura of having been vacant for some time, not the bustling hive Ryson had first imagined.

O'Neil led the way to under the fuselage just aft of the external cockpit section, then marched up a spiral staircase that ascended into the plane's dark belly. The motion sensors then switched on the interior lights.

Despite the plane's enormous size, they had entered a relatively small space. Judging by the four sets of computer console stations, this was a battle-management quarters mock-up, crammed between a pair of fore and aft bulkheads connected by a heavily shielded conduit.

Stale air permeated the quarters, bearing hints of unknown chemicals that irritated Ryson's sensitive nostrils. O'Neil headed for a nearby computer to retrieve a classified file, which depicted the full-blown airborne laser in flight.

"Here is how everything works," he pointed at the illuminated screen. "As you know, LASER is an acronym for Light Amplification through Stimulated Emission of Radiation. Thus, to generate a laser beam, you start by stimulating a *lasing material* so it emits radiation, i.e. light."

"Naturally," Ryson said.

"Lasing materials can come in many forms, solid like a ruby gem, or gaseous like helium-neon gas, but their unique property is that when the right amount of energy, such as electricity, is applied to them, the material's electrons are stimulated to release energy in form of a photon particles stream which is then concentrated to a laser beam, in a process called lasing."

"Thanks, but you should feel free to skip ahead."

O'Neil continued. "After that, it is a matter of collecting and focusing these laser lights into a larger beam powerful enough to burn a hole in the desired object. Like the outer structure of a missile. All you need then is a good tracking system to aim the laser beam and poof, you have a weapon. That essentially is it in principle, but in actuality, it's not an easy task."

"Why?"

"To maintain peak operational performance, a laser requires an ample supply of energy, such as from a nuclear reactor or hydro-electrical dam, but to get the thing airborne, we needed a light-weight material that could generate a lot of energy—more bang for the buck, so to speak."

"And how did you solve this riddle?"

"We came up with COIL."

"*Coil?*"

"Yes. Chemical Oxygen Iodine Laser."

Ryson shook his head. "How does it work?"

"We mix chemicals that produce a tremendous amount of heat for their weight. This thermal energy is fed into a lasing material which then produces numerous laser bursts, as I described."

"Sounds like it's more complicated than you're letting on."

"Not in principle. Let me show how it's done."

O'Neil had a schematic drawing appear on the display screen.

"It all begins at the gas generator," he pointed to the octagonal top box. "First we mix in chlorine gas with a pre-made mixture of liquid hydrogen peroxide and potassium hydroxide to produce electronically excited oxygen "O2" molecules.

Next down, these energized O2 molecules are mixed with the iodine gas in a second chamber then fed into the lasing cavity 'gain' region. Here, the oxygen's energy excites the iodine gas atoms which then quickly 'cool off,' releasing their energy as photons, the building particles of light and lasers. You with me so far?"

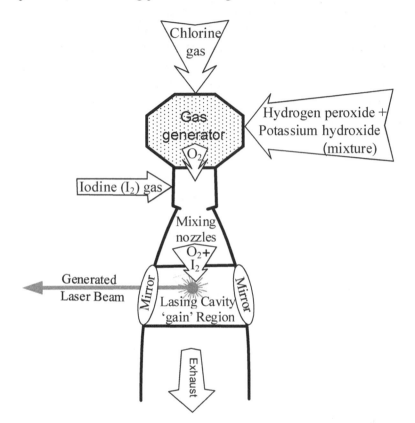

Ryson nodded, peering intently at the screen to fully comprehend the diagram. "So then you collect these released photons in these set of parallel laser cavity mirrors," his fingers traced further down, "which amplify the photons to be discharged as a laser beam."

"Yup," O'Neil nodded. "A megawatt class laser, too."

"What's special about the chemistry of these materials you're mixing in?"

"Nothing special, that's the real genius behind it. None are exotic or hard-to-produce materials, just everyday drugstore chemicals. Liquid hydrogen peroxide is basically hair bleach. Potassium hydroxide is used to unclog drains. Chlorine is your fabric-washing bleach or swimming pool water protector. Iodine is a typical skin disinfectant."

"Jeff, let me get this straight. You created a *mega*watt military-class missile-killing laser out of household chemicals?"

"That's right, old buddy."

"So some chemistry student can get all these ingredients from a local discount store and mix them up to create a weapon class laser fuel?"

O'Neil put his right hand on Ryson's shoulder and shook gently.

"Simple in concept only, but a devil in implementation," he pointed back to the diagram. "The mixed hydrogen peroxide, potassium hydroxide, and chlorine gas must be atomized first. The exact mixing ratio is key and classified. The mixture's resulting excited oxygen atoms are singlet delta oxygen which, along with the iodine gas, must be fed into the laser cavity at near supersonic speeds using customized mixing nozzles. Only then will you get your precious photons."

"'Near super-sonic mixing,' how?"

"With a specially developed super-fast turbine-pump. If you fed it water, it's powerful enough to fill up your average household pool in less than two minutes."

Ryson's lips curled in amazement. "That thing must be huge!"

"You would think so, but we are short on space in the plane, thus we built one so compact it can fit atop my office desk," he said. "Let's take a closer look." He opened a small door in the aft bulkhead which led to the weapons section.

Venturing deeper into the fuselage along the narrow, dimly illuminated access-way, Ryson found the 747's voluminous inside to be surprisingly cramped. Its tubular fuselage had the claustrophobic feel of a Navy nuclear submarine Ryson had once toured. After passing by various compartments, they arrived at the back of the plane, to a half-dozen huge modules.

"COIL modules," O'Neil remarked, "juxtaposed like a V-6 car engine, three to a side. You are looking at center aisle of the 'V.' We nicknamed it 'the laser vale.'"

"Cute," Ryson said.

O'Neil pointed to a peculiar looking device in one of the modules. "This is what all the hoopla is about: the FLM, Flight-weighted Laser Module. It's what makes COIL possible."

Ryson studied the oddly shaped device. It appeared as a maze of metallic pipes not unlike an oversized heating radiator, connected to a collection of intricately configured optical lenses.

"It's as big as an SUV!" Ryson exclaimed.

"Yeah, about 6,500 pounds per FLM, which is why we picked a 747-400 to lift it all up. Their interconnected cascaded format enables the power of the laser to be successively amplified by each FLM to the megawatt range."

Ryson saw that the pipes from each module seamlessly meshed with others to a mind-boggling tubular conduits grid, which struck him as both a plumbing masterpiece and nightmare.

"What about the waste from all the chemical reactions?" Ryson asked.

"Some benign heat, water, potassium salt, and oxygen; we recycle the hydrogen peroxide until it's used up." He headed for a staircase that took them underneath the giant V of the laser vale.

Ryson faced a colonnade of six funnel-shaped conduits coming down from the bottom of the 'V,' each funnel nearly as thick as the body of a nearby technician.

"These are the single tube ejector exhausts for the COIL, installed below the modules, so gravity pulls the gaseous waste down through them and then out to the sky from the plane's ventral."

As they walked back up the corridor, O'Neil motioned to a series of large upright polished metal cylindrical tanks, resembling the so-called 'Sherwood Forest,' the rows of missile silos in a nuclear-strike submarine.

"These pressurized tanks store laser fuel chemicals. Firing each laser shot consumes hundreds of pounds, per second. But a 747 can store 30,000 lbs. of it."

"So about forty laser shots worth?"

"Yes. And each shot costs only a thousand dollars. It's a basement bargain savings, costing less than 1% that of an anti-missile missile."

"And a hell of a lot more accurate too," Ryson surmised.

O'Neil nodded.

MOSCOW, RUSSIA

Trostov cursed as his luxury sedan was once again stuck in the heavy traffic for which the narrow aging surface grid of the former Soviet capital had never been designed to accommodate.

Trostov saw countless soaring modern structures, the many symbols of newfound wealth. Prosperity without proper regulation had led to corruption and provided shrewd opportunists like Trostov a path to undeserved riches.

During the Soviet era, Trostov had used his military status to create a shadowy network to smuggle fine western items into the luxury-starved state. Immediately following the formation of an independent Russian state, the hitherto sternly policed communist economic system lay in free-market disarray. Unemployment and inflation ran rampant, with goods even scarcer than before.

This environment had fueled the expansion of the general's domain into a lucrative underground empire, which repeatedly ten-folded his wealth. Eventually, as order supplanted economic chaos, Trostov legitimized his vast fleet of cargo ships under registered maritime corporations, though mainly as a tax shelter.

On the surface, Trostov was a sharp-dressed, respectable businessman who provided much needed infrastructure to a fledgling economy. Underneath, he was incorrigibly corrupt, trafficking for hefty profits any contraband: drugs, prostitutes, stolen luxury cars, and ransacked historic artifacts. But his favorite smuggled items of all were instruments of war: tanks, guns, artillery, and even fighter jets were sold to the highest bidders. Those who dared oppose him or offered consequential competition were violently put down by his allies in organized crime.

He recently had focused on the more lucrative business of industrial espionage, particularly in acquiring the billion-dollar military secrets of major western powers. He sold them to eager nations able to make use of such information, mostly China and a resurgent communist-sympathizing Russian government, which allowed him to continue operating with impunity.

Now he was finally in possession of what no one else had ever dreamed, cryptically named "crystals" to throw off any prying electronic eavesdroppers.

Excited about the next steps, he dialed on his cell phone a longer than normal sequence. A foreign beeping pattern filtered in before the other side picked up.

"Hello?" The male voice had a thick Chinese accent.

"We have them."

"And are they absolutely clean?"

"Reasonably certain, regardless, this completes our contract's first phase," Trostov pushed.

"Agreed. Give me our meeting location then."

Trostov read off a set of encrypted numbers. They only meant something to the person who could translate them into a geographic location.

"Goodbye," the man said curtly.

Trostov smiled. A big payday lay ahead if all went well, and he saw no reason why it wouldn't.

AT THE ITF COMPLEX

O'Neil continued rambling on excitedly about the mechanisms and control systems of the laser in minute details. By the time they had made it back into the battle management quarters, Ryson's brain was nearly full of technical jargons. But his curiosity was still not satisfied on some of the laser's more key aspects.

"You mentioned this laser operates at a 1.134 microns short wavelength?"

"Yes, to reduce the laser degradation caused by the atmosphere."

"But laser beam operations are sensitive to air pressure differences between various altitudes. Just how did you account for this critical aspect in your ground tests, seeing that the forty thousand feet operating ceiling of the COIL is way up there?" he asked, pointing skyward.

O'Neil looked mildly disappointed. "You are underestimating me Ian."

"Certain things just cannot be done on the ground," Ryson said defensively.

"Can't they?" O'Neil challenged. "Follow me." He headed back down the staircase and then exited the hangar on the opposite side of the SIL.

Ryson squinted at the bright outdoors, then focused on a most peculiar structure towering about a hundred yards in the distance.

It was an enormous white sphere, over eleven stories high, held aloft by an array of slender vertical supports mating to its equatorial belt. The ensemble reminded Ryson of a giant elevated municipal water tank, but one of a wider spherical storage, and a far different purpose. He recognized it as the same structure he had caught a mystifying glimpse of right before landing at Tanaris.

"What in the world is *that*?"

"The Ground Pressure Recovery Assembly. It solves your air density issues."

"How does it operate?"

"It simulates the lower pressures existing at up to forty thousand feet. The spherical chamber you see is a negative pressure vessel that sucks out by-products of the COIL, like heat and water vapors, which can otherwise snuff out the laser generating chemical reactions in the SIL. It also changes the SIL's internal air density, based on how much air we suck out, so we can conduct our research as if we were at that altitude's air pressure. As you can see, a duct connects the chamber's south pole to the SIL building for quick venting."

Ryson followed the trail of a huge pipe tall enough to accommodate an upright six-foot-tall man, with headroom to spare.

O'Neil gazed up at the massive dome gleaming beneath the midday sun. "350,000-cubic ft of air volume capacity, over 1.5 times what goes into a blimp. And it's just as airtight!"

Ryson mulled the unorthodox design of the giant structure and its special purpose. "So what you really have made is the world's biggest vacuum cleaner."

O'Neil led out a burst of laughter at Ryson's often wry yet accurately observant humor. "Yes indeed! And the most expensive one, at nearly 19 million dollars."

"Nothing comes cheap if it's military," Ryson remarked. "And where are the targeting optics for firing the laser from the plane?"

"They were outsourced to our off-base specialists, then mounted directly on the operational prototype. We're nearly done with the testing phases, and duplicates of everything you saw in the SIL was implemented in our existing prototype ABL."

"I like to see the actual operational model. Seeing is believing," Ryson offered.

"Right now the bird is out on an eight-hour test flight. How about tomorrow?"

"Fine," Ryson said, and followed his mentor to their parked Jeep.

As they sped away, Ryson's mind remained preoccupied with the strange buildings he had seen. They had no earthly business being on an airbase.

Half a mile out, he turned to take a last look at the entire mystifying complex.

The front cockpit portion of the SIL's mock plane caught his attention again, and suddenly he realized what had been bothering him since first seeing it up close. It resembled the ghastly severed head of the aerial tanker he had encountered a few days ago at the bottom of the dark Atlantic, with a dead crew inside, in sharp contrast to this bright and serene desert.

There was a connection between the two, Ryson was sure of it, and men had died because of it. Perhaps more would perish if he could not timely complete his task. He turned and refocused on the road. In the distance, the asphalt shimmered under the hot afternoon sun. And though temperatures soared past one hundred degrees, Ryson felt a cold shiver run through him.

THE WHITE HOUSE

When Edward Fleisler and General Norton arrived at the Oval Office in response to the urgent request, they found the commander in chief seated behind his desk poring over an engrossing document that had caused his somber expression.

Fleisler politely knocked on the opened door and the president looked up, somewhat startled, as if being shook from a deep trance.

"Oh, come in." He listlessly invited them to shut the door.

"We came as fast we could, sir."

"Thank you. I wanted to hear the latest updates in person."

Fleisler cleared his throat. "Well, Mr. President, we paid Admiral Connelly a personal visit and without disclosing the black-classified nature of the plane in question secured his cooperation in searching the seabed more thoroughly."

The president nodded appreciatively. "How long before we can get some feedback from the old skipper?"

"Two more days, considering our plane's elusive characteristics," Norton said.

"That's what I'm most worried about," he said, falling into a brooding silence.

Fleisler raised an eyebrow. "What is on your mind sir?"

"I asked the National Security Advisor to prepare me this briefing," his fingers began drumming atop a sheet of paper. "It's an appalling summary of serious military security leaks we've had in just the last few years."

"Sir—"

"A couple years ago, FBI arrested one of our trusted India-born stealth bomber engineers for selling his stealth cruise missile technical know-how to China."

"I am familiar with the case."

The president sighed, peering over his reading glasses. "Last year, a California defense contractor engineer was arrested for selling submarine propulsion technology, also to China."

"Yes sir, he was convicted and is serving 25 years," Norton added.

"And few months ago, a Canadian citizen of Chinese origin, sold to the Chinese Navy our fighter pilot training software. The jury gave him just two years in jail."

Fleisler wanted to interject but kept silent, noting the rising anger in his superior's voice.

The president's fingers balled into a fist; the paper crumpled inside it. "China, and other determined rivals are relentlessly after our military secrets. We have been too late to detect these breaches. God knows what else is going on."

"Sir, do you think Chinese military espionage is behind this bomber accident?"

The president shot a glance at the Secretary and pounded his fist on the table, the crumpled report still tightly squeezed between his fingers. "That is exactly what I think!"

"But sir," Fleisler said, trying to maintain calm, "this is too bold, even for China or Russia. Buying documents is one thing but stealing a functioning strategic weapon from our airspace could well be construed as an act of war. They know we would come looking for our missing bomber."

"Unless we are led to believe it has already been destroyed in an innocuous accident."

"My God, do you think that this whole event has been staged?"

Releasing his grip on the paper, the president simply looked into the distance.

"By whom?" Norton challenged. "Colonel Gorik would never have ordered it."

"Maybe not," the president said distantly. "But what do you know on the pilot?"

The president had a point. When it came down to it, not much was known about the pilot, besides Gorik's dubious explanations. "God help us," Fleisler muttered.

"Let's look at it from another angle," Norton surmised. "Only two countries in the world have the interest *and* the capabilities to make use of the bomber's technology, and if exposed, to survive a U.S. political or military backlash."

"China and Russia," the president mused.

"Yes sir. So any place in between would just be a refueling point, or a parking lot till the heat was off, before the plane was delivered, maybe in pieces. The intermediate refueling locale must be at a half-way distance to those countries."

"It can't be in Europe, too conspicuous" Fleisler said.

"So what's left?" asked the president.

"Africa's northern Sahara" Norton said. "I doubt it got parked in the desert. But the Russians could have sent in a tanker, and aerially refueled it for a flight home. Not much radar coverage on most places over the Sahara. It would be perfect."

"Makes sense," the president said, uneasy at the direction matters were headed.

"We need to look at all recent aerial military activity in this region. If anything unusual has been going on, I want us to know about it," Fleisler said.

"And pray we don't come up with anything conclusive," the president interjected. "If a Russian or Chinese military tanker was covertly used, then it was government sanctioned. That would be an act of war, World War III."

The two men gazed at the commander in chief, whose mood had now gone as dark as their own hopes for a peaceful ending to the crisis.

"Let's just hope our man Ryson can find out something useful, and soon."

APPROACHING TANARIS

"That hydraulic oil pump I replaced is doing well in this flight," commented Albert Maines, the helicopter pilot.

Ryson, in the passenger seat, silently nodded. The thump of the chopper's engine permeated the orb-shaped canopy, making conversation somewhat difficult. He peered at the jaggedly grooved desert unfolding below, first made familiar from his years at Tanaris.

But his mind was on Evertt, the ill-fated bomber's pilot. Ryson was returning from Evertt's apartment, in a city fifty miles out. He was unable to find any identifying clues, not even fingerprints, as the place had been evidently wiped clean, presumably by Gorik's orders.

The only encountered items of interest were a trio of empty picture frames on a living-room end table. All had been cracked, leaving behind broken panes and strewn glass shards, with a black ribbon and half-wilted rose next to one.

A thought occurred to Ryson. "Albert," he addressed the pilot. "What did you want to tell me the other day?"

Maines hesitated for a second. "First, tell me the craft-type Evertt piloted."

Ryson disliked breaching security protocols, but perhaps he could bend the rules a little.

"It was an ordinary bomber."

Maine shook his head. "That can't be. You see, one day a nasty weather front rolled in and caught us off guard. I wanted to turn back, but he took the helm and flew us through that horrible storm, negotiating turbulence with uncanny precision. I never told anyone about that."

Ryson considered the story. "Lots of pilots here can do that in a chopper."

Maines raised an eyebrow. "No, that kind of turn-on-a-dime maneuvering is not something a heavy-bomber pilot is trained for; those large birds simply ain't built for such agility. *I* sure didn't learn that. This fella's talent level usually doesn't end up in a bomber."

Ryson cast him a look and discerned an intriguing glint in Maine's eyes. "Perhaps, but I have a feeling there is more here you are not telling me."

Maines suddenly looked apprehensive, as if fearing being overheard. "I did not want to say this. But something *did* happen on our last flight."

"What?"

"He pulled out a picture trio from his flight suit and gazed at each for a long while. Never done that before."

"Go on." Ryson found his curiosity piquing.

"I took a peek. Two were of men in flight suits by a military plane. I gathered the courage to ask him on them. To my surprise he spoke for the first time."

"What did he say?"

"That they were his brightest wingmen and best friends. And then there was a portrait of a lady, prettiest thing you ever saw. He said she was his wife. I dared again, to ask him what happened to them. And then he did the unthinkable."

"What?"

"He lifted the visor to reveal his eyes, in a gaze that sent shivers down my spine. They seemed like a possessed man's, burning with some untold fury."

"Amazing."

"Then said she was killed in a freak accident in South America, nine years ago on February 20th, the date stuck with me for some reason. And that is all he spoke, before he closed the visor and tucked the pictures back in his flight suit."

Ryson reflected on the story. "He must have loved her deeply," suddenly feeling a connection between him and Evertt. "Is this the man?" he asked, presenting Evertt's file photo.

"Don't seem like him, I only saw his eyes, they weren't anything like in this picture. Listen, if anyone asked, we never spoke of this," Maines half-pleaded.

"You got it," Ryson reassured, then quickly fell back into a pensive silence.

Ryson deduced that Everett's sudden break of no-communication protocol with Maines meant he was not intent on coming back, which gave credence to the thought that his any role in the tanker's destruction was not due to a drug-induced panic, but pre-meditation.

Still, Ryson knew that a one-facetted perception of a person's characters rarely provided an accurate complete picture of the whole. His own life was proof of this axiom. His intuitive scientific talents were the envy of his peers, who seemed to assume he lived in a Nirvana where solutions to complex problems appeared before him, on command.

Ian's father was a race car engineer, and their weekends at the track had influenced Ian's fascination with engineered speed. But Ian wanted to fly. Years later, when being awarded in a high school science contest, an attending U.S. Air Force recruiter had exuberantly encouraged him to become a flight-test engineer: a hybrid of a test pilot and aeronautics engineer who improves a prototype plane's flight characteristics. Ian quickly took it to be his life's calling.

Following high school, Ryson enrolled in the U.S. Air Force Academy and began the required educational trajectory by attending both engineering and Test Pilot schools. It was the most fulfilling period of his life to date. But as his uncanny mastery of electromagnetic wave theory became increasingly evident, his superiors decided that he would better serve the USAF if devoted exclusively to the upcoming field of stealth design. He had simply become too valuable to be lost to a flight test accident. Despite his vehement protests, he had been phased off the flight line and placed in pure R&D.

Recognizing that he would never fly futuristic fighter craft, he disappointedly left the Air Force in favor of a private aviation manufacturing powerhouse, a supplier of cutting-edge military aircraft. That way he would at least enjoy the normalcy of civilian life.

After a brilliant start in the private sector, however, he discovered that the company was financially failing, and was soon laid off. Without work for over a year, he was coaxed at his lowest point to join the Black Squadron, a decision he would ultimately bitterly regret.

And then his life was rent by that one calamitous day.

Ryson shivered, and his head shook with short spastic motions as if suddenly doused by a bucket of ice water.

"Hang on," Maines said. "Getting bumpy with the evening winds picking up."

Ryson nodded appreciatively for the rescue from his own bitter thoughts. He suspected he had unwittingly played a greater role in the Evertt affair than he cared to admit at this point, especially to himself. The familiar Tanaris crater came into view, and somewhere in it lay the answers he was seeking so that he could return to his girlfriend before it was too late.

"Land us by plant 9," he hollered back, Maines confirming with a nod.

The chopper flew over the crater's rim in a shallow arch, heading straight for the heli-pad. In the distance, Ryson caught the glint off a huge white plane approaching the runway. It appeared civilian from afar, though he knew its nature to be anything but that.

BARCELONA, SPAIN

Sluggishly, the tourist-filled cable car left the stone and concrete hub dug inside Montjuic recreational Mountain adjoining the panoramic Mediterranean and set out for the other side of the Barcelona harbor.

From the restaurant perched atop the cable car's station, Trostov followed the gondola's leisurely pace, before returning to the business at hand with the official sitting across his table.

Xendong, a bespectacled round-faced man in his fifties with receding wispy silver hair, was staring at Trostov with calculating eyes. "What an inconspicuous location you picked us."

"I'm a shipping magnate," Trostov reminded. "Besides, I like the view." Trostov, had loved it ever since his first visit in 1980, then as part of a high-ranking Soviet delegation.

Trostov knew that for Xendong, a China native, such sentimentalities played no role in a cold business world. Xendong regarded the flamboyant life-style of the former Soviet general a liability to the otherwise chess-like planning that went on behind those steely eyes. But as a black-market veteran who had withstood countless attempts on his life, Trostov seemed unfazed. The Russian slapped some thinly sliced Jamon Iberico, a local cured ham delicacy, onto his tomato-pasted bread and invited Xendong to do the same.

Xendong sighed. "Stop wasting my time."

"The deal is: deposit $1.5 billion to my off-shore accounts, evenly distributed."

"My investors need to know the merchandise has not been tracked."

"The shelter's metallic fish-net covering creates a Faraday cage. No radio transmissions get in or out. Otherwise they would have come for it by now."

"Maybe it's their waiting trap for you," Xendong warned.

"This is too important to them to wait just for me," he said. "I assure you, it has not been traced." He wrote a sequence of encrypted Global Positioning Satellite coordinates on a napkin and shoved it across the table.

Xendong was the only man with the decipher key. "This is the meeting place?"

Trostov nodded. "Yes. In two days. And don't be late."

TANARIS

Standing at the flight line's edge, Ryson beheld the ponderous Boeing 747 elegantly touch down, then wheel to a halt a mere hundred feet away. The roar of the four powerful engines reverberated in Ryson's ears.

A pair of low flying F-18 fighters suddenly appeared overhead, but in relative silence, their normally earsplitting jets unable to acoustically penetrate through the ABL's howl. Ryson watched the fighters zoom gracefully over the edge of the Tanaris crater and out of sight. Then he returned his gaze to the tarmac.

A small flat-top tow vehicle approached the white leviathan, a mouse before an elephant, its tentacle gripped the 747's front wheel shaft and backed the behemoth into its designated parking area with surprising ease. Only then did the ABL's engines whine died down.

"There she is my friend, in all her glory," O'Neil declared, arms extending out toward the giant plane, as if for a lover's embrace.

Ryson's perception was less passionate. He focused on the unusual bulbous contraption attached to the plane's nose cone.

"We call it the Big Eye," O'Neil had spotted his curiosity. "It's where the laser exits to engage targets. Let me show you." Using a cordless CB, he instructed the plane's control room.

A huge cornea within the Big Eye rolled vertically to expose on its reverse side a massive and highly polished glossy lens running the spectrum of colors as it rotated into position.

"It's the world's largest air-borne turret," O'Neil said, "weighing in at 7 tons."

Ryson regarded the contraption's aptly named conformal window, with apprehension. The swiveling targeting lens and its glimmering iridescent sheen mimicked a giant roving eye, of perhaps a science-fiction alien predator peering intently at him, capable of unleashing enough energy to burn him to cinders.

O'Neil continued. "Took us six years to build it to its exacting specifications. The optical coating enables usage as both a firing platform and a receptor."

"A receptor?"

"Yes. ABL really has four lasers. Two track and beacon for target acquisition and illumination, a 3rd measures atmospheric turbulence so we can adjust COIL's power to compensate. Their reflected beams are received in its mirrors as feedback. All lasers operate at different frequencies to not interfere with each other."

"That nose-tip turret must have wreaked all kinds of aerodynamics havoc with flight performance," Ryson remarked.

"It did at first. But with computer modeling and wind tunnel simulations we solved most of it. She still won't fly like its intended commercial airliner design," O'Neil allowed, looking up with a stiffened neck, hands clasped firmly behind his back. "But then again we are not hauling passengers here. She will circle the battlefield, blast out Scuds, and then come down."

"Isn't the laser sensitive to the plane's vibrations?" Ryson asked, cocking his head at the 747.

"Very much," said O'Neil, "All laser related devices, even the 6 COIL modules, had to be painstakingly isolated from the airframe with state-of-the-art spring load vibration isolation benches, to dampen the shakings to acceptable levels."

Ryson did some quick mental calculations. "I remember a demonstration module back in mid-90s that had only multi-hundred-kilowatt power. It had a weighty platform, pushing the limits of the plane's lift thrust. Now at your current increased megawatt levels, the laser platform would become too heavy and bulky to lift with any plane."

"Have a little faith," replied O'Neil. "That laser was made over a decade ago, old news. We now use compact lighter materials, aerospace grade stuff integrated into the essential hardware elements. And using several laser modules provides synergy to increase laser power, reducing weight and volume. Altogether we are packing *only* 200,000 pounds into the airframe."

"And it all works?" Ryson asked, a hint of skepticism seeping into his voice.

"Beautifully!" O'Neil said cheerfully. "It outputs 110% of the power it was set to generate."

Ryson let out a whistle of pure astonishment, looking at the gleaming monster with newfound respect. It was filled with marvels that until now had belonged to the realm of pure imagination. But it was all real, though perhaps still too heavy in the context of this mission.

"So you essentially put *two* B-2's worth of weight inside the ABL."

"Uh-huh," O'Neil nodded.

"But none of the B-2s can be retrofitted to carry so much mass, nor carry such a nose-mounted turret without losing its stealth capability."

"True, but the SuperCOIL is *not* a retrofitted B-2. It's a new plane designed to accommodate all that."

"Now listen to me," Ryson said, his tone serious. "It's damn near impossible to build a whole new stealth bomber without thousands of contractors ..."

O'Neil silenced him with a hand wave as a technician approached within ear shot, and urgently motioned to the Chief Engineer.

"I have to go now but come by my office later to chat." Before Ryson could say anything, O'Neil was off, leaving Ryson with more questions than answers.

GORIK'S OFFICE

Kessler stepped out of the special access elevator, which opened directly into Colonel Gorik's top floor office. Unlike the ornate conference room, the colonel had configured his working environment to be a highly functional setting for tackling everyday tasks. Large flat-panel computer displays, and state-of-the-art telecommunication and surveillance gear allowed access to virtually anyone, while keeping eyes on every inch of Tanaris.

"What's the report on Ryson?" Gorik asked, not taking eyes off his readings.

"Seems all the interviewed base personal told him the same thing, as expected."

Gorik gazed pensively at the far wall. "Any one of high rank?"

"Just one: Jeffery O'Neil."

Gorik's eyes darkened. "He wasn't to be contacted!"

"O'Neil is a technical person, sir," Kessler said. "He knows nothing about

Evertt. The two never met."

"O'Neil knows too much about all other aspects of our operations. With his help, Ryson might be able to piece things together." Gorik fell silent for a time and then said, "I will handle this myself. Just keep your eyes open. If Ryson starts to cross certain thresholds, I will have to ask you to do something decisive about it."

RYSON'S QUARTERS, TANARIS

Ryson dimmed the lights which, all things considered, felt apt as it closely mimicked his prospect of investigative success so far. For the moment, however, the missing B-2 was not his foremost concern. His unsettling thoughts returned to Evertt, who had bore the burden of a tragical loss of his wife, and it all gnawed at Ryson's subconscious.

Whatever the mystery behind Evertt's motives, this facet of his life had evoked an unwelcome feeling within Ryson that had been growing unchecked for the past few hours. He could not allow it to continue.

He flipped his suitcase open to a large stack of files, but instead reached for a secret custom-made compartment, a relic of the Cold War, used for hiding classified microfiche.

Ryson opened the complex lock and produced a small container of liquor. He twisted the top off and took a long swig. The hard drink hit the back of his throat with a mild sting. As it inched down, a pleasant warmth soothed his mind, like an ointment applied to a surface burn.

He lay down on the bed and gazed at the slowly rotating ceiling fan. He let the cool airflow wash over him and yearned to be back in his girlfriend's arms.

Soon as his eyelids had closed, however, a different, terrifying vision began to form. Ryson took a deep breath then reopened his eyes to dispel that picture though it remained, as if projected onto the ceiling, his mind replaying a horrible past day from which he could not escape. His mind's ears now heard the loud clangor of the twin-engine propeller plane in which he and his fiancée had been sitting, more than ten years ago.

Exactly three years prior to that date he had met her on a sunny beach in San Diego while on leave from Tanaris. An outdoors, adventurous person with whom Ryson shared many interests, she was a pure delight and the two quickly fell in love, a prelude to the best years of his life.

They had recently partaken skydiving, and Ryson thought it the perfect setting in which to propose. After the dive, they would celebrate at a romantic ocean-view restaurant.

As the airborne plane neared the drop zone, Ryson got down on one knee. Holding the ring, he gazed into her eyes and asked with a trembling voice if she would marry him. She said yes and eagerly slid the ring onto her finger. Then the two embraced and shared a passionate kiss.

Soon they arrived at the drop zone, and the crew opened the side door. Gusts of winds swirled through the fuselage. Decked in helmet and goggles, they shared another loving kiss before the jump. She exited first, followed by Ryson.

The duo settled into arch position, descending in tandem from 9,000 feet. From his vantage point, Ryson's eyes followed the beautiful white-clad figure hovering gracefully below, arms extended wide as she sailed smoothly in the azure sky. Her long golden hair flowed out from under her helmet, undulating in the rush of fresh outdoor air, glimmering softly in the evening sun. A multicolor tapestry of landscape sprawled beneath, a breathtaking backdrop to the flight of his angel.

Ryson committed the magnificent scenery to memory. It was an indescribable feeling this aerial buoyancy, a sense of stillness despite the falling, made indelible by the mesmerizing sight of his fiancée. He wished they could stay afloat forever, two beings in love, living among the clouds, free from the mundane worries of the lands below.

The beeping of his altimeter interrupted his reveries: time to deploy their chutes. Ryson waited for hers to deploy, to slow her just enough for him to catch up, enabling a side by side landing in the drop zone, now for the first time as her fiancé. Their post engagement time on the plane had been far too short. The rest of their lives were just beginning to unfold, and he could not wait to reach the ground to start that life.

But looking down, he noticed something was wrong. He saw her reaching for and pulling the release cord on her chute. Nothing happened; the chute pack was unresponsive. She pulled again, then again, but still nothing. To his horror, he realized a malfunction must be preventing the parachute from deploying. She was falling helplessly, something had to be done.

His mind froze at the thought of the ghastly eventuality, as if it had already transpired. A paralyzing fugue gripped him, and he was unable to summon motion. Within seconds however, the paralysis had passed just as inexplicably, and he had full control of his body, allowing him to devise a plan. He would go to her, and save her with his own parachute.

They had both reached the terminal velocity of 120 mph, and air drag prevented further acceleration while in a free-fall belly position. It would be impossible to cross the five hundred feet separating them if he could not descend faster than her.

But Ryson, an experienced skydiver from his flight engineer training, knew how to outwit gravity. Orienting his torso head-down he increased terminal velocity to the maximum of 180 mph and shot downward like an arrow.

Zooming down, the wind whipped furiously against his face and the g-forces mounted, but he kept his eyes focused on her and willed himself closer, as the ground was springing up at a horrific pace. He was almost upon her, and his hands were outstretched to within inches of her jumpsuit fluttering wildly in the wind.

Just a second or two more and he would have her.

He yelled out to her, but his call was ripped away by the wind.

Ryson lurched the last inches forward by mimicking a swimmer's breaststroke, and his right fingers grabbed the tail end of her jump pants. He felt immense relief and thrust his left arm forward to secure a firm hold on her ankle, intending to clamber along her body and grab her in a tight embrace, then deploy his chute.

But something unexpected happened. Rather than lunging forward, he was violently tugged upwards, hoisted with great force as if by a giant hand. Her slick nylon suit slipped out of his tenuous grip, and his left arm, already in mid swing forward, fell inches short of her ankle.

He was going up, away from her, against his will. To his horror he saw his parachute unfolding up above. He must have crossed the minimum deployment altitude, and the altimeter-controlled emergency safety mechanism had automatically opened his chute. Devised as a safeguard against a skydiver's loss of consciousness following a jump, it had now triggered with opposite effect. The air rushed into the parachute, lifting him like a marionette in the wind.

"No!" he screamed in agony, writhing within the straps, eyes bulging with the shock of being helplessly carried away, robbed of his one chance to save her.

Looking down, he watched as her arms flailed helplessly as the inevitability of death became clear to her. Before his eyes, the love of his life slipped away, ever further out of reach.

She receded still further, a fast diminishing dot in the landscape, and then was swallowed up by a green cluster of trees. In a brief glimmer of hope he wondered if the branches had dampened the 120-mile-per-hour impact of a terminal velocity freefall to somehow forestall a certain demise. That sliver of hope, however irrational or unrealistic, forced him into steering the parachute near the crash site.

Landing less than two minutes later, he spotted the prone body a hundred feet away, helmet and gear still intact. Heart in his throat, he hastily released the parachute and broke into a run. When he reached her, he knelt down and checked her for vital signs, a faint pulse, heartbeat or shallow breathing.

There were none.

Her body was smashed, neck broken, skull fractured with blood flowing from the helmet to pool into the diving goggles. Her eyes, however, were wide open, those vibrant green gems he regarded as the most beautiful in the world and into which he had so lovingly gazed just minutes earlier, now harbored no life. The expression on her face was one of supplication.

He gently placed her head on his lap, and carefully removed the goggles; softly he ran his palm over her face, closing the eyelids. Tightly clasping her left hand, he caressed the finger on which he had put the ring and thought of the future that now could never be.

Tears welled up and head turned to the sky, he sought answers he knew would not come. Anguish boiled to unbearable levels, everything blurred in a lurid haze; he was only vaguely aware of the subsequent events, the wail of ambulances, the rushing paramedics, and the trips to the hospital, and the morgue, as if it all happened to someone else.

Forever burnt in his eidetic memory was her last pleading expression; the same helpless plea he had heard in her final screams. Perhaps she prayed for survival seconds before the impact. But Ryson's ravaged mind interpreted the gesture as a plea for help directed solely at him, the man she had hoped would save her from the inevitable when all else had failed.

And he had let her die.

What would have happened if those precious seconds were not lost while he remained locked in that frozen, shock-induced stupor?

Months later, the psychiatrist had explained it was not his fault. He had suffered from a rare and hitherto undiagnosed psychological condition, an involuntary reaction triggered in even the bravest individuals when the life of a loved one was placed in mortal danger.

The sound medical reasoning proved devastating nonetheless, only affirming his belief in his inability to act when a loved one needed him most. He became convinced that his love had literally killed her and had reasoned that without such deep love the event's impact would not have triggered the virtual freeze, which deprived him the time to save her. It did not matter that he had never experienced such paralysis before, not even when facing death while test piloting the most unwieldy of fighter jets past their envelope.

Held captive by a growing sense of self-imposed guilt, Ryson's wall of confidence when performing perilous tasks gradually shattered, subconsciously dismantled brick by brick, in an effort to never be placed in another such situation. So did his volition for lasting intimacy or true love. If he did not love, he could not hurt by failing to save a loved one's life if called upon again.

A guilty subconscious is an avid taker; the more he nurtured his guilt, the more it spread like cancer until it had nearly consumed him. Over time, his enfeebled condition had exacerbated to fuse with most aspects of his life, even at nights, to render his dreams as pure nightmares.

In those frightful sleeps he would vicariously experience his fiancée's final writhing moments, a terrifying falling sensation to the bone-shattering end.

GENERAL NORTON'S HEADQUARTERS, LANGLEY AIR FORCE BASE

General Norton had just unsuccessfully combed through the voluminous comprehensive intelligence report on detected aerial military activity of interest within the disappeared bomber's range, when his phone rang.

He answered, it was Admiral Connelly's voice, absent its usual abrasiveness.

"My fleet has completed scouring the seabed. They recovered every piece of the tanker, but nothing belonging to a stealth bomber."

"So your boys came up empty handed."

"They are the best, and if they said it's not there, then by God it is not."

Norton thanked Connelly, then hung up and reclined, rubbing his tired eyes.

He then returned his gaze to the large wall-mounted world-map, hopelessly attempting to pinpoint the elusive bomber's whereabouts within its maximum flight range, a vast expanse which constituted one tenth of the whole planetary surface. It was akin to searching for the proverbial needle in a haystack, and a task unlike anything he had trained for. The stealth project was conceived to pose an unsolvable detection riddle to the enemy. Norton never thought the day would come when he was looking for one on his own radar scopes.

But he had always presciently feared as such, from the first day when the stealth bomber wing was officially placed under his command following their service entry. To fully familiarize himself with the singular characteristics of these phenomenal flying contraptions, he had met with Ian Ryson, the stealth guru, for a detailed briefing. He recalled their captivating discussion.

"I still don't fully understand how it works, it's all like magic to me," the future head of Air Combat Command asked Ryson.

"It's not magic sir. It's stealth, and it's all science," Ryson replied.

"Suppose you explain it to me, easy."

"As you know, radar is an acronym for radio detecting and ranging. A radar dish emits invisible radiation, like a lighthouse, then "spots" an aircraft by its reflected radiation. So in a nutshell, to be stealthy, an aircraft must not reflect radiation back to the radar station."

"Yes, but how is it all done?"

"In two ways: you correctly angle a surface to bounce most of the radiation energy away from the radar source, while you absorb the rest within the body of the aircraft like a sponge."

"*Absorb* radar radiation, how?"

"You cover the surfaces with RAM, radar absorbing materials, such as the Iron-ball paint that converts the received radar energy into negligible heat, via tiny metal-coated spherical particles suspended in thick paint."

"So then why not just simply absorb all of the radar radiation with RAM?" Norton asked.

"Because that much RAM makes the aircraft too aerodynamically bulky to effectively fly, hence the need for radar deflective shapes as well, which themselves also pose great obstacles to stable flight. The big challenge is that stealth principles and implementations are often at odds with aerodynamics'."

"Meaning anything shaped really stealthy is not flyable?"

"Yes, until recently," Ryson said.

"And what is so dauntingly difficult about angling the surfaces so they are not like a head-on mirror to reflect radar energy back to its source?"

"An aircraft has countless differently-angled aerodynamic surfaces along its wings, stabilizers, fuselage, tail fin, rudders and engine intakes, and also its wing-mounted missiles and bombs," Ryson remarked. "Radar waves bounce at different angles off each such angularly-varied surface, making the determining of an overall radar-evasive surface configuration for an airworthy airplane very difficult.

"Thus, a fundamental theoretical understanding of how electromagnetic radar beams reflect off a plane's intricately linked surfaces was desperately needed. Fortunately, we got some serious help from the most unlikely source of all."

"Who?"

"The Soviets."

Norton's eyes popped open. "Our own mortal enemies of Cold War??"

"Yes sir. A Soviet scientist, named Pyotr Ufimtsev, devised equations that accurately predicted how electromagnetic radiation reflects off any given geometric configuration. He explained this breakthrough in his 1966 classified paper entitled the 'Method of Edge Waves in the Physical Theory of Diffraction', which earned him the highly coveted State Prize of the Soviet Union."

"Whoa."

"But at this critical juncture, the Soviet military just shelved his work."

Norton's curiosity piqued again. "Why?"

"Because Ufimtsev's equations were considered by the Soviet airplane designers to be at total odds with aerodynamics, and only led to an unflyable plane with just flat surfaces. Plus, the equations were too calculation intensive for the contemporary computers to effectively tackle.

"Then in 1970s Ufimtsev's work was declassified and the USAF Foreign Technology Division translated it but without realizing its true portents."

"Go on."

"The translation was studied by our aerospace powerhouses, including Northrop and Lockheed, as part of clandestine Project Harvey, to devise military aircraft that could seep into the impenetrable Soviet defensive radar net.

"A genius engineer at Lockheed's top-secret facility nicknamed 'Skunk Works' figured out how to effectively use Ufimtsev's equations for an optimal stealth airplane shape."

"Good old 'Skunk Works'!" Norton praised. "Those guys had for decades churned out state of the art legendary spy aircraft: the U-2 in the 1950s and SR-71 Blackbird in the 1960s."

"Right, and this time, using Ufimtsev's work, they removed the largest theoretical hurdle on how to reduce a plane's radar cross section, or RCS, so it be virtually undetectable."

Norton silently nodded in agreement. He knew how overly dependent modern designs are on computers, but the fact remained that computers can only calculate, not theorize principles.

Ryson continued. "A plane's RCS determination was still a very prodigious calculation task. But recent advances in U.S. micro-chip technology had made computers just powerful enough for calculating two-dimensional flat shapes. The resulting aircraft could thus have no curved surfaces, contrary to almost every aircraft design to date. And all the flat surfaces, or facets, had to have the fewest end-points: three, which reduced the plane to a set of triangles.

"A cleverly designed Lockheed computer program called "Echo-1" then calculated the RCS of each triangle which then got summed up to a whole, for the entire plane."

"I assume it was successful?"

"Yes. Testing showed that Lockheed's model achieved RCS ten times lower than Northrop's, and 100,000 times smaller than a B-52. Next to a B-52's barn-size RCS, the Lockheed models appeared no larger than a golf ball."

"That's incredible!"

"Indeed. Lockheed thus won the government contract in 1976 to develop the first stealth fighter, the F-117. The entire secretive project now code-named 'Have Blue', was placed in the Black, where even its very existence would be unacknowledged.

"But building the F-117 still became the ultimate challenge in conforming the exotic stealth principles to aerodynamics', with stealth pre-empting all other considerations, such as any performance degradations in maneuverability and speed, all sacrificed to achieve reduced RCS.

"This transmogrified the aircraft's traditional shapes into a pyramidal facetted envelope with all flat surfaces." Ryson then imaged a frontal close up line-drawing view of the F-117.

Norton observed the outline of the fuselage's stepped pyramidal shape that culminated at the severely pointed apex to a planar cockpit. It was flanked near its serrated base by grated engine intakes resting atop razor-thin, swept-back wings whose obtuse-angled leading edges bounced radar energy away. The entire plane was facetted with flat intersecting triangular surfaces and vaguely resembled origami, with no two surfaces made at right angles to each other, even the twin rear fins were made V-shaped, all to deflect radar energy. Absent from this view were ordinances, tucked deep within internal bomb bays to prevent radar returns.

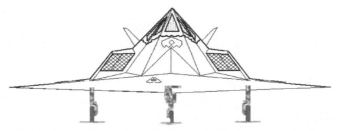

"Hmm, that still looks pretty unflyable to me," Norton remarked.

"And it was. All the faceting had resulted in the most unstable flying platform ever built whose erratic movements along pitch, yaw and roll rendered it virtually unflyable. But new sophisticated fly-by-wire computer control systems with rapid enough reaction time, could now make the unruly F-117 platform flyable."

"Impressive."

"Yes, except the F-117's small airframe limited its range for deep strike missions into the Soviet Union's vast expanses to cripple its inner military infrastructure."

"So why didn't they just make it a bomber size?"

"Beyond the F-117's existing dimensions, the faceting configuration still rendered the plane's aerodynamics too unstable, even with a fly-by-wire system. The need for stealth and aerodynamics to coexist in perfect symbiosis mandated a far different approach in developing a bomber-sized craft," Ryson said, hinting at things to come.

"The B-2."

"Yes."

"I recall the U.S. Air Force had some lofty expectations: a 40,000 lbs. payload delivered to any target in the world from U.S. bases, without refueling."

"Correct. And only one configuration could successfully marry low observability principles to that of long range and heavy payload, which funneled both Northrop and Lockheed to a conceptually identical design: a flying wing."

"Makes sense, a tubular fuselage provides no lift, only increased air resistance."

"True, and from a stealth perspective, its bulky shape and airfoil junctions also detrimentally create radar reflector surfaces. A flying wing on the other hand lends itself to stealth since the relatively thin wings offer little frontal surface incident angle to a radar wave. Much like air, most of the radar waves would simply flow around the wings."

Ryson then had the B-2's frontal view schematic pop up, showing the seemingly impossibly thin flying wing design, in contrast to the F-117's soaring pyramidal shape.

"Looks like Jack Northrop's 1940s propeller YB-35, and YB-49 jet," Norton reminisced.

"Very much so, and after using all the modern complex algorithms and simulations, the B-2 optimal wingspan came out to be 172 feet, exactly the same as its two 1940s predecessors."

"Interesting coincidence. But those predecessors were decommissioned due to aerodynamics instabilities of a wings-only design, especially after decorated test-pilot Glen W. Edwards was killed flying one over Murac, before it was renamed to Edwards Air Force Base."

"That was over 40 years ago, sir," Ryson remarked. "Sophisticated fly-by-wire systems have now rendered the flying-wing a stable platform as well. In fact, the B-2 boasts an impressive 136 embedded fly-by-wire computers tasked with the internal flight functions of a bomber so intricate it surpasses the Space Shuttle as the world's most complex flying craft. And the advance avionics enables flying as low as 200 feet, and a sub-sonic 650mph top speed."

Norton let out a whistle. "Impressive, but what about the stealth aspects?"

"The advent of super-computers capable of calculating billions of instructions per second finally enabled computing the myriad RCS points along smoothly curved surfaces. The rigid discrete flat facets used in the F-117 could now be curved and then uniformly integrated with others into a continuous crease-less panoply, in a design concept called 'continuous curvature'."

"A *what* now?"

"Continuous curvature, it effectively turns the aircraft's entire hide into a single smoothly flowing and uninterrupted giant surface, like that of a manta-ray. Radar waves would flow smoothly around the plane's curving hide and encounter no disruptive sharp creases."

Ryson brought up a picture showing the smooth layout of the B-2. Norton could clearly see how the plane's perimeter outline was governed by straight lines intersecting at predetermined angles to give it the distinctive boomerang shape design, while the top and bottom surfaces were smoothly curved to exacting geometric measurements, all for affording the greatest elusiveness to radar.

"Lockheed's bomber design was stealthier, but this time the Air Force opted for Northrop's larger payload and range, thus granting them the lucrative contract for 132 B-2s."

"Yes, I remembered that," Norton nodded.

"But Northrop's structural specialists would also soon face daunting challenges in actually building a continuous curvature design to its mathematically optimal computer model."

"What were the problems this time?"

"For one, radar waves are notoriously unforgiving of even the minutest deviations from the perfect theoretical geometric image, and so building the plane's continuous curvature hide needed the precision of forging an optical lens, but on surfaces orders of magnitude larger. Hand-shaping these expansive facades would simply not pass the muster of such unerring tolerances.

"So innovations in automated manufacturing techniques, such as computer-aided manufacturing and design, had to be made before continuous curvature principles could be effectively employed. The B-2 would thus had to be virtually configured from the outside-in.

"Because range and payload were of major considerations, new and exotic carbon-based materials such as carbon fiber epoxy composites and carbon-reinforced plastics were used for the B-2's skeletal framework. These were not only structurally stronger and lighter than metal, but less prone to fractures and rusts, as well as capable of being molded into more stable shapes.

"More importantly, these dielectric carbon-based composites also inherently functioned as RAM to further reduce the B-2's radar signature."

"Does it use any externally applied RAM?" Norton inquired.

"Yes, but not comprehensively as with the F-117. RAM could now be limited to the plane's leading swept-back edges, which bore the brunt of radar assault."

"And what about the engines and bombs?"

"As you can see from these pictures, all ordinances are carried in weapons bays inside the stealthy fuselage. The engines are also buried, for the B-2 at one engine-diameter lower than the air intakes to reduce direct exposure of their highly reflective rotating turbofan blades to radar waves. And the air intakes are top-mounted, so shielded from ground radars by the plane's ventral. These embeddings and some shielding, also reduced the plane's thermal and sound emissions from infrared and acoustic detectors."

"But what about the engines' exhaust?" Norton asked. He was referring to the circular metallic exhaust nozzles and the blazing-hot 2,000F exhaust gases gushing out the tail pipe, which maximized the plane's thrust but also presented its biggest target for IR-guided missiles.

"Look behind each plane: the traditional circular nozzles are flattened into dual elongated rectangular openings so the emerging exhaust heat evenly distributes across a longer duct surface, which reduces temperature at any given point. The flat nozzles are also made of cooler non-metallic composites, heat absorbent ceramic tiles originally developed for the Space Shuttle."

"Don't you lose thrust that way?"

"Yes, but there's still plenty, and both planes are subsonic to not be given away by their trailing sonic booms."

"Nice. And what about the cockpit?" Norton asked on the notoriously radar reflective cavity. Sitting prominently high on the fuselage and cluttered with non-stealthy features such as instruments, and ejection seat, it provides a fertile ground for radar return. The cockpit's transparent canopy is also clear to radar waves which can both enter and reflect back unhindered. The F-117's incredibly reduced RCS meant the pilot's helmet alone appeared larger to radar than the rest of the plane. But RAM paint could not be used as it offered no visibility to the pilot.

"The cockpit windows were coated with a fine transparent gold layer, which as an electrical conductor obstructs the radar waves yet allows for normal visibility."

"In the B-2," Norton observed, "the entire centrally located cockpit seems reconfigured to a gentle hump on the plane's mid-portion in conforming to the continuous curvature design."

"Correct. The F-117's was made in flat panes to conform to its faceted design."

"Where are the control surfaces and tail fins?" Norton said, referring to the elevators and aileron flaps, critical to ascend, descend and turning.

"The B-2's enormous size allowed for control surfaces to be made large enough to be placed at various locales along the trailing edges of the flying wing, so no tail fins were needed."

"Whoa, this thing is amazing," Norton remarked, having fully realized a truly strategic bomber was created that combined stealth with long range and heavy payload. Aside from a range of 11,500 miles with one aerial refueling, it had achieved or exceeded all its other initial criteria. And the third leg of the United States offensive nuclear triad was finally restored.

But stealth had not only changed aviation warfare, it altered the world history when just a few months later, its effectiveness was first demonstrated in 1991 during the Operation Desert Storm, over Iraq.

Norton recalled the F-117 fleet flew 1299 flaw-less precision bombing sorties against the most advanced Soviet-designed Integrated Air Defenses to date, without a single F-117 even nicked, which helped bring a rapid end to the war.

The implication of the stealth's ruinous effects was not lost to the Soviets. Their own hitherto impenetrable air defense wall was now deemed hopelessly rife with huge radar gaps to a devastating projected fleet of 132 B-2s. Such a decisive strategic military weakness led to a swift demise of the Soviet Union.

His attention reverting back to the present, Norton cracked a wry smile at the irony: that the Soviets had spent billions on a globally unrivaled radar defensive network, only to see it all be undone by the mathematical works of one of their own. It was like a banker who had constructed the most impenetrable vault but left unguarded the blueprints for its master key.

Norton's mood however quickly turned sour, in realizing yet another ironic twist: the same valuable weapon had now suddenly become a double-edged sword.

"We needed the damn things and built them," he muttered under his breath, knowing that searching for a radar-invisible craft posed as great a challenge to its own creators as to all those whom it had been intended to harry.

Having hit two dead-ends, with the flight report and the sea-search results, the decorated Air Force general reached for the phone and dialed for the only man who could help him now.

THE CARGO PORT AREA, NEAR LAGOS, PORTUGAL

The industrial bay bustled as hordes of workers scurried about anchored merchant ships, each representing a sizable bounty in charged service fees. Time was money.

Standing a few yards from a large moored vessel was Xendong. He had traveled incognito across the Iberian Peninsula to meet with Trostov, who stood nearby.

An agent of a contemporary Communist regime, Xendong was a firm believer in China as a future superpower. It had already claimed that role in the economic arena, and now aspired to the same militarily, with a little unwitting help from the United States in some key technologies, hence his pairing with this eccentric ex-Soviet man. He turned to Trostov who had kept an interested eye on the ship.

"It's not the prettiest, but this old lady can really haul," the Russian admired.

Xendong looked at the immense flat-topped vessel, its upper deck loaded with giant rectangular shipping containers.

"I have seen bigger ones built in China," he commented apathetically.

"Sure you have. Our old lady here should have no problems carrying us."

Xendong suddenly understood. "We are not traveling on *that*!"

"No one would be looking for us on a cargo ship."

"Why not fly there just as inconspicuously?" Xendong protested.

"No airports where we are going."

Xendong looked surprised. "Odd, considering what you claim to have for us."

"I will explain later," Trostov replied. "Let's get on board." But Xendong froze, as if sentenced to Chinese water torture. "I get violently seasick easily. There has got be another way!"

Trostov laughed, clasping his right hand on Xendong's shoulder. "There *is* no other way my Asian friend, but we have plenty of motion-sickness medication on board. You won't feel a thing the whole trip. I promise. Just focus on the end prize, it will make it all worth it."

Xendong took an apprehensive look at the paint-chipped vessel and tried not to think of the gut-wrenching times ahead. If what Trostov purported to have in store was genuine, it would indeed all be worth it. If not, he would personally see to it that his ruthless Chinese agents had the Russian's head delivered to him on a plate.

TANARIS

Ryson was cursing the searing desert heat that had turned his jeep into a veritable furnace when his ear-piece cell-phone began ringing in an urgent tone.

"Ryson here."

A voice crackled over the encrypted wireless link. "This is Edward Fleisler."

"Yes sir."

"Lieutenant, how is your investigation on the pilot proceeding?"

"Sir, I'm afraid my orders forbid discussing the situation with you."

"It's okay, son," the president's voice cut through, nearly causing Ryson to veer off the road. The commander in chief's distinct resonant voice he had publicly heard was unmistakable.

"Sirs, it's an honor to be speaking with you," Ryson stammered.

"Any finds on the identity or motives of the pilot?" Fleisler chimed in.

"Nothing conclusive yet, but I am making progress," Ryson replied sheepishly.

"We cannot allow for this weapon to fall into the wrong hands, at all costs," the commander in chief insisted. "Might be time to proceed with Operation Gold."

"*Gold*?" Fleisler interjected. "You mean it had a WT-100 unit?"

"Yes," the president somberly replied.

"Good God, no! It's too close to the Florida coast!" Fleisler said.

"What is a WT-100 unit?" Ryson inquired innocently.

A long, stunned pause set in, as if the duo had forgotten he was still on the line.

"No need to know Lieutenant," was Fleisler's eventual bold reply. "Keep us informed of any finds," and the connection was cut.

Ryson yanked the hands-free receiver off and threw it on the passenger seat.

Whatever the WT-100 unit was, he surmised it could only imply a device lethal to many. He realized a perhaps most pernicious aspect of the missing bomber had been withheld from him all along. The consequences of failure on his part now seemed far more grave, not just for him, but perhaps for countless innocent others.

The impossible urgency surrounding his mission had suddenly doubled.

THE ASSEMBLY FACILITY, TANARIS

Jeffery O'Neil was immersed in study materials neatly laid out on a large slanted drawing table, the kind once used to create blueprints. The computer-design age had made such boards' usage all but extinct in high-technology manufacturing, yet O'Neil had managed to keep a few. He considered portable computer screens simply too damn small.

A knock came on his open door. O'Neil looked up to the sight of Ian Ryson, and waved his old buddy in. "Coffee?" he asked, eyeing a percolator in the corner.

Ryson generously poured a cup, and sipped the dark liquid, a most welcome awakening feeling, considering his fitful sleep.

"What can I do for you now?" O'Neil asked.

"Tell me how exactly you build the SuperCOIL."

O'Neil placed his hands on his waist. "Ian, I am kinda busy now," he said with a mild frown. "Can we do this later?"

Ryson didn't buy the theatrics as he met his old mentor's gaze and sensed an inexplicable hint of discomfort and sympathy lurking behind those eyes.

"I have a mission to accomplish," he countered sternly. "I need useful data."

"What kind?" O'Neil asked, a bit taken aback.

"Like how you built a brand-new stealth bomber without anyone finding out."

O'Neil exhaled at length as his shoulders stooped again. "Okay, let's go," he said resignedly, heading out. Ryson eagerly followed, wondering why a person so excited to show the more classified laser materials was suddenly being so elusive.

The duo walked briskly along the concrete apron to a nearby massive seven stories high hangar that dwarfed man and machine alike, spacious enough to house two indoor football fields, or a number of 747-sized planes lined up wingtip to wingtip.

The hangar's 200 yards broadside consisted of huge corrugated sliding doors, each larger than a regulation basketball court.

Security guards let the duo pass on the count of their black-lined "all-access" badges. Inside, an elevator took them up four flights. They stepped onto a berm, floored with see-through metal grids that ran the cavernous hangar's full length.

Pacing along the clanking narrow ledge, Ryson took a bird's-eye view of the bustle below, focused around a half-dozen fighter jets which on a quick glimpse bore a fairly close resemblance to the F-15 "Eagle" on count of their broad-bodies, twin tails, dual engine intakes and large trapezoidal-shaped wings. But Ryson knew these weren't F-15s.

Their front fuselage was broader, the twin tails were canted outward not straight up, the dual engine intakes angled inward, and the plane's overall sleek physique demonstrated a more advanced design. These fighters were configured for stealth.

O'Neil observed Ryson curiously gazing the aircraft.

"F-22 'Raptor', the world's most advanced fighters," he said. "*True* stealth fighters, not like the F-117s. They can dogfight better than an F-16 and can go supersonic without afterburners, meaning a sustained supersonic thrust that won't drain the fuel tank in minutes."

"So they got supercruise?" Ryson asked as he eyed this third incarnation of the stealth aircraft. Ryson recalled that during 1980s, USAF was in need of an advanced plane to outmatch the next generation of Soviet fighter aircraft. Initially code-named "ATF," this futuristic Advanced Tactical Fighter incorporated two avant-garde features: stealth and supercruise.

O'Neil nodded. "I see you have been keeping up with your readings."

"Yes, who could forget how Lockheed and Northrop once again competed over a lucrative stealth contract. It took each over four years and $2 billion to develop their prototypes."

"YF-22 and YF-23."

"Right, if I recall correctly, Northrop's YF-23 design was actually stealthier because they adhered more closely to continuous curvature. Sleek seamless curves of constantly changing radii all the way, that was one decidedly radical and futuristic looking bird."

"But Lockheed's YF-22 design vaguely evolved from their F-117," O'Neil remarked. "As you see before you, it is more angular and conventional-looking. Thanks to better understanding of stealth, heavy RAMs could now be localized to only key areas, such as leading edges, or gaps and cavities in the hide."

"You left out their vectored thrust, superb integrated avionics and phenomenal thrust-to-weight ratio, two engines each outputting 35,000 pounds of force."

Ryson further recalled how vectored thrust was achieved via movable louvers placed on the twin engines' output, to direct their thrust up or down from level flight position. This enabled the YF-22 to turn vertically much faster, thus affording it far greater dogfighting agility.

Northrop had decided against the flaps as they increased the plane's radar signature from behind. Thus, Northrop had designed a stealthier aircraft with a fighter's speed, while Lockheed had created a true dogfighter that included its own stealth features.

The Air Force ultimately chose the superb agility of Lockheed's YF-22, which would be renamed "F-22 Raptor" in the mid-1990s.

This selection had raised curiosity on the winners in the three stealth contests: For the F-117, Lockheed's stealthier platform had won; for the B-2, Lockheed's stealthier platform had lost to Northrop's larger payloads design; and in this third go-around, Northrop's stealthier platform had lost to Lockheed's more agile design. This demonstrated that the USAF's stealth purchase decisions were not predicated solely on an aircraft's degree of stealthiness.

"Marvelous aircraft," O'Neil praised, "and right here at our disposal."

Ryson took in the sophisticated fighter's deadly features admiringly but wished they had not been placed at the hands of an ethically corrupt Black Squadron. He also noticed the activity that was going on around them bordered on assembly.

The ceiling trusses supported railings for aerial cranes moving heavy parts, like the engines, to be lowered onto a specific plane. Each plane had its own rectangular service area, unofficially delineated by mesh covered, open drainage channels.

"Such complex machines," Ryson remarked, drumming his fingers on the raised protective railings.

"That's right," O'Neil affirmed. "Each Raptor has in excess of a million parts. It took a Lockheed Martin team of over a thousand highly skilled workers to churn out just one plane every month or so."

Ryson nodded absently while looking down at the throngs of technicians swarming about the F-22s. They milled seemingly at random, but to an expert observer it was a well-choreographed affair where each performer group stayed within its invisible boundary area, here designated by their access badge colors.

"It seems you still have quite a retro-fit assembly going on," Ryson observed. He knew the white-lined badge workers on the periphery were not permitted physical contact with the plane. Next up were the darker-colored badge technical crews who could tinker with the airframe and systems but not being privy to most of the plane's secrets. The next tier was the gray badge, worn mostly by the pilots who worked on F-22's critical features such as the radar cross section or enemy radar detection modes. Above all that was the coveted "all access" black badge.

"Ah, yes," O'Neil nodded. "After taking delivery we do home-grown customizing, that suit our particular black-classified needs. It's still a lot of work."

Ryson raised a curious eyebrow and said nothing more.

After passage through a number of additional security checkpoints, O'Neil led them into a high-tech presentation room sporting a wall-sized flat-screen display.

He had Ryson take one of the movie-theater styled seats, then activated the display equipment from a raised control console's sensi-touch panels.

"Sure you are ready for this?" he asked.

"Of course; nothing you're showing here would shock me."

Don't be so sure, O'Neil thought. "Well, here it is then," he deadpanned.

Abruptly, a head-on view filled the entire screen, of a stealth bomber which could have been easily mistaken for a conventional B-2. But not to Ryson, as he held his breath.

This plane was monstrous, nearly jumping out of the flat display as a giant aquiline-beaked pre-historic flying beast, ready to pounce. Since it was airborne, there was no surrounding objects to scale it against, but to Ryson's trained eyes it was dimensionally larger than a normal B-2. Ryson carefully examined its details with utmost skepticism.

"Is this picture computer generated?" he asked.

"It is real, but computer enhanced to make it interactive."

"I'd say its one-and-a-half times a B-2." He drew an imaginary aerial outline of the on-screen plane with his raised index finger. The observation made him immediately uncomfortable.

"Very close," O'Neil praised. "Spot any other differences?" he quizzed.

"Slightly portlier, to lodge the big COIL chamber and its chemical reservoirs."

He knew with continuous curvature a plane's size per se was not a theoretical hinderance to its achieving low radar observability, so the B-2's flying wing shape could be made larger to house a COIL. To Ryson, the real enigma was how it was all actually built.

More than ever he was eager to delve into the technical schematic portion, seeking answers to some of his long-standing questions since first being thrown into the thick of things.

"Where is the lasing turret? The bird's beak looks as a normal B-2." Then he discerned a shallow bulge on the planes' mid top-portion, a convex translucent curvature so darkly tinted as to blend inconspicuously with the plane's black stealth covering. "Is it that bump up there?"

"Yes, it's a top-mounted turret," O'Neil said, tapping the screen. The computer automatically peeled off the image's top portion, revealing an inside cut-out view.

Ryson could now see the graphically exposed turret tucked neatly beneath the top-hide, yet ingeniously conforming to the plane's overall smooth contours.

O'Neil continued. "The telescope and beam directors implemented here are more complex than the ABL's, requiring some trickery to all fit inside, but they work just as well."

"Except for the laser's range of course," Ryson corrected.

O'Neil nodded again. "There were power penalties associated with accommodating everything into a boomerang-shaped plane rather than one with a straight tubular fuselage."

"How much penalty?"

"About 60% of the ABL's laser range, though it can fire more laser shots."

Ryson peered lower, and to his amazement spotted a second turret in the SuperCOIL's ventral. "You have *two* turrets?"

"Yes, to cover areas above and below, each turret weighs less than half the ABL's single turret because it's configured differently."

Ryson was still trying to take in the whole image and its significance. At some level he still could not believe it, but here it was, despite all his reasoning as to how it could not be.

"You have clearly done the impossible," he said grudgingly, "but how?"

"Without using thousands of sub-contractors, you mean?" O'Neil voiced Ryson's last shred of doubt.

"Yes. I bet you need a book to explain that."

"Hardly," O'Neil said. "Just need two words: Virtual Prototyping."

"You mean CASD?" Ryson asked, referring to using computer-aided simulation and design, rather than drawing boards, rulers and pencils, as in the pre-Vietnam War era, to design a plane. Most of the original B-2 was drawn up using CASD, a 1980s state of the art concept that shortened the B-2's development cycle by years. But on many fronts, CASD was insufficient to develop a plane as complex and secret as the SuperCOIL.

O'Neil cleared his throat in a short cough. "CASD is now like an ancestor of Virtual Prototyping. Today, computers are invoked on all fronts, to streamline the manufacturing processes, improve production tooling, and even develop better composite materials, like the SuperCOIL's new RAM. Our deeper understanding of stealth has also reduced overheads of its airplane application. Things now go from Virtual Prototyping straight into production tooling, which is perfect for such geometrically precise designs to deflect radar waves. In short, we can now virtually build a plane on this baby," he patted the computer console, "top to bottom, even fly it, all before cutting the first sheet of metal for its airframe."

Ryson listened to the explanation but his gaze remained transfixed on the plane.

There was something about that image which still bothered him. "And it all works out as you suggest?" he asked skeptically.

"Yes, you just saw the proof of concept in those F-22's parked in the hangar. All their stealth designs were made on the computer. In fact, achieving low radar observability is now just a minor portion of an overall development expense."

"That's incredible!" Ryson whistled.

O'Neil offered a punch line. "And with all these advancements, the need for your *thousands* of sub-contractors has shrunk to just a few dozen and we got most of them home-grown in Tanaris, at least for the critical components. In fact, we didn't even have to use a real-life mockup of the bomber to fit in the laser the way we did for the ABL. All the COIL's laser concepts were proved in the SIL; then we rearranged the same laser components into a stealth bomber airframe via VP. Saved us a bundle in cost, efforts and time."

"So that is how your manufacturing managed to stay below the radar."

"Good pun, Ian," O'Neil cracked a smile. Knowing Ryson's wry humor, an indication of an intended pun meant just the opposite.

Ryson had a point. The Chief Engineer was too enamored with his accomplishments to care about anything else. "Building the SuperCOIL was no mean feat, it required overcoming all the hurdles of laser power generation and accurate in-flight tracking, precise shaping to exacting tolerances of the stealth equations and the aerodynamics limits of an airborne platform, and the keeping of all of the above stealthy. It was the perfect storm of technological challenges, but our ship came out with flying colors," he gloated.

Ryson had other matters to address. "So are you going to tell me the *real* story now?" he sprung his ultimate, and most serious question.

"What do you mean?" O'Neil asked, caught off guard.

"You have only shown me manufacturing stuff. You know damn well even the best computer programs cannot conjure up an original blueprint for this baby. The core is missing."

"You are absolutely correct," O'Neil's voice sounded strained. "It was our best resource, human ingenuity, which did that part."

Ryson became alarmed. There was something about this he had not liked from the start, and now it began to dawn as to what it might be. He felt light sweat glistening on his palms.

"I'd like to see the blueprint," he said.

O'Neil paused to weigh his options. "Ian, that is not important here. Let me show you more on how the SuperCOIL was manufactured."

Ryson sensed evasiveness in O'Neil's demeanor, it stood out for such forthright a man. He got up in time to see O'Neil readying the system for an early shut down.

"Show me the blueprint!" he said, heading toward the control area. O'Neil tried to block the way a foot short of the panel. "I can't; it's restricted," he reasoned.

"Nothing here is restricted to me!" Ryson replied, pushing past the befuddled Chief Engineer, reaching for the controls.

"Ian, please don't!" O'Neil implored.

Ryson was not listening, as he began to tap on the panel. With each touch the computer stripped the bomber of a component, reaching toward its inner skeletal core. When an entire portion was gone, contoured blueprint outlines filled its place.

Ryson's heart thumped faster in recognizing the now exposed unique underlying design signatures. His breathing became shallow and irregular.

There were many parts to display at this sequential rate, so O'Neil decided to shorten his friend's anguish. Reaching in, he jumped the program ahead, to the full bare bone design blueprint of the bomber.

As if beholding a ghost, Ryson shocked face went pallid. Before him lay a concept that was never meant to be and had existed only in a theoretical study completed years ago.

O'Neil opted for a bright angle. "You should be very proud, Ian," he said and clapped his colleague's left shoulder.

It was futile.

Speechless, Ian Ryson's stomach had leapt to his throat. Staring him directly in the face was the blueprint of a creation he knew more intimately than anyone in the world; because he had designed it.

GENERAL NORTON'S HEADQUARTERS, LANGLEY AIR FORCE BASE, VIRGINIA

Norton was deep in a phone conversation with major Giraldi, in charge of monitoring readouts from the myriad NATO radar stations strewn along the North Atlantic rim. Norton had just asked Giraldi to alert all his listening posts to a certain type of unusual signal.

"Look Ben, I know this sounds weird," Norton said, sensing Giraldi's puzzlement, "but I have a feeling that the object I am seeking may only be found by this method. Here are a set of frequencies to focus your search on."

"But still an awful lot of junk signals out there to sort through," Giraldi said.

"Let's hope we get lucky."

"My men are experts. Maybe we won't need luck," Giraldi offered.

"Amen to that," Norton said, though not sharing the major's optimism.

AT THE ASSEMBLY FACILITY

Ryson felt his irregular, shallow breathing pace normalizing, as his mind slowly recognized his distorted reflection in the bathroom's slightly warped mirror. He only vaguely recalled a frantic rush to leave the display room and passing startled technicians along the way.

The ghastly image of the blueprint he had designed years back, and now fully implemented, had struck him like a hammer. Deep down however, he had long ago suspected as much, but subconsciously chose denial over remorse. Now he could no longer live in that self-created illusion. The veil of darkness had been pulled aside, and by his own persistence no less.

It had all started years ago when a young Ryson, disillusioned with the US Air Force, opted for a private defense sector job. He had seemingly arrived at the perfect time, during a ramp up to compete with six aero-space developers for the Air Force's contract on the world's first long range, heavy payload stealth bomber.

Ryson had worked feverishly to complete the simulations for his stealthy new bomber design. Due to the aerodynamics and Ufimtsev's mathematical constraints, all the competitors involved had invariably arrived at the same general shape; of a flying wing.

The devil however, lay in the details, which determined the airplane's desired overall stealth, and bomb-load capacity.

Ryson's design offered double the payload lift of the closest competitor, though at fifty percent size increase and triple the cost. But the company's cost-minded executives forced Ryson to scale back his design.

When the day of reckoning finally arrived where all competitors demonstrated their bomber prototypes to the Air Force brass, their cross-town rival Northrop edged all others, primarily on the basis of having a larger lift capacity design.

Ryson was furious. He knew the implementation of his original vision may have well awarded his company the contract on the basis of payload. Worse yet, the board of directors now maliciously placed the blame for the doomed the project on his aviation engineering judgment, not their own top-level corporate blunders.

Facing shareholders' anger for losing billions of dollars in lost contract revenues, the company decided to lick its wounds and exit the stealth production business altogether in favor of conventional military aircraft, laying off the entire stealth research division, Ryson included.

Once again disillusioned, Ryson initially looked for silver-linings to this forceful change in his career. But life on the outside would not prove any kinder.

Stealth research is military work with only few companies receiving large government contracts. A non-competition clause prevented him from working elsewhere in the field for five years and knowing of no other life besides military technology he would soon become penniless.

It was at this low juncture in his life when Ryson was approached by McCane who needed his expertise on electromagnetic wave technology to work on a new form of stealth.

McCane had shrewdly laid out an offer too good to pass up. Ryson reluctantly accepted it and for the next four years became part of a team whose research had brought about some of world's most advanced stealth materials and designs to date.

But it was also a most curious era as no actual products ever seemed to emerge from his research. McCane had often explained the nature of Ryson's work as government funded feasibility studies only. Of particular interest to McCane was Ryson's prior work on the heavier-load flying wing concept.

Ryson would ultimately conjure up a bomber design even more effective than before. The plane's load capabilities were augmented, to stand at 2.5 times a conventional B-2, but with still only a fifty percent size increase.

Despite his success, Ryson would grow to disdain his life. All along, it had come with a latent high price tag, facing tight deadlines and Gorik's unbearable demands. And, it seemed nothing he designed would ever get built.

By this time, he had met his future fiancée, and attained a degree of balance between a seemingly dead-end work and a fulfilling personal life headed toward lasting happiness.

Then the calamitous sky diving event struck like a hammer, and that delicate equilibrium shattered before his eyes. With the joys of a blossoming romance turned into unbearable grief, the last safeguard against a total melt down was removed. Soon, he would have no choice but to leave Tanaris.

Ryson splashed water on his face, then took deep breaths to regain his composure.

"Ian, are you okay?" O'Neil's soothing voice filled the room.

Ryson shrugged him off, still feeling betrayed.

O'Neil stood quietly under the ambient flicker of fluorescent lighting.

"Why did you turn *my* plane into that—abomination?" Ryson said, avoiding eye contact.

"Relax, you didn't mind it so much as someone else's design. Be proud!"

"Of what exactly?" Ryson pounded his left fist into the side of the porcelain sink so hard that a small crack formed, "that my bomber design was perverted into a killer-laser platform and caused the death of an entire tanker crew?"

O'Neil's eyes rolled. "Ian, it was an aerial accident, it's in the nature of aviation. I have a feeling this has more to do with hurt pride than humanitarianism."

"What are you talking about?" Ryson massaged his aching left hand.

"After all you finalized the SuperCOIL's design for us."

"I only undertook a research study of a bomber before I left," Ryson protested, turning an angry face to O'Neil.

"Nonsense; all the follow up questions we sent, what you think they were for?"

"A simulation, just like everything else!"

"But you also provided us the theoretical underpinnings, which we fed into computers, to number crunch an actual working model."

"To build the SuperCOIL."

"Yes. Wish you could have seen that baby fly with my laser on it!"

Everything was making frightful sense to Ryson now. After he left Tanaris he was rehired by McCane, as a remote consultant on certain key aspects of the bomber. Once again with nowhere else to turn, he had accepted McCane's very generous offer out of financial desperation.

But the purpose of this second tour of duty had soon become an even deeper enigma. He was constantly asked aerodynamic and stealth constraints questions that clearly lay outside the specs of his previous bomber work. And then there were the really strange questions, ones involving the resistance of the stealth coating to thermonuclear blasts, or lasers' thermal spikes. Gorik had kept him completely in the dark as to the real purpose of his work.

Now that the veil of secrecy was finally lifted, he was both deep-down thrilled to see his vision realized, and resentful of its perversion by people he hated most.

"Why the need to put a laser into a stealth bomber? Wasn't ABL good enough?"

"You have to ask Gorik that. Anything else?"

"Yes. What is this WT-100 unit installed on the SuperCOIL?"

O'Neil made no reply though his face blanched. At that very moment his cellphone began to ring, and he answered it. A brief conversation ensued.

"I'm sorry, Ian," he apologized after being done, voice trembling. "Something has come up." And he was out the door before Ryson could inquire further.

UNKNOWN LOCATION

A figure took quiet steps in the dark wilderness, stopping regularly to take his bearings, and make sure he was not being followed. On his broad, muscular back he carried a military-camouflaged duffle bag.

High above, he caught glimpses of the moon playing hide-and-seek behind the fast-moving clouds, casting intermittent reflections on a nearby lake. He hoped the sky would stay clear long enough for him to get an accurate dead-reckoning read on the orbiting body overhead.

After wading another hundred yards through the undergrowth, he arrived at his carefully scouted destination. It was a natural hide-out formed by the convergence of massive volcanic rock slabs. In the middle was an open area into which he crept wraithlike, unheard and unseen.

He pulled out a shoebox-sized electronic device from the bag, extended its retractable tripod legs and pushed the tips into the soft mud to secure it in place.

On the device's topside lay a set of neatly stacked, wedge-shaped thin metal plates, which he unfolded like a hand-held fan, into the full circle of a transmitter dish. With the flip of a switch, the device came to life. He retrieved a small card-sized circuit board from his vest and inserted it into a slit on the device.

Instantly, the transmitter dish swiveled on its mountings with a soft *whrrrr* and began searching the skies for a satellite thousands of miles above.

The figure looked upward also, as if trying to pinpoint the elusive object with his unaided eye. The satellite would be overhead soon, only to disappear over the horizon fifteen minutes after, and not reappear for another six hours. This was the man's one chance. He could not make an unnoticed journey here in broad daylight.

A strong wind swirled between the volcanic slabs, and the nearby grass rustled. He peered out from the rock openings but spotted no one. Looking up, he saw that high gales were quickly moving the lumbering clouds; and soon the clearing he was hoping for appeared.

The satellite was directly overhead now. He could almost feel it. The transmitter dish finally acquired a solid lock-on it would not lose again, no matter what the weather. The man typed in a specific code, and the machine began transmitting a predetermined sequence. It would do so once a minute for fifteen minutes, at every six hours interval when the satellite was overhead, then shut down to conserve power and reduce chances of interception.

The figure huddled in a corner for another ten minutes till the satellite had passed over and the device shut down as preprogrammed. It would awaken again in exactly five hours and forty-five minutes.

He would not be here then but knew the machine would not fail him.

WILSON'S OFFICE

Standing in front of Sergeant Wilson's desk, in one hand Ryson held up a model of the aerial tanker with its boom extended to a refueling position which almost touched the model of a trailing B-2 he held in his other hand.

"Imagine for some unexplained reason the boom breaks off during refueling, causing a fire that blows the tanker apart," Ryson was saying.

Ryson was there on a nagging hunch, for which he needed the aircraft engineer's technical corroboration. Following his shocking meeting with O'Neil, his thoughts were once again on the bomber's fate. That night, while lying in bed, he had envisioned the tanker's horrible explosion with such vividness that he almost felt the heat from the blast scorching his body. The fiery tanker fragments then shot straight down and shredded the B-2's stealth hide, inflicting catastrophic integrity failures that plunged the bomber into the Atlantic. Now he was presenting the same scenario to Wilson, using the models on aircraft engineer's desk.

"What are the odds for the tanker's fragments damaging the bomber's stealth covering to make it visible enough to our powerful radars trained on its exact location?" Ryson asked.

"Very high," Wilson responded, "if no evasive action by the bomber's pilot."

Eyes still focused on the models, Ryson nodded. "What type of evasive action?"

"Quite drastic. The pilot has to disengage and go into a virtual dive, then gun the engines to outrun the falling debris."

Ryson moved the models to mimic Wilson's narrative, which seemed very plausible, but Wilson added, "bombers however are not geared to perform such maneuvers, and more importantly neither are their pilots. Such maneuvers can only be executed in a fighter plane and by a highly adept fighter pilot, not by a bomber."

"Maybe not by a conventional bomber," Ryson remarked, "but wouldn't the B-2's flat-line characteristics allow for such maneuvering to dodge debris collision?"

The sergeant mulled the question as Ryson watched him.

"I suppose if you somehow kept the B-2 at the correct vector to the explosion source, most debris could pass above or below it. But again, it's nearly impossible," Wilson insisted.

"Why?" Ryson pressed.

Wilson frowned. "Because unless the pilot had anticipatorily prepared the maneuvering systems for such a dive, there wouldn't be enough time to set it after the explosion." He momentary paused in thought and scratched his head. "I don't see it happening, not even with the best trained bomber pilots."

"So the only issue here is how the pilot could see it coming?" Ryson asked.

"Yes," Wilson replied with growing annoyance.

Ryson had heard all he needed. "Thank you, Sergeant," he said, then placing both models on Wilson's desk before leaving.

Ryson was in deep thoughts as his footsteps echoed down the hall. No doubts now that the pilot had anticipated such dive, but there was more. And then, thanks to Wilson's assertions, it dawned on him: if the SuperCOIL had survived the tanker's explosions unscathed via such aerial maneuvers, then it could have been commanded only by a highly adept *fighter* pilot.

REMOTE LISTENING OUTPOST, NORTH ATLANTIC OCEAN

Beeping most peculiarly, the multi-frequency scanner elicited a curious look from the radar operator. Manning this remote listening outpost on the Atlantic Ocean's fringe had not made for an exciting year, until a few days ago when Central Command asked the operator to be on the lookout for any unusual transmissions.

A minute later the scanner beeped again in the exact same tone, followed by thirteen more chimes at precisely one per minute, then suddenly stopped. The operator was intrigued, yet unconcerned. Any emergency rescue call would have transmitted more frequently. Besides, this odd signal appeared as unintelligible background noise, if not for its precise occurrence pattern.

The operator decided he had yet no conclusive proof to justify a report, which required filling lengthy official forms, and perhaps immediate follow-ups.

His 12-hour shift was almost up, and his replacement had just pulled up in the parking lot. He jotted down the information, turned on an automatic recorder to the frequency of the spotted signal, and made a point to pick up on it the next day.

RYSON'S OFFICE

The eerie glow from the flat-panel monitor cast reflections on Ryson's tired face as he sifted through Tanaris fighter-pilots database, convinced that the chosen pilot of the SuperCOIL was in fact a seasoned fighter jock.

Such selection now made sense to Ryson. He believed the SuperCOIL's bomber designation was a misnomer, of which aviation history was fraught with. For instance, the F-117 'Fighter' could only drop payloads so was in reality a mini-bomber. Ryson deemed the SuperCOIL, with its pinpoint shoot-down aerial weaponry and no bomb payload, as really a fighter. And despite lacking a fighter plane's veritable mark, of nimble dogfights maneuverability, Ryson saw the SuperCOIL as an aerial weapon which could achieve greater air-to-air kill ratios than any fighter plane. But by any designation, this liminal plane was a formidable weapon on the verge of ushering in the largest revolution in military aviation since the advent of the jet engine. And he firmly believed it was stolen by a fighter pilot.

Unfortunately, his only close finds were of three fighter pilots who had spent significant time flying conventional non-stealth bombers, and all three had reported to duty that fateful morning.

As Ryson rubbed his watering eyes, a thought occurred to him. He quickly examined Evertt's history file in the system and discovered a picture update to Evertt's digitized finger-print files, made just the day before the B-2's disappearance. Curiously, it was only of Evertt's right thumb, which called out to Ryson's investigative nature as an enigmatic message, and different than the fingerprint on his paper file provided by Gorik. It left Ryson with no choice but to re-enter the new thumbprint into the system search. To his surprise, a second matched record popped up for the right thumb.

But Ryson's excitement quickly evaporated. The inactive record belonged to an airman killed years ago in combat. And not just any aviator, but one Ryson had long considered an idol.

He originally dismissed this strange, if not impossible, coincidence as data-entry error. Yet as he compulsorily examined the deceased aviator's record, he found many of his physical characteristics matching Evertt's, more so than anyone else at Tanaris database.

Ryson printed out the man's picture, to corroborate it with chopper pilot Maines, the only man who had actually partially seen his face. His excitement rising, he dialed Maine's number. An unfamiliar voice answered.

"Is Captain Maines available?" Ryson asked.

"Sorry, a fatal helicopter accident claimed him yesterday."

"How?" Ryson exclaimed, genuinely shocked.

"Report showed his chopper's old hydraulic oil pump malfunctioned…"

Ryson quickly hung up, as his heart pounded, and knots formed in his throat at the sudden realization of what had really happened. Maines had replaced that pump just the day before and tested it in their flight. He was being told a cover-up story.

Trying to remain calm, he dialed others germane to the case, and each had been sent on remote assignments. Desperate, he called O'Neil, his last resort, but strangely even the indispensable Chief Engineer had left Tanaris, incommunicado.

Ryson leaned his forehead on the cold, indifferent surface, closed his eyes and breathed deliberately through his nostrils as he tried to make out the slowly forming picture of events that had led to what he believed was the theft of a super-weapon. He refused to believe the disaster had been the result of pilot error. But what would have caused one of the best and most loyal pilots in America to intentionally destroy its most prized possession?

His rational mind soon prevailed. If access to everyone below him had been deliberately cut off, he had but one place to seek answers: at the very top, from Colonel Gorik himself.

TANARIS HEADQUARTERS

The expansive top floor bay windows offered a commanding view of the multi-colored sedimentary lined walls of Tanaris crater. From this high ground, Colonel

Gorik regarded the vast military network his genius had created from a once semi-derelict airbase in this remote inhospitable corner of the American Southwest.

Originally a major, he had quickly risen to a colonel rank. Gorik was a fearsome man, having ruthlessly disposed of anyone of consequence who had dared oppose him. Even his best colleagues had not been spared. It had been an arduous journey of ascendancy. Now he stood above it all and perused his domain from an empyrean vantage point.

"Lieutenant," Gorik authoritatively addressed a waiting Ryson without turning his head, "I thought I made it clear that you are not to bother my men."

"Where are Jeffery O'Neil and all others?" Ryson asked.

"On remote assignments."

"I must talk to O'Neil immediately," the lieutenant re-emphasized.

"You are wasting my men's time, they are facing tight production deadlines on matters which are beyond your authorization."

"I'll let the president decide that," Ryson waved his orders, "unless *you* can answer my questions."

"Ask then," Gorik said, like a teacher talking down to an obtuse pupil.

"Why did you secretly build the SuperCOIL, wasn't the ABL's laser enough?"

"The short of it is," Gorik said, pacing along the windows, "the ABL is rather worthless, more a science experiment than militarily practical, a dog and pony show for the top brass. It's most likely non-survivable in a real battlefield."

"What do you base that on?"

"The ABL is designed for a high-altitude holding pattern over friendly territory to scan the enemy skies for launched missiles. Its laser has a few hundred miles range, impressive, but still can't reach missiles launched too deep within a hostile terrain. We cannot send the ABL further in, because a 747's very large radar signature will pop-up on enemy trackers like a flying barn. Not only will it be exposed and vulnerable to their fighters' air to air missiles, but the enemy can then simply not launch its SCUD missiles from sites within the ABL's range."

"But a stealthy platform with a laser cannot be detected while it creeps in close inside enemy territory to surprise their launchers, fire dozens of shots within seconds, then disappear without ever being tracked," Ryson extrapolated.

"Precisely," Gorik raised an eyebrow.

"Then why not just ask for the SuperCOIL to begin with? Why the ABL charade and diversion of funds?"

"As you know, the B-2 program turned out to be a financial white elephant." Gorik recalled how the B-2 program became a victim of its own vaunted success. With the Soviet Union's total disintegration in 1991 which was in part attributed to the advent of the B-2, the Cold War precipitously ended, and so did the B-2 production budget to counter the communist menace. By 1992, the B-2s numbers were cut from 132 to only 21 planes, which amortized the B-2s' enormous development cost to a skyrocketing 2.2 billion dollars per plane, making each craft literally worth double its weight in contemporary gold. "They did not want to fund another such acquisition for an even larger stealth platform, especially when the underlying laser aspects were not proven to work yet."

"But they still went for the ABL?" Ryson asked.

"Yes, pure laser research on a modified existing 747. Easy to sell concept."

"Though it is rather useless in actual battle."

"Right. And their eventual realization of it would be a major blow to my plans; unless I had already delivered a working alternate solution."

"The SuperCOIL," Ryson said.

"Yes."

"But you're already the king of your realm," Ryson said. "What's in it for you to partake in such a high-risk venture?"

Gorik's gaze turned back out to the distant horizon where a formation of F-16s were making a tight nose-bleed high G-turn, fuselages glinting in the bright desert sun. He briefly relaxed his guard. "I have been confined to this airbase for far too long, kept out of sight on the account of secrecy. My only ticket to become a general and enter the mainstream of the Air Force is to deliver an ultimate weapon, one that can radically change the face of aerial warfare altogether."

"Very ambitious," Ryson said with a hint of sarcasm that infuriated the colonel. "But why you got the president involved?"

"The SuperCOIL has some specific parts which required outsourcing, and so needed absolute manufacturing secrecy. Only the president could assure that."

"And he agreed to all this?" Ryson was astonished.

Gorik's visual focus shifted back inside. "Once I had told him the ABL would turn out to be a huge flop, and that he would be blamed for championing the program, he had no choice but to go along with my Plan B. It put us in the same boat so to speak. He is up for re-election, so he went with it for a share of the glory or avoidance of political defeat—however you want to look at it. The budget was already allocated because the ABL's inflated price covered the SuperCOIL, so no red flags to the Congress, or even McCane, who was duped like everyone else."

"Including me," Ryson said in a hushed voice.

"Yes, though you were actually a great help to us."

The taunt appeared to hit Ryson like a violent punch.

Gorik went on. "The President then left it all in my hands. It was a colossal feat to design, integrate and make airborne the world's most advanced air weapon in such a short time, and under utmost secrecy. I came through with flying colors."

"Except for your selection of the pilot of course."

The colonel's mood turned to anger. "Did it not occur to you why the president, who knew of this project all along, is acting surprised to hear of the SuperCOIL in front of his own inner circle? The president might use me as a scapegoat if needed, but I am not as defenseless as he might think. So your presidential mandate is not as carte blanche over me as you believe."

"You are in effect blackmailing the president for making a bad decision that you pushed on him as a good one in the first place."

"I prefer to call it firm persuasion. And it's only fair since its being played in both directions. Come now," Gorik said. "Your visit's real purpose is to serve as a reminder that I am not immune to being removed. The President wants this mess solved quietly just as badly as I do, but in a way that covers his ass too. You just happen to be caught in the middle."

"Solved *quietly*? Is that why you disposed of Maines?"

"What subsequently happens to those you involve in this case at your own discretion is not my concern," the colonel stated coldly.

"And O'Neil?" Ryson asked.

"He is safely far away now, but should I be forced to recall him, then who knows. No form of transport is accident free as you saw with Maines. You two go way back, O'Neil speaks of you as a friend, it would be a pity if your insistence on seeing him caused his untimely demise. He has a wife and family, as do most others who have been sent off-base."

Gorik seized on Ryson's dismayed silence to declare the meeting over, showing the lieutenant the door with a parting advice. "Just go with what you have in the time you have left to you, so your job here will be done soon."

THE REMOTE LISTENING OUTPOST, NORTH ATLANTIC OCEAN

The scanner beeped again, in the same ominous tone as the operator had first heard it the day before. This time he pursued it with genuine interest.

As before, each mysterious auditory burst was a noise-like garble and the only indication of artificial generation was in its precisely-timed transmission pattern. He glanced at his watch, still 9 hours to go on his shift; plenty of time for sleuthing.

He compared the signal against the one he had recorded the day before and found both signals were curiously transmitted every six hours, in only fifteen bursts of one per minute. What kind of randomly generated natural noise could do that?

This was now definitely something worth reporting. He filled out the lengthy forms but held off on sending them in order to perform a final verification.

Five hours and 45 minutes later, the beepings resumed, on the dot, and precisely followed the same routine as before. The operator was convinced it had man-made origins, though unsure of its purpose.

He dispatched the completed report to Central Command, marking it as urgent.

UNKNOWN LOCATION

In the moonless night, two men climbed along the narrow passage that led up a steep hillside, though at noticeably different paces. The front man, thanks to years of military training, negotiated the rock-strewn path with relative ease. The trailing figure, in contrast, paused frequently to recover his breath and feel his pulse rate dip to safe levels.

"We'll be late at this rate," Trostov teased his lagging companion from uphill.

"Go to hell," Xendong replied in mid-exhale, causing the Russian to chuckle.

The Asian businessman had not expected such physically grueling activity. Worse, he still suffered from the effects of his ocean voyage on the cargo vessel that now lay out of sight.

A furtive powerboat ride had landed them on these mysterious shores. Stripped of all his electronic gadgets in Portugal on Trostov's orders, Xendong was also unable to gain an astral bearing on their geographical location due to cloud cover.

They had sailed for only two days at cargo-vessel speeds, but their warm lush-green surroundings hinted at neither Northern Europe nor the Africa's deserts. So where were they?

Xendong laboriously followed the fit Russian to the crest line. The trek was then mostly downhill, enabling him to keep pace more easily.

An hour later, Trostov stopped to dial numbers on his radio device's dimly glowing screen. A Russian voice crackled through, and Trostov spoke an authorization pass code, then fell silent.

"Now what?" Xendong asked.

"We stay put, it's been your favorite activity of tonight."

Xendong was indignant but lacked the energy for unproductive arguments. He sat down on a nearby flat rock and let the ocean breezes wash over him. He could faintly hear the waves again but knew on this side of the ridge they could only be coming from a large lake.

Gently massaging his leg muscles, his thoughts soon shifted to the prize ahead, and its significance to his Chinese employer.

For some years now, China's People's Liberation Army Air Force, had been secretly developing its own stealth bomber counterpart to the B-2, code named H-8. Xendong knew the H-8's estimated range of over 8,000 miles placed the U.S.

within striking distance of its laser guided bombs and air-launched nuclear tipped cruise missiles whose 2,000-mile range further enhanced the bomber's reach.

In many respects, the H-8, whose program had commenced back in 1994, resembled that of the B-2, not surprising since most of its so-called indigenously developed features had been copied from its U.S. counterpart. It had been a time-consuming process acquiring, fabricating, and reverse engineering the most complex flying contraption ever built.

Nonetheless, Chinese officials had quietly boasted behind closed doors that their new strategic bomber exceeded the B-2 on many fronts. But Xendong had not bought into these vaunted claims, and for good reason.

He knew with increased computing power and better understanding of a low observable layout, an airplane designed with a modicum of stealth characteristics, such as an overall flying-wing shape, had become more achievable than before. The main bulk of stealth research was now focused on the craft's onboard systems, such as avionics and low probability of intercept radars that enabled stealth craft to see air and ground targets without being spotted.

In these aspects, China still clearly trailed the U.S. Thus, Xendong knew better than to think of the current H-8 as anything more than an ersatz B-2. And despite best efforts for over a decade, many of the B-2's vital details had remained elusive to China's foreign espionage. Which is why he had been sent on this perilous mission and instructed to follow Trostov, to the ends of the earth if need be.

LANGLEY AIR FORCE BASE, VIRGINIA

"What do you make of it?" General Norton asked Alan Parker, Langley's chief communication intelligence officer, of the report received from a remote station in the North Atlantic indicating interception of odd transmissions.

Parker, donning a set of headphones with hands pressing tightly on the ear pads to block out ambient noises, lifted an index finger to ask Norton for additional moments of silence.

"Very strange," Parker finally replied. "Data analysis confirms it's a man-made signal, not noise. It's spread spectrum transmission: a normal message signal is mixed in with random noise so the result sounds like background noise."

"Making its detection impossible to an unintended recipient," Norton deduced.

"Precisely. It's very effective. I have thrown every single military decryption key at it, yet no luck. But why send us a message we cannot understand?"

"I have an idea. Leave everything here."

The communication officer quickly exited as Norton dialed his phone.

Fleisler's voice came on. "I gather you've come across something, General?"

Norton quickly explained the situation. "We need the right decryption key."

"We gave you all the keys we have."

"Not all," the general said calmly. "You left out the Tanaris-specific codes."

"You know we cannot give those out. We have to send it to them for analysis."

"Suit yourself. I'm transmitting the signal to you now."

RYSON'S OFFICE

Ryson slammed the cover closed on Evertt's docket, then gently massaged his temples with kneading fingers. The adrenaline laced vigor from his vehement argument with Gorik had long since ebbed, leaving behind a fatigued mind.

The ruthless colonel had not denied that Maine's death was a homicide of his doing, which told Ryson that he too might not be safe for very long. And Gorik knew that Ryson could not burden yet another human loss, this time a friend. Plus, Gorik had the president effectively blackmailed. But how could Ryson let down the commander in chief, and more importantly, his country? Ryson felt as if he could neither pursue his cause, nor back down.

His mind harked back to the finger-print anomaly in Evertt's file which had led him to another deceased aviator's file. If that was a purposely placed hidden message, the trail might not have had to end there.

Galvanized, he pulled up the deceased aviator's system history file. To his surprise, the long-dormant record had too been recently altered, in the format of a new finger-print file. He queried the computer for this new print.

This time, it took Ryson a few minutes of staring expectantly at the screen before he was presented with its improbable match.

THE UNKNOWN LOCATION

Xendong felt as if he had been sitting on the damned volcanic rock all night, but a glance at his watch indicated only a twenty minutes hiatus. His mind raced with restrained excitement.

He heard rustling in the brush ahead, from which then emerged dark silhouettes, of camouflaged armed men wearing infrared night goggles, which had picked up the heat signature from Trostov's lit cigarette amongst the dense undergrowth.

They silently led the duo down a hidden path into the hillside. Only then did Xendong discern the outline of an entrance to a bunker. It was cleverly burrowed into the cliff and nearly covered with ivy and other vegetations that must have grown on its cement hide for decades.

The company went past a rust-covered heavy iron gate, and down narrow corridors until they had arrived at the bunker's main complex. In this series of interconnected rooms Trostov's team had set up camp.

Jury-rigged wire lines studded with lights provided ample overhead illumination to a number of compartments. Xendong spotted a radar operator station, several ordinance storage areas, and crude living quarters.

The bunker appeared to have been otherwise abandoned for well over half a century. On the concrete walls Xendong spotted faded stenciled insignias of Nazi Germany, which added to the locale's curious oddity.

"Never seen such an elaborate smuggling set up," Xendong observed in earnest.

"Extraordinary opportunities call for extraordinary measures my friend," Trostov stated. "So would you like to see the ultimate prize?"

"Don't tell me it's chopped up and stacked in one of these rooms," Xendong said, as his gaze swept about the bunker's confined layout.

Trostov laughed. "Follow me." He took a turn at a juncture into a musty corridor and headed along its narrow path to an iron door, then swung it open with loud metal-grating noise.

Inside was pitch dark but judging by the fresh airflow Xendong guessed it a cavernous space opening directly to the outside. Trostov flipped on switches to bathe its front area in projected light.

The area was fairly spacious, but with a much lower reinforced-concrete ceiling than most hangars. Its size, however, was not what now had Xendong's undivided attention, but rather the ominous machine that occupied most of the space.

Situated directly in front was a strange yet familiar looking aircraft. It was dark, sinister, and unconventional to say the least, a pair of expansive wings converging to no real fuselage to break their flat uniformity, only a gentle bulbous centerpiece that melded smoothly at either end into their planar canvas. Above them sat curved glass panes, as monstrous eyes flanked by a pair of menacing air intakes, resembling a beast's nostrils. It was inconceivably black, and defiant to all light that shone upon it, like a void perceivable only by its boundary.

This aircraft was the stuff of dreams—or nightmares.

"Good God!" Xendong exclaimed, the enormity of Trostov accomplishment finally dawning on him.

Xendong barely heard Trostov's follow up remark. He was in a different world, a Nirvana of sorts for a man in his profession. At long last, China would be in possession of a living breathing B-2 bomber, one that would be disclosing all its secrets and making a truly superior Chinese stealth bomber a reality many years ahead of its time.

"This is fantastic," Xendong finally uttered, still flabbergasted.

"Sure is. Dark as coal on the outside, but harboring technologies more precious than diamonds," Trostov remarked, "my crystalline *diamonds* have arrived!"

"You deserve all the credit," Xendong said, finding a new respect for the Russian.

"Not *all* of it," Trostov teased.

Xendong felt the Russian was being genuinely modest for once, perhaps to some degree humbled by the success of the improbable feat.

"Now, I would like you to meet the brave pilot who really made this possible," Trostov said. "You may come forward comrade!"

From the darkened ends of the cavern, a solid set of footsteps came marching forward. Xendong inexplicably felt a knot tightening in his throat. The tread grew louder until finally the source of the footsteps crossed into the light. Xendong nervously scrambled for his pocketed glasses, putting them on with shaky hands. A shock rent him in recognizing the ghostly face that now appeared before him.

"No! This cannot be!" he shrieked.

RYSON'S OFFICE

Ryson's ears instinctively perked up, as if apprehensive of getting caught. In front, his computer displayed a secret personnel record not meant for him to see: a portrait of an older man who strangely bore no associated name, just an identification number. His date of service had begun nine years back, but there were no previous activities record, or even a birth date. It was as if the man had not existed prior to that, nor any indications of what he did since.

Was his purpose at Tanaris to serve as a pilot, or something else? It struck Ryson as the most curious of oddities. Not one to back off easily, he studied other information in the file.

Then he juxtaposed the older man's portrait next to the dead aviator's. Each seemed of a different man. The dead aviator portrait was of a serene fair-haired pilot, with a youthful charismatic fly-boy smile, and eyes glinting in anticipation of a bright future. Ryson realized that this man must have not updated his portrait since joining Tanaris.

Ryson dug deeper into that pilot's file, feeling almost sacrilegious considering his near reverence for the man. The file stated the pilot's wife had died some five years after his demise, on February 20th, in an accident in South America. Oddly, just as with Evertt's file, that information was added the day before the SuperCOIL's disappearance. Otherwise, the file had remained dormant for years, since the pilot's death. The February 20th date sounded familiar to Ryson, but he could not readily recall why.

He then turned his attention to the older man's portrait, which conveyed a far different story. It was of a man aged beyond his years, with anguished face punctuated by hardened eyes brimming with vengeful conviction. Drawn into the images, Ryson searched facial features of each man, eventually discerning of special shared peculiarities.

Slowly he drew irrefutable conclusions his heart did not want to believe: that these men were one and the same.

The older man was indeed the renowned 'dead' aviator who had obviously not died at the time his file indicated. But a deeper question now arose: how did that man relate to Jonathan Evertt, the SuperCOIL's purported pilot?

Suddenly Ryson recalled his talk with Maines, the chopper pilot with whom Evertt had briefly spoken of his wife's death nine years ago on Feb 20th in South America, an exact match in date and place to the death of the storied pilot's wife.

Assuming Maines statements were genuine, there remained only one explanation: the SuperCOIL's real pilot was indeed the aviator who appeared in both photographs.

But Ryson felt more betrayed than triumphant, in discovering the man behind this whole sordid affair. That man was none other than the Alpha Squadron's former revered commander, Ryson's long-time aviation idol, declared as dead in combat over Iraq along with his entire attack wing following a tragic ill-fated black-classified mission during the Operation Desert Storm; a man once known as Captain Jack McDermott.

TANARIS

"Do you have it?" McCane asked impatiently.

"Yes sir," the communication commander confidently replied. "The signal was coded with our encryption keys; our decryption code will turn all that gobbledygook into plain English."

"Do it," McCane ordered with ambivalence, not knowing what the signal forwarded to them by Norton would reveal on the mystery of the missing bomber. The computer console beeped and flashed a message.

"Here it is," the commander stated. McCane's heart nearly skipped a beat. He eyed the screen but saw only an unending sequence of numbers.

"This is what you call 'plain English'?" he groaned.

"It's a numeric-only message, no words. It contains two parts. First is a long authentication sequence that matches the pilot's most recent identification code."

"So we know it's from him," McCane mulled out loud. "And what else?"

"The second part is the geographical coordinates where messages come from."

McCane's ears perked, his mouth suddenly parched dry. "Where?"

"Just verified the location with the receiving satellite. It is coming from near one of our own bases." He tapped a map on the screen with his finger. "Right here."

TANARIS

Ryson's cell-phone rang. It was McCane.

"Gorik needs your progress report for our meeting with the president."

"Where and when?" Ryson asked, surprised.

"Headquarters, 2pm sharp!" the general ordered, then hung up.

Gasping for breath, Ryson arrived at 1:58p.m., and found himself amidst a heated teleconference debate. On one side of the ornate conference table sat Gorik, McCane, and Kessler facing a wall-sized flat-panel display whose live high-definition image was so crisp and scaled to proportions that seemed a trans-dimensional portal had opened directly into the White House.

Then the conversations were abruptly cut short and all stood to attention as the president entered the Situation Room. He strode to his designated spot at the head of the mahogany table, under a prominent wall-mounted seal of the commander in chief.

"Please be seated," the president said in a composed demeanor, but wasting no time in getting matters underway. "First, let's hear on Lieutenant Ryson's finds."

"Same here," Gorik said, smirking at Ryson.

Ryson steadied his gaze on the commander in chief, who had assigned him to this vital but miserable task.

"Mr. President, I firmly believe foul play was involved, and by a person of sharp wit and unparalleled piloting skills." He intentionally kept his eyes on the White House crowd but felt Gorik's gaze boring a hole in the nape of his neck.

"On what basis? And don't mince words," the president demanded.

"Physics, sir." He saw that the statement brought curious stares and murmurs arising from both sides of the view screen.

"*Physics?*" McCane repeated.

"Yes, sir." Ryson then summarized how the boom had been precision cut by a laser beam. But the White House audience appeared less than impressed.

"Couldn't the laser beam have come from another source?" Fleisler asked.

"No, Mr. Secretary, only from the SuperCOIL, purposely fired to blow that tanker out of the sky. And I believe the bomber wasn't destroyed," Ryson stated, then paused for effect.

"But it *must* have been!" Fleisler exclaimed.

"Unlikely," Ryson said. "The event-timer registry proves the explosion occurred seconds *after* the SuperCOIL had detached, sufficient time for an adept pilot to place a safe distance between the two vessels."

"But no real proof the bomber survived, Lieutenant?" the president asked.

"No, Mr. President," Ryson replied. "Just theories that fit the facts."

The President ruminated, then nodded without any despondency. To Ryson, it seemed as if his explanation had given credence to an alternate theory. But which?

"Sir, if I may speak freely, I believe there is more to this story than I am being told. I *must* know. It is essential to my assessment of the situation."

"I think it is time," said the president, "we gave you a full briefing. Norton?"

Norton put up an image of a cigarette-box-sized device. "This is the pilot locator," he said. "The pilot can activate it in the event of a crash. The device obtains its location via a Global Positioning Satellite and transmits it in a rescue message. Three days ago, we received a signal from our reconnaissance satellite orbiting over the Atlantic. The signal contained unique identification that matched the SuperCOIL's pilot locator," Norton said.

"You believe this confirms our bird is at the bottom of Atlantic?" Ryson asked.

"Perhaps, but the locator is on the pilot, not the plane, and its signal did not come off the coast of Florida either."

Ryson looked dumbfounded. "Where then?"

"A spot off the African coast, over 3,000 miles from Florida," Norton said.

"Where exactly?"

"The Azores."

"The Portuguese islands?" Ryson asked, incredulous. "We have an Air Force base there."

"Perplexingly the signal is coming from a different isle in the chain," Norton continued, "that airbase did not pick up the signal, as it was deliberately directed to a special satellite. Nor is it continuously transmitted as a pilot locator is programmed to, but in short bursts used by our Special Forces to reduce detection."

"Someone must have tinkered with the locator's transmission form but not its message," Ryson deduced out loud.

"Yes, and we'd like to know why," Fleisler added.

"It was meant to be discovered only by us," Ryson conjectured. "But I question the motive."

"No motive, just a pilot who has gone mad," Gorik surmised.

"But we don't even know how he got to the Azores," Norton remarked, "if he is still alive, or more importantly where the plane is."

"Why not put a locator on the SuperCOIL itself?" Fleisler questioned Gorik.

"It can compromise its location," the colonel explained impatiently. "In a fatal plane crash, we would have to remotely activate it, and so might an enemy during its mission flight."

"And what if the enemy got to a downed SuperCOIL first?" Fleisler pressed.

"We prepared for that contingency too."

"How so?"

"Operation Gold," Gorik said coldly.

"What's that?" Ryson asked, having now twice heard the alarming term.

"That information is classified," McCane told him.

"Perhaps the pilot activated it inside the plane, before he died?" Fleisler asked.

"No, he must have gotten out," Ryson said. "The device was given a relatively large directional antenna, and special spread spectrum encryption circuits which resequenced the signal. Doesn't sound like the work of a man who has gone mad."

"The pilot must be in hostile hands," Gorik said, taking a more cautious stance.

"I agree," McCane said. "He did not want to alert the airbase because their normal search and rescue mission would also alert his captors to move or kill him. No, he wanted for only us to go there, with precision and care."

"If a hostile situation, shouldn't we resort to Operation Gold?" Norton asked.

"There is no reason to regard the Portuguese islands as hostile territories, or to think the plane is even there," Gorik said calmly. "Our terrain study shows no place on that isle to land a plane that size, or even a crash site."

"What's your proposal?" the president asked. "Getting tired of conjectures."

"First recon the site," Gorik stated. "If the plane is irrecoverably in hostile hands, then we re-evaluate the Gold option. We be ready to face any contingency."

"This is a job for the Special Forces," said the president, turning to Norton. "How fast before units can be flown to the scene?"

"SEAL Team Two is stationed in Germany. They can get there within hours."

"Mr. President," Gorik interjected again, "due to this mission's ultra-secret nature, I recommend using the Black Squadron."

The president nodded after some thought. "You get the first crack," he said, "but if you fail, we'll send in everything we've got! Are there any questions?"

"Sir," said Ryson. "Why bring me here if you had already heard from the pilot?"

"To corroborate the pilot's foul play. And we also need a stealth expert on this mission. I will leave the logistics details to Colonel Gorik."

Ryson's eyes widened. He loathed embarking on another assignment, especially an overseas one, but feared he would have no choice in the matter.

"Gentlemen," said the president, eyes sweeping across the room. "Our nation depends on your efforts. This weapon must not fall into enemy hands! Clear?"

Everyone nodded and the meeting was over.

The view-screen went dark, and Ryson felt alone again, like a sheep abandoned in a den of wolves. McCane set out to arrange for the forces, leaving Ryson with Gorik and Kessler.

"Well, Lieutenant," Gorik said, "seems we will be working together for a while longer. I did not however appreciate your assessment of the pilot to the president."

Ryson garnered some inner strength to gaze at the colonel. "Is that why you immediately volunteered the Black Squadron?" Ryson said, watching Gorik's puzzled expression. "So if you happen to find the pilot alive, no one else will know about him, or what you will do to him?"

"What are you getting at?" Gorik asked.

"It be a shock to outsiders to find a living Captain McDermott behind all this."

Gorik face became livid. "That pilot has been dead for over a decade." He looked at a nodding Kessler. It was not enough to convince Ryson, he desperately wanted closure on whether the ace pilot was alive, by hearing it from Gorik.

"You deliberately misguided me, it's a federal offense," Ryson continued.

"Just for argument's sake," the colonel countered, "even if your crazy theory is right, the case is black-classified and cannot be discussed in any judicial venues."

"Justice will be served, somehow," Ryson said diffidently.

"Served for whom? I certainly would not be implicated for any of the pilot's actions. Besides, I can assure you he is none other than Jonathan Evertt."

The door had barely shut behind the parting lieutenant when Kessler turned to Gorik. "He was only hoping for us to tip our hand."

"Which we didn't," Gorik said smugly, though still angry. "Assemble our best commando team for this mission and take Ryson along."

"What if we do run into McDermott on the island?" Kessler asked.

The colonel barely hesitated. "Kill him, then dispose his body where none will ever find it."

"And Ryson?"

"Him, too. The more the merrier."

APPROACHING THE AZORES, THE ATLANTIC OCEAN

The four inflatable high speed-boats, in tandem formation to reduce head-on radar signature, rapidly sped toward the island destination at night along a pre-charted path. From the rear of boat number three, Ian Ryson ducked apprehensively behind a phalanx of heavily armed commandos wearing camouflage outfits that blended in with the backdrop of the black skies like invisible cloaks.

Ryson lay nearly flat against the deck to shelter his pallid face from constant splashing by the rough briny swells. The gut-wrenching, wave-hopping forty-minute trip felt like hours. His only real companion had been the quiet whirr of the electric boat motor specially made to minimize its acoustic signature.

Now and then he peeked at the silhouette of the island's high volcanic walls that loomed ever larger on the darkened horizon. He tried not to think of what terrors may lay beyond those mysterious ramparts of granite, or that he was resting on sacks of C4 high explosive ordinance.

The veteran Black Squadron commandos seemed unaffected by these details. As if just another day at the office, their focus lay perpetually transfixed on the approaching target, and only occasionally turning face to offer the lowly lieutenant a troubling reptilian sneer.

Ryson tried his best to hold on, taking deep calming breaths and thinking of Kathleen to avert an onset of the nightmare. He wondered if he would ever see her again. This question had plagued him during the last adrenaline-filled, sleepless eighteen hours since the hurried departure from Tanaris with Gorik's finest commando team. They had boarded a C-2A "greyhound" cargo transport bound for Admiral Breneman's aircraft carrier off the coast of the Azores.

It was a bumpy, noisy ride on the monster "COD"—Carrier Onboard Delivery— the C-2A's mission nickname, which enabled carrier landings and take-offs. The C-2A was reasonably fast for a turboprop that could haul more than ten thousand lbs. of cargo, including 26 crew and Special Forces members. After several aerial refuelings en route, the greyhound touched down on a carrier deck amid rough seas, along with squadrons of F-18s flown covertly in from Tanaris.

Following a final mission briefing, the commandos embarked on high-speed vessels at nightfall toward this elusive locale, one of the more remote islands of the Azores chain.

Yet Ryson doubted they would find the SuperCOIL. The satellite topography maps showed a mostly craggy isle devoid of any flat areas suitable for the landing of a bomber-sized plane.

And then he felt the boat slowing. The engine whine switched to a lower rpm, and the waves felt less choppy. Looking up, sheer cliffs towered overhead.

They had arrived.

There was a sense of renewed energy, even mild agitation, rippling through their assault group. Each member fixed their eyes on the challenge of the rocky ramparts, against whose granite-slab base the wind-driven waves broke furiously with thunderous roars.

The boats turned starboard while closely hugging the cliff base. The squad leader, doubling as the navigator, checked bearings on a portable GPS device, then silently gestured the engine operator to take a more westward course.

Soon the mini-armada reached an improbable break in the solid walls where a small bay lay in sight. Without a word, all four teams veered into the crescent sandy beach, quickly off-loaded equipment, and dragged their boats out of the water, hiding them behind volcanic megaliths.

They grabbed pre-assigned rucksacks and all munitions they could haul, and silently started down the narrow path leading into the island's interior.

AT THE RUSSIAN HIDEOUT, AZORES

Trostov sat at the edge of the make-shift bed in his damp quarters. He took a deep soothing pull from his cigarette, then exhaled into the dim room, watching the cloud of white smoke waiver like a dispersing ghost. Soon payment would be transferred to his Swiss account, and the bomber be then flown to mainland China.

It would be the culmination of a project that had been virtually sprung on him nearly three years ago. "What could you possibly have," he had asked the American man offering a lucrative partnership, "to be worth tracking me down?"

"An item of great interest for a resourceful person like you," the former fighter pilot had replied. Then he gave Trostov the big picture while omitting the plane's laser weaponry aspects. The stealth features alone had astonished Trostov, who realized it was worth a fortune beyond his wildest dreams.

But paying the man's demanded $120 million upfront would nearly cripple Trostov's smuggling network until the bomber's finalized reselling, and his Chinese partners never advanced anything substantial.

Black market weapon dealing was a perilous venture of myriad variables, the riskiest of which was establishing trust between the delivery and payment parties. All the while he had to stay steps ahead of the world governments' intelligence operatives with a price tag on his head as hefty as the profits he hoped to make.

"What if this bomber I have never heard of is just a trap to lure me to your CIA?" Trostov had asked.

"You think I have any love left for those people? Look, as a good will gesture, I will cut my advance fee in half to sixty million, with another sixty upon delivery."

It was a feasible offering for Trostov, and as always, he could devise safeguards against betrayal.

"What you'll do with all that money?" he had prodded the former fighter pilot.

"Buy a new identity and live the good life. Now, when and where you want it?"

"Soon as your bird is ready to fly. I'll arrange a suitable interim hide-out."

"Why the interim bull crap?" The American asked.

"The agent is the soul of discretion. His government competes with the United

States militarily but doesn't want to kick off Armageddon. At least not while behind the curve."

"Hence the third-party strategy?"

"Right, and they have always paid a premium," Trostov said, extending a hand.

"Done," the American shook back firmly.

During the next three years, Trostov had been meticulously cautious in dealing with this mystery client who had promised him a technological equivalent of the proverbial moon. He had taken extensive measure to verify his real identity, and to avoid detection only irregularly communicated with him. The only key information conveyed to the pilot was the configuration of the destination runway for him to covertly perform landing practices at Tanaris.

No information was given as to where the secret strip lay. The pilot was only told to fly east after stealing the bomber and contact Trostov's agents on an encrypted channel. Only then was he provided with the actual destination.

ON THE LAKE FRONT

Despite lack of weapons or gear to haul, Ryson marched laboriously to the squad's rear. Panting, he struggled to not trip on loose rocks in soft earth muddied by a recent rain fall.

Like everyone else, his eyes sported low-light goggles which turned the dark desolate surroundings into a greenish surreal landscape that could have belonged to an alien world.

Ryson followed the team down a grassy path to a lakeshore, at where they set up camp behind volcanic boulders. A few reached for scuba diving suits stowed in their backpacks.

Kessler, the mission commander, motioned Ryson to approach his station. Ryson reluctantly set toward him, while careful to not to trip over anything along the way, and soon he stood before the major, who held out an extra scuba "wetsuit" outfit. He gestured for Ryson to don it.

Ryson shook his head in defiance, terrified. "Absolutely not," he replied in a low shaky voice, "I know nothing on scuba diving in combat, it was never a part of my mission here!"

"Well it is now, and that is Colonel Gorik's order."

"I don't believe it!"

"Take it up with him when we return. Now get into that suit!"

"Major why are we doing this?" Ryson asked.

Kessler's eyes narrowed on Ryson, who saw their wolf-like gleam even without the aid of night vision. "The transmitter whose signal we intercepted is on the far side of this lake. As of our last read ten minutes ago, it was still sending messages."

"And so why the need to swim to it?"

"It's the fastest, least obstructed way. We'd rather not go around these monsters," he pointed to the sharp vertiginous cliffs bordering the lake. "Don't have that kind of time."

Resigned, Ryson yanked the scuba gear from the commander's hand.

The cold water was deep, the visibility appeared poor to non-existent, and the motivation for his teammates to save him was rock bottom.

And this time there would be no pods to protect him should his paralysis return.

AT THE RUSSIAN HIDEOUT

The stencils on the dumbbells read 110 pounds each, yet they were steadily hoisted along perfectly symmetrical parabolic paths that converged atop an imaginary arc, the arms' length of Captain Jack McDermott.

The pilot held the dumbbells high over his head, with their flattened ends in parallel but not touching, then lowered them synchronously to his hip-line, in an optimal three-seconds time.

Taking a deep breath, McDermott laid down the weights, then got off the inclined bench and wiped his glistening forehead with a towel. He had not forgone his daily exercise routine even in this remote locale's Spartan accommodations. Trostov had brought in the weights to help his men maintain peak physical shape.

The captain massaged his neck to ease a dull aching from his last lift repetition. It was an old injury, a nuisance reminder of a bitter past, but at least it no longer threatened to permanently rob him of the ability to walk.

McDermott vividly remembered those days, as his gaze caught site of a page-size portrait of his wife on the desk against a far wall. A flower rested at its base, one he had picked that day while venturing outside. At his home, every day since her passing he had placed a fresh flower next to it on his end table, even in winters.

Next to hers was a second picture, of a fighter pilot group donned in flight suits, all members of his Alpha Squadron, and posing by an F-16 Falcon bearing the emblem of the once-noble Black Squadron. McDermott, the former squadron leader of that fiercely loyal and patriotic aerial combat unit winced at recollections of the dreaded events that had led him to this place.

"Captain Evertt?" the nurse spoke in Italian-accented English. The year: 1991.

"Yes?" McDermott answered to his assumed name. He was in an intensive care unit in Riyadh, Saudi Arabia's capital, where he had rested for the past three days.

A medical chopper had flown him here, from the field hospital by the Iraqi border where he was taken while unconscious after ejecting from his F-16 following a ground-missile attack on his squadron. His last memory was of uncontrollable tumbling into an outcropping of rocks, with his parachute wrapped around him, denying the protective use of his hands. Then the snapping sounds from his neck had reverberated in his ears, and all had gone dark before his eyes.

But fate had once again smiled on him. An Italian patrol vehicle on an unscheduled tour had spotted his parachute and rescued him. His true assailants must have fled at the sight of the armored company, though his fall had almost finished the job for them by fracturing his neck.

That he had survived such an injury was a miracle. Even as he had lain in the ICU after emergency surgery, he could only partly feel his toes, and was unable to stand upright.

The intense pain, however, paled in comparison to his grief. His mind drifted back to the squadron members whom he felt he had personally let down, despite the attack having come as total surprise to all. For three days now, he had been held immobile, with nothing but anguish to pervade his weary mind.

All things considered, he wished he had died along with his friends. Only his curiosity had kept him going, the burning desire to one day discover the truth behind what had actually happened and strangle the culprits with his bare hands.

"You have a visitor, sir," the nurse stated.

"Another government inspector?" he asked.

The nurse shrugged.

"Send him in," McDermott said. His only reply to each inquiry by Italian investigators was a pre-approved cover story: that he was Captain Jonathan Evertt, a U.S. Air Force pilot returning from a classified combat mission.

The nurse hurriedly left. Minutes later a set of heavier steps echoed down the hallway, not of hospital staff's soft-soled shoes, but of combat boots marching to a standard rhythm that only another military man's ears could register. It was a familiar tempo, one he had heard countless times at Tanaris.

McDermott spoke as soon as the man had reached the front door.

"Glad you finally showed up Major," he said, though unable to see who he was addressing. The restrictive hard-shell brace that firmly held his neck in place allowed only an upward view of the white hospital ceiling.

"Your ears still working just fine," Gorik's voice filled the room. He stepped to the bedside. "You survived," the major stated. His tone hinted at disappointment, not admiration.

"Surprised?" McDermott asked.

"Not really. I knew a rare breed like you would not be had so easily. Wish I could say the same about the rest of your men."

The back-handed compliment struck McDermott's heart like a knife. His eyes glazed with tears for the first time in his military career. But his feeling for his doomed men ran deep. It was as if he had lost three brothers. "What happened?"

"I don't know, we are still investigating," said the colonel.

McDermott's eyes shifted away, looking for solace.

"I would have come sooner," Gorik continued, "but frankly your assumed identity worked a little too well with our non-U.S. forces, so locating you took a while. Even then I had to see you to be sure."

"I rather you had not seen me like this at all."

"You may recover, at least partly."

McDermott had not found that an appealing prospect. The top-notch Italian neurosurgeon flown in from Rome was only cautiously optimistic. And any recovery mandated a lengthy and grueling rehabilitation and physical therapy.

"Assuming so, what's going to happen now? I don't want any bullshit."

Gorik put his hand on McDermott's left arm, feigning a comforting gesture, and took a deep breath. "You asked, so I am going to give it to you straight," he stated. "This does not look good, in fact it's terrible. We have a decimated elite squadron with three dead men. I don't know if it's the pilots or planners to blame, but the high ups have asked me to decommission you," Gorik said.

"I am their scapegoat," McDermott said, having predicted as much. "It's ok, I was retiring from flight anyway. I will just do my desk job and train the future generation of fighter pilots."

But Gorik shook his head. "You don't understand Jack; they are asking you to leave Tanaris and black-classified life, *completely*."

"What?" McDermott winced in pain, his sudden reflexive motion yanking the many sutured incisions. "They can't leave me out on the street like this!"

"They wanted to, but I prevailed on a few concessions, namely Alpha Squadron's integrity."

"What are you getting at?" McDermott asked, unsure if the Major had fought for the fallen men or his own career.

"After all your years of exemplary service, our men at the base should remember the Alpha Squadron as heroes," Gorik said with an air of righteousness. "We decided to cover this incident up, and report that you and your men died honorably in combat."

"My men *did* die honorably, it was for their mission!" McDermott protested.

"Yes, they did die, but not you."

"I don't like where this is heading."

"Records will indicate that you died as well. The circumstance of death would be 'shot down over the target area.' Your men will receive the highest recognitions of valor, and you will be given an assumed identity and a generous pension to live the rest of your life, with your wife."

"That would be a lie!" he protested vehemently. "My men succeeded in destroying the targets and took a few bastard MiGs down too."

"True," Gorik stated. "But ours is a better story than one of being shot down at a desolate spot by enemy commandos. It's not exactly the glamorous ending one hopes for heroes."

"To hell with your fabricated hero scenarios, my men fought and died with courage, and those are the characteristics every hero is made of. It's all that matters," McDermott argued.

"I guess we see things differently then," Gorik replied.

McDermott knew Gorik was unflinching, as he mulled the macabre proposition. There had to be another way.

"And if I refuse these cover-ups?"

"Then we will have to file this under a Class-A," referring to accidents caused mostly by pilot error resulting in death, or loss of the aircraft. "It will not bode well for your deceased men's reputation. I will also not be authorized to give their families additional secret funds to make up for their losses, of which they would need every penny," Gorik said.

When the major returned later that week seeking a response, a physically and mentally broken McDermott reluctantly accepted the offer, and solely for sake of his peers' families.

McDermott was later flown stateside for additional corrective operations. Then for over a year, the former Special Forces lead who had run six miles daily was confined to a wheelchair. His days were filled with physician visits, and grueling rehabilitation programs. It would be another eight months before his body could graduate to a set of crutches for movement.

Eventually he made a full physical recovery against all odds. But his scarred mind was not so quick to heal. Enduring thoughts of his lost comrades haunted him, and bore heavy on his shoulders. Worse, he had been unable to resolve that fateful day's mysteries via insider fact finding, as he was no longer "in the black."

In an attempt to allay his grief, he had gradually resumed his once vigorous active life, partaking in swimming, running, even hiking. Each time the anguish of his past was too great his wife would nurse him back from the borders of insanity. Her sight alone instantly calmed him, and she was the focal point on which his new civilian life revolved, as she had been in times past.

Five years later, Gorik again caught up with McDermott. He found the once severely debilitated captain climbing the sheer face of a hundred-foot cliff.

McDermott's muscular arms and legs found secure holds as he nimbly made his way up to the cliff-top, and then back down to the riverbed again. The colonel waited patiently during the descent, then made his approach.

"Your full recovery amazes me," he commented loudly from the distance.

McDermott was not surprised at the sight of his former commanding officer. He had spotted Gorik's camouflaged uniform from the crest line, the same way he had visually picked out low flying enemy aircraft in his fighter jet from ten thousand feet. Nor had the fact that the former major now bore the new insignia of a colonel escaped him.

"Why are you here after all these years?" he asked, gulping water from his plastic bottle.

"To bear good news," Gorik paced to within a few yards, crunching small pebbles and rocks under his heavy boots. McDermott cast a suspicious sideways gaze at a man who had so abruptly returned, and at such an unexpected locale.

He wiped his mouth on his sleeve. "Let me guess. You found out who killed my squadron?" he addressed the only thing that still mattered to him, a wave of fresh pain sweeping over him. "I don't believe those were Soviet made missiles," he said, alluding to his mystery assailants. "They were too accurate and agile."

"Jack, you are not in the black anymore," Gorik lowered his visor a bit to keep the low sun off his face. "I cannot officially discuss this. Now since you and I go way back, off the record I can say we could not conclusively prove anything."

McDermott grimaced at Gorik's blatant insincerity. "More like you didn't *want* to prove anything. Any unpleasant truth found wouldn't bode well for your career," he replied bitterly.

"Let the matters of the past rest there. Focus on the future," Gorik said in a preaching tone, taking a step closer.

"Whose future... mine or yours?"

"Both. I have a new project, and I can get you the necessary flight clearance."

"From the same people who originally demanded my removal? You're insane!"

"We have a new commander in chief, and many of those old generals in charge have since moved on or retired. I just need to know you're in for sure before giving out any details."

McDermott turned towards the sun setting over the high cliffs. The craving for air combat still coursed in his veins but had inextricably intertwined with the demise of his close friends. Ultimately, it was a closed chapter he would rather not reopen, especially in light of his new life. "I'm sorry, Colonel," he said at last. "My focus is my wife now. She's the only semblance of a normal life I have left. We're celebrating our tenth anniversary soon and planning to start a family of our own. I can't just walk away from all that for the sake of a plane."

"This isn't an ordinary plane," Gorik teased.

"None of them are," McDermott said wistfully. "At any rate, I've moved on from that life." He expected further hard selling, but the colonel replied in a surprisingly accepting tone.

"I understand, Jack. You're quite lucky to have such a loving woman, sticking by you throughout a taxing decade, first your hot-dogging career, then a lengthy physical recovery, and now living under assumed identities. Where are you going for your anniversary?"

"South America. An affordable vacation in paradise."

"Make sure it's a good one."

"It will be."

"Captain?" a male voice addressed him in Russian-accented English, bringing him back to the present.

"What is it, commander?" McDermott growled.

"General Trostov requests your presence at the surveillance room at once, sir."

"For what reason?" McDermott inquired.

"We've got uninvited company on the island."

THE SURVEILLANCE ROOM

"What do you make of them? Regular divers?" the camera operator asked, peering intently at the reddish thermal images on the monochrome monitor, fed by a hidden camera on the nearby lake, one of many Trostov had deployed along the likely approaches to the base. This infrared camera captured body heat, but its murky underwater resolution revealed only generalities of a quad diver formation advancing with uniform precision behind their underwater motorized craft.

"Not regular divers," McDermott said, hiding his true observations. "They're using special self-contained underwater breathing apparatuses, and only two groups use such equipment."

"Who?" Trostov eagerly asked.

"One is deep-sea treasure hunters, but this lakebed has no sunken ships."

"And the second group?"

"The U.S. military," McDermott stated coldly. The comment made the astonished Russian's head pivot in his direction.

"Looking for this secret base?" Trostov was incredulous. He had complete faith in his own ability to pull off covert operations undetected.

The camera operator chimed in. "Might be cadets on a training exercise from the Lajes Field." He referred to the U.S. Air Force transport hub in the nearby

Azores island of Terceira.

"Or a highly trained SEAL team searching for their missing bomber," McDermott countered. "Let's take a look," he motioned two others to follow him.

"Be careful; if they're just cadets then we don't want to alert them," Trostov cautioned. But McDermott was already out the door.

THE LAKE

In the depths, Ryson began to feel his old hydrophobia stalking him like a predator. He had subdued its once-paralyzing grip during the incident in the pod, but as his trio team plunged ever deeper into the black void below, he feared such a reoccurrence would spell certain death.

He forced his focus on sensory stimuli, particularly his frigid medium. The cold-water sensations that had started as skin prickles had now permeated deep, freezing him to the bone despite his wetsuit. It was a mystery how a semitropical island would hold such an oppositely tempered lake; perhaps it was replenished from subterranean cold-water wells.

Ryson tried to marshal his besetting thoughts of the nightmare, the mission, and his curios environ, as he eyed the men in front, and the torpedo-shaped propeller device he clung to.

Amid all that, he had not seen Kessler secretly creep into the lake behind him, carrying a Heckler & Koch P11 underwater gun.

Some fifty feet aft, Kessler calmly observed the progress of his heavily armed team. Each member rhythmically stroked his trained legs behind a diver-carrying-vehicle (DCV), torpedo-shaped craft a diver could latch onto for a ride.

Despite their superb physical fitness, Special Forces avoided unassisted submersed swims of a length exceeding five hundred meters. These four men, swimming in a finger four formation with a lightly suited Ryson at the far right, struck Kessler as a quiet flock of ravens, and thanks to their rebreathers gave off no telltale bubble bursts.

Kessler took measured breaths from the mouthpiece of his rebreather, which was like a scuba, except it released no exhalation bubbles to the outside. It was also very efficient, since three-quarters of the oxygen inhaled remained unused by a diver's body and exhaled out with the carbon-dioxide. His rebreather simply routed this mixture via a mouthpiece tube to a CO_2 scrubber filter, which separated the oxygen for another inhalation by him. This effectively quadrupled his oxygen tank's capacity. Unlike leisure divers, each man carried his rebreather on the front, for easier manual valve adjustments and freeing their backs for other loads.

Kessler took his bearings from a special compass and gazed at the depth meter. In anticipation, he reached for the gun strapped to his waist as he accelerated to close the distance with the front swimmers. It was almost time to say farewell to an unwanted member of his team.

A few hundred feet to the front and side, McDermott, clad in scuba gear and flanked by a pair of ex-Spetsnaz Russian naval special forces mercenaries, checked his motion sensor, which warned of the approaching assault team. The trio pumped their legs and lurched forward, relying solely on muscle power because of virtually no heavy loads and a shorter distance to intercept.

They had run full speed from the base to the water's edge, donned gear in record time, and disappeared beneath the surface.

Hauling minimal weapons, McDermott was equipped with a Soviet-era SPP-1 underwater pistol, which operated more like a nail-gun than its conventional surface firearm version whose bullets' range was drastically reduced in liquids to a fraction of an airborne shot, usually no more than fifteen feet. Worse, with the barrel filled with impeding water, the ammunition of a normal bullet could burst the gun, resulting in injury. The SPP-1, much like the Heckler & Koch P11, relied on shooting darts at relatively low velocity, which nonetheless proved fairly accurate and lethal. Each gun however was unwieldy and carried only five bullets.

Motioning his team to veer left and attack on the mark, McDermott set for a broadside approach of the target. On account of their specialized gear, he had readily recognized them all as members of Black Squadron—except for the one swimming to the far right.

This one peculiar diver hauled no load and his rather awkward struggling body lacked the graceful thrusts of the accompanying trio. He instantly placed the figure as an outsider, maybe a demolition specialist, or technical expert of some kind sent along for the ride. Perhaps he was the man McDermott had been hoping for all along. He would find out soon enough.

Kessler had just come within gun range of his prey when the clouds parted, and the lake was suddenly bathed in penetrating moon rays that turned the dark waters to shimmering silver.

The major welcomed the clearer visibility, which improved firing accuracy. Extending his right arm in front, he held firmly to the German made P11, then grinned murderously as he secured aim at the body of an unsuspecting Ian Ryson.

It wasn't until the ambience became abruptly lit that McDermott discerned a fifth man in the target company furtively catching up from the distant rear. His outstretched arm was holding a gun. Oddly, it was trained at the outsider man in his own team.

Though the man's head was entirely covered by the neoprene helmet and face mask, the all-too familiar physique and swimming style left little doubt about his identity. Despite the frigidness of the water, McDermott felt himself growing hot under the suit as he recognized the opportunity for revenge was finally at hand.

But the time had not quite arrived for his grand plans: the familiar figure was only an agent of the man he ultimately sought. And so he deftly aimed at the figure's arm and squeezed the trigger on his SPP-1. A four-inch bullet sailed out.

Milliseconds before he had hoped to dispatch Ryson, Kessler felt a sudden sharp pain in his right forearm while his eyes caught the blur of a metal object swish by mere inches from his face mask. Several things then happened in quick succession.

The induced muscular reflex loosened his grip on the gun. It quickly disappeared into the void below, though not before the pulled trigger discharged a nail bullet. It shot high past Ryson, who instantly noticed it along with the now alerted trio ahead. The forward members then instinctively scanned the surroundings, caught sight of McDermott's company sweeping in from starboard, and took a defensive posture, leaving Ryson at a loss for guidance.

Observing the battle space with clarity, McDermott gestured his escorts to engage the forward target team, except the struggling man on the far right. Quickly retraining his own gun at Kessler's DCV, he fired two more shots. The nail bullets, with their tips intentionally blunted to create hydro-cavitating, sailed in silent tandem toward their motorized target.

Blood poured out of the exposed surface wound on Kessler's forearm and dispersed in the cold water. Ignoring his injury, he jerked his head left to trace the trajectory of the nail bullet and immediately spotted the trio of unmarked divers approaching from broadside, each holding an SPP-1. Seeing that his men had already set to engage he weighed his own chances.

Still aft of his own pack, now without a gun and hampered by a heavy load, he would have little effective agility to be a match for the armed assailants. There could be more hostiles on the way, and knew his team had no reinforcements.

The armaments type and maneuvering tactics used by the assailant also hinted at a highly trained team which they could not easily subdue especially from their disadvantaged and outgunned defensive position. There was only one sound tactical option left.

"Retreat!" He commanded through his acoustic wave transmitter.

He set his DCV to aft, but a pair of metal slugs pierced into its outer hull incapacitating the electric motor. The propellers ground to a full stop. Kessler cursed under his mask and ditched the defunct vehicle as it began a slow descent to the bottom. His sight shifted to his approaching armed assailant, realizing it would be not be long before he would be upon him.

Deprived of his DCV, there was now little chance of making it back to the base with the heavy load, so he released the cargo's latch and wiggled out from under it. Tightly pressing his arms against his torso to reduce drag, he stroked the muscular legs and flappers to accelerate away.

McDermott regarded Kessler's escape run with ambivalence, half-wanting to chase down the fleeing man to a mortal fight. But before the temptation to pursue could get the better of him, the moonlit wash disappeared behind covering clouds and Kessler's body vanished into the darkened water like a ghost.

Unfazed, McDermott turned to join the forward fray. One of his men was already on the way down, blood gushing from his throat, a victim of a fatal knife wound from his adversary. Further below him floated the body of the Black Squadron commander who had taken two nail shots in his chest and back.

The remaining ex-Spetsnaz had spent all of their five SPP-1 bullets. The other two divers, each brandishing a knife, were closing in on him. There was no sign of the group's outsider man, but his fate did not matter now.

With swift agility, McDermott swam to the aide of his outnumbered man, discharging his remaining two nail bullets into one of the attackers. One barely missed but the other slug smashed directly into the facemask, penetrating the skull for an instant kill. The last assailant, now realizing the hopelessness of his situation, attempted to retreat but was cut down.

A shocked Ryson found his breathing intensified and heart pounding involuntarily. He had been barely missed by a bullet and witnessed the intense fighting that had erupted without warning. Not being in his element, the only instinctive logical place of safety was up.

Before realizing what had happened, Ryson had his DCV pointed to the surface, set at full power, his legs spastically flailing to further hasten the ascent. Somehow he kept the hydrophobic nightmare at bay by focusing on the depth meter, just as he had done in the pod. He paid no attention to the aquatic combat below. He had no fondness for the Black Squadron and knew nothing of the others' intent. For some unexplained reason they had paid him no attention.

Now within just few meters of the surface, he regained full control of his senses. The return of mental clarity was mixed with the anticipation of stripping away the face mask for a deep breath from the fresh air above, and then to weigh his options.

But things did not happen that way. Without warning, his brain precipitously slowed as if shutting down into deep sleep. His eye lids became heavy and a severe headache pounded his skull. His fingers became unresponsive and limp. He let go of the DCV. His vision narrowed and went out as he lost consciousness.

Then he plunged into darkest oblivion, *falling, falling, falling* . . .

AT THE RUSSIAN HIDEOUT

"What happened out there?" Trostov demanded.

"Visitors," McDermott stated flatly. He had returned minutes earlier and changed out of his dripping wetsuit, now hung in the corner.

"Those were Navy SEALs!" the incredulous Russian pointed out. "They know we are here and could be on us any minute!"

McDermott walked behind the desk in his cramped quarters. "Relax. It was only an expeditionary force," he said. "I doubt they know our precise location here. Besides, we killed them all. It will be a while before the rest of them figure out what happened to their buddies and make another attempt."

Trostov wasn't so optimistic. "Why you think they don't know of this base?"

"Because that was the dumbest approach path, or they'd be inside here by now. They are most likely combing through the whole island. Luckily for us they started at the wrong end."

"What tipped them off to this locale in the first place?" asked Trostov.

"Someone must have tracked your movements to here."

"Certainly not!" the Russian protested. "How did they get so close unnoticed?"

"You tell me, you set up surveillance."

Trostov mulled the jab. There was heavy sea and air traffic in the area, a fact he had leveraged as he had taken over this derelict forgotten base and set things up undetected under the Americans' noses. But the same factors were now also hampering his ability to see the other's approach. Besides, he had to rely on passive systems such as infrared or listening devices with shorter reaches than active systems like radar, which would have served as a beacon to their spot.

His best defensive strategy was to remain undiscovered in the first place and allow them time to escape. With their cover blown, they were on borrowed time now, and all that mattered was how much of it they had left.

"Can we determine the size of their force?"

"Maybe," McDermott drummed his fingers on the desk. "We brought back a prisoner who might be able to give us some more information. He is out cold in the next room but should be coming around shortly. I'll interrogate him."

"What should I do?" Trostov asked, hoping the American had a better idea.

"Evacuate! Send your men to clear the runway so I can take-off for China."

"But the money has not been transferred yet..." The Russian voiced his main reason for wanting to stay put.

"That is *your* issue; talk to Xendong. I am sure between losing the plane and hastening the funds transfer his countrymen will go for the latter."

"This could be a disaster," Trostov remarked.

"Or the perfect opportunity to get your money even sooner."

Trostov reflected on the American's shrewd take and then grinned deviously. "I'll get on Xendong right away."

"Before that," McDermott said sternly, "get a defensive perimeter set up, focused on protecting my exit route. And have that runway up and operational!"

Within minutes of Trostov's leaving, the base came intensely alive, men running about, arming themselves with assault weapons, gearing for combat. McDermott remained in his quarters and made no attempts at mobilization.

Instead he grabbed the portrait of his wife that sat inches from his right hand. He drew it close to his chest and gazed intensely at her angelic face. His fingers reached to caress her golden hair behind the glass, and his thought shifted to the calamity that had forever taken her away. Unbidden tears fell.

About a decade ago an explosive-packed truck bomb blasted through their vacation hotel in Bogotá, Colombia. The hotel was an especially popular stay for U.S. citizens who frequented the place and thus a prime spot for a notorious drug cartel to message Washington to cease all covert military drug-war activities in this South American country.

The blast's force brought down the building like a house of cards. McDermott's wife had been in the first-floor lobby then and was instantly buried under five stories of concrete rubble.

McDermott had gone out for a morning jog then, but on returning to the disaster site had refused to give up hope despite the unremitting gore of the rescue efforts. On the third day, he heard that a woman had been found alive on the first floor. She owed her miraculous survival to being pinned a few feet beneath a huge intact support beam. But she was not his wife.

It would be four more days before the rescue workers reached her, or what was left of her, nearly at the bottom of the debris pile. The coroner told McDermott that she had been partly crushed and had likely died slowly as the lifeblood drained from her body.

For many months following, McDermott lived in a sort of haze, neither awake nor sleep, usually half-conscious of his surroundings. His mind was preoccupied with grief, and hatred toward the drug cartel. He wanted to avenge her death, to raze the cartel's camps, and kill with his bare hands every single man involved in the event. But he also began to blame himself, for not having been there to somehow protect his wife, for having vacationed in an apparently volatile foreign land, even for having joined the Air Force in the first place, where he had met her.

His mental condition was noticed by the U.S. Army psychiatrists, who had McDermott, still known by his assumed identity, immediately returned to his home base near Dallas, Texas.

After months of intensive therapy, he was deemed cured of his suicidal and vengeful fantasies and accepted the loss of his wife as an unfortunate incident beyond his control. He finally managed to persuade the Army psychiatrists to return him to normal life. But secretly, his self-loathing continued unabated.

McDermott gently placed the portrait on the desk and wiped his watery eyes. Then, as if suddenly aware of his surroundings, he leapt to action with lethal purpose.

IN THE DARK

The upscale restaurant boasted an expansive terrace that jutted prominently over a panoramic hillside. Ryson took in the romantic scenery with exhilaration.

The softly lit ambience and myriad twinkling stars far above had made for an enchanted evening. He gently squeezed the silky fingers of his enthralled girlfriend. Soon their faces turned to each other, and their lips met in a loving kiss. Ryson watched the candlelight dance in her aquamarine eyes.

"You have excelled again in the romance department," Kathleen told him.

"Nothing but the best for my girl," he said, gently firming his grip on her left hand, then sneaking a wistful peek at her naked ring finger.

"Don't worry Ian," she said. "Whenever you're ready, I am."

Ryson knew feigning denial was of no use. He had already told her of his past, and she had reacted with supportive understanding.

Throughout their four years together, Ryson had noticed his nightmares softening, and increasingly she had appeared in them, often at abyss's edge to throw in a rescue rope.

It had been a strange sensation. Kathleen was both loving and sympathetic on exceptional levels. Ryson, who felt his life had shattered into a million pieces after his fiancée's demise, was now finding Kathleen's ardent love slowly melding the pieces back into a new whole. *If only he could take that last leap*, he thought.

And yet he felt something else as well, a strange sense of déjà vu, as if everything having already unfolded once, exactly as he now perceived it.

With that unsettling recognition, Ryson's eyes twitched, and opened. His drooping chin was resting on his chest, and the after-effects of a splitting headache pounded against his skull with each heartbeat. A musky odor filled his nostrils, and he struggled to see in the darkened surroundings, devoid of any panoramic restaurant views, or Kathleen.

Slowly, he recalled he had been shot at on a lake mission and tried to reach the surface before all had gone dark as he fell to the depths in a seemingly fatal plunge.

He was not dead, but as he tapped his foot on solid concrete, realized he was not in a tent at the base camp either. He was seated on a wooden chair, which creaked softly from his body movements. His arms were restrained by handcuffs holding his wrists behind his back.

Everything was dark, and he could only hear faint unintelligible murmurs of faraway conversations, not unlike the ambience in the restaurant; expect they were not in English.

He was damp from head to toe, though his scuba suit had been removed by someone. He had no idea how he had gotten here, where he was, or for how long. If the lack of soreness in his shoulders from being bound was any indication, he could not have been here for long.

All things considered, he was surprised not to have perished in the lake after seeing his team decimated. Someone hostile must have saved him, but who—and, more terrifying, why?

Regaining full command of his senses, he realized he was not alone. He could almost hear low breathing and had the feeling of physical proximity, as if being visited by a ghost.

"Who's there?" he uttered in the dark.

In hearing the flick of a switch, bright light poured into his eyes. His head reflexively wheeled away from the overhead lamp, as he squinted at the abrupt change in ambience.

Someone approached him, and he raised his head to the sight of a broad-shouldered figure, a man who until now had existed only in a classified database of deceased pilots.

"Well if it isn't Lieutenant Ian Ryson," the man said, sizing him up. "I wonder why a combat inexperienced man was sent on such important covert operation."

Ryson said nothing, too shocked by the powerful presence he faced. The figure pulled up a chair and sat directly in front. "You compromised the whole mission," he half admonished, "and nearly got yourself killed. But here you are now."

The two men stared at each other without speaking, while Ryson gathered his courage. This was not the way he envisioned his first encounter with the idolized man he had chased through a maze of secrecy and misinformation.

"I don't suppose you could take off these handcuffs?" he asked.

"Depends on how cooperative you want to be."

"I don't have the information you want," Ryson stated.

The man leaned closer so that his face almost filled the lieutenant's line of vision. "Why are you here?"

"To find out why *you* are here," Ryson replied.

"So the old colonel wants to know where his Captain Evertt has gone."

"No," Ryson said, feeling renewed vigor. "Just on why Jack McDermott stole his plane."

The man was unfazed in hearing his real name. "Gorik told you that?"

"I found that out on my own, with help from Maines, your chopper pilot."

"A helpful guy."

"Your pals got him."

"Those SOBs will pay!" he raged. "Your team boated from a carrier, right?"

"Yes," Ryson blinked. No point in denying the obvious to a former veteran.

"And what did you expect to find?"

"We intercepted a pilot locator signal, it had your signature encoding."

McDermott's eyes glinted with satisfaction. Ryson saw it as an opportunity to shed some light on this whole affair.

"We feared you were in hostile hands, but I see you are not alone, or captive."

"My foreign friends are with us."

Ryson pressed on an ethical angle in hopes of reaching McDermott. "I cannot believe you have sold yourself to them," he said.

"Not my own self," McDermott replied, in an all business tone. "Just the plane."

"And where is it?" Ryson asked, not really expecting an easy answer.

To his surprise McDermott was accommodating. "They say a pilot never ventures far from his plane while away from home."

"But there aren't any runways on this island!"

McDermott chuckled, which momentarily softened his expression a bit.

"You think I flew over four thousand miles here only to parachute out and show up empty handed for my customers?"

Ryson tried to shrug against his restraints. "I still don't believe it's here."

McDermott raised a curious eyebrow, considered a few scenarios, then decided there was no substitute for a visual option.

He reached for a set of keys in his side pocket, uncuffed Ryson's hands from the chair, though still not from each other, then helped him to his feet. As soon as the lieutenant had steadied himself, McDermott headed for the door.

"Follow me," he commanded.

THE LAKE

Kessler administered first aid from his waterproof kit bag before the swim back to base, during which he struggled to ignore the almost unbearable pain in his leg muscles from massive lactic acid build up. Years of brutal training had taught him to disconnect his mind from corporal warnings. Sheer fortitude powered his last few hundred feet of the mile-long trek. On reaching dry ground, he took off his flaps, latched them to his front webbing, and set out for the camp.

A camouflaged man emerged from the ferns and guided him back to base.

"The radio!" Kessler ordered, on entering the makeshift command center.

The man handed him an AN/PRC-112 Unit, standard Special Forces issue communication gear. It was a small, six-inch flat rectangular device with an external pivoted antenna, allowing secure communication from forward positions with the base. It took Kessler a full minute to get connected across the Atlantic Ocean to the one man he currently least wanted to have a conversation with.

"What's our sit-rep?" Gorik voice crackled over the wireless link.

"We had company," Kessler chose his words with care. "Three men missing."

There followed a few seconds of silence that seemed endless to Kessler.

"Who was behind this?" the colonel asked.

"Our person of interest, and his new friends. I can spot his style a mile away."

"And our guest?"

"Lost as well, but not as planned," he said cryptically.

"You were intercepted. How?"

"Hidden surveillance I assume."

"We're facing an organized team," Gorik surmised. "Forget recovering the transmitter. We need to attack with full force."

"I'll call for reinforcements," Kessler said. "The choppers should get here from the carrier fairly quickly. We'll hunt them down like rats."

"That's more like it. Now one more thing. There's an abandoned naval air station on this island. It hadn't come up on any active-base searches, but it is not far from the transmitter's coordinates. This must be their stronghold's location."

"Send me the layout, I want to know how to best approach it. Any intelligence data on the size of the force we're facing?" the major asked.

"No, but they can't possibly outgun you. Just make sure no one comes out of there alive," Gorik commanded and switched off.

The radio went dead in Kessler's hand.

AT THE HANGAR

"Holy Mother of God!" Ryson exclaimed. He was experiencing a genuine goose-bump moment as he cast a stunned gaze at the massive frame of the SuperCOIL.

Up until now, it had existed only in blueprints he had drawn up long ago, and computer-conjured images. Swept by waves of giddiness, Ryson felt like the kid in a movie whose comic sketches had suddenly come to life and sprung off the drawing board and into reality.

"Quite a feat indeed," McDermott remarked, pacing toward the black beast. With outstretched fingers he softly caressed its smooth radar absorbent hide in a gesture of both admiration and strange affection.

Using a small handheld flashlight, he began touring the bird's exterior. He stopped regularly to illuminate specific parts beneath the plane's all-encompassing severely dark coating and interestedly inspected each portion.

"How does she handle in the air?" Ryson called out as McDermott disappeared behind one of the plane's larger flaps on its trailing wing edges.

"Amazingly well," McDermott hollered. "Even better than a normal B-2."

Ryson beamed. His realized design was given high marks by one of the best aviators who had ever lived. This would have been a moment of technical pride if not for the circumstances.

"It's a fantastic weapon," McDermott said. He squatted by the nearest of the three-wheel wells and shone a beam of light up the undercarriage. Above, the SuperCOIL hung like a vast black void, as if ready to descend upon him like a bird of prey whose impenetrable dark hide soaked up the rays of his diminutive flashlight by its tri-cycle talons.

Ryson regarded the SuperCOIL as an engineering beauty. He admired the smooth elegant contours imparted by the exact geometries of a continuous curvature airfoil design. And he couldn't agree more with McDermott's weaponry assessments on a purely tour-de-force basis. But his conscience was not quiet.

"One day it may be," Ryson commented. "Right now, it's a *dreadful* weapon."

The remark stopped McDermott, who stood upright and approached to within few feet of Ryson. For a moment, the only sound was that of a gentle breeze flowing through the hangar. "And how do you determine just what kind of weapon it is, Lieutenant?"

"By who controls it."

McDermott cocked his head to the left. A wry smile half-broke across his face. "You probably think I'm insane," he chuckled as if in confirmation, then strode towards the SuperCOIL.

McDermott checked the hot spots along the wing's leading edges for cracks in the integrity of the RAM, knowing his life depended on it.

He regarded the dark plane as one of his most captivating sights, despite its macabre appearance. He had felt that way for years, since attending a low-key presentation of it by Gorik. The immense hangar doors had parted on an unlit runway under a moonless, cloudy sky, and what had been revealed was imprinted on McDermott's mind henceforth.

He stood before the manta-ray shaped craft, which even in the dead of night remained perceptibly black, a thing of untold malice. Its enormous pinions seemed to dissolve into the encompassing darkness. He felt engulfed by its almost supernatural aura, and the immense cavernous hangar opening before him like the temple of a pagan god of destruction.

"Captain, I present you the SuperCOIL," Gorik gloated.

Up until then, McDermott had flown it only in simulations. But with a gut-wrenching sensation similar to what Ryson must have just experienced, he finally encountered it in the flesh.

The wily Gorik had hidden the plane's laser capabilities till an operational airframe was delivered. Now as he divulged what the creature would harbor in its belly, McDermott felt that a wild fantasy was fast becoming reality. In the craft's unbelievable powers of doom, he perceived what a decade of torment had been unable to bring to his soul: salvation.

And for the first time in years, McDermott felt joy.

"You certainly have pulled off the greatest high-tech caper of all time," Ryson remarked, breaking McDermott's train of memory. "I take it you'll be flying out within few hours?"

"Why do you think that?"

"Because your team knows it is no longer alone here," Ryson said. "And you're doing a preflight check." Ryson referred to a pilot's pre-take-off ritualized inspection of the control surfaces, wheels, and cockpit innards. In the case of stealth, it also meant scouring the radar-absorbent hide for any tell-tale cracks.

"You have a knack for the detective. Someday it might get you into trouble," McDermott wryly remarked. He again peered at the intricate patchwork of the RAM that constituted the plane's comprehensive and impenetrably dark stealth sheath whose novelty had never dwindled in his mind.

The blackness of the plane constantly impressed upon him the fantastic frightfulness of the craft. It struck him as an enormous griffin, reincarnated in a hybrid of lasers and stealth, rendering the best of both worlds in one singular fighting machine. The plane could fly undetected and strike with devastating blows from great distances. Even the mythological beast did not boast such powers.

McDermott's face hardened at the thought of what he commanded, feeling an uncontrollable surge of desire for vengeance course through his veins.

Ryson sensed the flaring of hatred in the captain's eyes and tried to reach out to dissuade him from whatever it was he intended to do. If they could only establish some common ground. "We were both used, you know: me to design it, you to test fly it," Ryson called out again.

"An interesting coincidence isn't it?" McDermott asked rhetorically, without taking eyes off the inspection. "But you overlook the irony."

"Which is?"

"It's your own life-long creation that has led you here and it may end your life as well."

Ryson reflected on those words. No hint of threat in the captain's voice.

Yet he had no doubt as to what McDermott referred to. Minutes earlier, when he had followed his captor down the narrow concrete corridors, he had committed to memory every turn and wall markings hoping it would enable him to find his way back to the hangar with the rescue team before McDermott had taken off.

Based on their mannerisms, armaments, and outdated uniforms, Ryson placed the others in the compound as ex-members of Spetsnaz, the dreaded Russian special forces. This was no two-bit operation he realized, but a meticulously planned affair, with some of the world's best-trained ex-military mercenaries.

Ryson drew on his military history recollection to place this strange base. Early in World War II, the Portuguese had allowed the Germans the use of this island in the strategically situated "Hawk Islands" Azores archipelago, for naval refuelings. But along with fuel depots and a hardened command center, the Germans had also constructed a secret airstrip for launching reconnaissance planes to help the dreaded U-boat Wolf Packs hunt for Allied cargo convoys.

By 1943, the resurgent Allies had occupied the Azores and to accommodate their larger cargo transport planes, had turned to the relatively open expanses of the nearby Terceira Island to build the Lajes Airbase, with longer runways. The inadequate German secret base on the small remote island was abandoned, and its runway soon overgrown with vegetation.

This heavily camouflaged hangar now also became less mysterious to Ryson. He recognized it as a makeshift Russian transportation shelter used for temporary bomber bases. The volume of fresh ocean air that breezed in from the hangar's obscured ends signified a large outside opening. In case the plane carried a homing device, the hangar's interior was covered with extensive fish-net metal wire, thus creating a giant Faraday Cage from which no transmissions could be made.

But still mysterious to Ryson was how a plane the size of the SuperCOIL could have landed there at all.

In fact, the old German runway was revamped to a landing field custom-fitted along its length with three strips of metal set 22ft apart, the exact distance between the wheels of the SuperCOIL's tricycle undercarriage. McDermott had honed the required precision landing skills in Tanaris by secretly spraying the tarmac with 3 innocuous paint blobs 22ft apart and repeatedly touching down right on the mark.

Each metal strip consisted of discrete camouflaged planks, with low-lying shrubs placed in between to enhance concealment from satellites and reconnaissance flybys. Unlike most other planes, the SuperCOIL's engine intakes were mounted on its upside which naturally eliminated the danger of low-lying vegetation being sucked into the intakes.

The main challenge lay in the runway's short length. The SuperCOIL's expansive flying wing design, however, afforded superior aerodynamics lift so that a trained pilot could land the bomber at relatively very low air speeds without risk of plummeting to earth on runway approach. Thus, a much shorter runway would suffice. The same held true for take-offs, as the all-winged design naturally took to the air quickly, unlike the smaller F-117s—or any other aircraft, for that matter.

For the logistics of setting things up, Trostov, a shipping tycoon, had used his vast freight fleet as a cover for piecemeal delivery of parts, especially the runway strips. He had even opted for planks of lighter aluminum, in place of steel ones, so they could be carried by smaller, less conspicuous boats. Cargo was unloaded late into the night and ferried to the island while the mothership remained offshore.

"Are you working for the Russians now?" Ryson asked.

"Alliances have to be made sometimes."

"You mean arrangements that betray your country."

"Betrayal is in the eye of the beholder. Judge me when it's all over."

"Why did you bring me here?" Ryson pressed.

"To let you see what you created," McDermott replied.

EN ROUTE TO THE TARGET

Kessler matched his GPS position, shown on his device, against his team's actual location in their cross-island trek. They were off only by ten feet.

Almost one hour now since he had contacted Gorik, and the support choppers, flying at wave-top level, had furtively approached to disembark a full complement invasion force. Matters were progressing smoothly.

This time Kessler had opted for the relative concealment of a land route. His newly provided maps had revealed a more direct level path to their target, to which they would now arrive in under two hours. Then it would be a matter of effective deployment in that tactical environment before going hot to penetrate the base.

The major peered at his platoon of over forty commandos, divided into three files, of men who moved like wraiths in the dark, unheard and unseen, each carrying a deadly load. None, however, was as intent as Kessler to make McDermott pay with his life.

AT THE RUSSIAN BASE

McDermott strode down the musty corridors, after returning Ryson to his holding cell and handcuffing him to a chair.

He considered it a sordid affair, incarcerating a fellow American ex-serviceman in a den of Russian mercenaries. Just a few years back he would have died fighting these very combatants to free such a civilian captive. He cringed at the thought of this loathsome transformation.

He had once been a compassionate man, but the death of his wife had cast him within an inferno of hatred. That cauldron was stoked with vengeance. He hated himself now, and Gorik above all, for bringing it about.

"I have nothing left, no place to go," McDermott had somberly told the colonel shortly after his wife's funeral.

"Come back to Tanaris, Jack. It's your home, always has been." Gorik's tone was fatherly.

"But I'm supposed to be dead."

"What if I told you there's a plane for which you would need no crew, or even a co-pilot? No one will see you," Gorik enticed.

"How?" McDermott asked with defiant curiosity. "Fighters fight in formation, bombers have many crews."

"This plane is singular," Gorik smiled. "All computerized, even the weapons systems."

McDermott's weary expression lightened somewhat. "What type of plane?"

"Let's just say it flies like a bomber but deadlier than a fighter in air combat."

"A fighter-bomber?" McDermott asked, referring to the likes of the British Tornado, with a fighter chassis but better suited to air-to-ground attack than to direct aerial combat.

"Not even close," Gorik said, noticing a growing interest on the captain's drawn face. "But you won't need any squadrons or crew, at least not in a manner which will identify you."

"What is the clearance level?"

"Beyond Black."

Gorik then explained how McDermott would remain concealed in his helmeted G-suit and communicated by text or voice alteration software and replied in kind.

McDermott mulled the information. It might be workable, but there was something there he couldn't trust. Gorik had figured out the details from all conceivable angles, as he always had with every such venture. McDermott just wanted to get a better taste of what the base commander had cooked up before purchasing his meal. Only one question remained.

"Why me?" he asked.

"You're the best there is," Gorik said. It was a fact, not flattery. "And since you officially don't exist, you're the perfect man to fly a plane that doesn't exist either. Do you read me?"

"Loud and clear," McDermott said, convinced. "How long is my stint?" His fly-boy inner voice was telling him to do this just long enough to allay the crushing grief of bereavement. He knew however, that it would not be that simple.

Gorik shrugged. "About three to five years, till the first model is fully operational. Then others can take over your work if you choose to leave."

Anguished anew, McDermott gazed into the distance. The last time he had retired from the armed forces was not an easy decision. "And what would I do afterwards?" he asked.

"Jack," Gorik said, clapping McDermott's back, "this is Tanaris. There'll always be another next generation superplane with your name on it."

"And if I don't work with you this time?"

"Then you're free to return to civilian life. Live away from the black projects."

For a split second, the colonel's unguarded expression revealed that he believed himself about to checkmate his most difficult opponent. And in a shock of realization, McDermott understood that Gorik had been behind the demise of his squadron over Iraq, and later his wife.

In time, he would come to discover it all by gleaning and probing every piece of information in Tanaris' secret databases. McDermott had an innate ability for sleuthing, a skill for which Gorik had never accounted in his machinations.

XENDONG'S QUARTERS,
THIRTY MINUTES EARLIER

Xendong ran a clammy hand over his balding head, ignoring the profuse sweating that dampened his palms. He was in shock of sorts, over what he had just heard.

"Those were American Special Forces your men encountered?"

"Yes," Trostov replied. "Don't ask me how they located this base."

"What's next?" The Chinese man's voice trembled. He had never trusted Trostov, and now especially after discovering McDermott as the pilot, whose Black Squadron roots had struck a sudden fear in Xendong's heart.

"The operation is off. We must evacuate at once," Trostov announced.

"But the plane…"

"We can't timely clear its runaway now, so I am leaving it here."

"What?" Xendong protested in disbelief. "You're quitting after all our efforts?"

"Our American pilot and I have made plenty on this deal as it is," Trostov said coldly. "No need risking a death trap here. You can join us, of course."

"How? The ocean is now too well monitored to take the boat back."

Trostov cocked an eyebrow. "I have a small deep-sea submersible in the old U-boat bay. Its electric motor is silent and can get us to the next island without detection. From there we can safely escape."

"Safely?" Xendong asked in desperation. "My superiors will have my head on a stick for failing to deliver them a super-weapon after they already spent so much on acquiring it. There has to be a way to get this plane to China!"

"Perhaps there *is* a way," Trostov replied. "My men may die if they stay to fight off the Americans long enough for the plane to take-off. So there'd be a price."

"Name it."

"Full payment deposited in my Swiss bank at once."

"My superiors will never agree!"

"Then it's their loss, and your head too," Trostov said, running his index finger across his throat.

A few seconds later, Xendong's frail fingers reached out for the portable phone Trostov held out to him. Inside three minutes, the ensuing heated conversation concluded as beads of sweat glistened off his pronounced bare forehead.

"They will deposit one billion in your accounts within thirty minutes," he said.

TANARIS

"What is the situation Colonel?" McCane asked, deep frowns carving his forehead.

"My team will be tightening the noose in a few hours," Gorik replied.

"Call me when it's show time."

"As you wish General," Gorik said, watching his superior disappear behind the bend in the hallway. For the first time in his career, Gorik envied the puppet general, who could simply deflect blame to his subordinate colonel. That bore especially true now, when McDermott, once indispensable to the colonel's success, seemed on the verge of undoing all his accomplishments.

Gorik had worked exceptionally hard to attain his current status ever since he was only a major in the Black Squadron ranks. He had patiently bided his time, then staged a silent political coup by falsely attributing unfavorable events to the Black Squadron's founder, resulting in his ouster. He then had assumed the title of base commander.

Gorik relished the Black Squadron, whose originally devised role was carrying highly covert operations involving genuine matters of national security. These included behind enemy lines intelligence gathering, deep penetration search and destroy missions in the Vietnam War, and generally curbing military ambitions of communist sympathizing world governments.

To this end, Gorik had assembled a superb crew around a gifted and charismatic individual, Captain Jack McDermott, whom he had personally converted from the U.S. Air Force. McDermott was selected as a "fast burner," - an exceptionally experienced and capable pilot with the potential for rapid rise through the ranks.

Gorik had then allowed McDermott the free hand to select a team from his former Air Force squadron top-notch aviators. Within a year, McDermott had molded his gathered Alpha Squadron into the most well-trained and formidable fighter unit in the country, if not the world, and trained to fulfill other covert dimensions of their new employer. Their subsequent unbroken chain of operational success in turn propelled Gorik to new heights.

Soon however, a new threat would loom for which Gorik was ill-equipped: the abrupt end to the Cold War. With the demise of the Soviet empire imminent, his organization's perceived usefulness could be greatly diminished.

The entrepreneurial Gorik could not let his well-constructed enterprise simply wane. Worse, he was facing an internal perceived threat. Captain McDermott, despite his invaluable contributions, often did not see eye to eye with his colonel. Gorik sought the success and survival of Black-Squadron at all costs. The unwavering McDermott, always true to his Air Force roots, wished to operate only within the law and morality. On more than one occasion he had persuaded Gorik to select ethics over opportunity, to the detriment of the colonel's career. Gorik had constantly endeavored to sway the loyalty of his prodigy, but to no avail.

The pressure reached a flashpoint when an impressed president offered McDermott a command second only to Gorik to oversee the operations and trainings of the next generation of Black Squadron pilots.

It was a role McDermott had agreed to take only following retirement in a few years. Gorik had sourly regarded the event as a death knell for his unscrupulous ambitions, perhaps an outright attempt to be replaced by McDermott. Suddenly feeling as if between a rock and a hard place, he desperately sought the next military opportunity to sweep all opposition aside.

His sinister wish would be granted on August 2, 1990, when the Iraqi forces rolled into Kuwait unprovoked, occupying the small oil-rich country within hours.

Gorik regarded the ensuing onset of the Operation Desert Storm as a long-sought ticket to a rise in ranks. He even quietly nicknamed it his "war of ascendancy," envisioning his elite Black Squadron to shine in various covert mission roles, just as they had during the long Vietnam War.

But as the Iraq war became an increasingly lopsided affair for the Allies and with a quick cease-fire in sight, Gorik had endeavored to protract the conflict by any means necessary. And so when secret intelligence surfaced of the true nature of a sandy fortress by the Iraqi airbase near Ur, he saw it as his best chance to achieve a number of career goals all at once.

As a prelude, he had the Patriot missile guidance codes corrupted to enable an Iraqi SCUD missile to penetrate their intercept zone and reach an Allied base, killing more than two dozen American servicemen. Not only did this act bring an immediate call for stepped up efforts by the Black Squadron to destroy these mobile menaces, but it served as the justification for an air attack on the fortress by Ur, where the SCUDs were erroneously deemed to have been launched from.

Covert Allied agents had pegged the site as a chemical weapons depot constructed initially during Iraq's eight-year war with Iran in 1980s. Gorik concluded an Allied air offensive against such a site would spur the Iraqis into launching the dreadful weapons in a "use it or lose it" scenario, thus adding a new and terrifying dimension to the Gulf War.

The effects would be an escalation and prolongation of the conflict, with further calls for the Black Squadron to neutralize such depots all over Iraq. Gorik did not want Iraq to prevail, only to be given enough teeth to draw out the war, so to boost his prominence among the upper echelons of the armed services.

And there were even more gains to be made.

The aerial assault proved a perfect opportunity to bid Captain McDermott and his crew farewell. For the colonel knew McDermott's hand-picked and incorruptible Alpha Squadron would inevitably discover his own sinister plans.

Gorik was ambivalent on dispatching his prodigy, whom he at times regarded as an unruly son.

But the colonel's career advancement was paramount. He needed men whose blind loyalty lay with him alone. And he had seen in Kessler, the commander of the archrival Beta Squadron, a younger version of himself, who would unfailingly carry out his most heinous orders.

McDermott's assigned attack team had been purposely uninformed of the fortress' chemical weapons stash. The captain never witnessed a secondary high-explosive blast from the silos or from the SCUD warheads, because they contained chemical agents, not explosives.

Gorik had seen to it that the squadron flew non-stealthy F-16s and carried minimal air-to-air missiles so to be heavily outgunned by Iraqi air and ground defenses. Their interception by the enemy was then more plausible and less consequential to the stealth program than if 4 F-117s had been shot down in their first full-scale war, a disaster that would have been credited to Iraqi fire power.

When these precautions proved inadequate to seal the fate of the Alpha Squadron over the target area, Gorik executed Plan B, in which Kessler's beta team interdicted McDermott's returning squadron from the ground. Using guided shoulder-strapped SAMs, the commando unit locked onto the frequency of each F-16's homing beacon, which was secretly fitted beneath the cockpit to ensure that no aerial evasive maneuver or countermeasure could foil the missiles.

Despite long odds however, not only did McDermott's team prevented any chemical-tipped SCUDs from launching, but to Gorik's chagrin McDermott also managed to cheat death.

And there was still collateral damage. A chemical cloud dispersed from the depot's wrecked silos blew southward over portions of the allied ground forces. In wind-diluted amounts, the poisons' trace quantities were not immediately lethal or even easily detectable, to be considered the major chemical counter-attack Gorik had hoped for. The exposure, however, led to the long-term debilitating effects seen in the mysterious Gulf War Syndrome, whose symptoms many affected vets considered a fate worse than death.

When the colonel later found a severely debilitated McDermott in hospital, he opted to afford his brilliant pupil one last chance, disguised under an offer of complete retirement from military, to which McDermott reluctantly acquiesced.

During the following years, with Kessler at his side, Gorik ruled Tanaris unopposed. Having consolidated his power, he transformed the airbase into a top-notch research and development facility for the next generation aircraft. The colonel was a shrewd businessman who realized such transitions in a post-Cold War era would help keep his airbase a main focus for government funding—funds for which he had alternative plans, as he aspired to even loftier ranks.

Once again, however, McDermott became vital to the success of Gorik's next gamble: the creation of a stealthy airborne laser platform. If the colonel could limit McDermott's involvement to just flights, then he could take advantage of his superb piloting skills to test fly the greatest aerial weapon of all time.

All that remained in his path was the captain's new marital life. Staging the death of an innocent wife as a drug lord attack in a volatile foreign land, however, required minimal planning. And Kessler had, expectedly, carried it out without question, bringing down an entire building and killing countless others so that media attention would not be focused solely on her death.

After that, it was a matter of time before a despondent McDermott could be manipulated back to the flight line, toward the realization of Gorik's grandest dream: the SuperCOIL.

AT THE RUSSIAN BASE

When McDermott entered his quarters, he found Trostov settled in a chair at the far left. McDermott headed directly for a footlocker to retrieve his helmet and oxygen mask, then immersed in working on the gears with his specialized tools. He said nothing to the visitor.

"Don't you want to know why I am here?" Trostov said in his barely-accented English. His words echoed dully off the barren cement walls.

"The greedy glint in your eyes says it all," McDermott replied.

"You're an observant man. The payment delivery is complete. I had your share, sixty million dollars, deposited into the separate accounts, as you requested."

A long silence followed, as McDermott performed life-support check, part of his preflight operation routine. He had always performed the chore himself, believing rank to be no excuse for losing one's edge—especially when one's life literally depends on the technology.

Trostov approached and placed his hands on the back of McDermott's chair. "We've done it, and now we're both rich!"

McDermott attempted to swallow his distaste for the Russian. In many ways, he regarded Trostov as no different from Gorik: opportunistic mercenaries who would resort to any unscrupulous means. As for his own gains, McDermott had arranged for all of his millions to be secretly given in the near future to the families of his fallen wingmen and his slain wife.

"Did you hear what I said?" Trostov asked.

"I'm not deaf. All the world's money won't save me if this oxygen mask fails during flight."

Trostov sat on the desk's corner, near the picture frames, and looked at the American. "I know. You forget I'm a former Soviet Air Force pilot. So what did you gather from our captive?"

"Not much," McDermott lied, poker-faced. "Just that his team was only at expeditionary strength, not enough to overtake this base."

"Then why rush to leave?"

"I don't trust his story," McDermott said. "I'm sure there are a lot more of his SEALs team lurking around than he's letting on."

"So make him tell you the truth."

McDermott cast the Russian a curious gaze. "I don't do torture. I'm a pilot."

"You disappoint me. Back in my day, I'd have had that information already."

McDermott exhaled impatiently. "Then why don't *you* go and make him talk?"

"Not worth being positively identified when I'm so close to having it all. The Americans would then seriously do anything to hunt me down."

McDermott put the helmet on and strapped the oxygen mask on his face. The long end of the corrugated oxygen hose dangled from his chin, and he hooked it into a testing device on his desk, then flipped a few buttons to make sure the hose and the rest of the life-support gear was working properly.

"Cold War of nuclear weaponry is a thing of the past," said Trostov, "but cold war of economics is in full swing. Russia needs technology to sell. And since we're no longer shunned as communists," he added, "everyone can come to us now. Our *prize* will bring many interested investors, if through the right channels."

McDermott knew that ever since the F-117's success was undoubtedly demonstrated over Iraq in 1991, countries had been engaged in developing counter-stealth technologies. Fortunately, none had yet netted a reliable defense system, in large part because no such weapon was ever allowed to be tested against an American stealth craft. But with a live bomber representing the latest in U.S. stealth technology, the Chinese and Russians could test all sorts of weapons against it and sell those results for hefty profits. Either could also use the plane as a test bed for refining its own stealth planes, such as the Chinese H-8, or the Russian SKAT, an unmanned stealth drone which resembled a scaled model of the B-2.

"How's the runway preparation?" McDermott asked, removing the oxygen mask and helmet.

"It's ready," Trostov replied. "All the camouflaging shrubs been cleared out."

"Good. I'll be airborne shortly, then."

"Are you sure that thing can take-off from such a short runway?"

"You underestimate the fly-wing's ability to get airborne swiftly," McDermott said with deep pride. "It's an awesome design."

Trostov couldn't disagree with McDermott's assessment. He had marveled at the plane's capabilities and was proud that it had been made possible by Pyotr Ufimtsev, a Russian scientist. He then cringed at the thought that Ufimtsev's visionary stealth insights had come to pass in a communist nation whose technology could not possibly realize its potential.

Trostov recalled first seeing a portrait of a young Ufimtsev, a sharp-eyed and bespectacled man whose circular glasses and slicked-back hair gave him more than a passing resemblance to a famous character once played by Harold Llyod, the iconic American comedic actor of the silent film era. Except that nothing about Ufimtsev's work was cause for levity. Quite to the contrary, it provided a blueprint that, when perverted by military minds, had ushered in the deadliest air combat vessels yet devised. Unfortunately for the Soviets, this particular perversion had been brought about by their most powerful nemesis: the United States.

During the Cold War, many NATO experts belittled Soviet air-weapons industries as only capable of plagiarizing the western designs into erstwhile Eastern Bloc fighters, a stance that outlived communism to mar all future Russian designs. The Soviets had been humiliated by lagging far behind the superior American ingenuity in airplane research and development, but in case of stealth they could not so easily hide behind such an excuse.

But as Trostov saw it, fate has a strange way of evening things out. Once more, the Russians were in possession of what he believed was rightfully theirs—and now in its most advanced form.

What he had failed to anticipate, however, was how far the U.S. stealth program had progressed with the advent of the SuperCOIL. McDermott had not shared with him the plane's laser capabilities and instead misrepresented the aircraft as a mere bomber. Only Xendong had so far noticed the flattened dark bubble on the plane's ventral, which housed a laser turret, as was told by McDermott that it contained a new Low Probability of Intercept radar.

The Chinese saw the LPI radar as tremendously valuable, but McDermott had not allowed either man inside the plane. He kept secret the access code to the bomber's sole entrance as safety insurance before a deal was reached. Trostov, who had often noticed that McDermott spent prolonged periods inside the plane, wondered whether he was performing system checks, tinkering with internal equipment, or just standing guard by his flying castle.

The American held all the cards, but so long as Trostov would get paid big, he had no serious concerns, and a lowly Xendong had no choice in the matter.

It was a pity, Trostov thought, that unlike China, Russia currently had no covert state sponsorship for such a massive undertaking. A patriotic part of him longed to see it touch down on the land in which its very theoretical underpinnings were conceived. But maybe the motherland could still do one better.

If caught, Trostov had no official authorization from the Russian government. But he had struck secret deals so that once the Chinese had dissected the plane, he would repurchase valuable information from them and resell it to the Russian military—for a profit of course. From a business standpoint, it was double dipping. It only made the whole affair that much sweeter, while bringing the dreams of an indigenous Russian stealth bomber closer to reality.

Trostov suddenly missed the heady days of the Cold War. He had been a young pilot then, his mind filled with a fervent sense of patriotic duty during his beloved Rodina's tantalizing technological struggle with the West. Ambition came at a terrible cost, however, as aircraft were test-piloted that failed to live up to their design potential and that claimed the lives of many young aviators for whom pushing the envelope was a way of life.

He had known that American efforts during the same struggle also were not fail-safe, though with much lower mortality rate. He gazed at one of McDermott's framed photographs: a group of pilots in front of a newly developed aircraft.

"We, too, had a great many test pilots die," Trostov remarked, sensing the photograph was a memorial. "All in hopes that the great Soviet Union might one day become capable of dominating the air."

"It's the price of war," McDermott said. "Each side exacts its own share of human life, even if it is a *cold* war."

"And in the case of our secret organizations, often not even their own countrymen will ever know of their sacrifices," Trostov remarked on the unsung heroes of wars, a truth that transcended all national boundaries and ideologies.

McDermott returned to his work.

OUTSIDE THE HIDDEN ENTRANCE

Andre Krelonic pressed his night-vision goggles against his face and listened. He had just heard a slight rustle in the low shrubs by the narrow path leading to the bunker's steel door.

He was relieved when a flapping bird took to the air out of the suspect spot, then he glanced at his watch. He had been out here for over three hours, deployed as a quad team of ex-Spetsnaz commandos to guard the bunker's rear gate. Other units were mainly clearing the makeshift runway on the other side, leaving Krelonic's team as the only sentries to this concealed pass.

With his radio, the ex-Spetsnaz commander alerted the three others hiding in nearby vegetation at carefully selected locations so that all who approached the entrance came within the collective "arcs of fire" kill zone of their assault rifles. There came another soft rustle in the bushes ahead. He peered through his goggles but spotted only the same stupid bird that had nested there and was returning from a nightly forage. The thought of food made him hungry, and he gazed down into his rucksack to fish out a packed sandwich.

A single dark mass, blotting out the sky, quietly lowered itself from a high tree branch above like a spider. With his head down, Krelonic saw no shadows in the moonless night; he only felt a pair of powerful hands on his temples from aft, and with a swift jerking motion, his neck twisted violently. Instinctively he raised his hands in self-defense, but the sound of broken vertebrae filled his ears like thunder. In seconds, his limp arms and body fell into the manhole.

The assailant quietly lowered himself into the hole, then unhooked the nearly invisible long nylon tether hanging from his back. After checking Krelonic for vitals and finding none, he and raised his own team on the radio for an update. He learned that Krelonic's men had met the same fate as their leader.

AT THE RUSSIAN BASE

Under the dimly lit low ceiling, Ryson sat alone, his hands cuffed to a wooden creaky chair. His mind was racing with thoughts of the mission, seeing the SuperCOIL, McDermott's enigmatic behavior, but mostly with the prospect of not surviving to see Kathleen again—and, if he did, where their lives would lead. He felt another panic rush, on the paralyzing nightmare that had rendered him unconsciousness in the lake. Somehow, he was caught in that lifeless state, and brought to this dreadful place.

And all this after believing the experience in the pod had enabled him to control at least his nightmare's severity. Even in the lake he felt capable in keeping it at bay, at least until the very end, when everything had suddenly fallen apart.

His thoughts were interrupted, as McDermott strode into the cell wearing a full flight suit.

"I guess this is the big goodbye," Ryson remarked.

McDermott sized up his captive for a few seconds. "Do you fancy yourself a brave man, Lieutenant?" he asked.

Ryson shook his head. "Not really. Only a tendency for getting thrown into situations that call for bravery. I seem to have failed this one miserably."

"Considering all the data you gleaned about me, I say you've done quite well."

Ryson was thrown off by the unexpectedly encouraging words. He mulled them over. "Maybe on the technical sleuthing," he countered, "but put me in a lake and I can't even protect myself from drowning."

"Well it's not easy to do when your own men are trying to kill you."

Ryson looked up at him in disbelief.

"Come now," McDermott continued. "Surely you must have realized the trajectory of the bullet which swished just inches over your head meant it was not aimed or fired by us."

"Kessler…" Ryson uttered. "Then why did he miss?"

"Because I shot him in the arm first," McDermott replied, "to prevent him from killing you."

"Guess I owe you one."

McDermott raised a couple of fingers, "actually you owe me *two.*"

It took Ryson a second to catch the hint. "I went unconscious," he said.

"Indeed. It's called the deep-water blackout," McDermott explained. "When you rise too fast out of deep water, cerebral hypoxia shuts your brain down usually right before you surface. You would've drowned, but not the way you're thinking."

Ryson pondered the significance of what McDermott's words. "So it was purely a physical phenomenon that made me go out?" A wave of relief came over him.

"You thought it was your nightmare?"

Ryson's left eye responsively twitched by exposure of his most secret fears.

"While at Tanaris," said McDermott, "I read your rather tragic file. It did not quite spell it all out for me, but I knew . . ."

"How exactly?"

McDermott's face abruptly hardened as he replied, "I suffered from nightmares too, when my wife was murdered. I, however, faced mine with fortitude because before long I had found a new reason to live."

"Vengeance," Ryson said softly.

McDermott nodded, "looks like you also have found a new sense of purpose."

"Kathleen."

"Right. It's time to let go of the past weaknesses. Focus on a strong future."

"But how?" Ryson shook his head despondently. "It hunts me at will!"

"Then you must hunt it back," McDermott said sternly. "Even harder than it has ever hunted you. Why don't you try to face it for once? The next time it comes around, don't run or veer away. Just dive in head-first and dare it to do its worst, instead of trying to escape its grip like you were a trapped rat."

"It will never work," Ryson said, lowering his gaze to the concrete floor.

"Have you even tried it?" McDermott challenged. "*I* have, because I *conquer* my problems. I confront my worst fears. I hunt *them* down and make trophy heads out of their carcasses for my showroom up here," he said, tapping his right temple with his index finger. "It's the first lesson they teach you in Special Forces but perhaps the last thing some ever fully learn: that fortitude defeats any adversary. When all your physical strength has drained, and your mind is assailed by every negative possibility, fortitude is what gets you through. Try it the next time that son of a bitch chasm gapes at you. Harden yourself! Jump in and take control, bring yourself out of it like you would do with a plane that has gone into a flat-spin."

McDermott's words came to Ryson as an epiphany. The captain was obviously more than just a masterful aviator. He had a will tougher than steel. And now some of that resolve seemed to have passed into Ryson's mind. Staring at McDermott's unflinching face, Ryson tried to discern from his wizened features the shades of the compassionate man he once was. There was an unmistakable glow of virtue within the captain, but in a mind in which love and hate had fused for the sole purpose of vengeance, it was hard to see where one ended and the other began.

"Tell me," Ryson said, feeling that the time was right for a bit of probing. "Why are you doing this?"

"It's the best way to get back at Gorik."

"For what?"

McDermott's eyes suddenly flashed with rage. "For beginners, his killing off my squadron over Iraq."

"I don't believe it," Ryson said. Deep down, however, he knew that Gorik was capable of such brutality; after all, he had ordered Kessler to dispose of him during a combat operation.

"I have the proof!" the captain exclaimed. "While working on the SuperCOIL efforts for close to a decade, I also covertly searched Tanaris databases. I discovered that my F-16s were all shot down by American-made missiles aimed to track secret homing beacons installed on our planes, also learned our targeted Iraqi site stored chemical weapons. The released gas contributed to the Gulf War Syndrome. And there is more."

"What more can there be?"

"My murdered wife..." McDermott looked away, "she was 3 weeks pregnant."

"I'm sorry," Ryson said, at a loss for words, then tried refocusing on the future. "I guess you will be in Russia then in a few hours."

"No, China," the captain replied, searching through his tools. "At least that's what those fools think. But I would never lead a top-secret American plane to either place, trust me."

"Then where *would* you lead it to?"

"To Peterson Air Force Base, where else?" McDermott said flatly. "That's where all the evil comes from."

"You're going to *NORAD*?" Ryson asked, referring to the North American Aerospace Defense Command facility that had once been buried deep within Colorado's Cheyenne Mountain for protection from nuclear attacks during the Cold War. It had since been moved to the nearby open-air Peterson Air Force Base, some ten miles away. But NORAD was still the nerve center of many defensive responses, and a heavily defended target. Its destruction would create deep impact on the general civilian psyche as well.

"Yes, the one and only," McDermott replied.

The swift and stern nature of the reply caught Ryson by surprise. Ryson had always prided himself on his ability to detect deception, but it was impossible to tell with McDermott. And those cold, unrevealing eyes of his remained devoid of emotion, as if they were of an obsidian statue. The insightful captain had outmatched him in more ways than one.

"You mean you didn't know?" McDermott asked, probing Ryson's expression.

"Even a neophyte would have known, let alone a special investigating officer. Well, I figured the entire U.S. Air Force would be there to greet me. That's why I needed such a powerful vessel to deliver me to my goal."

"And what are you going to do when they show up?"

"Destroy them, one by one."

"Then what? You can't stay afloat forever."

"I'll punch a big crash hole in the base with the B-2. It will be the world's most expensive tombstone."

"Killing yourself is not the answer."

"Your opinion. The only question is how many others I can take with me."

"Suppose no one decides to show up to 'greet' you while your fuel runs out?"

"Oh they will, trust me. Seeing that Denver International Airport is not far off."

"What are you talking about, for God's sake?"

"Shooting down civilian airliners, so the Air Force will have no choice but to confront me."

"That is madness! If you're after Gorik at least take your revenge to Tanaris," Ryson pleaded.

"There are no civilian airbases near Tanaris. No major population centers for me to make my compelling case for the Air Force to confront me. No one would know what happened."

"Your killing actions make you no different from Gorik then," Ryson reasoned.

"Won't it? There is a difference, Lieutenant. If a soldier kills during war, he is a hero; if he does it during peace, he is a murderer. I am killing the evil in *my* war. Gorik kills the good, as well as the good in all of us."

"Then why didn't you do this right after refueling off Florida?"

"To let the gravity of the situation sink in for the imbeciles in Washington, give them time to realize they would have no alternatives but to meet me in the air. It will cause them to suffer, a taste of what I have been enduring for the last decade."

Ryson looked at the captain in disbelief, and realized that this was no mercenary act, as he had initially thought, but one driven by pure vengeance. It was abhorrent, what McDermott was about to embark on, but the man had nothing to lose; for the past decade he had lived only for a promise of future revenge. But his evident inability to take direct aim at Gorik would subject others to an unjust punishment.

McDermott glanced at his watch, as if expecting a delivery, and then reached for his CV and raised the four guards to the outside hidden entrance. When he received no response from any, he reached to drop a small electronic memory stick into the lieutenant's shirt pocket. "All the information you will need to know the truth is in that device. When at Tanaris, compare it to their secret database records, which is where these documents came from."

"Why not do that yourself? I can promise to get your voice heard."

McDermott did not respond but simply placed the keys to the handcuffs on the far desk. "Well it's time. So long, Lieutenant. I wish you happiness," he said, and headed to the door.

Desperate, Ryson implored, "What about your wife?"

McDermott stopped mid-stride.

"How would she feel about your becoming a murderer, especially when it involves innocent civilian people?" Ryson rambled on. "Just think. If she were alive today, would she still love you for what you are about to do?"

McDermott turned a furious gaze to Ryson, who felt his body stiffening with fear. Before the junior officer could say another word, McDermott swooped toward him with the swiftness of a hawk and grabbed him hard by the throat.

"How dare you speak of my wife?" he said in a low, hoarse voice, his fingers tightening around Ryson's neck. "You imbecilic military bureaucrats don't even know the *meaning* of love. All you care about are regulations!"

Ryson desperately sought air, his eyes widening with McDermott's hand nearly encircling his windpipe, as his body began to convulse. "Why did you have to bring her into this?" McDermott shouted. "I should just end your worthless life right now!" The sound of a death rattle escaped Ryson's throat, and McDermott suddenly released his grip, as if disgusted by what he was touching. Ryson's limp body slumped into his chair and the sound of gasping filled the room.

"I don't believe we have anything more to say to each other, Lieutenant," McDermott said.

Ryson leaned back and heaved a labored sigh as the captain slipped out of view, his footsteps fading on the slate floor.

OUTSIDE THE HIDDEN ENTRANCE

The figure pressed Krelonic's corpse against the manhole wall to give himself more room. He had watched Krelonic from above for over an hour before striking, timing his attack to right after the Russian's periodic reports to the command center. He now lay in wait, expecting the main assault force to arrive any moment.

He got busy unloading his backpack. He retrieved a half-dozen brownie-sized blocks of C-4 explosives and stuck metal detonator rods into their putty-like material. It was imperative that the rods be properly inserted and for each detonator mechanism to provide the right amount of discharge voltage. Otherwise, the explosion would fail to rip apart the closed metal entrance.

Despite being called "high" explosives, C-4s, like most other plastic explosives, were actually very difficult to detonate without the right means. Sheer movement, or even taking a hammer to it would not trigger an explosion and setting it afire via a dynamite fuse would only make it burn with an extra bright glow. But these attributes also made it a safe material to transport on one's back and to form into different shapes.

His radio chirped, and he spoke few terse sentences into it, then heard heavy footstep behind him. Major Kessler, in his black-camouflage uniform, approached accompanied by three commandos who eyed the array of C-4 blocks lined up neatly just inside the rim of the manhole. The major gazed up to take a final night view of the high crests of the landmass covering the mostly underground base.

"Is everything set?" he asked, eyeing the entrance to the sole access tunnel on this side of a large hill.

"Yes sir," the commando leader replied.

"All our men are positioned for attack. You may begin."

The commando leader, joined by Kessler's "breacher" squad, grabbed the deadly explosives and headed toward the door in the hill. Each malleable pack was pasted into or around the metal obstacle's weak points, most notably the hinges. Within only a few minutes, all the material was packed into place, and the men backed away to a safe distance.

In the dark, Kessler spotted the commando leader's silhouette with couple fingers raised to indicate two minutes until detonation. Kessler relayed a short encrypted SITREP message to Tanaris on the imminent assault and ordered his men down to the ground. Then like a blood-thirsty wolf, he marked the time in anticipation of the carnage ahead.

THE HOLDING CELL, MINUTES EARLIER

Ryson's breathing had slowed to almost its normal rate in minutes since he'd been nearly choked to death by powerful fingers of a man he now knew to be utterly insane. McDermott had to be stopped at all costs from his crazed mission, of that he was convinced.

The touch of cold steel against his wrist, however, reminded him that he was a prisoner. Seeking any form of escape, his roving eyes quickly caught sight of the key McDermott had set on the desk before hurrying away, perhaps to tease his poor captive with something tantalizingly beyond his reach.

But first, Ryson had to break free of the bolted down chair. He began swaying his torso. The old chair's wooden frame creaked louder with each side push until it crash-landed, along with Ryson, and broke into pieces, freeing its captor. Ryson quickly clambered to the desk for the tiny key and snapped the cuffs open.

He next unlocked the foot restraints and then stood and stretched his arms and legs a bit to get some more circulation back into his extremities. He would need all his strength and flexibility if he were to confront McDermott.

Grabbing a long wood piece of the broken chair—his only available means of self-defense—Ryson had just made a move toward the door when the deafening sound of a sudden blast barreled down the corridors. It sent violent shockwaves deep within the base, knocking him flat onto the dark gray concrete.

AT THE RUSSIAN BASE

A stunned Trostov emerged from his quarters to a scene of mayhem and realized his base was under attack. The explosive opener to a surprise assault had sent his disoriented crew running frantically around the narrow corridors in search of safety. He rushed toward the operation center. The place was in shambles, the earthquake-force blast had sent everything flying off the shelves. He addressed a dazed mission officer and a radio operator.

"What's the SITREP?" Trostov demanded, trying to tally the damage.

"Intruders have penetrated the compound from the north entrance," the officer replied. "Our men there are being overrun by superior weapons."

"Don't just stand here then!" Trostov barked. "Take all available to guard that passage. No hostiles are to penetrate the inside grid. We need those routes kept open for escape. Understood?"

"Yes sir," the officer said before running off to join the fray.

Realizing that far too few troops were available inside the complex, Trostov picked up the radio to call for reinforcements from the bulk of his team guarding the runway. "Unit Two, report!"

The radio crackled in response to a mix of explosions and heavy-caliber machine gun fire before the field commander came on. "We're drawing a lot of fire from all over," the commander said. "Got to be two dozen men out there paired into ten or twelve buddy teams."

His voice was surprising calm, all things considered. It instilled some hope in the Russian general that not all his mercenaries were blind-sided by the attack. "What is your condition?" Trostov asked.

"A few dead. The rest are pinned in their manholes, but not letting anyone through. Any idea who these guys are, General?"

"No," Trostov replied in half-truth. "Keep them from the runway at all costs," he yelled so he could be heard over the racket on the other end. "That is an order!"

"Da," the man replied in Russian.

Trostov realized that no help was arriving from the outside. He was reasonably sure who the assailants were but surprised they had shown up this early. Something was obviously wrong with the tactical assessments he had been provided by the one man who should have known better.

Ignoring the discouraging sounds of the approaching enemy, he headed down the dim corridors in the opposite direction.

From the makeshift field command setup, Kessler monitored his men's progress into the cement structure. Following the initial breach, his commandos had volleyed a dozen tear gas canisters and flash grenades down the corridor, then charged ahead in gas masks and night-vision gear. The passageway had led them to a rather steep path, deep within which they met their first serious resistance.

Kessler had split his troops into two groups. Twenty men were thrown into the frontal assault. Another twenty had fanned out trying to circumvent the steep hill above the mostly-underground base but had not made it much past the ridge before drawing heavy fire from Trostov's men assigned to defend the runway at all costs.

The major looked at his watch, then motioned the reserve commandos, armed with light bazookas, into the bunker. Leaving only the radio operator and a sentry outside, he followed in behind the last man, his weapon drawn with the safety removed, intent on killing every occupant of the base, including McDermott and that pesky lieutenant.

Cooped up in his quarters, Xendong was terrified. He had never envisioned being on this remote island, much less caught in a life-and-death firefight against a formidable enemy. The distinct rattle of 9-mm rounds from MP5K submachine guns—the signature close-quarters combat weapon of the U.S. Special Forces—had made it clear what Trostov's men were up against.

Knowing that his side lacked the ammunition for a drawn-out combat, it would be only a matter of time before the underequipped Russians were defeated, but hopefully not before the rogue American could fly off with the prize aircraft and for himself to escape via Trostov's submarine. At the moment, however, the treacherous Russian general was nowhere in sight.

McDermott put on the last of his flight gear and headed toward the hangar, ignoring the rumbles of the fierce battle that raged fewer than fifty yards away. Instead, he focused on what lay ahead. Soon he would be airborne and free of this miserable hive of misguided mercenaries.

He had made it only a matter of yards toward the hangar when he was addressed by the very man he had hoped to avoid.

"You betrayed me," Trostov bellowed at him from behind.

The captain turned a side glance at the Russian, whose hands clutched a semi-automatic aimed directly at him. But given the circumstances, he didn't bother denying anything, or hiding his contempt for the Russian.

"Your greed betrayed you," McDermott said icily.

"I should shoot you right here," Trostov said with a flash of ire on his face.

"Go right ahead," McDermott rejoined, turning toward Trostov, with arms accommodatingly spread out to expose his full torso. "Hope you can fly that plane to China by yourself."

Trostov raised his gun, its muzzle aimed at McDermott's heart, execution style. His fingers visibly tightened around the trigger. But the American showed no signs of fear or remorse, as if he was being done a favor.

Trostov gritted his teeth in frustration. Feeling defeated, he lowered the weapon. McDermott grinned condescendingly at his weak-minded adversary, then wheeled in his boots and disappeared down the smoke-hazed hallway.

A livid Trostov stood there a moment while contemplating chasing down the pilot and finishing him off after all, but once again his business logic took the upper hand as he still wanted McDermott to deliver the loot. All he had to focus on now was fight his way to the submarine, then navigate it to safety, so he turned and ran back down to command his men.

The sound of distant explosions eventually rang loudly enough in the ears of a semi-unconscious Ryson to cause his eyes to open. His mind emerged from the shock of hitting the hard concrete, and he realized where he was. To the rattle of gunfire coming from the far end of the bunker, he awkwardly rose to his feet. Considering how quickly he was becoming lucid, he assumed he hadn't been out for more than a few minutes. He then remembered why he was there: to stop a madman. He grabbed the piece of wood and headed out of the corridor.

Acrid smoke from the gas canisters had crept deep into the hallways, stinging his eyes to make it difficult to find his way back to the hangar.

McDermott's references to attacking civilian airlines echoed in Ryson's mind, and his heart began pounding furiously.

Trostov arrived at the front lines to find the situation worse than anticipated. Despite fighting fiercely, his men had been pushed back so far down the main hallway that the entrance to the corridor leading to the submarine lair now lay in a no man's land between two opposing forces.

He took cover in one of the wall recesses as bullets whizzed past, and came upon the mission commander. "What the hell happened?" he asked the man.

"They have state of the art weapons, blasted their way in with anti-tank guns."

Trostov peeked down the darkened tunnel but spotted no one. The attackers had shot out all the lights on their end to remain concealed, and they relied on infrared to return fire. A single bullet struck the cement wall just a few inches from his face, forcing him to jerk his head back inside.

"Sons of bitches," he growled, not even having seen the shooter. "Where are our night goggles, Commander?"

"Our outside units have the few we brought."

"Why isn't there enough gear for everyone?"

"We weren't coming here for a heavy combat mission, so we packed light."

Trostov cursed under his breath. No point in dwelling on his own short-sightedness. He had to focus only on escaping. "I need to get to that corridor!" He pointed at the juncture.

"That's impossible," the commander said. "You'll be gunned down. Best we can hope for now is to stall them here."

Trostov eyed the man with disdain, despite finding his combat tactical assessment solid. But Trostov was a driven businessman for whom the notion of *impossible* had often carried no meaning. Before long, he had devised a way out.

"I have a plan to get to that corridor," he said. "Trust me."

"Does that plan include me, too?" A Chinese-accented voice spoke from the far corner of the recessed wall.

Trostov turned to see a black-clad Xendong standing there, just a few feet to his right. "When did *you* get here?" he asked.

"Just in time to see your men get decimated. Didn't you say they were the best?"

Trostov gave him a hostile look. "I like to see your countrymen do better," he retorted. "Anyway, we're almost out of here."

"'*we*?'" Xendong shot back. "You vermin were going to escape by yourself!"

"I can still do that, you know."

"Oh, no you won't," Xendong said with a smirk.

Trostov caught sight of the glimmer of the silvery pistol aimed in his direction. "Are you going to shoot me, old man?"

"I will, a fitting end for a filthy rat, if you ever try to leave me behind again."

Trostov mulled over the situation. His devised plan hinged on quick physical action. No part in it for a slow aged man, especially one so inclined to shoot him from behind. It was an easy decision for Trostov. All he needed was a distraction.

As if on cue, one of his men stepped out of cover and blasted at the assailants, who in turn returned fire immediately. Bullets raked the wall overhead, showering them with metal caps fragments and chipped concrete. Xendong instinctively recoiled, momentarily turning his head to avert the raining debris. It proved enough time for Trostov to pounce.

With surprising agility, he wrested the weapon from Xendong's feeble hands by using a sharp wrenching move that cracked multiple bones.

Xendong screamed in pain. "You broke my wrist!"

"Don't worry," Trostov said calmly. "You won't be needing it anymore." He reached for his semi-automatic and delivered a dozen rounds into the man's body, which promptly fell.

"Take that to your bosses," Trostov spat, tossing the puny silver pistol onto the blood splattered corpse.

In the darkened end of the corridor, Kessler's night vision goggles picked up the strange thermal spectacle of a man firing into a corner of his own hideout. It wasn't until the lifeless body of an elderly Asian man fell into the open that he realized what must have happened.

Kessler took it as a sign of dissent among the ranks and opted to exacerbate matters by pointing out the spot to a squad member, who directed a series of long bursts in its direction.

The machine gun fire claimed a cluster of men, all thrown back a few feet by the impact. The ceiling lights were also hit by bullets and exploded in a shower of sparks. The rest momentarily dimmed, as if from a power outage, and then flickered and came back on, though in far fewer numbers.

Having barely survived the latest assault, Trostov resorted mostly to hand signals to direct his men over the cacophony of combat. Besides, judging by the blood oozing down some of the men's earlobes, he knew most of them had suffered blown ear drums. They were tough soldiers, Trostov reminded himself: trained by the Spetsnaz to withstand far worse punishment than this. If only he had brought enough weaponry for all his men...

Another round of heavy machine gun riddled holes on the opposite wall, cutting down a commando who had emerged from his cover to return fire to a previous volley. Trostov hoped his Kevlar vest would fully protect him in the seconds ahead. His life depended on it.

Seeing an opportune moment, he waved directional gestures to the soldiers and then sprinted forward behind the cover of two men emerging from their wall recess. "Cover us!" Trostov ordered the aft commander with a special hand signal.

Salvos of intense suppression fire were let loose to keep the assailants at bay as the trio made their way toward the mouth of the escape corridor. Trostov was barely a yard away from the juncture when, in the darkness ahead, countless muzzles sparked to life with deadly flashes.

A fusillade of bullets riddled his front escorts. The two men dropped in quick succession, and he in turn felt sharp pain in his right shoulder and then left knee. Trying to ignore the unbearable pain, he kept moving forward and then, in one final effort, lunged into the corridor's opening and out of the line of fire.

The explosive outdoor battle sounds came through the makeshift hangar's cavernous opening and echoed off the thick concrete walls. Standing beneath the plane's massive pitch-dark carbon-composite wings, McDermott took a long calming drag off a just-lit cigarette and then crushed it under his boot, it reminded him of a condemned man's last act before a firing squad. Even so, he considered a single puff from a freshly lit cigarette a symbol of good luck. Like many fighter pilots, he was mildly superstitious when it came to combat flights, and so had followed his usual pre-flight ritual.

He quickly climbed aboard the SuperCOIL from its ventral ladder and then took his place at the helm, the sole crew member of this one-man vessel. The beast seemed to acknowledge its master via a mild short-lived rumble in the soft monotonous hum of its idling engines. Soon, as he settled in the pilot's seat, his mind was swept clear of all outside concerns. Once more, amid the cockpit's familiar environment, he felt at home, the only place he could now truly feel that way. Over the past grievous decade, that small instrument-filled compartment had increasingly become his most comforting haven, an inner sanctum where his mind felt free of all the intrusions of a treacherous world.

Here, his unparalleled aviation skills bestowed on him absolute control over its faithful electronic systems. He knew that no machinery would ever purposely betray him. Underneath the protective stillness of the transparent canopy lay a placid sanctuary of rapport between man and machine, where malice gained no entry. When viewed from his airborne refuge, whatever conflict raged outside might as well have been happening in another universe—far too distant to cause him any harm.

With complete composure, McDermott did a quick pre-flight checklist and then counted the seconds to take-off.

A gravely injured Trostov staggered a few feet inside the escape corridor, just far enough to stay clear of any ricocheting bullets, and then, yelping in pain, he fell to the hard floor. At least a half-dozen bullets had struck him, and been absorbed by the Kevlar vest, but two had hit unprotected body parts. He gingerly ran his fingers over his right shoulder and felt his collar bone had been pierced close to the rotator cuff. He could barely move his arm.

Worse, his left knee had taken a direct frontal hit that had shattered the tissue into a soup of bone fragments and blood which soaked his pants down to his ankle.

With monumental effort, he ripped off his right sleeve, and secured it as a tourniquet around the left thigh. No medics were around, but the first-aid kit in the submarine contained enough morphine to tie him over until he could escape to a place with a hospital. He would have to crawl through the long tunnel on his sole working leg, with only one arm to pull him along the concrete.

Just minutes earlier, Kessler had observed the daring breakout of a trio: two had been shot—obviously, fatally—with one narrowly succeeding. He took the escaped man to be the team leader; no one else could garner the suicidal support of his comrades for such foolhardy attempt. Without anyone to effectively urge on the other side, Kessler saw the situation as relatively favorable for a final attack, so he motioned his men to commence an all-out assault.

Just minutes later, his squad rushed forward, each raising an aimed bazooka. Almost in unison, four anti-tank projectiles sailed out of their launchers with a distinct *woosh*. Within seconds, tremendous blasts spewed out of the distant walls' recesses in a scattering field of body parts, concrete chips, and weaponry that was dispersed all over the tunnel.

The remaining Black Squadron members charged forward in two-man buddy teams, their weapons drawn to cut down anyone in their path. All resistance disappeared in the ensuing carnages. Kessler ordered his men to split up and chase the fleeing enemy. No prisoners were to be taken.

Not one to miss out on the pleasure of the hunt, Kessler opted for a specific corridor that would reward him with the biggest trophy.

The thunderous barrage of approaching automatic rifle fire that had followed a series of devastating explosions made it clear to Ryson that the Russian resistance had all but collapsed. He ambivalently wondered whether the victors would treat him any better than the men they had so mercilessly tracked. He tried to block out the thought and concentrate on his own chase in the narrow galleries that led to the elusive hangar. It was difficult to spot the correct passage in the darkness and smoke, but he remained reasonably sure he was getting closer with each step.

And then his ears picked up a new sound amid the mayhem. In the distance, from a group of powerful jet engines, came a low whine that was slowly rising toward a full-fledged roar. He had heard the familiar crescendo all too often; the ominous sound of a B-2 bomber preparing for take-off. But this time, the sound literally made the hairs on his forearms stand on end.

He turned into the right corridor and ran at full speed toward the source.

It didn't take long for Kessler to find his prize, by simply following the blood trail that had started at the corridor's mouth and still glowed warm on his infrared scope. Its origin soon came into view as a lone crippled figure crawling slowly along the floor. Like a predator seeking fresh meat for a kill, Kessler was pleased to find his prey was alive.

Kessler pulled out his Beretta M92F side arm and kept it trained on the wounded man. "Stop!" he commanded.

The figure rolled over, his left shoulder pressed against the wall, his face a ghostly shade. Kessler saw that the man was unarmed and breathing laboriously, with froth appearing at the corners of his mouth. He stepped closer and shone his flashlight at the man.

"Who are you?" Trostov asked him, eyes averting the flashlight's intense beam.

"No one of consequence," Kessler replied.

"I will give you ten million dollars if you let me go," Trostov pleaded in between shallow breaths. "Anything you want."

"Where is Captain McDermott?" Kessler demanded, ignoring the offer.

Trostov gazed at the masked commando, a mere silhouette behind the bright light. He knew that unless he could strike some sort of bargain with this man towering over him, he would not live to reap the rewards of his well-laid plans.

Trostov could not bear the thought of dying so unceremoniously in this dark, squalid place, like a hunted sewer rat—not after having pulled off one of the greatest capers in military history. No, he had been too damn shrewd in his life for it all to end here, of that he was certain. His arms dealings had taught him that every man has a price. He just needed to find out what this one's was.

"Down in the hangar," he said, not caring whether his assailant could somehow forestall the plane from taking off. All he cared about now was getting out alive.

Kessler eyed the man with disdain, correctly assuming that without his involvement, none of this would have happened, at least not the way it had. He raised the muzzle of his Beretta and aimed it at the weakened man's forehead.

"No, please," Trostov pleaded, feebly waving his left hand and then coughing up blood. "I'll give you *twenty* million, anything you want . . ."

Kessler's eyes narrowed. "I want our stealth bomber back, you Russian asshole." He then pulled the trigger, and a single 9-mm round left the barrel in a muzzle flash that briefly lit up the corridor. A moment later, Kessler stared down at Trostov's lifeless body with intense satisfaction.

With almost mindless dexterity, McDermott ran his fingers across the extensive cockpit controls in his preflight check. He pressed the array of buttons and switches with the ease of a concert pianist as he confirmed that all systems were ready to go: the oxygen pump, the fuel gauges, the computerized avionics, and most importantly, the weapons and targeting systems of the lethal COIL. He finalized the powering-up of the aircraft. Until now, the engines' soft hum had been soothing to his ears, almost symphonic, but he would hear and feel their enormous power soon enough. Moving the rpm lever forward, the plane trundled ahead, rapidly gaining speed.

Nearly out of breath, Ryson scurried into the open expanse of the hangar, but he had arrived in time only to catch the riveting sight of the wings of an enormous black beast soaring over his head.

As soon as McDermott punched the afterburners to full thrust for take-off, the engines roared to a deafening crescendo. The plane forged ahead with incredible grace and agility. The gathering acceleration pressed his back against the seat as everything in his peripheral vision turned to a blur, including a small figure that had suddenly appeared to his far right.

The figure had arrived late and, as a result, was inconsequential now. The front portal gates had swung wide, the Faraday netting removed, and within an instant the winged creature had cleared its concrete pen for the last time.

There followed a brief precision dash along the shortened runway, and then the SuperCOIL took to the sky, piercing the firmament like a black arrow lunged from its quiver, set on vengeance.

OFF-SHORES FROM AZORES

The expansive deck of the aircraft carrier came into view under the rapidly brightening predawn sky. In the few minutes it had taken for the transport helicopter to land on the flat top, the sun's first rays had broken over the watery horizon, casting a yellowish tint on the flight deck.

Sitting silently next to the chopper pilot, a ruminating Ryson watched as a formerly distant speck grow to enormous dimensions. It was hard to grasp the massive scale of the aircraft carrier, even with a dozen fighter jets resting on its deck like flies.

Ryson had arrived at the hangar just in time to behold the SuperCOIL's wings soaring right over his head. Caught in the plane's powerful wake turbulence, he was tossed into a stack of cargo boxes by the sidewall.

Soon the fading roar of the bomber was supplanted by ear-piercing sounds of close-range gunfire. The impact had knocked him to the ground, so he remained out of the bullets' path.

Before long, however, he was staring into the business end of Kessler's assault rifle, as the Black Squadron commandos converged on the hangar from all sides, after evidently having killed every single Russian on the base, and on the field. Ryson had expected Kessler to finish him off just as swiftly.

"That was our plane, right?" Kessler asked.

"Yes," Ryson said evenly. "And you just missed it."

"Lucky you," he muttered, then lowered his rifle and motioned Ryson onto his feet. Ryson realized now that the rogue captain had fled with the ultimate prize, the major must have assumed that the lieutenant had gained some insight into McDermott that would prove useful for Kessler's pursuit. Ryson deduced he was worth more alive than dead, at least for the time being.

The loud grating noise of the chopper's door sliding open broke Ryson's trance. A salty breeze swept through the cargo section, where Kessler sat with his commandos. The company got out swiftly, and Ryson was led along the deck to the superstructure island.

Kessler quickly headed downstairs. After a few turns in the steel corridors, he arrived at a special communication center, set up for this secret mission, ordered everyone out except Ryson, put on a headset and switched the transmitter to the preselected encrypted frequency for call to Gorik, who picked up right away.

Shortly into conversation, Ryson noticed Kessler's face turning pale. Gorik was obviously displeased by Kessler's failure to recover the aircraft or its pilot.

"I will put him on," Kessler replied. He motioned Ryson to don an earpiece.

"Tell me, Lieutenant," Gorik said, "what did the captain reveal of his plans?"

With some lingering reluctance, Ryson told Gorik of McDermott's scheme to attack NORAD and commercial airliners. Gorik took the grave news rather calmly.

"McDermott has gone utterly insane," he remarked, then ordered Kessler to disconnect Ryson.

The major continued the conversation for few more minutes. Contrary to Kessler's worst fears, Gorik had commended him for leaving Ryson alive. Nonetheless, Kessler was in no better mood after the call had ended. He switched off the radio, and they headed upstairs. Reaching the artificial metal runway, the major looked about, spotted the air boss, and approached him. He spoke a few words into his ears over the howl of a fighter preparing for take-off and then hurriedly left in the direction of his squadron, leaving a hesitant Ryson behind.

So much the better, the lieutenant thought before the air boss stepped closer to him. "You are ordered back to Tanaris immediately!" the man said in a deep voice that cut through the background noise.

Ryson could not believe his ears. "But I just came from combat, on that damn chopper!" He feigned disappointment, hoping to stall his departure until he could contact Norton, and to review the contents of the memory stick McDermott had stuck into his shirt pocket.

But the air boss would have none of it. He cast Ryson an indignant look. "That is a *Helo* son. It's what we call them contraptions in the Navy. And I don't care what you been through. You are ordered out ASAP, and I am to make sure of it."

His no-nonsense tone made Ryson back down. "Okay you win. Should I get on board the greyhound?" Ryson asked, eyeing the nearby cargo aircraft.

The air boss shook his head. "I am afraid this calls for something a lot faster."

COMBAT AIR PATROL,
THE ATLANTIC OCEAN,
130 MILES SOUTHWEST OF AZORES

The brace of F-18/C "Hornet" held to a close formation, flying steady at twenty-five thousand feet, as indicated by their above-ground level readout—only that they were above the Atlantic Ocean.

Captain Larson, flying in the lead, barely a plane's length ahead of the second Hornet, gazed out of the surrounding bubble canopy and found nothing but his aft wingman in all that blue sky, which confirmed his AN/APG-73 pulse-Doppler radar scope read. He knew he would have better success visually spotting his prey than relying on cockpit instruments which indicated an empty electronic horizon.

Since taking off from the carrier a little over an hour ago, they had remained on a southwesterly course, flying at a fuel-conserving 330 knots to extend the range of their combat-air-patrol flight mode. Except this CAP was not the normal sentry of the carrier's defense zone, but a search and destroy mission.

It was 6:27 a.m. The sun was still rising behind him. He tried not to think of the other two Hornet pairs heading southeasterly, both in search of a radar elusive prey.

The three Hornet sections had been told they were hunting a conventional B-2 bomber, which explained why his Hornet's pylons were filled to capacity with air-intercept missiles. Yet how would AIMs be effective against an adversary who failed to register on either radar or infrared guidance scopes? Perhaps he would have to use the laser-locking features instead, which required him to come close to his prey, though not a big concern, since the B-2s lacked an air defense system.

Tired of watching an empty radar scope, Larson opted for a higher vantage point. He reset the elevators to ascend, gunned the afterburners, and climbed to forty thousand feet, followed closely by his wingman.

ABOARD THE SUPERCOIL

The giant flying wing flexed one of its enormous articulated surfaces along the starboard trailing edge, and the entire airfoil began a graceful swing in a wide curved turn. In the cockpit, McDermott monitored the multifunction display as he eased the control stick to set a new course.

Since escaping the Azores some ninety minutes earlier, McDermott had flown southeast, toward the African coast, then made a westward turn in direction, toward the United States.

McDermott had plied these routes aboard a conventional B-2, as part of the NATO bombing of the invading Serbian Army in 1999, which had honed his B-2 bomber skills in a real mission while gathering flight data for the SuperCOIL prototyping. As usual, McDermott's identity had remained hidden. He had welcomed the anonymity afforded by the flight suit and helmet, which concealed him from what he regarded as a cruel and unfair world. He also, however, failed— or refused—to see how the uniform ensemble served as a personal prison.

There was a time when he was deeply aware of the distinction between that uniform and the man who wore it. A time when he possessed a compassionate soul, and the synergy of love and duty was his highest calling. Only when called on would he don that suit, and valiantly perform his tasks for the service of his country, which he loved so dearly, almost as much as he loved his wife.

Unlike Gorik, McDermott had no interest in war for war's sake, and if everlasting peace were someday to occur, he would gladly retire that uniform, even if it meant never flying another fighter jet again.

But all that had changed when Gorik robbed him of his greatest love, leaving him armored with a hatred he could never remove. In the wake of his crushing griefs in bereavement and discovery of his unwitting betrayal of his country, he had come to despise his own existence. His compassionate spirit had steadily wizened to a shadow, at first a numbing emptiness that was later replaced by a consuming desire for vengeance. His warrior skills were all he had left, and he was determined to use them in his last 'mission', one he saw as of true honor to rid his country of a hidden blight that was Gorik and his organization. And, unable to bring back his wife, he would join her. All he had needed was a plane capable of delivering him to such destiny, and the SuperCOIL, sprung in his path as if out of sheer karma, would do just that.

A blinking light from the vast console snapped McDermott's attention back to the flight. He took a quick read of his position and concluded it was time to re-activate the low probability of intercept radar which allowed him to see others without being seen. Before long, the furtive LPI scope revealed what he had sought. With a tug on the control stick, he veered the bomber toward the objects on the scope and soon came within visual range of a pair of nimble grey specs in the far distance, whose pilots had no doubt already spotted his much larger aircraft.

COMBAT AIR PATROL,
THE ATLANTIC OCEAN,
200 MILES SOUTHWEST OF AZORES

Larson had just ordered a return-to-carrier, and his plane was turning in a sweeping easterly arc when he saw it in the corner of his right eye. A growing black dot had suddenly announced itself against a rising sun and moving on a clear trajectory.

He recognized the visual as a plane. And, judging by its size from such a distance, it was massive, and unusually sleek. He checked the multipurpose color display scope and still found nothing on either radar or infrared.

But the thing was real and crossing the broad horizon at speeds just below the transonic boundary. There was also an uncharacteristic absence of IFF—Identification Friend or Foe—transmissions, and his own calls requesting the information had gone unanswered.

"Do you see what I'm seeing?" Larson asked his wingman.

"I sure do," said the latter. "But my scope says my eyes are seeing things that ain't there."

"It's real, I assure you. Stay in formation and follow me."

The captain maintained the turn, keeping the Hornet rolling until it came around full, then zoomed in the optical magnifiers at the bogey. The read on the plane's unique features left him no doubt as to its type. It was a B-2.

Larson, who had considered the search mission akin to finding a needle in the proverbial haystack couldn't believe his serendipitous find. He sent an encrypted message to the carrier along with his coordinates, and awaited instructions.

The reply came swiftly: he was to maintain pursuit from long range, while the two other Hornet pairs were vectored in on his location. It would not be long before all six aircraft would be in position to intercept the lone bomber heading west.

EN ROUTE TO TANARIS

Some 1700 miles west of Larson's position, another squadron of F-18s sped away over the Atlantic Ocean toward the U.S. coastline at just shy of Mach 2, their fighters' limit. Ian Ryson was back-seating behind Kessler on a D-model Hornet, the only two-seater in the group. He looked passively out the bubble canopy at the blue expanses of ocean and sky, which merged almost indistinguishably in the distance. Looking around, he could see the rest of the tightly formed five-plane entourage in a staggered close-knit wingtip to nose formation that stretched back two planes' length in either direction.

If Ryson craned his neck, he could still spot the diminishing outline of the KC-135 tanker from which they had refueled minutes earlier. With a ferry range of just over two thousand miles, the Hornets were already on their second aerial refueling since leaving the carrier near Azores. Even so, they had covered close to three thousand miles at breakneck velocities and would soon be in visual range of Savannah, Georgia. They would then go feet dry, flying over land to Tanaris.

Shortly after takeoff, soon as they'd leveled out of the climb at 30,000 feet, Ryson had examined the contents of McDermott's memory stick on a personal digital assistant which he had retrieved from his locker upon return to the carrier.

The PDA's decryptor software had enabled him to read all the stored files, which appeared to be genuine reports drafted in formats unique to Tanaris. Still, given the outlandish accusations involved, he remained skeptical of their authenticity until he could view the originals at Tanaris.

Glancing at the multipurpose color display, Ryson wondered about the rogue captain's proximate whereabouts. With its digital moving-map, the display provided locations of any known friendlies and bogies, as well as flight data and positional references for the purpose of augmenting combat effectiveness, so to put the pilot's mind at ease. But against a radar-invisible adversary, the empty display only increased Ryson's anxiety.

He tried to conjecture on McDermott's most likely route to NORAD. He quickly ruled out a northern route through the desolate Arctic Circle, knowing the brutally low arctic temperatures could invariably affect the operation of the COIL, damage the stealth coating, and make noticeable the engines heat trail that was normally undetectable in warmer climates.

Eliminating a northern route, however, still left an expansive southern approach through which the plane could slip undetected. Ryson was trying to eliminate other possibilities when the radio cracked to life.

"Unit One, this is the Base." It was Gorik's voice.

"Yes sir," Kessler said.

"We have a development. One of the patrols has reported a confirmed sighting."

Ryson perked up as if the sighting were of a UFO.

"What location, sir?" Kessler asked.

Gorik read the encrypted coordinates. "I knew we would hunt that rat down. Nothing escapes our grip."

"Should we redirect to engage?" Kessler asked eagerly.

"Negative. You're too far out of range, and not carrying any missiles."

Ryson could almost hear Kessler's grumbling. To lighten the weight for their supersonic trip home, none of the planes were fitted with missiles. They would now have to land, re-arm and head back, by which time they would arrive too late to the SuperCOIL's current location.

"What's the plan, sir?" Kessler asked, sounding frustrated.

"Our local team is converging on the target for a direct intercept. Maintain your current course and speed. Return to Tanaris ASAP. Base out." The radio went back to static, and Kessler switched it off. He must have known Ryson had heard everything, but he said nothing.

So far Kessler had barely spoken to his back-seater, for which Ryson was grateful. Ryson looked up the coordinates on his scope and found them surprisingly close to the Azores, which didn't account for over two hours of flight time for a bomber purportedly en route to NORAD. And then there was the matter of an ace pilot such as McDermott allowing himself to be spotted so easily. Perhaps he had been sighted out of sheer luck, coming in range of a wandering sentry fighter.

Stranger things had happened to pilots, despite their skills.

TANARIS

"How long before they are all in range?" a worried McCane asked, looking at the large digital clock display.

"The diverted F-18s have just gone supersonic after their mid-air refueling, should be in range in 25 minutes," Gorik replied calmly, but getting a bit annoyed at the general's persistent inquiries since the SuperCOIL was first spotted.

"Is the target still in sight?"

"Yes. No way a subsonic bomber can outrun a Mach 2 fighter. We are just long-distance shadowing him till we are full force. Then we'll shoot the bastard down."

"You're going to destroy your own prized fifteen-billion-dollar bomber?" McCane asked, astonished.

"We have no choice. You heard what that son of a bitch is going to use it for."

McCane wanted to say something but thought it pointless to argue—except for one matter. "Six Hornets against the SuperCOIL... is that going to be enough?"

Gorik grinned. "Let's hope not," he said, confounding McCane further.

IN PURSUIT OF THE SUPERCOIL

Captain Larson's long-range radar scope bleeped to life at the supersonic approach of his fellow squadron members.

The two Hornet sections dropped out of Mach a few miles aft of his formation before synchronizing speeds to 550 knots. Larson, the mission lead, issued a Judy call to the base on his coordinating an intercept strike on his tracked prey.

"What is the mission, boss?" one of the wingmen asked.

"To shoot that thing down," he commanded. "Orders from the colonel. Don't ask why." His tone emulated Kessler's, whose ruthlessness he admired.

"Split up in pairs, approach from flanks," Larson directed his flight mates. "You are clear to fire at will." He watched his squadron disperse like a pack of wild hyenas ready to bring down an African buffalo. The two sections peeled off with afterburner bursts, setting for positions north and south of the target. Larson rolled to the right, in unison with his wingman, put the black bomber squarely in the middle of his head-up display, then set on a lag pursuit.

The heading would approach the target from directly behind, for the best probability of obtaining a thermal lock on the plane's heat exhausts. Not one to purposely limit his options, he also reset the AN/APG-73 pulse-Doppler radar to maximum power discharge in the hope of homing one of his radar guided Sparrow or AMRAAM missiles.

He knew that the elaborate boxing-in of the bomber by a half-dozen fully-armed fighters was mainly an air show. All really needed to bring it crashing down was a single missile, and he alone had a panoply of such hard-points under his wings. A B-2 was defenseless once air-intercepted, capable of neither flight nor fight, which is why stealth bombers had solely flown night combat sorties, to cover their Achilles heel regarding visual spotting. This one, however, seemed to have boldly ignored that cardinal rule.

From the SuperCOIL's cockpit, McDermott attentively tracked the fighters' movements on his threat scope. Their IFF designators had all the markings of a Black Squadron fighter wing. He was now surrounded. Two fighters were at his aft six o'clock and closing fast, with a second and third pair flying high to port and starboard, then turning toward him in pure pursuit mode.

It was a nightmarish one-to-many intercept scenario for any fighter pilot, who would, ideally, jockey to face all attacks on one side of him, preferably to his front, where his missiles could easily lock on. As it stood, however, his only open space was to the front, and he well knew that his heavy bomber could never outrun the nimble Hornets.

But there was no need to run.

Without hesitation McDermott's eyes raced across the control panels, a complex array of computerized multi-purpose display units each subdivided into esoteric clusters tasked to certain operations. Some of the cockpit instruments had rectangular screens with a grid-like array of push buttons underneath, resembling oversized pocket calculators. One such cluster, though, was especially prominent: the weapon and targeting systems that operated the mighty COIL. McDermott quickly reached for the laser controls.

Larson scanned the approached bomber on his HUD, its slim yet expansive wingspans now seemed to connect the HUD's vertically angled framing pylons that jutted out like goal posts. He felt as if chasing a thrown boomerang at top speed. The bomber however had not change in course or airspeed and continued on a straight flight in arrogant defiance of the deadly arsenals that floated about.

Larson ordered the flanking planes to split, with one fighter in each pair aiming directly at the bomber and the others taking position at the front and sides at ten and two o'clock. In less than a minute, all birds were in attack position, and Larson gave the go-ahead for the flanking pairs to converge at the bomber from high in the air, like a pincer, and connect a pair of missiles at its center. All he had to do was lie back and watch.

The threat indicator bleeped louder in the SuperCOIL's cockpit. The LPI radar was now picking up two Hornets approaching from sides. McDermott paid them no heed as he ran his fingers over the weapons control buttons with such agility as to appear to be skittering. Within seconds, the targeting computer had all six fighters tracked and entered into the fire-sequence queue, with the top priority given to the fast closing flankers. Sensing a burning rage welling, McDermott pressed *engage*.

In a fraction of a second, the low-power range-finder and tracking lasers shot out. The computer determined the atmospheric turbulence from their reads, adjusted the main laser power and actuator targeting mirrors to compensate, then unleashed the full power of the main COIL from the bomber's top-mounted turret at the fighter approaching from the starboard side.

The flanking Hornet's pilot was given no forewarnings. His radar was silent as always and his own eyes deceived him. Suddenly, the transparent canopy of his cockpit turned a glowing crimson, and the air inside grew scorching hot. His flight suit was set ablaze, and he felt blood boiling under his skin. But there was no time to react to the excruciating pain. In an instant, his mind rushed to a blinding delirium and was abruptly silenced in flames as the SuperCOIL's laser sliced its way through flesh and metal alike, blasting the fighter in a huge fireball wreckage, a blazing shower of incandescent smithereens dispersing in myriad ways.

Larson witnessed the spectacle in profound shock. The wavelength of the chemically-powered laser made it invisible to the human eye, so the Hornet's explosion came unexpectedly, as if blown up from within by a fuel tank mishap. There were no telltale missiles plumes, and no parachute appeared in the aftermath.

A quick scan of the infrared, however, conveyed a far different story, of a huge thermal spike registering in the IR scope. It was a massive energy beam. Larson could not believe it had emanated from a terrestrial source, and he was tempted to search the skies for UFOs.

His eyes were still on the IR scope when the second F-18, flanking the bomber's port, was also torn to pieces in a fire ball. The same thermal signature reappeared, but this time he could clearly observe a searing ephemeral connecting line between the doomed F-18 and a semicircular spot atop the bomber.

"Holy mother of God!" he exclaimed as he fully realized the bomber's offensive capabilities, of a type he had never even heard of, much less encountered. He knew he had to react fast. "Shoot that son of a bitch down *now*, with everything you got!" he ordered his wingman.

"I have no radar lock, and we are out of range for laser-targeting or guns!"

"Aim manually then, get them close and they'll find their own lock!"

The wingman obediently let loose a pair of missiles, a heat-seeker AIM-9 Sidewinder followed by a radar tracker AMRAAM, while doing his best to line up the sight with the bomber's impossibly thin profile. Larson quickly followed suit.

The missiles leapt out of their railings, ignited their main boosters, and soon exceeded Mach 4, dashing straight ahead. If the bomber made no sudden moves in the next dozen or so seconds, it would remain right in their paths for impact. With a little luck, the heat-seeker Sidewinders would catch the faint IR signature of the engines at very close range and guide themselves into the nacelles for a certain, "no-luck-needed" kill.

The high-pitched Missile Launch shrill echoed in McDermott's helmet. His innate fighter pilot instincts warned reflexively that immediate evasive action should be taken, but those instincts were quickly held in check by his new training discipline, reminding him that he wasn't flying an F-16. As he pressed the *targeting* and *firing* buttons in this singular craft, so many air combat rules changed. The four missiles were computer-identified, ranged, and queued. There ensued slight rumbles in the cockpit as the COIL sequentially fired four shots, this time with less intensity but the same uncanny accuracy.

A quad of consecutive explosions quickly supplanted what was, until an instant earlier, a salvo of hurtling missiles in Larson's scope. The blasts came in near unison, giving the illusion of the projectiles having simultaneously struck an invisible wall, perhaps a force field of sorts. Larson shook his head at that far-fetched conjecture, but at any rate knew he now faced a far superior enemy than he was originally led to believe.

"All units take evasive actions!" he commanded, pitching the Hornet's nose into a twenty-degree dive and watching the ocean well up. As he did so, a thought occurred to him on how to bring down the feisty bomber. He had little time to consider his options, however; to his aft, a bright blast erupted from the center of his wingman's fuselage. The same deadly thermal read reappeared on his scope, this time closer than ever. The explosion's shockwaves buffeted his Hornet from above as he gunned the afterburners, accelerating his descent.

With three manned targets destroyed and one fleeing, McDermott set his sight on the Hornet duo in front, which had now taken different trajectories. They were peeling away from the flanks at top speed, spewing dark afterburner plumes in their wake. That put the fighters at a ninety-degree roll, exposing underbellies of fully armed missiles hanging from their pylons. Mindful of his limited supply of lasing fuel and the added expenditure for penetrating a fuselage, McDermott opted for a more economic approach in directing the targeting computer.

In a display of frightening power, the craft unleashed its lethal beams only milliseconds apart, each beam directed to a single missile mounted at a fighter's ventral midsection. Each warhead exploded instantly, its shards tearing into the airframe and setting off internal fuel tanks and other wing-mounted missiles. The expanding chain reaction resembled a roll of firecrackers going off in rapid succession until nothing was left of their host plane but a collection of barely recognizable falling debris.

The ocean rushed full speed at Larson, who was not about to lose control, not yet. He took a deep breath through his oxygen mask to counteract the dizzying effect of the vertiginous descent, yanked the center stick to level out of the dive two thousand feet above the water, then reset the elevators and ascended almost vertically, toward the bomber, on full blowers. If his hunch was right, there could be a big payoff for such boldness.

He had seen energy beams shoot out of the B-2's topside and reckoned his only chance of success lay in staying clear of its reach by sweeping under it, from an angle that was difficult to detect, then head sharply upward to come within gunfire range, or a missile lock.

With the 34,000-pound thrust of dual GE-402 turbofan engines on his back, the mounting g-forces pinned him down in his seat. The bomber's angular profile grew rapidly as a jagged blackhole that had rent the sky. It was a menacing sight as Larson slewed the targeting crosshairs over for a visual lock before he grasped the gun trigger and marked the seconds until he was in effective range.

McDermott refocused attention on the last remaining Hornet barreling up like a dagger aimed for his underbelly. He could have easily shot down the intruder from a few hundred miles out but preferred not to spend more of his precious laser fuel than necessary, so he waited for a closer, less wasteful shot. The Hornet was almost within its gun range when McDermott set the COIL to automatic track and destroy.

In the aft, energized oxygen molecules were mixed with iodine gas and injected at supersonic velocities into the six laser chambers before the computer fired the generated blistering multi-megawatt beam at the pursuing plane, this time from the ventral turret. The entire sequence transpired more tersely than the fractional-second lapse in Larson's reaction to the locked-onto signal to press the firing trigger on his Hornet's Vulcan gun. But the infinitesimal delay proved an eternity compared to the incomprehensible speed of laser light. By then, Larson's F-18 was already an expanding ball of superheated shards scattering over the Atlantic.

TANARIS

"Any survivors?" a chagrined McCane asked as he gazed at the view screen in stunned disbelief. The six blips representing the Hornets had disappeared, at times in such rapid succession that he was tempted to attribute it to a display malfunction.

"I seriously doubt it," Gorik said. "The SuperCOIL is the perfect weapon." The colonel seemed exceedingly pleased by the bomber's effectiveness, more so than being fazed by his failed attempt to vanquish an adversary.

"Any updates on the plane's location?"

"None. If McDermott maintained his westerly course, he's by now reached the edge of a weather front covering most of the mid-Atlantic. We'll never visually find him in there. It'd be like trying to track him at night."

"We need to inform the president then," McCane said.

"Send a secure message. Tell him to stand by for a live discussion in two hours."

"You don't tell the commander in chief to remain at your whim, Colonel."

"Then couch it in whatever politicians' language you normally use."

EN ROUTE TO TANARIS

It was dark again now. The night had crept abominably from the west, and only in the extreme aft could tinges of purple and dull gold be seen from a sun that was 'setting' fast behind the eastern horizon. Traveling at Mach 2, the fighters had literally outpaced the Earth's rotation. Ryson saw the eerie phenomenon as it unfolded: the western sky's blue had dissolved into darkness, as the fighters outran the day and reentered a mortifying world of shadows and gloom.

Soon, the sole illumination came from the monochrome multipurpose display scope for the "GIB," the guy in back, which reminded Ryson of the small portable black-and-white TV he had once received as a college gift from his uncle.

A moment later, the encrypted dial radio came on again.

"Unit One, acknowledge," the speaker device crackled.

"Unit One here, proceed," Kessler replied.

"Our plan did not succeed," Gorik said flatly. "Confirmed 100% casualty rate."

Kessler frowned behind his visor. "And the bogey?"

"Contact was lost."

"Should we turn to search?"

"Negative, maintain course for the base, understood?" Gorik said firmly, leaving no room for discussion.

Kessler paused again. "Roger that," he said, then switched off the link. The cockpit suddenly became deathly silent, with only the dull roar of the turbofan engines to fill the acoustic void.

The downed pilots aside, the lieutenant had now his own worries. For him, the significance of this relatively isolated event lay on a far wider scale, one that heralded another momentous turn in the history of a stealth bomber platform whose future was troubled even before they had entered the service in the early 1990s.

The costly B-2 had come too late for the Cold War, for which it was principally designed. Within months of the fall of the Soviet Union, their production was thus cut to a mere 21. Cheaper embodiments of stealth technology such as the F-117 and, later, the F-22 had gravely eroded the justification for a $2.2 billion bomber. But the advent of a potent airborne laser had suddenly brought a new variable into the stealth bomber equation.

This laser could now be inducted into the offensive aerial arsenal as a weapon in its own right. The SuperCOIL was designed to track and shoot down dozens of ground-launched enemy missiles. But McDermott had just shown that if set against enemy planes or their launched missiles, a handful of SuperCOILs could decimate the entire air force of any country, even that of a superpower. Nothing ever devised in the realm of air-to-air interception was capable of shooting down so much with such surgical precision and a comparatively inexpensive energy medium.

The frightful reality was that the top speeds of neither a fighter nor its Mach 7 missiles were any match for the COIL's so-called laser bullets, which, at 186,000 miles per *second*, traveled at light speed, or Mach 900,000. This meant a virtually zero launch-to-impact time so that acquired targets could be instantly hit, allowing no time for any defensive counter measures. McDermott, the SuperCOIL's only test pilot, likened the swiftness of the laser bullet's response to killing a target with a first glance, so being tracked now meant being instantly destroyed.

In many ways, Ryson regarded the SuperCOIL as a weapon born out of a "perfect" technological storm, since such breakthrough developments required not only advancements in different engineering fields, but also their intersection at the right time in their developmental maturity. The SuperCOIL, the supreme realization of that vision, represented the merging of three of the world's most advanced technologies: computers had made its aerodynamic design possible, stealth had made it invisible, and the laser had made it seemingly invincible.

To McDermott, this historic technological convergence had come to form a high-tech arrowhead—a lethal spike he would drive into the hearts of those who had wronged the people whose lives he had held dearer than his own.

For Ryson, such dreadful implications posed a more profound question: had the United States, the contemporary deity of military air supremacy for more than half a century, inadvertently built an air weapon the country itself could not defeat?

ABOARD THE SUPERCOIL

McDermott checked the LPI radar scope and found no evidence of hostile aircraft, or any activity, this far out over the ocean. The cloud cover had reduced outside visibility to a few feet, rendering any attempt at visual scanning useless. Of course, this also meant no one could spot him either, his main reason for taking this route.

His eyes shifted to various other instruments in the cockpit, especially the fuel gauges. On jet fuel, the multipurpose display unit, or MDU, positioned to the left indicated an ample stock remaining for his long-range craft to reach its target, still more than nine hours away, if it survived the air defenses. This brought his attention to a more serious matter: the laser fuel gauges.

A special-purpose MDU placed near the center panel revealed a distinctive feature of the SuperCOIL. The MDU graphically displayed a laser fuel read of nearly 70% full on both oxygen and iodine gas counts. He had used more than ten shots' worth to destroy six planes and four launched missiles. The fuel reserves had an estimated capacity of forty shots, but the true count depended on the range and power level of each laser burst. Attacking the fighter's thicker fuselage had incurred a higher fuel expenditure than normal. He would need to utilize the remaining shots judiciously so as not to squander his sole means of defense.

In an encouraging sign, the plane had lived up to its promise, destroying half a dozen Hornets with pinpoint accuracy. As the sole person responsible for this deed, he felt only bursts of excitement over the bomber's unparalleled accomplishments. This, of course, was not the first time he had taken lives in combat, but it was the first time he would be unable to use the chain of command as an excuse.

And he felt no remorse.

TANARIS

The parallel strings of dotted lights defining the 12,000 ft runway glowed brightly in the clear desert night as the F-18 squadron made its final landing approach. Their above-ground level indicators, which had decreased steadily to one hundred feet, suddenly shot back up to a thousand as the desert dropped out from under them, into the crater's floor. Turbulence picked up dramatically below the ridgeline of the crater's rim, where the howling wind furiously swirled about the walls.

Kessler was undaunted, but in the back seat, Ryson pulled his straps a bit tighter to not get bounced around the small cockpit area if the landing got rough. It was his first fully conscious act in the last few hours.

Gorik had earlier made a video transmission to Kessler, who shared it with Ryson. The horrifying recording was a collection from the IR cameras mounted on the doomed Hornets. After analyzing the tapes, the lieutenant now had a new set of questions for the loathed colonel.

Kessler's lead Hornet landed with surprising smoothness on the cement airstrip, followed by the others, who all rolled out to their lit hangars. Ryson unsnapped his oxygen feed as soon as the canopy was raised, and he took a deep breath of the desert air. It was dry but smelled genuine, not like the stale stuff he had been breathing through the rubber hose.

The crew hauled a set of ladders out to the fighter. Kessler managed his dismount briskly, unlike Ryson, whose legs made numbingly stiff after hours in a cramped space, nearly caused him to fall down the steep rungs. The duo then headed for a nearby open-topped Jeep. Taking the driver's seat and gunned the idling engine as if he were still in the Hornet, Kessler made such a sharp left turn out of the hangar that an unbuckled Ryson nearly fell out of the door-less vehicle.

On the way to headquarters, Ryson noticed every hangar was unusually running on high alert, with fighters being fitted with weapons. As he gazed up at the star-filled sky, he realized that in just a few hours' time it would be dawn—*again*.

Following a quick elevator ride up the headquarters edifice, Kessler marched to Gorik's office door and stood at attention. Gorik waved them in.

"Welcome back, Lieutenant," Gorik said, unfeeling to Ryson's cold stare. "So our good en route captain is going to wreak more havoc."

"Yes, and you can't stop him," Ryson said.

"I have a way. Trust me."

"Then why did you opt to kill your own men?"

"Excuse me?" Gorik replied, suddenly seeming indignant.

"By not telling those pilots about the SuperCOIL's weapons," Ryson pressed.

"What makes you think I didn't?"

"Because no sane squadron commander would deploy his fighters in such a way against a bomber if he knew the target could strike!"

"I'd blown that bastard out of the air with all I had too," Kessler interjected.

"And cost your entire squadron?" Ryson shot back.

Kessler was about to retort when Gorik laughed aloud. "No worries gentlemen. Our friend won't even make it to the U.S., let alone cause us any problems."

"Captain McDermott would beg to differ," Ryson said firmly

A grin broke across Gorik's face. "Why don't we ask the captain of his stance?" Ryson's eyes widened. "And just *how*?"

"Simple," Gorik said as he activated the transceiver switch. "We'll call him."

ABOARD THE SUPERCOIL

A sole crimson indictor light blinked innocuously among the cockpits array of instruments. To McDermott, it stood out like a lighthouse beacon as it heralded an encrypted communication request from Tanaris, from Gorik no doubt.

The signal was received from an overhead satellite with replies projected back into space on a tight beam. This severely reduced the interception chance by any ground or aerial units, so being detected during communication didn't worry him.

McDermott felt a deep satisfaction in letting Gorik know that his cherished plane had been abruptly taken—just as his own beloved wife had been taken from McDermott. He flipped open the channel. "Your commando boys failed," he said.

There was no reply for a few seconds, though faint murmurs could be heard in the background. Gorik's voice finally came through.

"Jack, I know how you must feel," the colonel said in an obvious effort to sound compassionate. "But stealing a prized plane to attack NORAD or civilian airlines with it isn't the way to go."

"I see the good lieutenant has lived to fill you in on the details of my plan."

"He is right here. Now do us all a favor, and help yourself survive, too."

"Survive so I can go on being your tool?!" McDermott felt a surge of vengeful intentions rise to the surface, and he wished he could somehow reach into the radio and choke the life out of the man on the other end.

"Perhaps a suitable arrangement can be made?" Gorik asked.

McDermott laughed bitterly. "And what would that be?"

"Anything you want Jack. Money, security, you name it. Just land that plane safely somewhere and walk away."

"All that you're offering, I already have. Or don't want or need."

"Then what do you want from me?"

"To turn yourself in, then leave Tanaris. Maybe then I won't hunt you down."

"Jack, be reasonable. That won't solve anything or bring back anyone you've lost. It will only force me to destroy the SuperCOIL before you reach NORAD."

"Enough with the cheap talk," McDermott said. "It's me and you now, Gorik. Come get your precious plane if you can find me. I'll kill everyone who stands in my way, just like you killed my squadron in Iraq, when they stood in yours," he said, furiously switching off.

TANARIS

The transmission ended abruptly. "McDermott is blaming me for all his life's failures, and now he's insanely making others pay for that," Gorik commented.

Ryson nodded, though he agreed only with the latter part of Gorik's observation. A pity, Ryson thought, for such a brilliant pilot to have crossed that fine line between genius and madness. Or had he really? The captain had been a deep enigma from the start.

An aide briskly walked into the room. "Sir, we have the plane's location!" the young officer announced with a rush of excitement.

"Excellent," Gorik replied. He turned to face a befuddled Ryson.

"We had programmed the SuperCOIL's GPS system to transmit the plane's location automatically while the encrypted channel he used is activated," he explained. "It's a little secret we'd kept from our taunting pilot friend."

"Even so, it's just not a worry to him," Ryson said.

Gorik gave him a puzzled look.

"By the time he comes out of all that cloud cover, he'll be thousands of miles away from where you last tracked him."

"Let's just say that the plane has an even bigger secret of which our friend is also unaware," Gorik said. "A secret deadly only to him." He turned to the aide. "Make sure my conference room is primed for our call, with McCane present."

"Yes sir," the officer replied before rushing off.

"Whom are we talking to?" Ryson asked Gorik.

"The president."

ABOARD THE SUPERCOIL

McDermott felt a sense of betrayal, an unsettling premonition that set in soon after he had switched off the transceiver. The disturbing feeling reinforced his uneasiness about the SuperCOIL's Global Positioning Satellite system, an addition to the old-fashioned but trusty Astro-Inertial Unit, first developed in the early 1960s for the avant-garde Blackbird.

Unlike GPS, which obtains its location from data provided by an orbiting satellite, the optically based AIU had a computer-controlled tracking telescope which locked onto the astral maps of the heavens, which were then matched against the stars' pre-selected position stored in a database. Remarkably accurate, AIU was fully passive, with no telltale transmissions. The SuperCOIL's AIU was on the cockpit's portside, with its glass cover made flush with the plane's hide to minimize radar reflectivity.

Regardless, McDermott was unfazed by Gorik's threats, as he had long ago ceased caring whether he lived or died. To him, the black plane might as well have been a flying hearse carrying him to his beloved.

As such, he could not help but feel as if being borne on the mighty shoulders of Anubis, the jackal-headed ancient Egyptian god who led the dead to the halls of Maat, their place of judgment. And before that higher judgment he would stand, without any compunction or plea of clemency for what he had recently done or was about to do. For whatever the verdict, it could doom him to no worse an existence than his current torments. He was prepared to face that afterlife, but not before he avenged his loved ones. It wouldn't be long before Colonel Gorik, too, would face that same moment of judgment, and for far worse deeds.

SITUATION ROOM, THE WHITE HOUSE

General Norton walked briskly down the basement hallway of the West Wing, en route to the Situation Room. He was three minutes late already thanks to the unpredictable D.C. traffic, as he now made his way past numerous stately portraits in the ornate corridor.

Arriving at the Situation Room's reception area, he followed the time-honored security protocol of depositing all his wireless communication devices, including his cell phone, into a lead-lined cabinet designed to prevent signal transmissions from the devices in case they were bugged.

Inside the Situation Room he found a seated president and Secretary of Defense engaged in conversation. Both men wore grave expressions on their faces, especially the president, who motioned him to sit down.

The Air Force general sat near the end of the large mahogany table then pulled out a set of documents from his briefcase. "Wonder what our wily colonel is going to say this time," he remarked.

"Seems Gorik will recommend Operation Gold," the president somberly stated. Norton's jaw dropped slightly. "That would be insane!"

"Normally yes," the president said. "But evidently we are also dealing with an equally insane pilot. Either way, Gorik better have a convincing argument."

An incoming call came from Tanaris.

The president nodded and then Fleisler picked up.

The image of Tanaris's main conference room appeared on the large display screen. Norton stared at a quad of McCane, Kessler, Ryson, and Gorik seated at a massive horseshoe table in a mostly dark room that was only directionally illuminated so that the colonel's imposing figure stood out even more prominently. Norton felt like he was gazing at an elaborate TV studio set.

"Mr. President, we have a situation," Gorik began. A wave of anxiety uncharacteristically appeared on his face.

"Indeed," the president said impatiently. "What are the recent developments?"

"Thirty minutes ago, we contacted McDermott," Gorik explained his GPS ruse.

"And what happened?" Fleisler inquired.

"He seemed quite unhinged and only confirmed the lieutenant's initial report that he is to attack NORAD, and civilian airliners in the vicinity of Denver International Airport."

"You believe he would actually go through with it?" Norton questioned.

"No doubt. If his merciless decimation of my F-18 squadron is any indication."

Ryson cast a dubious look in Gorik's direction but kept his silence.

"What is he after?" the president asked.

"Revenge. He seems to somehow blame the Air Force for both the loss of his squadron during the Operation Desert Storm and, later, his wife by a drug cartel."

"That makes no sense!" Norton snorted.

"I understand, General," Gorik replied. "But a deranged mind cannot be reasoned with. All we can hope for now is to stop him at all costs."

"I would like to know," Norton said angrily, "why you assigned such a 'deranged mind' to pilot that plane in the first place?"

"Gentlemen," the president interrupted. He contemplated the circumstances a moment before glancing around the room. "Right now our top priority is to contain this crisis, so let's focus on that. Colonel, what's your assessment of the pilot's approach to either target area?"

Gorik worked the controls to project a digital map onto the screen. It covered North America and large parts of the Atlantic Ocean. A red dot appeared over Azores and then moved in a southwesterly direction while tracing a solid slightly-arched line behind it. It stopped at a point some two thousand miles east of Miami.

"The red streak shows the conjectured path of the plane in the huge Atlantic cloud covering that reaches the Florida's tip," Gorik continued. "We can safely assume this path because it offers McDermott greatest protection from visual sightings, which during the day is his aircraft's main vulnerability."

Gorik traced a dotted line on the map to illustrate a trajectory to the Florida Keys. "He won't risk traveling directly over Florida or south over Cuban airspace. Once over the Gulf of Mexico, however, he will have lost the protection of the clouds, so I believe he'll try to stay over that body of water and make land somewhere between New Orleans and Houston."

Gorik briefly paused to let the information sink in for the listeners. "His path from there to NORAD could bring him over Dallas, Oklahoma City, or in an alternate route, Houston. Either way, he could end up over Albuquerque or Santa Fe. The opportunity to down civilian passenger planes could kill hundreds, or even thousands, of innocent people."

"What if we send a few dozen intercept squadrons when he attempts to go feet dry?" Norton asked.

"It could still be difficult to spot his plane," Gorik said. "Especially with a pilot skilled at evasion, who can now shoot down more fighters than we can timely amass in any location to stop him, and it won't go unnoticed by the press."

"What do you propose we do?" Fleisler asked.

"Activate Operation Gold while we still can," Gorik said, mainly addressing the president, the only person who could authorize it.

A moment of silence followed as all eyes turned to the commander in chief.

"There's got to be another way," the president said, leaning forward as he pressed his fingers against his temples.

"No sir," Gorik said emphatically. "All other alternatives would be too horrific to even contemplate."

"But I find it hard to believe McDermott would do this."

"It's the truth, Mr. President. This is not a rash decision on his part. That man has meticulously planned this for years. He even allied himself with rogue Russian ex-military personnel and betrayed them, too, in the end. In the process, he has caused the death of my tanker crew, commandos, and a half-dozen F-18 pilots, all in cold blood. We can't reason with him in the limited time we have left."

The president nodded with dismay. He looked around the Situation Room, only to see so many empty seats normally occupied by the war-staff—military advisors made absent in this decision due to its black-classified nature. He would have liked their moral support, as he was simultaneously skeptical of and swayed by Gorik.

"Lieutenant," he addressed Ryson. "You interacted with McDermott in Azores, do you believe his mindset is to carry out this threat, so to justify our implementing of Operation Gold"?

Ryson took a deep breath and then looked the commander in chief in the eye. "Mr. President, with all due respect, I cannot answer that question unless I know what Gold is."

Norton looked at the president, who gave him a go-ahead nod.

"Lieutenant, do you know of WT-100 Units?" the general asked.

"No sir."

"It's the code name for a top-secret tactical nuclear weapon, the size of a small briefcase, with a kilo-ton level yield developed specifically for this task. It doesn't have an ICBM's multimegaton warheads that can wipe out entire cities but can still evaporate a few city blocks."

"And you want to use it to destroy the SuperCOIL while it's in flight?"

"Yes."

Ryson frowned thoughtfully. The concept was unorthodox but hardly novel. In fact, as far back as the 1960s, entire nuclear-tipped surface-to-air missile defense systems had been deployed, premised on that a nuclear blast high in the atmosphere could destroy scores of invading Soviet aerial formations. But that strategy's effectiveness hinged on using large tonnage devices, and the knowledge of the enemy's exact whereabouts via radar.

"How do you plan to accurately deliver such a limited yield device when we don't even know where exactly that plane is?" Ryson asked.

"We don't need to do that, son," Fleisler said.

"And why not?"

"Because the device is already on board the aircraft."

ABOARD THE SUPERCOIL

McDermott knew at that very moment, in a faraway location, a great debate regarding defensive options against him were being feverishly weighed, particularly on his indicated target.

The NORAD facility, originally buried deep within Cheyenne Mountain, bordering Colorado Springs, was once the vibrant nerve center of Cold War vigilance. Built in 1961, the underground command center was a virtual garrison fortress burrowed beneath 2,400 feet of solid granite and shielded behind 25-ton nuclear-proofed metallic doors. From this impregnable center, ICBMs could be launched, bombers made airborne, and Armageddon unleashed at any confirmed signs of a Soviet preemptive strike.

But with the fall of the USSR, the costly tunnel complex, with $250 million annual operations cost, was set to a standby mode, and essential functions were migrated ten miles out to the open spaces of Peterson Air Force Base.

McDermott had no doubt that the president knew quite well that everything of consequence in NORAD now lay wretchedly exposed to an attack by a plane that could approach it undetected—a plane he now piloted toward its destiny.

SITUATION ROOM

The president intently observed Ryson's shocked face on the wall-mounted screen.

This was not the first time that a top-secret plane had slipped out of the U.S. government's hands. The first ever downing of a U-2 spy plane was by the Soviets on May 1, 1960, when its pilot, Francis Gary Powers, flew a reconnaissance mission over the Sverdlovsk military installation in central Russia.

Soaring to over 70,000 feet on a 103-foot wingspan - above the reach of the Soviets' contemporary interceptor aircraft and missiles- the avant-garde U2 was equipped with state-of-the-art cameras that for five years captured with impunity otherwise unobtainable images of military complexes behind the Iron Curtain.

All that changed, however, on that fateful morning when Colonel Powers' plane was met with a barrage of the Soviets' new SA-2 missiles, one exploding close enough for its shockwaves to destroy the high-flyer's tail fins, forcing Powers to eject to safety. It was the first ever downing of any plane by a SAM.

But in his frenzied efforts to eject, Powers failed to activate the explosives' time-delay fuse to destroy the cameras contents, and most of the plane, all of which were recovered by the Soviets and used as proof of U.S. spying. The U-2 program never fully recovered from the ensuing publicity.

With the U-2 debacle still in mind, incorporating a self-destruct mechanism into the design of the covert F-117 was strongly considered for the Operation Desert Storm in 1991. A loss over enemy territory would have revealed the plane's stealthy design and RAM composition. The self-destruct idea was ultimately rejected in favor of obliterating the remains of any downed craft with friendly fire from the air, but since F-117s were used on the most heavily defended targets, this would expose the later "mop up" fighters to the same intense enemy fire.

In the end, the F-117's overwhelming success in the Desert Storm, where not even a single F-117 had been damaged by intense enemy fire, only helped create a myth that stealth technology made planes invincible.

But all that would change, just as it had with the U-2.

The war in Kosovo in mid-1999 marked the first downing of an F-117, via a single shoulder-mounted surface-to-air missile. Even more disturbing was that the wreckage had remained in enemy territory and not been destroyed by friendly fire. Ryson vividly remembered images of civilians celebrating atop large chunks of the F-117's wings with its RAM coating intact. Such images, however downplayed by the NATO allies, secretly resurrected the notion of fitting the stealth craft with self-destruct mechanisms.

While, by the early 2000s, the United States no longer had any serious concerns on an accidental disclosure of primitive F-117-type RAM composition, which it could detect by classified means, the sophisticated one used to coat the SuperCOIL was a revolutionary design virtually impossible to detect even by U.S. radars. It therefore became imperative that if such a plane were to fall into enemy territory, it be obliterated, preferably without leaving a single molecule of RAM intact. And the only device capable of assuring such total annihilation was a small nuclear charge. Its blast would efficiently vaporize all traces of the plane and its coveted overlay with minimal collateral damage. Even in a worst-case scenario—say, a crash within an enemy city—the blast would level no more than a few city blocks.

Ultimately, the previous president had agreed to the idea, knowing the 'last resort' final decision on a GO command would rest solely with him. This came straight out of the Doctrine for Joint Nuclear Operations, stating "the decision to employ nuclear weapons at any level requires explicit orders from the president."

"Well, Lieutenant?" Norton said.

Ryson waved his hand while he decided what to report. Rubbing the fresh strangulation bruises on his neck, he recalled McDermott's hand tightening around his throat in a murderous rage. In the end, it came down to weighing the consequences of action versus those of inaction. Absent more evidence, giving McDermott the benefit of doubt could be tantamount to gambling with innocent civilian lives. He had lost his fiancée to inaction and felt a miscue now could make him responsible for deaths of thousands more, an unbearable prospect.

It was settled then.

Ryson's lips parted as he caught sight of the tense expression on the president's face. "It's more likely than not that McDermott would carry out his threats," he said cautiously.

The president audibly sighed. He couldn't entirely trust Gorik, but under the circumstances, he now felt he had no choice.

"This is definitely the most opportune moment for such action," Gorik pressed.

"How so?" a weary president asked, eyeing the video-conference monitor.

"The cloud envelope in which the SuperCOIL is hiding," the colonel said, pointing to the map, "would virtually limit the radioactive fallout to a small area, to be absorbed by the surrounding moisture and later deposited harmlessly back into the ocean in the form of rain. In addition, the SuperCOIL's route is far from those taken by any commercial passenger or cargo planes whose electronic systems could otherwise be rendered inoperative by the blast's ensuing powerful EMP."

Gorik paused for effect. Against a backdrop of countless achievement plaques and insignias, his imposing figure seemed larger than life when viewed from across the screen, making it harder not to heed his words.

"Finally," he continued, "the clouds will obscure visual sightings of the blast's source." Gorik gazed into the video cam. "Which ensures continued secrecy."

The President remained contemplatively silent, his chin in his hand.

Like a shark sensing the blood of wounded prey, Gorik seized the moment to drive home his point. "If we forego this opportunity now, we could be faced with no alternative but to resort to the same later, over U.S. soil, most likely in populated areas on McDermott's flight path."

"Why don't we ground all air traffic in the area?" Norton asked. "He'll have nothing to shoot at then."

"Doing so only forces him to seek targets elsewhere," Gorik explained, "with most of the U.S. within his flight range. We can't afford to ground the whole country and have a nationwide panic set in, especially because of a home-grown threat. It'll be political suicide."

The president had slipped into a gloomy silence.

"Mr. President," Gorik continued, "perhaps by sheer serendipity, we have come to know his proximate whereabouts—a safe location for our purpose, I might add. We may never be afforded this chance again."

The president glanced around the room and then looked at Gorik again. "Proceed with Operation Gold," he said, his tone resigned.

TANARIS

"About damn time he gave in!" Gorik said as soon as the screen switched off. "Let's kill this bastard once and for all."

"But why destroy the SuperCOIL?" McCane asked, who like Ryson, had not bought into Gorik's sophistries to the president.

Gorik ignored the general as he had a video feed piped in, of a communication officer located at Tanaris. "Stand by for the nuclear Go command."

"Yes sir," the officer replied sternly.

Ten seconds passed. The colonel managed to avoid eye contact with the others.

"Nuclear Go command received," the officer added a moment later. "Satellite uplink established. Awaiting transmission go ahead, sir."

Gorik smiled at a perplexed McCane, then sneered triumphantly at Ryson. "Commence transmission," he ordered, with an almost feverish anticipation.

Any second now, the radiation display meter would come alive, inundated with the tremendous level of electromagnetic energy emanating from the nuclear blast source. Gorik imagined the event: a blinding explosion resembling a brief false dawn that would violently disrupt the serenity of the blue Atlantic. No creature would be there to see it, save for a vaporized pilot and a few marine life forms that would, no doubt, never see anything else again.

His fantasizing, however, was interrupted by his own vigilant mind. The display had remained placid as ever, as if nothing had happened.

"I said commence transmission!!" he barked at the satellite operator, infuriated by the prospect of being robbed of his fantasy.

But the operator's reply was even more disturbing. "Transmission commenced 14 seconds ago," he said.

"Send another!"

"It's being sent on a fast re-transmit cycle. So far sent more than 1500 times."

"Then why the hell is nothing happening? Confirm the radiation display meters and cross-check their readout with the Atlantic fleet."

The operator once more peered at his console. "All systems are operating within normal parameters," he stated matter-of-factly. "The Atlantic fleet input is also negative. There has been no explosion. Could be a malfunction."

"Impossible!" an irate Gorik shouted. "That system has 100 percent reliability, especially against in-flight malfunctions!"

ABOARD THE SUPERCOIL, MOMENTS EARLIER

The special reception instrument on the main console display blinked, and the recording device registered an incoming signal that was to herald his demise. But Captain McDermott's face only broke into a mild grin, one of wry satisfaction.

The last major uncertainty in his plans had fallen neatly into place. From now on, he controlled his own destiny, which he was now eager to face more than ever, as he powered the SuperCOIL to its maximum speed.

SITUATION ROOM

"You mean that thing is still airborne?!" the president asked, incredulous.

"I'm afraid so, sir," Gorik replied.

Clearly disgusted, the president eyed Norton. "Now what do you recommend?"

"We order the AWACS to start a comprehensive search. There is one airborne already over Florida, and I can get two more over Houston and New Orleans. This should cover the southern sector of the projected path."

"Do it then," the president ordered.

E-3 SENTRY AWACS, THIRTY MILES NORTHEAST OF MIAMI

Captain Dugan received the alarming call through his earpiece. Until then, his Airborne Warning and Control System had been lumbering in a routine aerial exercise, but had picked up mostly commercial aviation signals from Miami.

The radar data were being fed to them by 13 AWACS specialists sitting in what would normally have been the passenger section of a commercial airliner—except this militarized Boeing 707 off-shoot resembled nothing of the sort. The main area had 14 command-and-control consoles designed to perform highly specialized functions for AWACS's main C3 airborne surveillance objectives of command, control, and communication for strategic defense and tactical engagement.

Dugan raised his chief radar operator on the intercom. "A new assignment was sent over the secure line," he said. "It's being fed to your terminal."

A moment later, the radar operator finished scanning the message. "You've got to be kidding me! Is this for real?"

"Appears so. Our asses are on the line here. We can't let anything get through."

Dugan turned to his perplexed co-pilot. "Keep your eyes open, too."

"We have the most powerful airborne radar on the planet riding on top, chief," the co-pilot said, pointing up at the huge 30-foot diameter radome disk mounted atop the fuselage, the signature feature of an AWACS. "Our eyes are always open."

"I meant the ones in your eye sockets. They're better suited for this task."

The co-pilot still appeared perplexed. "Just what kind of a plane, exactly, are we looking for?"

"You'll know it when you see it. If it has no authorization, report it."

The co-pilot nodded, scanning the clear horizon in search of their elusive prey.

SITUATION ROOM

"The additional AWACS are being deployed Mr. President," Norton said. "In 20 minutes, we should have the Florida and Gulf coastlines completely covered."

The president, however, had his doubts.

"We are better off tracking him from the ground," Ryson said from across the view-screen.

All faces suddenly turned to him. "And with what?" McCane asked impatiently.

"Our radars, of course."

"But that plane is radar-invisible!" Fleisler exclaimed.

"Not really," Ryson replied.

"Lieutenant," the president interjected, "I have personally seen that plane's radar cross-section," referring to the drawn circles used in illustrating how big a plane appears to a searching radar. "It's RCS is a thousand times smaller than a B-52's, like a dot on a paper in comparison. This plane could be standing right in front of the radar and it would not register!"

"Mr. President, reduced RCS of course plays a major role in hampering radar's detection ability," Ryson diplomatically replied, "but contrary to popular belief, this reduction does not linearly translate into radar's inability to detect each plane."

He now encountered a collective blank stare.

"Let me explain," Ryson said. "The RCS circles are not how a radar actually sees a plane, but merely a graphical representation: of a circular cross-section of a hypothetical aluminum sphere with the same pre-determined RCS as that plane.

"Moreover, RCS is only a measure of a plane's radar reflectivity, which is based on a plane's shape and composition, not its actual size. For example, a large B-1B bomber has a much smaller RCS than a MIG-27 fighter."

Ryson typed a few commands on an electronic console, and a mathematical equation was projected onto the main view screen for everyone to see:

$$\text{Radar's reduced range} = (\text{Reduced RCS percentage})^{0.25}$$

"Suppose you tell us more but go easy with the math!" the president stated, eliciting mild, short-lived laughter from the audience.

"Let's say a radar could detect a B-52 at 100 miles out," Ryson continued. "Because the exponent on the equation's right-side is 0.25, reducing a plane's RCS by say a factor of a thousand reduces the radar's range by 82 miles, meaning it can still track the plane when within 18 miles from it, not from a mere 160 yards, which is one thousandth of its original range. Thus, reducing RCS by a thousand does not reduce a radar's range by a thousand."

"Only reduced by 82 miles?" the president asked.

"Yes sir," Ryson replied, "but it is ample space for a B-2 bomber with a wingspan of only 172 feet to fly through. Allow me to demonstrate."

Ryson switched the image to a computer-generated electronic map of a simulated battle space. It displayed a rectangle marked as "target," and secondary set of points denoted as SAM, the launch sites of surface-to-air missiles protecting the target. For each SAM site, a set of concentric circles appeared, the outer circles of each overlapping those of other SAM sites; when combined, the sites nearly covered the entire display area.

"A SAM site uses a number of radars with different ranges and frequencies for tracking an aircraft at different distances," continued Ryson, as he had a moving boomerang-shaped plane appeared in the lower right-hand corner.

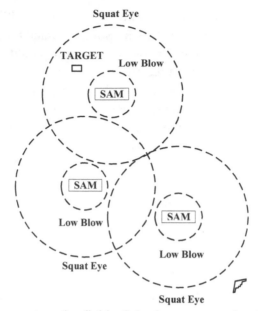

"When an airplane enters the field of the longer-ranged radar, such as Squat Eye, shown here by the outermost circle, it's automatically detected by that radar, locked onto by its SAM missile, and marked for destruction when it comes within range of the inner circle radars, such as Low-Blow. The diagram here is the range of each of these radars for a conventional airplane, such as an F-16 or a B-52.

"But stealth blunts the detection ability of SAM's longer-range radars."

Ryson switched the display to a stealth screen. Suddenly, the SAM sites' coverage field was drastically reduced in area to a set of non-overlapping circles.

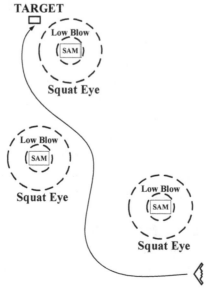

The SAM sites now resembled sporadic scattered blots, as tiny islands strewn in a vast sea of unprotected airspace through which a stealth craft could sail undetected to its target, but only while using the right navigational path.

"A plane's reduced RCS in effect makes the ground radars near-sighted but not totally blind. It turns a blanket coverage area into a minefield, so still a threat."

"Only if a stealth plane flies too close to those radars," Norton observed.

"Exactly," Gorik added. "Which is why it's imperative to know these enemy radar locations in advance, with our intelligence gathering tools like satellites and ground operatives."

"Has any stealth aircraft been destroyed this way?" the president inquired.

"Yes sir," Gorik replied. "In 1999 an F-117 was shot down over Serbia during the NATO war there. A shrewd commander named Dani Zoltan managed to predict our daily flight paths, which had become far too routine, and placed a SAM unit on one of those paths, then shot it down. It was still a bit of luck, if you ask me—but it did happen."

"I assume McDermott knows of all our radar sites?" the president remarked.

"That's correct, sir. The SuperCOIL was on its maiden combat simulation flight to sneak back to Tanaris undetected. Its Data Transfer Module database was programmed with the comprehensive list of all our military radars from Florida coasts to Tanaris, just as it would with an enemy terrain in real combat."

"Christ!" Fleisler exclaimed. "The man is clever, all right. He waited till we handed him our defense plans on a silver platter."

"As if he needed our help," the president said curtly.

Ryson knew the president was alluding to a deeply disturbing issue: the virtual absence of any anti-stealth measures in the defensive arsenal of a Superpower.

With the demise of the Soviet Union, many U.S. leaders assumed that the U.S. would remain the sole designer of stealth technology for decades to come. As a result, no effective stealth countermeasures had been developed. In fact, such countermeasures were secretly banned, for a simple reason: not only they proved even harder to develop than stealth itself, but they could also serve only to jeopardize U.S. interests should the technology fall into the wrong hands.

Well over half a century earlier, that same mindset had ushered in the dawn of the nuclear weapons age, which had placed humanity perilously close to extinction. Perhaps the idea of an ultimate weapon can never die.

"We can change those plans, in ways he wouldn't expect," Gorik suggested.

"It's a long shot still," Norton said. "The radar site must be almost underneath the B-2 for this to work."

"Yes, if the same transmitting radar is to detect the plane. But there is another way," Ryson offered.

"Another way?" the president asked.

"Yes sir. It's a simple matter of detecting energy dumping," Ryson said. "You see, most radar energy isn't absorbed by the plane's stealth design. It's simply redirected, i.e. dumped, elsewhere, away from the transmitting radar source. We need to use another set of eyes to track this dumped energy to find the plane."

"Sounds too simple," the president replied. "What's the big catch?"

"The trick is to know where to stand in exact relation to the radar source to provide it with these added sets of eyes. Since the plane's exterior surfaces are our reflective radar mirrors, detection depends on knowing the plane's precise reflective characteristics and geometry. It's not so easy for an adversary to do in practice since most of such information are classified."

"But not classified to us," Gorik remarked.

"Yes, so we can then set up a multi-static net to spot it," Ryson added.

"A multi-what?" Norton asked.

"We deploy mobile radar-receiving stations, each positioned at a precise distance from its transmitter radar. They'll receive the transmitter's radar energy, which is reflected from the B-2, and then alert us," Ryson explained.

"We then direct enough saturated firepower to blast the B-2 out of the sky," Gorik assured.

"So we'll move the mobile units into positions that aren't programmed into the plane's computer with the hope that it will fly over one of the 'mines'?"

"That's basically it, sir. We'll also synchronize the units to extend their range."

"And where should we deploy these—mines?"

Ryson examined the map, taking into account the plane's projected paths and ultimate heading. "Our best bet is along the New Orleans and Houston corridor."

The president turned to Norton. "How long before all of this is in place?"

"Two hours or so, sir," the general replied.

"Then let's get to it!"

ABOARD THE SUPERCOIL

From the cockpit of his radar-invisible plane, McDermott calmly waded his way through the alabaster cloud cover. Concealed from his vision were far more violent worlds, one from which he had so narrowly escaped and the other toward which he so eagerly raced.

The constant trail of white mist that swirled its way about the flight deck's bow windows produced surreal scenery. Now and again, the denser bands would take on uncanny forms that seemed to him as apparitions of loved ones long gone, whose sight induced both joy and grief. Over the years, he had come to feel a strange oneness with this numinous vessel, which at times seduced him into an almost mystical trance.

The thunder of air rushing against the massive wings were as gentle caresses of his wife stroking his hands, the mighty engines output flowing hot as silent fury, and each passing moment bringing him closer to his fate.

TANARIS

General McCane momentarily shut his eyes in anguish. He had felt a splitting headache coming on. But when he glanced at the colonel, the latter appeared to be unexpectedly upbeat.

Gorik noticed McCane's melancholic gaze. "Did someone die?"

"Something did," McCane said sharply. "All of our careers, especially yours!"

Gorik smiled coyly. "Patience is a virtue. It will all work out, in good time."

"Time is precisely what we don't have!"

"On the contrary, we'll have plenty of it once we kill our rogue friend."

McCane looked at the colonel as if he were insane. "Even if you actually destroyed that plane, you've really only shot down your own ticket to glory."

"There's so much you don't understand."

"Perhaps you explain . . ."

"Later. I've got to focus on tracking the SuperCOIL once it enters our airspace."

McCane glared at the colonel but said nothing.

Gorik headed for the far side of the conference room, to a wall-projected defense map which displayed radar sites and fighter bases that could be thrown into battle at a moment's notice. He focused his attention, however, on the resources of the Black Squadron. He considered destroying the SuperCOIL a small price to pay for keeping his command of Tanaris while disposing of McDermott. The latter plan was right on schedule.

By demonstrating the SuperCOIL's capabilities in live combat against the world's best trained pilots in advanced fighter craft, McDermott had unwittingly advanced Gorik's objectives. Gorik had spotted that opportunity early on, and then intentionally sent a selected portion of his men to their deaths. In doing so, he tested the SuperCOIL's combat effectiveness under real battle conditions without having to resort to subpar flying drones or unconvincing computer simulations.

And with all the costly proof-of-concept base research already completed, additional SuperCOILs could be assembled within a year at a fraction of the original's expense. He conjectured that a handful of SuperCOILs could bestow unique preeminence to American global air power. The USAF had not enjoyed such supremacy since the closing days of WWII, and that was achieved mainly through the staggering number of American airplanes produced.

By contrast, only a dozen or so SuperCOILs would achieve the same level of air dominance, thanks to the United States' unique monopoly on laser-stealth hybrid technology. Just a few years earlier, this aspiration had been seen by many top-ranking military figures as an unattainable dream. Whether implemented in bombers or fighters, the advent of airborne lasers would revolutionize air combat. And if Gorik played his cards right, this new air force would be formed under his command. At last he could leave the confines of Tanaris and take his place at the head of the most elite of the Air Force.

Only one man stood in the way of his path to glory—a former prodigy who had uncovered evidence that could expose the colonel's dark side to the world. He would have to be killed, all traces of him erased.

E-3 SENTRY AWACS, SIXTY-FIVE MILES SOUTHEAST OF MIAMI

A mentally exhausted co-pilot suppressed a yawn, then turned to Captain Dugan, whose somber expression was evident even from behind his military issue sunglasses. "Seen anything yet, boss?"

Dugan shot him an annoyed look for the subtle sarcasm. Still, he couldn't really blame his flying partner. They'd been at sentry over four hours now, near the Gulf of Mexico, and seen nothing of consequence—which offered little reassurance considering the looming cloud blanket that blocked out their southern sky.

Equipped with pulse-Doppler scan radars, AWACS' fuselage-mounted circular radar disk, with a center white band painted in a huge 'Do not enter' traffic sign pattern, could scan the skies at an impressive six revolutions per minute, and pick up a small bird from hundreds of miles away. It was the sheer volume of the scanned areas, however, that proved its weakness against stealth.

Back in the White House Situation Room, Ryson had elaborated on why a radar's range did not linearly correspond to the aircraft's RCS size. He had, however omitted mentioning the difficulty in acquiring a target in the first place, a tracking prerequisite. Acquiring such an elusive target was difficult for a rotating ground-based radar dish that, like a lighthouse, could cover only one portion of the sky above at a time with its narrow search beam, but even more difficult for an airborne radar which now had to sweep both above and below the craft. It was like a blind-folded person swinging a bat at a fast-moving fly in an arena the size of a football field. Ryson would have mathematically summarized this situation as follows:

$$\text{Radar's reduced range} = (\text{Reduced RCS percentage})^{0.75}$$

Because the exponent on the equation's right-side is 0.75 for a volume search, rather than 0.25, for tracking, reducing a plane's RCS by say a thousand, now more linearly reduces the aerial radar's range, to 0.006 of its original range. For Dugan, his AWACS' 200 miles radar range would spot a stealth plane only when within 1.2 miles from it. By contrast, human optical spotting could extend to 50 miles at flight altitudes in blue skies. Today, however, the sky was clear only to the north.

The captain had pushed his plane to the edge of the cloud cover but wasn't optimistic. He checked the time and jotted it down on a pad strapped to his left leg. According to his instructions, they would have spotted the plane by now. So he concluded that the plane had either taken another approach or slipped past them hidden inside the cloud cover.

Dismayed, Dugan reached for his headphone and reported his observations through a secure relay to General Norton.

ABOARD THE SUPERCOIL

McDermott applied the elevons and rudders with ease as he steered the deceptively thin bomber on a 15-degree roll southwest. The maneuver was graphically shown on the Multipurpose Display Unit above his right knee.

Unlike the traditionally roomy B-2 flight deck designed for a two-man team of a pilot and mission commander, the one-man SuperCOIL had every space used to accommodate the massive COIL. The cockpit's instruments, however, were almost identical to a B-2, with the exception of the prominently displayed COIL MDU.

McDermott glanced at his watch. During the last four hours he had headed southeasterly and soon would be circumventing Cuba from its underside, to the chagrin of those in the Situation Room. It was a circuitous path but safer now that he was no longer flying within the cloud cover.

The arching path had brought him to the outer rims of the Caribbean islands, providing him one last recollection of time he had spent with his wife. Shortly after, a vast pelagic spectacle came to full view. Miles of breathtaking coastlines appeared below, the expansive but gently undulating ocean shimmering under the sun's warm rays. He knew it from memory.

And yet he saw little of that dazzling beauty now; the cockpit's tinted shielding filtered the life out of the vivid panorama, rendering it a somber gray, mimicking his own mood. Long ago, the notion of beauty had become intimately associated with his beloved wife, and he could no longer bear experiencing it.

Soon he had flown within visual distance of their coastal honeymoon hamlet. But here, too, all looked alien and beyond his reach as he gazed down at the town in wistful longing. The houses that had once made for a romantic backdrop now struck him as lifeless; for to his eyes, love, that quintessential essence of life, had vanished from them. Like fallen bodies they remained, but held no soul.

SITUATION ROOM

"Well, General?" the president asked Norton. The parties on both sides of the view screen had convened again to reassess the situation.

Norton relayed the just received discouraging news from Dugan.

"It's useless then," the president said, shaking his head. "And so are the other two birds flying over Houston and New Orleans. They'll never spot McDermott."

The president had a strange realization that the United States' air defenses were in uncharted waters: they were virtually impenetrable to aerial intrusions, with just one exception—the one that mattered the most now: stealth.

"Where do you think he could be, Lieutenant?" Fleisler asked.

Ryson nervously cleared his throat. "He should have reached the Gulf of Mexico by now. But not sure from which precise entry point."

"Then he no longer has clouds to hide behind!" Norton shouted.

The president nodded. "What have we got to visually sight him?"

Norton quickly scanned the military map. "Outside New Orleans, the 159 Fighter Wing has F-15 squadrons that can be armed to go under 20 min."

Gorik rolled his eyes. The deployment would dangerously straggle the AWACS and F-15 fleets in an over-exposed front in a long-shot hope of a visual sighting. "Sir," he interjected, "the F-15s could suffer the same fate as my Hornets."

"We have no choice," Norton said.

"This operation was designated a Black Squadron project," Gorik reminded.

"Not anymore," Norton fired back. "Our nation's entire airspace is at risk right now. That's a job only the Air Force can handle. My boys were trained for this."

"With all due respect, General, your boys are just that: boys. They can't go up against a plane like the SuperCOIL."

Norton bristled. "Don't forget your team originally came from *my* backyard."

"And I trained them in ways the Air Force never could have!"

"To be scheming bastards, like you?"

"I won't stand for this insolence!" Gorik exclaimed.

"Let's maintain professionalism," the president broke in. "I'll decide this."

Both sides quieted down, and all eyes turned to the commander in chief.

"Under the circumstances," the president said, "I have to agree with General

Norton's assessments. The Air Force will lead this operation. Black Squadron's role will be limited to Tanaris defense, should that need arise. Is that understood?"

"But sir," Gorik began. The president raised a palm to cut him off. "That is an order, Colonel, and not open to debate." He abruptly ended the call, leaving an infuriated Gorik gaping at the darkened screen with his fists clenched.

NAVAL AIR STATION, NEW ORLEANS, LOUISIANA

Captain Preston's F-15 "Eagle" was still ascending from take-off when he received the finalized destination coordinates on the Heads-Up Display. The glowing green digits foretold a three hundred miles flight over the Gulf of Mexico before touching base with a patrolling AWACS for further instructions. At the airbase, Preston was given only a ten-minute briefing on his top-secret assignment involving a possible shooting down of a B-2, as now confirmed by the live ordinance hanging under his sleek fighter's pylons. The Eagle was packed with air-to-air missiles, mostly of the infrared kind, such as the AIM-9 Sidewinder.

Hauling a full complement of firepower, however, decreased airspeed due to the air drag placed on the exposed armaments, so his Eagle would fly subsonic and needed aerial refueling en-route. Already Preston could feel the extra toll on the twin Pratt & Whitney F-100 turbofans, invoking full fuel-guzzling afterburners to compensate for the heavier load.

His lead Eagle, now set for level flight at 2000 ft, was joined in tandem by five armed wingmen. The six F-15s then flew in a synchronized holding pattern over the airbase while Preston obtained the clearance to proceed from the control tower.

"Keep your eyes peeled, your lives will depend on it," Preston addressed his squadron. "Climb up to fourteen thousand feet in formation."

"Yes, sir," each wingman replied.

Preston swung his Eagle over the airstrip in a wide arc, the wingmen in tow. The ascending fighters then banked sharply, briefly exposing their deadly underbellies to the control tower before leveling back in a tight formation and heading thunderously toward the horizon.

TANARIS

"Major, prepare your men for immediate deployment," Gorik ordered sternly.

Kessler nodded and left the conference room.

"You are sending Kessler after him??" McCane said resolutely. "The president was quite clear that it's now exclusively an Air Force matter!"

"I'm still allowed to defend Tanaris," Gorik replied.

"Over the far away Gulf of Mexico?"

"General, I believe the best defense is a good offense, no matter the threat."

"Our last squadron got easily shot down. McDermott will spot these ones too."

"No, he won't. The F-18s are visible to his radar, but not the F-22 Raptors."

McCane's mouth dropped open. "Of course," he said. "F-22s are stealthy too!"

"They thus have same stealth advantage as the SuperCOIL, but nimbler."

"What's your plan?" McCane asked, with sudden renewed interest.

"We'll intercept the SuperCOIL over the Gulf, then send that son of a bitch to a watery grave. No one will know we were even there."

McCane stared at Gorik in amazement. It was a brilliant idea. Nice and clean. Given the vastness of the gulf and the lack of radar sighting of a stealth plane, its wreckage would likely never be found, and the matter would quietly disappear.

"Then let's hope your men can spot that plane."

"It won't be long," Gorik said, glancing at the map.

ABOVE THE ARIZONA DESERT

Major Kessler snapped on his oxygen mask and then increased engine thrust. The sleek Raptor responded by gracefully breaking the sound barrier without the roar of afterburners. It was a feat unrivaled by any existing fighter plane in the world.

Despite logging countless flight hours and mastering this aircraft, Kessler had never ceased to marvel at the F-22's many capabilities. Now more than ever, he was grateful that such a formidable craft had been produced, after all the development pitfalls. Against any other warplane, the F-22 was a clearly superior fighter in almost every respect imaginable. And it now served as the only aircraft that could stop McDermott from completing his malevolent mission.

TANARIS

Ryson took short sips from the piping hot cup poured from Gorik's grommet coffee maker. The rich aroma reminded him of exotic places at where he now rather be.

Playing a distant observer, he had kept quiet on his serious reservations about Gorik's simplistic plan as presented to a gullible McCane. To Ryson, using the F-22s against the SuperCOIL—or fighting stealth with stealth—offered a partial solution at best. The F-22's stealth provided concealment from the SuperCOIL's radar, but they still faced glaring problems in destroying that plane.

Like their conventional fighter siblings, the F-22s had no way of tracking the SuperCOIL from a safe distance. The pilot's only hope for success was to creep close enough to strafe the bomber with machinegun fire, or to shoot a missile directly into the bomber's airfoils, like an oversize bullet. But as the SuperCOIL's vital components were internally installed, a short machine gun burst would do little before the pursuer was blown out of the sky. And a successful hit from visually aiming a missile during flight depended far more on luck than on aviator skill. And all this only if a non-fatal visual contact could be made and maintained.

And in an aerial duel, the unleashed COIL could strike the F-22 nearly instantaneously, but the Raptor's rockets were unable to likewise timely reach the bomber's initial position.

With Gorik's career on the line, the colonel's plan was to compensate for this shortcoming by throwing in four of his precious F-22s at once to overwhelm McDermott. He hoped, out of sheer optimism or desperation, that one fortuitous silver-bullet in their salvos would bring down the infernal craft once and for all.

Ryson knew that Gorik was now beyond reason on the matter; the colonel was chasing a ghost plane piloted by a dead man.

ABOARD THE SUPERCOIL

The LPI radar furtively scanned the horizon and returned no signs of danger, displaying only few commercial airliners at beyond visual range. The SuperCOIL, after heading northwest along the 135-mile Yucatan Channel between Mexican and Cuban coasts, had now entered the open expanse of the Gulf of Mexico, the final body of water to cross before making land in the last leg of his journey.

McDermott wondered how his actions would be viewed. Would he be regarded as a hero or traitor? Odds were that it was a moot point; following the massive cover-up that would ensue, no one would ever know what he had done.

As long as he could carry out his task to its intended end, he could live with that until his final moment arrived.

OVER THE GULF OF MEXICO,
170 MILES NORTHWEST OF HAVANA

The lead Raptor's twin engines barely rumbled as Kessler pushed the F-22 to near its maximum supercruise speed, of Mach 1.54. His squadron had made excellent time in approaching their target area from Arizona. No other fighter plane could have covered such vast distances so quickly, without refueling.

He could easily surpass even Mach 2 if needed, but that would mean use of fuel-guzzling afterburners. Kessler knew the F-22 had not been designed to achieve any records in the world's fastest plane category. But thanks to its supercruise capability it maintained supersonic speeds without resorting to afterburners which consume over a thousand pounds of jet fuel per minute and quickly drain the fuel tank.

In a traditional sustained supersonic flight, the pilot judiciously engages the afterburners for a few seconds to go supersonic, and then again as air drag shortly slows the coasting plane down toward the sonic barrier. Yet the supersonic pace could still not be maintained for long. As such, fighter pilots typically reserve sustained afterburners use for only emergency situations, such as to outmaneuver a SAM or to disengage from a dogfight.

The Raptor, on the other hand, can sustain a constant cruising speed of well over Mach 1 for extended periods, like a marathon runner covering a long distance quicker than a short-distance sprinter. As such, without refueling, the Raptor could average 50% faster over total flight time than any fighter craft since the inception of jet-powered flight.

This astonishing capability was owed to remarkable feats in both aerodynamic design and engine performance. Supersonic air-drag was minimized by making the wings and tail sections thin, light, and swept back, which also had stealth benefits. The sweptback wings, shaped to an expansive trapezoidal "clipped delta", could hold 60% more fuel than a late model F-15C. Large drags from external weapons were also eliminated by adhering to the stealth mandates of carrying missiles internally, such as in the F-22's ventral and sides weapons bays. Finally, to power the aircraft past Mach 1 on just military power, the Raptor was fitted with twin engines each outpouring an impressive 35,000 lbs of thrust, equivalent to the P&W J-58, the world's only Mach-3 designated engine, used on SR-71 "Blackbird".

Although going past Mach 1 would leave a supersonic footprint for the listening ears, it was mostly offset by the F-22's ability to evade and dogfight, a feature lacking in the purposely subsonic F-117 and B-2. The Raptor could also fly subsonic when within range of known acoustic detection devices. And the lack of blazing afterburners would significantly diminish the plane's infrared signature, thus enhancing stealth while flying above the sound barrier.

The confluence of all such features had realized a plane of extended combat radius that achieved high speeds with a full weapons load. It enabled Kessler's trio of Raptors to compress their closure time to intercept McDermott, and to just as swiftly return to base.

A blip suddenly appeared on Kessler's main Tactical Situation Display, which laid out the entire battle environment surrounding the F-22 in a so-called God's-eye view by dividing the airspace into two concentric zones. The blip was quickly joined by five others, representing aircraft in tight formation. He didn't bother to look out of the canopy. The spotted squadron was in the outer zone of the TSD, well beyond visual range and too far out to be an immediate threat. Kessler therefore opted to furtively remain "lights out" by not activating his own radar.

TANARIS

Ryson had barely finished his coffee when the communication equipment crackled to life. It was Kessler. "We have a level five situation."

Gorik turned to Ryson. "You'll have to excuse us now."

Ryson hesitated.

"Get out!"

Humiliated, Ryson stormed out of the conference room. He touched his shirt pocket to make sure the memory stick was still there.

Gorik clicked the microphone back on. "Proceed to engage. No eyes but yours."

"Understood," Kessler said.

Gorik's last words translated to only one course of action in the Black Squadron's lethal playbook.

OVER THE GULF OF MEXICO, 500 MILES SOUTHEAST OF NEW ORLEANS

The fuel gauge read just over three quarters full on the lead F-15's cockpit display, though Captain Preston had mid-air refueled a mere thirty minutes earlier. Hauling all that ordinance under the wings had taken its toll, as he'd expected.

"Flight One, this is Lead Goose," he said. "Come in, please."

"One here," the AWACS controller said over the crackling radio.

"At the designated perimeter point. Request new surveillance coordinates."

"Stand by."

The controller on the other end sounded relaxed, Preston could even hear him sip coffee in between receiving and giving the new vectoring information to the fighters. Then came a final message: "Lead Goose, the new coordinates are beyond our maximum radar coverage range. Scour the designated area, then return to these bearings to re-establish radar contact."

"Affirmative," Preston switched off the transmitter. He knew his squadron would have communication with the AWACS despite being outside its radars' tracking radius.

He set course for the new search zone. The wingmen executed graceful rolls and followed his lead. Before long, with the intermittent use of afterburners for supersonic speeds, the squadron had come within the outer boundaries of their search sector.

Preston activated the powerful radome on the craft's nose, which showed no planes in the area. He decided to radio in his observation. To his surprise, he received only static. After several failed re-attempts, it became clear that his transmissions were being jammed across all communication frequencies.

A combat veteran and survivor of numerous simulations at Red Flag, Preston realized the jammings were conducted using U.S.-made equipment. Strangely, there was a complete lack of accompanying radar-jammings to hide the jamming source from the F-15s powerful radar. So far, his radar had operated unhindered, but unable to track any bogies in a seemingly empty sky.

Perhaps the B-2 was nearby after all. It was the only explanation that made any sense. Preston cautiously looked out the canopy at the deceptively uninterrupted surroundings. He saw that his wingmen were experiencing the same breach of communication. He hand-gestured them to follow him as he maintained his course toward the center of the search zone.

ABOARD THE SUPERCOIL

The radar warning receiver bleeped unexpectedly, then flashed warning icons on the multicolored scope—that tallied to a half-dozen symbols.

McDermott cast a puzzled gaze at the scope, wondering why his AN/APQ-181 Low Probability of Intercept radar had not picked up the bogey ensemble sooner. The LPI was furtive but its high microwave Ku-band operating frequency made it more susceptible to inaccuracies due to atmospheric attenuations.

Still, McDermott was grateful to have this special radar on a B-2, since regular radar blasts detectable radiation. For this reason, the stealthy F-117 had not been fitted with any active radar and relied solely on passive detection mechanisms.

It soon became evident that radar was indispensable to the more advanced B-2, and the dogfighting F-22. A variety of concealment tricks were thus used, such as pulse compression, decreasing the radar pulse's amplitude, widening frequency bandwidths, and reducing radar side-lobes with phased-array radars. These tricks disguised the radar pulse so it would appear as inconspicuous background noise in the cluttered landscape of radio frequencies.

In addition, the LPI radar was made to 'dance' across the frequency spectrum by rapidly hopping from one frequency to the next in a complicated pattern. Since enemy receivers are often set to specific frequency ranges, they're unlikely to detect the LPI radar, or to regard it as a threat—at least not until it's too late.

Implementation of LPI proved exceedingly difficult, requiring multiple antennas and sophisticated signal processing software to analyze the data returned by a beam of irregular shape and constantly-changing frequency patterns. The end result, however, is a stealth craft that can detect and track enemy radar without being betrayed by its own.

McDermott recalled his Air Force days, when he had test flown such fine craft to their envelope's limits. He had never envisioned then that he would one day become their adversary.

In any case, he would soon be out of range of his pursuers. His objective -and vengeance- lay elsewhere. Keeping the COIL at the ready, he increased speed so to exit the engagement zone as rapidly as possible.

APPROACHING THE "BANDITS,"
10 MINUTES EARLIER

The six circular symbols on the Raptor's attack screen were all green, indicating to Kessler a flight of fast closing friendlies. The Common Integrated Processor, the F-22's avionics brain, had received the information from the IFF data sensors, automatically identified the fliers as non-hostile based on their Identify Friend or Foe designation, and popped up a benign indicator icon for each on the attack screen. If the CIP could have read Kessler's murderous intentions, the symbols would have been turned into red triangles, signifying hostile bandits. Kessler's battle assessment interception request from the CIP must have thus confused its logic of over two million programming code lines.

Flying at Mach 1.35, the targets soon entered the inner zone of his Raptor's TSD's display, alerting him to increased Situational Awareness. The CIP had then passed the targets to the attack screen, where two more concentric circular zones further refined the battle space. The closing Eagle squadron quickly broke through the outer zone. Kessler was now given the options of avoiding the F-15s or engaging them before they entered the F-22's innermost zone, where his Raptor would be within their missiles' range. Kessler's trio of fighters had held to a tight formation, climbed to nearly 50,000 feet for a commanding view of the airspace.

It was at this point that Kessler began jamming the long-range communication frequencies so he could not be reported by his prey. Three tense minutes passed before he had the visuals on the six white specs, moving in a V-formation, that appeared on the distant horizon. He could have fired the missiles from fifty miles out, but he preferred the satisfaction of witnessing the carnage with his own eyes.

Kessler reached for the Inter/Intra Flight Data Link to synchronize the impending attack with his wingmen without tell-tale radio calls.

At once, the F-22s' stealthy ventral opened, then closed just seconds later. Inside that fleeting span, a brace of deadly AIM-120 AMRAAMs were jettisoned from each Raptor's internal pylons. Each rocket unfolded its stubby fins before its engine ignited in a blast of fury and accelerating the 335 lbs-missile to Mach 4 in seconds, with its onboard computer locked onto one of the unsuspecting F-15s.

"What the hell?" Captain Preston shouted when the Threat Indicator on his F-15 suddenly came to life.

"AMRAAMs heading our way," his wingman replied.

"I see it Two," Preston said, trying to project calmness to the others. "All birds, take evasive action." That was the only viable course, as they were well within the missiles' "no-escape" range, when fleeing via sheer speed was no longer an option.

Each Eagle broke from the pack on a different heading. Preston, with his wingmen in tow, went "lights out" and gunned the afterburners, climbing to nearly forty thousand feet along a skull-numbing high-g arc while dispensing radar-confusing chaff in their wake. The strategy worked, but barely in time.

"We got bounced," a wingman said of the unexpected attack.

Preston merely nodded.

The threat scope was empty again, and Preston rolled the plane 180 degrees to take a side-view tally of his squadron. He was horrified to see the fiery remnants of two Eagles falling into the waters below in smoldering masses of twisted metal. No parachutes floated below.

He spotted the surviving F-15s high above the crash sites. They were at his three and nine o'clock, each having lost a wingman to the sneak attack.

Some twenty miles aft, Kessler saw that his stealthy F-22s had flawlessly brought to the adversary an ambush, the optimal form of air-to-air engagement for achieving the coveted first look, first shot, first kill. But he had succeeded only in two confirmed kills by the trusty AMRAAMs. The squadron lead might have also been hit, but so far, he'd spotted no falling wreckage. The battle clamor had failed to register any such details on his radar.

All things considered, the AMRAAMs had done quite well, and the Raptors had revealed only one trick in their bag of many. A veteran dogfighter, Kessler cherished the thought, like a general waiting to send in the cavalry.

"Two and Three," he commanded over the IFDL. "We got us a mop-up job."

Each wingman replied by opening throttles to full, towards one of the low-flying Eagles. Kessler fell behind to monitor the battlefield, scan the skies for the remaining two Eagles, and continue the jamming while maintaining his front row seat to the next round in the aerial contest.

Flying at 20,000 feet, a rather startled Eagle wingman Andrew was trying to make sense of the sneak attack that had left his buddy buried at sea, when he spotted a fighter aircraft coming his way at four o'clock. It bore no radar signature on his scope, but the twin canted tails and diamond side air-intakes unmistakably identified it as an F-22 Raptor. The pilot breathed a sigh of relief, knowing that only the United States operated these craft. The plane must have arrived to provide additional air support against the elusive attackers.

"Captain," he raised Preston. "Spotting a friendly reinforcement on my four."

From high above, Preston gazed at the top profile of the F-22 with its sharply angled outline, and for a second, concurred with his wingman. But then he visually gauged its speed. It was too fast to be anything, but an attack run of a pilot hot for a dogfight, and he immediately recalled his deductions that the missiles must have been launched from a stealth aircraft. A second F-22 heading toward the other wingmen displayed the same aggressiveness.

"Watch out!" he shouted at both wingmen. "These guys are fangs out!"

"Roger that," Andrew affirmed, his optimism nearly depleted, then making a hard right in preparation for the coming onslaught.

Looking down from 45,000 feet, Preston had full view of the madness below, including two American planes shot down by their own. He made a quick visual survey of the horizon and spotted a lone Raptor some 25 miles out.

"Two," he said to the closest wingmen. "You got that bogey padlocked?"

"Sure do. Friend or foe? Not getting any IFFs."

"It's another F-22. Gotta be the squadron leader coordinating the attacks that are jamming our Mayday."

"You think he's seen us?"

"Probably not. The sun's directly behind us, must be blinding him." It was a fair assumption considering the Eagles' grayish-white color.

Preston's cockpit instruments showed that they were still twenty miles out from the bogey, and the angles read perfectly. Exactly as he had hoped.

"Let's pump-bracket that son of a bitch. Are you with me?"

"Yes sir," the wingman replied eagerly.

A bracket would trap the bandit craft between the two Eagles—a lethal position for the bandit—and in a pump, the wingman would serve as a decoy, giving Preston a clear shot at the F-22 while it pursued the decoy.

Flying in tandem, the two Eagles went to full military power and then broke formation as Preston soared in a wide arc away from the Raptor.

•

ABOARD THE SUPERCOIL,
MOMENTS EARLIER

McDermott peered curiously at his radar screen, which had continued tracking the F-15s as the SuperCOIL's plotted course steadily distanced the craft from their position. It wasn't the threat of displayed danger that now preoccupied him, but the presence of unseen evil.

The F-15 Eagles, which had followed a tight, orderly formation until minutes earlier, were now exhibiting a flight pattern akin to a gaggle of lost seagulls. Each craft had abruptly broken off from the pack, accelerated, and engaged in erratic evasive maneuvers to avoid invisible assailants, as if chased by ghosts. McDermott found no indication of attackers on his radar scope. The F-15s appeared to be putting on an air show with no spectators present.

Suddenly, two planes' radar signature expanded, each ripped into divergent trajectories of pieces descending to the waters below. A pair of missiles had popped up on his scope, as if out of nowhere, without any displayed launch planes, and connected to the ill-fated Eagles.

McDermott's gut tightened at the abrupt realization of what was transpiring. Pulling furiously on the HOTAS, he readjusted the plane's massive elevons so that they would shift toward an easterly course while he increased the engine thrust to full throttle. He then set the COIL's fire power to its maximum level.

ENGAGING THE "BANDITS"

From his F-22's gold-tinted cockpit, Kessler noticed with some surprise that a lone F-15 was coming at him full sail. It was one of the two lead Eagles that had disappeared from view. He assumed that the other had been destroyed, as he set his sights on this one.

A glimpse at his defense screen to the right of the TSD indicated that he was already within "normal" range of the Eagle's missiles, but he knew that the F-22's stealth and low IR signatures in effect drastically shrank the missiles' engagement envelope. He activated his own weapons systems, altered his course slightly, and set his predatory sight on the approaching F-15.

Flying unnoticed to the far left, Preston saw the F-22's rightward roll at his wingman as a sign that their bracket maneuver ruse had worked. Soon the wingman, acting as bait, would go into a tight change of heading and execute a high-G 180-degree "bat-turn," offering the pursuer the favorable position of shooting at his tail. Before the F-22 would be in range of the wingman, however,

Preston would furtively converge on the unwary Raptor from the left in a flanking movement that would position him for firing at the F-22. Preston was confident in the ability of his men and their aircraft, after years of flying the Eagle.

The death of his wingmen weighed heavily on his conscious, and the desire for revenge coursing in his veins threatened to overtake his rigidly disciplined combat training. He was also fueled by his resolve to add some F-22s to the tally of Eagles' exploits and, if nothing else, to deflate the hype about the Raptor's air superiority.

Maneuvering at the other end of the aerial bracket, Preston's forward wingman was too preoccupied to share in his captain's reveries. After observing the Raptor's swift change in course to intercept, he was now trying to predict its future trajectory. There were no radar locks on the Raptor, but with the two fighters on approaching head-on, which closed the interim distances at over Mach 2, he could not wait much longer. He marked an empty perimeter in the sky, which he judged the Raptor would be entering shortly, and fired an AMRAAM missile at its center.

The half-million-dollar projectile detached from the right-wing pylon and streaked across the sky, without a target lock. The wingman hoped it would acquire one at a closer range. The F-22 pilot, however, saw the approaching white-plumed rocket almost as soon as it launched from the Eagle. He rolled slightly to the left, easily side-stepping a fatal rendezvous with the blindly guided threat. The radar-homing missile never registered the stealth plane and sailed away to waste. The no-guidance launch, however, had served its main purpose of antagonizing the F-22 bogey into focusing exclusively on the wingman, evident by the Raptor's increased velocity in its journey toward the prey.

With his escape window quickly closing, the wingman concluded it was time to exit as quickly as possible. He broke left in a hard turn, momentarily reducing his speed to under 400 knots to minimize his turn radius until he had its tail completely at the Raptor, and then he blasted the blowers for three full seconds to go supersonic. As the Mach meter surpassed 1.2, the fleeing wingman hoped Preston would come through on his end, and soon.

Kessler kept an intent eye on the attack screen, which displayed the rapidly shrinking gap with his prey. His super-cruise, now set to its maximum, gave the F-22 a 0.3 Mach speed advantage over the Eagle. Sluggish from the supersonic drag from its external weapons and getting low on fuel, the F-15 could not keep up its afterburner for long and seemed to be pulled into the Raptor's weapons envelope.

In less than ninety seconds, the Eagle had fallen within range of the Raptor's AIM-9 Sidewinder. Kessler depressed the *firing* button to launch the heat-seeker missiles, which were housed internally but not in the ventral bay with AMRAAMs. The F-22 was fitted with two non-protruding side bays. The left bay opened and the specially made launch adapt unit LAU-141/A trapeze launcher railed out the Sidewinder into the airflow to allow for the missile's super-cooled sensor tip to obtain an infrared lock on the target, before the pylon jettisoned it at the Eagle, all in under two seconds. On cue, the F-15 leapt forward on full afterburners, its pilot no doubt getting an earful from the missile-warning blaring in his helmet.

To escape the pursuing projectile, the Eagle then vectored up in a steep and frantic climb toward the hot sun, which masked the plane's IR signature from the heat-seeker missile, before turning the nose down, and diving.

Inside the Eagle, the wingman breathed a sigh of relief over averting impact. He then checked his rear view just in time to see Preston's lead F-15 swerving to get into position behind the F-22.

Preston swung his F-15 toward the lopsided dogfight, but suddenly realized he had under-estimated the speed of his enemy. Recognizing the urgency of the situation, he gunned the afterburners and tried to make up for lost ground, acutely aware that the life of his wingman hung in the balance.

The defense screen suddenly alerted Kessler to the presence of a second aircraft, yet he remained focused on the pursued Eagle, which had managed to dodge the missile with vertical maneuvers. But in doing so, the Eagle had also lost horizontal speed, allowing the Raptor to creep even closer.

Kessler patiently marked the moment for the Eagle to level out of its dive and lose the sun's backing before unleashing a second AIM-9. The F-15 initiated another hasty evasive maneuver, but this time its engine nozzle, glowing red-hot from recent overuse of the afterburners, presented an even bigger IR signature to the AIM-9's heat detector. Before the pilot had time to eject, the missile sailed unhindered into the Eagle's tail pipe, the ensuing explosion reducing the fighter to glowing debris that fell toward the sea.

A stunned Preston was amazed at how quickly the battle had concluded for the Raptor pilot. He now desperately sought to repay the rogue pilot whose pursuit of the wingman had allowed Preston to swerve behind his F-22. The plane's scope had no radar read on the target, and the IR scope was ineffective due to no afterburner usage by the super-cruising aircraft. Going by the weakest of heat signatures, presumably in the Raptor's wake, he let loose a brace of Sidewinders, expecting the missiles to enter the Raptor's cone of vulnerability to acquire a lock.

It never happened.

The F-22, sensing the launch, merely shifted course again. All IR traces were swiftly lost to both Preston and his missiles.

Having made short work of the wingman, Kessler now aimed his attention on the lead F-15 fast approaching on full afterburners toward his 'elbow' position. But the surviving lead Eagle had arrived too late to effectively play his part in the bracket game. With the pursuer still nearly three miles back, well outside its effective gun range, Kessler executed a break. He veered sideways by manipulating the rudders, safely crossing the sky in front of the Eagle.

Feeling foiled, Preston quickly countered by turning with the Raptor. His Eagle, however, was unable to muster as snug a turn, and the high speed caused him to overshoot. He swiftly corrected his velocity and re-inserted himself back into the chase, though too late for a good attack position. The two adversaries thus began circling in a giant aerial loop in level flight, each seeking to position behind the other so to launch his weapons.

As a veteran fighter, Preston knew that all dogfights came down to achieving a simple goal: for the attacker to have the plane's nose pointed at the prey, either head-on, sideways, or—most preferably the backside—at his six o'clock. But it became quickly apparent to Preston that their current looping setup favored the much faster turning F-22, as it kept darting out of his HUD's frame.

With rising frustration, Preston realized he needed more speed, but lacking added engine thrust, his only recourse was to trade in altitude by rolling to a dive in a classic low-Yo-Yo maneuver. The Chinese-pilot namesake stratagem was fairly straightforward: the circling aircraft were akin to two marbles swirling along a bowl's rim. Preston would simply cut directly across by rolling his "marble" into the bowl in a down-up roller-coaster fashion, gaining the needed speed in the descend. He would then pull up and arrive at the rim's far side, right behind the still-circling Raptor, for a clean underside kill.

Not wasting any more precious time, Preston quickly rolled the F-15 to inside of the turn, dipped the nose under the horizon line, and began a sharp descent. The aquamarine Gulf rushed at him between his glances at the speedometer and altimeter, whose dials were quickly heading in opposite directions. As soon as the necessary velocity was reached, he pulled out of the dive in a precisely timed manner. He expected to emerge right on track to intercept the Raptor.

That's not what happened.

In seeing the F-15's dive, Kessler had held his course until the Eagle began its ascent. Preston had anticipated such a move but reckoned he would be safely inside the Raptor's turn circle before the F-22 could complete it. It was a reasonable assumption with any other pursued plane.

To Preston's disbelief, the Raptor invoked the afterburners for a brief second. Its twin narrow exhaust ports suddenly lit up, spewing flames like a demon's eyes.

It then swiftly inverted, the vectoring thrust louvers readjusted the jet plume by their full 40-degrees range, and the F-22 virtually pivoted in midair in an impossibly tight vertical turn that brought it barreling down on the climbing Eagle. The hunter swiftly became the hunted, as a bewildered Preston looked up through the canopy to the sight of the lethal bird of prey swooping at him from above.

On his HOTAS, Kessler flipped on the Vulcan Gatling gun switch. The Raptor's muzzles flashed with merciless fury, sending two-dozen rounds of 20mm bullets smashing through the Eagle's plexi-glass canopy, instantly killing Preston. The nearly decapitated F-15 quickly spiraled toward the Gulf, trailing a rotary plume of fire and acrid smoke in its terminal descent.

ABOARD THE SUPERCOIL

The radar scope now only registered one fighter, an F-15 Eagle still in evasive flight from unseen menace. But McDermott had come close enough for a clear visual of the battle area. His eyes found a total of four fighters. Two of the F-22s flew in the distance in a leisurely formation and appeared as mere spectators to the plight of the solitary Eagle chased by their third Raptor.

The SuperCOIL was still ten miles out, but at 60,000 ft had the altitude vantage over the aerial arena. None of the Raptors appeared to be aware of his presence. McDermott set in motion the targeting lasers. After years of patient waiting, he was now about to level a punishing blow on the flower of Gorik's air wing.

ANDREW'S F-15

Andrew's squadron had been decimated. After witnessing his other low-flier buddy crash into the ocean because of a Raptor wingman, he knew his chances of success were low. Still, against the odds, he had managed to survive this long, so perhaps if he could just shake off this pesky bandit, things could turn in his favor. So far, he had dodged two heat-seekers sent his way by breaking the AIM-9's thermal lock on his plane, and then he deftly kept his distance closer to the Raptor than its AMRAAM's minimal range to avoid another launch.

He conceded that the Raptor was a ferocious plane. Almost everything on it seemed to outclass the aging Eagle. But Andrew also understood the value of a pilot's timing and technique. So far, they had proven his most trusty ally. If only he could get behind the F-22, the table might be turned.

Applying airbrakes and cutting engine power, he slowed the Eagle, pitched the nose up, and then unleashed an afterburner burst that sent the F-15 hurtling up like a rocket. The Raptor pilot was not so quick to react and overshot his ascending opponent. Before long, however, he was in pursuit again, but not at the Eagle's tail as before. Andrew rolled into an upward spiral to keep the F-22 off his tail, but this time the Raptor instantly mimicked the move.

The two fighters were now ascending along intertwined helical flight paths parallel to each another. Zigzagging circularly across the sky as if caught in a massive whirlwind, each pilot jockeyed to position aft of the other for a clear shot.

From both climbing and turning, the g-forces were steadily mounting to more than six times normal gravity, but Andrew kept his wits about in this deadly aerial dance pointed toward the stars. He knew that the name of the game was who could *slow down* the most. In this, the F-22's 70,000 pounds of thrust actually worked against the Raptor, as its pilot was constantly forced to moderate his ascent velocity so not to overshoot the Eagle. But with its larger and canted vertical tails, the Raptor proved far more maneuverable than the F-15, and by invoking thrust vectoring, it could manage extreme angles of attack like no other plane on Earth.

With such superior turning capabilities, the F-22 pilot eventually gained the upper hand, at around 45,000 feet. He snuck deftly behind the Eagle at its elbow position and locked its Vulcan Gatling gun on the hapless prey.

"AMF," he said, bidding the target a pejorative goodbye.

Several things then happened. Thirty rounds of 20mm bullets leapt out of the Raptor's flashing muzzle, riddling the evading Eagle. In his murderous frenzy, however, the Raptor's pilot missed a growing dark form bearing down on him from 55,000 feet until it was too late. The form quickly enlarged to a menacingly vast shape, resembling a manta-ray. Andrew also saw it through the shower of bullets. A huge thermal spike then registered on his IR scope.

Inside the Raptor, the pilot must have felt the intense heat that took only seconds to tear past the F-22's titanium bulkhead, cutting the 16-foot support en route to the ammunition and fuel tanks. A huge explosion ripped through the fighter, disintegrating the Raptor in mid-air as its firing gun disgorged a last round.

Andrew regarded the unbelievable spectacle with ambivalence, feeling grateful for the Raptor's demise yet apprehensive at the prospect of being next. The reprieve however was cut short by the sound of countless internal dials indicating his Eagle had been mortally wounded by the aerial joust. All major avionics were failing, and the bird was leaking fuel. With some struggle in controlling the joystick, he brought the craft to level flight and descended to twenty thousand feet to eject.

The clear canopy then blasted away, followed by the charges in ejection seat, shooting him up into the open. As his chute unfolded, slowing his fall towards the Gulf, he wondered if he would be rescued, having been unable to report his last position to anyone.

ABOARD THE SUPERCOIL

The black beast was still in descent when the targeting computer automatically slewed over to the next entries in its queue: the two Raptors that angled at 60 degrees low in the front. The duo's wingtip-to-wingtip flight formation had made it impossible to tell which was the squadron leader, so McDermott instructed the computer to fire at random, and the electronic logic selected the target on the right.

Without warning, the B-2 unleashed its 5-megawatt energy beam toward the midsection of the targeted F-22. The Raptor's titanium hide could not ward off the inevitable for long. Within seconds, the searing laser turned the Pratt & Whitney PW-100 engine into molten metal and ignited the afterburner fuel into an aft explosion that blew through the fighter, sending it to a fiery death.

McDermott set the scope on the remaining Raptor but saw that it was already in a downward spiral, its ventral spewing wisps of smoke. In an uncharacteristic second-guessing of his instincts, he held back the COIL from firing. He was getting low on laser fuel, and needing the precious resource for the 1500-mile trek ahead. Besides, the F-22, clearly damaged from the proximal blast of its wingman, was in an unrecoverable spin that had already sealed its fate, and it soon disappeared beneath the low clouds. Feeling a rare sense of satisfaction, he spotted the floating parachute of the F-15 airman in the distance. With the communication jamming ended due to Raptors' destruction, the air waves were now clear.

McDermott relayed a brief anonymous transmission to the nearest Air Force search and rescue unit and then reset course toward his target in the United States.

TANARIS

The pop-up window on the computer console flashed a "Restricted Access Only" warning above a prompting password entry cursor, which Ryson quickly typed in. He queried the database for specific files that then appeared on the left side of a partitioned screen. Its right-side displayed contents of his inserted memory stick.

Feeling apprehensive, he matched the memory stick information to its counterpart on the left. Before him lay the irrefutable proof of McDermott's assertions. Gorik was indeed responsible for authorizing the killing of McDermott's squadron over Iraq, and later the captain's beloved wife in an assassination mission for the same area and date on which McDermott's wife had died. Ryson felt a knot in his stomach as he read the ghastly details of the incident.

He also found files on the Gulf War Syndrome. A meteorological map showed the southeasterly pattern of winds that had carried a large portion of the released nerve agents over U.S. Forces in Saudi Arabia.

But as Ryson delved deeper into Gorik's sinister world, he realized that McDermott's case was just one of many such illegal covert operations. Engrossed, Ryson continued scrolling through the incriminating data, while storing copies on the memory stick.

ABOARD THE RAPTOR

Kessler's blood-shot eyes momentarily gazed out the canopy at the blue expanse vertiginously swirling about him—it was not the sky but the fast-approaching waters of the Gulf of Mexico.

His F-22 was inverted, and in a flat spin that could turn unrecoverable any second. He had been flying alongside his wingman as a front-row spectator to the downing of the last Eagle, when the pursing Raptor was suddenly blown out of the sky. Within seconds he spotted the source: a great dark mass descending through the patches of clouds, trailed by a fine vapor set ablaze against the backdrop of the high sun. His immediate wingman was next to go. Kessler had no clear idea why McDermott had not selected him first but suspected that luck might have played a role. The scorching beam struck the wingman's tail with devastating effect.

Kessler had rolled to a dive when the adjoining Raptor exploded, sending showers of shrapnel and debris deep into his F-22's underbelly. The force of the blast spun the Raptor to full capsize, violently pushing it down toward the sea in an out-of-control horizontal cartwheel.

"Warning. Engine Failure," the ICAW's computerized audio announced. Out of sheer instinct, most pilots in any other craft would have ejected by now, though doing so while spinning inverted was fraught with unpredictable risks. After a minute, during which the Raptor plummeted another gut-churning 8,000 feet, he realized he should have been dead already at the hands of the bomber. Perhaps the F-22's impression of an unrecoverable spin had convinced the vengeful captain to save one of his precious laser shots for later. But whatever the reason, Kessler's focus shifted to surviving his current predicament.

He cut back power to the remaining engine, setting it in idle, then made use of his aerodynamic surfaces by raising the flaps and gear. Applying full rudders and aileron to the opposite of spin direction, he moderated the wild gyration to more recoverable levels, but he let the plane maintain its windmill motion until it descended past a stretch of low-lying clouds and into thicker atmosphere.

Now hidden from the B-2's perched view, he quickly re-powered the idled engine, angled the thrust vectoring nozzles to induce a nose-down position, and dumped fuel into the afterburner. With 35,000 lbs. of thrust suddenly kicking from aft, the Raptor punched out of the spin like a bat out of hell. It then rolled one-and-a-half-times about its fuselage along a shallow arc dive before Kessler regained full control at level flight barely 100 ft above the corrugated surface of the Gulf.

He quickly checked the functioning of all vital systems displayed on the ICAW, then kept to low altitude for his next hundred miles in flight. Like an angry, wounded beast, the Raptor roared across the aquamarine surface, the plane's powerful engine leaving an arrow-shaped aquatic signature in its sonic wake.

TANARIS

An anxious McCane rushed to the relay station panel, over which Gorik was already standing with a finger on the receiver. A brief crackling followed before the signal processors filtered out the unintelligible noise.

"Base, this is unit leader," Kessler voice cut through the static.

"What's the situation?"

"We were interfered with," Kessler replied over the howl of the Raptor's turbofan, then recounted the events. Gorik was furious.

"What's your bird's condition?"

"Lost an engine, but it's holding together," Kessler said. "Stealth was compromised, when my belly got the shrapnel. Taking an alternate path home with fewer radar sites en route, but need an aerial refueling point. The main tank seems to have been punctured, got a slow leak."

"It'll be arranged with the logistics crew. Base out."

His face reddening, Gorik shut off communications. "That son of a bitch captain will pay!"

"What are our options now?" McCane asked.

Gorik took a deep breath to regain composure. He spent a long moment in almost meditative silence as he collated the most recent data. Then his narrowed eyes flashed deviously. He crossed the room to the large map of North America. "We set a trap for him," he said finally.

"Where about?"

Gorik's finger tapped a spot on the map. "On a path to his intended destination."

"NORAD?"

The colonel shook his head. Sometimes McCane was so slow to catch on.

"His bearings show he bypassed the Air Force's set up off Florida, by circumventing Cuba, and through the Yucatan Channel."

No wonder, Gorik thought, that Norton's traditional dragnet searches had failed to net the elusive prey. McDermott's cunning stratagems had turned a once-impenetrable defense shield into a sieve through which his radar-invisible plane had slipped like a ghost, leaving no vestige of his passage. It was all becoming clear to the colonel. McCane, however, looked puzzled.

"He ignored the F-15s, and went after only the Raptors," Gorik continued. "Hell, he even saved the last F-15 from our grasp."

"So what?" McCane asked.

"Don't you see?" Gorik said, not hiding his contempt toward the obtuse superior. "He is *not* going to NORAD, to square off against the Air Force or down any civilian airlines. He's coming *here*, to this base. He's after *us*."

McCane looked confounded. "Then why all the stuff about the Air Force?"

"A ruse, meant to make us alert the president," Gorik said. "We played right into his hands. But so much the better, now that we know his real aim."

"Why is that better?"

"Because this base is far more heavily guarded than NORAD. After all, we have the most advanced air weapons on the planet here."

"That doesn't make any sense," McCane replied. "He knows he can get so much more publicity by going to NORAD. There's nothing on this base he can do much lasting damage to, even with his laser. And we can easily cover up the aftermath from outsiders."

"Revenge has made him crazy," Gorik replied. "Regardless, I shall enjoy watching his plane splatter all over the desert before he's even within range of us."

"How so, when you can't even spot him on radar?"

"We've not been able to spot him over water. But as soon as he's above land, it'll be a different story. It has happened before, remember?"

McCane raised an eyebrow. "McDermott wanted us to focus our mobile radar redeployments on NORAD so Tanaris would be more vulnerable?" he surmised.

"Precisely."

"So where are we moving our mobile radar 'mines' this time?"

Gorik grinned in delight. "I have a few spots in mind that could come as quite a nasty surprise to our vindictive friend," he replied.

TANARIS

The abrupt beeping of his cell phone broke Ryson's attention off the data he had been mesmerized with since first accessing the system. He had received a text message from McCane demanding he return immediately to Gorik's office. Ryson hastily downloaded the last few files onto his memory stick, logged off, and set for the hallway. Worries assailed him. If he could only get the data out in time, perhaps he could dissuade McDermott from carrying out his final plans.

Ryson found himself commiserating with the captain's losses to an extent he had not before, even grudgingly self-admitting that Gorik deserved to perish for his misdeeds. But he nonetheless wanted a legal judgment. In any case, it would do Ryson no good to confront Gorik with his newly uncovered trove of incriminating data, the colonel could immediately seal Ryson's silence with a bullet, and stage it all as an accident.

He took a deep breath as the ruthless nature of his adversary sunk in. He had to get off this base, and fast.

MOBILE SURFACE-TO-AIR MISSILE BATTERY, FIFTY MILES SOUTHEAST OF EL PASO, TEXAS

Major Trask switched on the command console's scope, which sent the roof-mounted antenna dish rotating on his recently camped mobile missile battery.

After an emergency airlift from Tanaris to a drop field near El Paso, they had taken dusty roads along the Rio Grande to this godforsaken secret location. The temperature outside was 110F, but it was even hotter within the metal confines of his command unit. Trask wiped the sweat off his forehead and took gulps of his canteen's lukewarm water.

When the console was fully powered up, he gazed intently at the radar monitor's circular display. A solid green line, representing the sector covered by his radar beam, was centered in the screen's middle, and swept about the circle like a fast-moving clock hand. Each time it would detect a plane via its radar reflection, a representative blip would appear on the screen. Typically, the plane's calculated radar cross-section was then compared to a table of known RCS values to determine the aircraft's model, and the defensive net was alerted to devise the best countermeasures for the identified craft.

But Trask knew that this was not a typical plane. A call he'd received from Colonel Gorik explained his assignment as akin to searching the sky for a ghost. Trask's two other units had camped out a few miles to his southeast and southwest at precisely calculated distances. The trio units represented the apexes of a triangle roughly angled like the B-2 bomber's layout but covering a much larger area.

Trask's unit played the role of the main radar source, with the other two units acting as detecting receivers to alert of any airplane reflecting radar energy in divergent paths away from the source, toward one of them. It was a tough-luck arrangement whose success hinged on absolute synchronization between all units.

Trask knew that the outlook for finding a B-2 wasn't very good from his ground position, but because he needed only to look upward, his odds for success were still five times better than those of the airborne AWACS. If Ryson had been present, he would have mathematically corroborated the area-search as follows:

$$\text{Radar's reduced range} = (\text{Reduced RCS percentage})^{0.5}$$

Because the 0.5 exponent on the equation's right-side is a square root, if a plane's RCS is reduced by a factor of a thousand, it reduces the aerial radar's range to 0.03 of its original range.

Trask uploaded the SAMs' operating profiles to confirm his reckonings, then shook his head in dismay. As an adept missile commander, he knew that even if the B-2 somehow stumbled into his radar net, there was little chance of it being successfully intercepted by any of his surface-to-air missiles. Since the B-2 would not be acquired until within 1.5 miles of his radar, it would already be close to the minimal distance required for any one of his SAMs to reach an optimal trajectory, where its guidance system could effectively direct it to the target.

A conventional aircraft is often picked up by long-range radar at its maximum range and then is handed over to shorter-range radars, which prep the SAMs for firing in time so that their guidance system is in full control for the kill. Stealth aircraft rob a missile of this opportunity by decreasing the range of enemy radar so it would pop up too late on its system for a launched missile to make a kill.

What all this meant to Trask was that even if the B-2 was spotted on his radar, it had decreased the fire-control of his SAM unit to the point that the B-2 can most likely continue unharmed. The best he could hope for was a radar glimpse of a B-2, and a report to headquarters.

Taking another gulp of unpleasantly warm water, he hoped for this assignment to end soon—preferably in time to haul his unit back to El Paso so they could catch that night's game while enjoying a frosty mug of beer.

TANARIS

Kessler cautiously flew the battle-scarred Raptor into the oval confines of the Tanaris crater. With only one engine operatioinal and despite the heavy damage to its underside, the F-22's expansive frame had helped minimize aerodynamic instability. Nonetheless, Kessler was forced to rely on his superior piloting skills in returning the bird to its nest. Now that he had almost arrived, the last hurdle was dealing with the occasional turbulence inside the crater.

Lowering the landing gear to go "dirty," he engaged whichever aerial brakes still worked to keep the Raptor steady and aligned with the runway. The Raptor's nose lowered, the front wheel made tarmac contact in a loud screech, then came safely to a full halt, and Kessler killed the power to the engine, much to the relief of dozen firefighters and trucks lining the tarmac.

Preoccupied with his failure to kill McDermott, he quickly descended the ladder that was just rolled to the cockpit, and angrily tossed his helmet to an approaching technician, then rushed to a waiting car, which drove him to headquarters. There, he logged into a secure terminal, where he found a system message waiting for him. It was a security video file whose silent digital recording Kessler began to play. The image was shot in low light with only a computer monitor providing illumination, but what he saw on the screen was clear enough.

As he set toward Gorik's office, the major grinned with the satisfaction of a hunter who finds heretofore elusive prey trapped in a cage.

ABOARD THE SUPERCOIL

McDermott gazed indifferently at the vast flatlands that made up much of Texas. After going "feet dry" in flying ashore, he had mostly darted along the Rio Grande basin. The land elevation had rapidly risen to above 5,000 feet, as he approached New Mexico. Not wishing for a daylight high-flying path, he kept the bomber at a modest 2000 feet above ground and course adjusted to a northwesterly setting.

One look at his scope revealed ample military radar activities. Some great search effort was underway, no doubt, but their weak signals indicated the source radars to be far inland. McDermott suspected a search focus closer to NORAD.

It seemed his ruse had worked and set in motion a rather predictable chain of ordered actions. He had always despised the insularity of many military decision makers, who staunchly did everything by the book, even long after those practices had become obsolete. But now, that lumbering dinosaur of command would prove his greatest ally. After years in the military, he had come to know that book by heart, and now, as a transient master of the skies, he was about to introduce to its cold-blooded authors its final terrifying chapter.

Only that his target wasn't NORAD, but Tanaris. Long ago McDermott had surmised that stealing the SuperCOIL was his only ticket to avenging his murdered loved ones. Killing Gorik with, for example, a gun, back at the base would've been too easy an exit for the colonel for a lifetime of deceit and murder, and it would never bring an end to the malignant environment Gorik had created on the base.

Exposing Gorik directly to the president or even the press would also not do. The colonel might use his influence on the commander in chief, who was indirectly involved in Gorik's affairs. The president might try to shield Gorik by appealing to national security considerations or even pardoning him.

No, McDermott wanted Gorik to experience the same degree of suffering that he had caused others. He would thus first deprive Gorik of his true love, the SuperCOIL. Then he would take a hatchet to the very roots of Gorik's power: no one of consequence would remain from that organization to become his successor.

And since there was no viable way to get to everyone from the ground, he would fight them from the air, at where he was the best.

The terrain-recognition scope indicated a flight path along the river basin approaching El Paso. He had selected, he believed, the best route toward his ultimate target. He would face no radars in these desolate spots, according to the classified information on his Data Transfer Module.

McDermott checked his bearings again, which placed him at seven hundred miles from the airbase. He felt a rush of adrenaline, knowing that from this point on, nothing would stop him.

MOBILE SURFACE TO AIR MISSILE BATTERY

Trask again tinkered with the console dials, picking up reads from various points, but so far, none were military in nature. He redirected it a few times but came up empty again. He was about to put his feet up and get a little shut-eye when the left monitor beeped, followed by the right. The reads were coming from the other two units in the multi-static triangle and signaled the approach of an aircraft. Strangely, nothing was registering on his own radar. He waited a few seconds to make sure this wasn't a fluke and then he placed a conference call to the remote units.

"Units Two, Three. I'm getting your receptor antenna feeds here. Verify?"

"It's correct, sir," a member from each unit replied, almost in unison.

Trask checked the reads' amplitudes. Each was half a normal direct return at that range. Whatever was out there, at this rate of increased signal strength, Trask reckoned it would be flying near his station at any second.

"Keep your ears sharp," he advised.

Grabbing a pair of binoculars, he stepped outside and glanced around at the vast cloudless sky. Only a moment after, he heard jet-engine noise so faint it must have been coming from many miles away. Always sharp-eared, Trask guessed the source and turned his head in its approximate direction. Then his jaw dropped.

It appeared like an apparition, much closer than its deceptively distant engine sound suggested, and far larger. But as quickly as it had materialized, the dark boomerang-shaped craft flew beyond the elevated horizon, and the engine sound quickly diminished to near silence. Trask looked at the missiles, a few had swiveled about their launchers, as if spooked by a supernatural presence that denied them any positive lock for firing.

Believing his eyes more than any radar read, Trask hurried back to the scorching mobile unit. As he typed an urgent message to the headquarters, he found his normally steady hands trembling.

TANARIS

"That is good news, indeed," Gorik said with a smile. He had just read the message from the SAM battery, one of a half-dozen 'radar mines' carefully placed along routes approaching New Mexico, but one on which McDermott had stepped over.

"Now we know he's coming to Tanaris for sure," Gorik added.

"Am I supposed to be happy about this?" McCane asked, wondering whether Gorik grasped the full gravity of the situation.

The colonel was about to reply when the main door swung open, and Ryson walked in. He was followed closely by Kessler, still in his flight suit and eyeing the lieutenant like a vicious watch dog.

"You made it back, Major," Gorik said, a hint of disappointment in his voice.

"That thing is impossible to kill!" Kessler said defensively. "Our missiles can't get a lock on the target before its laser decimates us!"

"I thought your F-22 could approach him undetected. What happened?"

Kessler's mouth parted to offer an explanation, but he was cut off by the urgent ringing from a phone connected to only one source: the White House.

Gorik raised one hand to order silence and put the call on speaker.

"Colonel Gorik?" the voice of an angry Norton boomed overhead.

"Yes, General."

"I want to know what happened to my F-15 squadron!"

"I beg your pardon, sir? I'm not following."

"Don't bullshit me. They've been shot down somehow!"

Ryson's eyes widened, though no one else present looked surprised.

"I can only assume that the culprit was our crazed friend McDermott," Gorik said calmly. "Were communications not established before engagement?"

"The com links were all jammed, on U.S. Air Force military frequencies!" Norton said.

"It verifies my theory," Gorik replied. "The SuperCOIL had those frequencies."

"But it doesn't make sense for a stealth craft to resort to that," Norton sighed audibly. "At any rate, we'll know more when our rescued pilot comes around."

"Rescued pilot?" Gorik said, chiding at Kessler who quickly averted his eyes.

"Yes, he was found unconscious in the Gulf, caused by a rough final impact on parachuted descend. We had him airlifted to a nearby base hospital. The really baffling part is someone who was there messaged us his location."

"Who?"

"That's why I am calling you, Colonel, to see if you might know."

"I don't. But if McDermott is behind this attack—and I strongly suspect he is—I suggest you double the air defenses around NORAD."

There was a long pause at the other end before the general spoke. "Agreed."

The line went dead, and harsh static filtered through. Gorik took his time hanging up, as if to inflict an auditory punishment on his audience, by whom he felt let down. He then turned to Kessler, who looked shocked and embarrassed.

"We'll discuss this later, Major," Gorik said sternly.

As a witness to the Black Squadron's attack on the Eagles, Gorik knew it was more imperative than ever to make sure McDermott did not survive his journey home. The surviving pilot was also a problem, but a commando team could dispose of him before he could talk.

"We have a rogue B-2 headed our way," Gorik said. "And from what Major Kessler was telling us only minutes ago, it's *impossible* to shoot him down. Any suggestions about how we can achieve the unachievable?"

The colonel glanced around but no solutions were forthcoming. McCane appeared lost in thought, Ryson looked bewildered, and Kessler remained angry.

"I expected so much more from such elite group," Gorik said contemptuously.

Kessler spoke, with conviction. "It is time we fought fire with fire! *Laser* fire."

"What do you mean?" McCane asked.

"Unleash the Airborne Laser!" Kessler shouted, his eyes rage-filled. "It can shoot that thing down from a hundred miles away!"

McCane shook his head. "The ABL can't make a beyond-visual-range target acquisition on the SuperCOIL the way it can with a radar-trackable ICBM. Not without being seen first and shot down, so it's worthless here."

"We *can* provide it that target."

A puzzled expression swept over everyone's faces.

"How exactly, Major?" Gorik inquired.

"Have an F-22 creep close for a visual fix on the SuperCOIL. It can then readily transmit those coordinates to the ABL so it can shoot the damn thing down."

"Are you suggesting we create a kill zone and then lure the SuperCOIL to it?"

"Precisely," Kessler said with a nod. "And the SuperCOIL can't shoot back at the ABL because its laser has only half the range."

Gorik rubbed his chin pensively. "Assume we can even get him to enter the zone, how do we get close enough for a visual sighting report before he blasts our nearby scout? We still don't know how he located your F-22 units."

Kessler pounded his fist on a desk. "It was the F-15s! Their flight pattern must have alerted McDermott to our presence. He would've never known otherwise."

"And?"

"We can do it again, this time to our advantage," he said, then pausing for effect.

"I'm not following you," McCane said.

"We'll set a bait. Fly in a fully loaded non-stealthy craft, say an F-16, to be picked up on his LPI radar just like the F-15s. As soon as he approaches the bait, we'll sneak up on his rear for a visual, and that's when we get him with the ABL."

"*Of course*," a convinced Gorik replied. "But who is to pilot a suicidal F-16?"

Kessler aimed a devilish grin at Ryson, then approached the bewildered lieutenant and pulled the memory stick from Ryson's front shirt pocket.

"This dog has been spying on us," he announced, holding up the device. "I caught a video tape of him downloading classified information on this device. The system alerted me that something was going on, so I installed a recorder behind that terminal and caught him in the act."

"What kind of information were you accessing, Lieutenant?" Gorik asked.

Ryson did not reply.

"Everything on McDermott since the Desert Storm, even information on the Gulf War Syndrome," Kessler said, tossing the memory stick to Gorik. "He was matching our records against information previously downloaded by that rogue coward before he fled in our bomber."

Gorik took a few steps toward a frightened Ryson and directed a piercing glare at him. "What did you hope to achieve by spying on us, Lieutenant?"

Ryson barely dared to look at his interrogator. "To know if McDermott had told me the truth," he said, no longer seeing any point in trying to deny what he'd done.

"And you needed this evidence to expose us, I assume." Gorik dropped the memory stick to the floor, and crushed it to pieces under his booths, like a roach.

"I believe in justice," Ryson said, staring at the shards of metal and plastic.

"And I believe in total devotion to my country's goals," Gorik's retorted.

"Does that include killing off your best pilots or murdering their leader's wife?"

Gorik turned away and strolled to one of the windows. "There comes a time in a man's life," he said, gazing outside, "when he has to ask himself what he values more: his own personal comfort or service to his country."

Ryson looked at him incredulously. "Are you referring to the sacred formation of a family through marriage institution as mere personal *comfort*?"

"When you are in the armed forces, the *military* is your institution. Nothing else should interfere. *Nothing.*"

"Captain McDermott had served his country for over 25 years in the most exemplary manner. This had nothing to do with your wanting him to serve his country, but with your wanting him to serve your own ends. This is the military, not the mafia. We serve the good of the *whole* country, not just a select few!"

Gorik turned back to the brash lieutenant. "My select *few*, as you put it, has kept this country safe for decades. You would understand that if you'd been in this business as long as I have. We deal in shades of gray here, not in the clear black-and-white moralities of civilian life."

"Murder is murder," Ryson shot back. "No matter what shade you paint it. And how is serving the military at the expense of civilians—hell, at even your own officers—anything but a rigid adherence to your own very narrow vision?"

"Tell that to your hero captain who's out shooting down Air Force planes."

"You ordered the killing of the F-15 squadron so there'd be no witnesses," Ryson said. "You are even more of a murderer now."

"Suit yourself Lieutenant" Gorik said dismissively. "Get ready for your flight!"

Kessler produced a gun from his donned G-suit, pointed its business end at Ryson and motioned him to move to the door.

"Are you mad?" A stunned McCane asked Gorik as soon as the duo had parted. "You're sending a presidential envoy into lethal combat!"

"Under the circumstances, do you have a better way of getting rid of him that we can pin on McDermott?" Gorik countered.

When McCane provided no immediate response, the colonel continued. "I want you to command the ABL."

"That's even crazier!"

"Is it really, General?" Gorik asked. "After all the free rides you've gotten from my success, it's about time you had a little personal stake in our ventures."

McCane did not argue. Instead he gazed at the far wall, where a projected map's markings displayed a possible path of the approaching SuperCOIL. The ever-shortening distance between the bomber and its target was like the tightening of a noose around their necks. Kessler's kill zone was now their only viable option.

McCane slowly lowered his head into his hands. "This better not fail."

"It won't," Gorik concluded.

ABOARD THE SUPERCOIL

It had registered as merely a short series of blips on the radar receiver and then faded fast as the bomber headed farther north, but the occurrence caused McDermott more concern than all the preceding events he'd encountered since leaving the Azores.

The SuperCOIL had no doubt briefly entered the field of a search radar—a mobile one, judging by its signal's strength. There had been no indication of acquisition or tracking. The oddity, though, was that the radar had popped up where none should have been according to his Flight Data Module. Someone had ordered a mobile unit to that remote location. Even worse, the deployment wasn't en route to NORAD.

The 600 or so miles that still separated him from his goal could become a death trap at any point along the way.

TANARIS

After they had dismounted the Jeep near a hangar, Ryson walked a few paces ahead of his captor, whose Special Forces training meant he could kill Ryson with a single neck blow.

In the pilots' dressing area Kessler sized-up the lieutenant, then tossed him a flight suit. "Put on the bag!" he ordered.

"You cannot be serious!" Ryson countered. "I am a presidential envoy, Major," he reminded. "What will happen when this gets back to the commander in chief?"

Kessler examined the lieutenant's face with piercing interest, like a poker player ready to call another's bluff in a high-stake game. "Lieutenant," he said in a soft but threatening tone, "I understand that you have a long-term girlfriend to whom you may be proposing marriage soon."

"What's that got to do with anything?"

"Maybe I would pay her a personal visit after we are done here. Send her to same happy place I dispatched McDermott's wife to."

Ryson's entire body stiffened. With the fury of one possessed, he clenched his fists then lunged at Kessler swinging. "You son of a bitch, stay away from her!"

Unimpressed, Kessler merely side-stepped the charging lieutenant, grasped his punching hand, and twisted it behind his back. The fight was over before Ryson had landed a single blow. Wincing in pain, Ryson reluctantly relented. "Now you listen to me," Kessler said hoarsely in Ryson's ear. "I can kill her without a second thought. But if *you* care about her, don't make her pay for your lousy decisions the same way McDermott's wife did for his."

"You think the president won't wonder why I'm suddenly piloting an F-16?"

"Don't be a hero," Kessler hissed, "just do as you're told, and it'll be over soon. You can go home free if you keep your mouth shut."

Ryson acquiesced silently though there was no reason to believe he would be allowed to live, even if he survived the flight.

Kessler released his captive with a small push and kept watch as they donned their G-suits and helmets. Within minutes they were back on the flight line, standing next to a fully armed F-16 Falcon, parked near the two Raptors.

"We'll be just a few miles behind," the major warned. "Deviate even an inch in your flight path and I'll personally stick an AMRAAM up your tail pipe. Got it?"

Ryson nodded and began to ascend the cockpit ladder. "This is a suicide mission you're sending me on."

"Don't worry," Kessler smirked. "We will take care of your buddy before he gets a chance to hurt you."

"And if you don't timely?" Ryson asked, hoisting his body into the cockpit.

"Then shoot all your missiles at him and pray they can fly faster to their target than his laser can get to you."

A grim Ryson said nothing more as the plexiglass canopy closed down on him. He felt as if he were being entombed under a transparent casket.

ABOARD THE ABL

Four black smoke plumes trailed the massive Boeing 747 as it reached its 10,000 feet cruising altitude. The engine roar subsided, and the lumbering plane leveled out of ascent on a direct path to its predetermined coordinates.

General McCane, seated in the lower deck's command center, headed up the staircase and opened the cockpit's door. Blinding sunlight pouring through the windows greeted him. Unlike the initial night-time test run, no coverings were needed for the panes on this daylight mission.

"ETA to our strike position?" he asked the pilot.

"Twenty-five minutes, sir."

"Keep your eyes open," he cautioned. "The radar is useless."

Feeling anxious in response to unseen danger, the general put on his shades in the bright setting. He gazed out at the enormous stretches of desert below and at the murky horizon lingering above. And he kept on visually searching, hoping to forestall the inevitable showdown with the shadowy craft he had helped create.

ABOARD THE F-22

With his flight helmet on, Major Kessler practically leapt over the cockpit's rim from the mounting ladder and into the Raptor's seat. He then swiftly connected the oxygen hose and other life support equipment. Satisfied, he touched a button and the 140-inch long monolithic polycarbonate canopy swung downward in a graceful motion that belied its nearly four-hundred-pound weight. It then slid forward smoothly and was locked in place with pins.

Knowing that time was of the essence, Kessler prepared for immediate take-off. Despite the Raptor's sophistication, it's pre-take-off details were surprisingly straightforward, requiring just three simple steps by Kessler: switching on the battery, briefly starting the auxiliary power unit, and setting both throttles to audit. The rest was automatic. The dual engines came on in tandem roars, as the APU powered down again. The computer then performed blazingly fast avionics tests and uploaded navigation data, and within 30 seconds of the engines coming on, the Raptor went from cold to full takeoff readiness as it taxied down the tarmac.

Glancing to the left, he saw the wingman pulling up to his side, and Kessler hand-gestured the go-ahead signal. Gunning the afterburners in near unison, the two accelerating F-22s took off from the runway, thundering to the sky in their rapacious pursuit of an invisible target.

ABOARD THE ABL

"Unit Two, this is Mother," McCane said via the secure satellite link. "We are positioning within range of the target area."

The short reply from Kessler came back only in the form of "copy."

The ABL set on a figure-8 holding pattern, just as it had in the test run, but this time with its radar off. Using it against a stealth craft would do no good other than alerting McDermott to their presence. Target acquisition would have to be made visually, and by proxy of Kessler's F-22 duo, which would creep close enough to get a fix on the SuperCOIL within the kill zone and transmit the coordinates in real time. The ABL crew would then search the localized area with their tracking lasers, to which the B-2 wasn't invisible, for a solid lock, then the B-2 could be quickly shot at with ABL's main laser.

McCane felt reasonably safe knowing that the SuperCOIL's lesser laser range meant it was unable to instantly return fire. The more he thought about the plan, the more convinced he became of its inevitable success.

All needed now was for McDermott to spot Ryson's F-16 and take the bait.

ABOARD THE F-22

Flying a mere 500 feet above ground, Kessler switched off the microphone after his brief exchange with the ABL. He glanced up at the underbelly of Ryson's F-16 cruising far above at 25,000 feet. The Falcon, loaded with threatening air-to-air missiles which also maximized its radar cross section to the SuperCOIL's LPI radar, would provide a tempting target.

The F-22 duo flew in ground-hugging mode to remain visually concealed amid the narrow gorges of northern Arizona while maintaining a decent view of the sky.

Kessler continually scanned the desert environs, for which the Raptor's canopy was especially well-suited. Unlike other aircraft, the F-22's bubble had no obstructing bows, even allowing for a direct aft view, if only he could swivel his head 180 degrees. Most dogfighters would be quick to point out that such a clear view of battlefield proved crucial in any air combat.

But, so far, Kessler saw no sign of McDermott, which did little to distract him from his own past failures at surpassing the storied pilot. He had failed twice now: in the Azores, and over the Gulf—thrice if he included the Iraqi desert years ago.

Kessler had always been enviously spiteful of the captain's innate superior fighting abilities, which had caused Kessler a loss of face during each encounter, and in the eyes of Gorik too, no less.

More than ever, Kessler was now determined to not come up empty handed again, even if it meant dragging McDermott with him to the depths of hell.

ABOARD THE SUPERCOIL

The LPI suddenly registered a potential threat. McDermott saw that it was a fully-loaded sole F-16 approaching from the northwest, and this close to Arizona border it could have flown only out of Tanaris. He had expected to encounter increasing resistance as he approached the base, but perhaps after being dealt some punishing defeats, Gorik was now using his resources more judiciously, employing lone scouts for directing larger formations in his direction.

McDermott considered bypassing the solo flyer, as a non-threat, but then he deemed this a perfect opportunity to ring Gorik's doorbell, to force a fear-laced colonel to send his remaining fighters into the fray, and none of them could prove a match for the mighty COIL.

Fresh rage welled up anew in the aggrieved captain at the prospects of eradicating the Black Squadron. His acumen, made cautious since the unexpected radar incident over Texas, was drowned amid an overwhelming torrent of vengefulness and invincibility.

He banked the SuperCOIL toward its prey.

ABOARD THE F-16

Ian Ryson checked his various scopes and found them all blank. *No surprise there*, he thought. The only sounds filling his ears were the Falcon's engine and his heart's thumping, the latter having dramatically picked up the closer he'd gotten to the kill zone.

The Falcon's cockpit, like most fourth-generation fighter jets, was relatively small and crammed with all sorts of instruments, consoles, and displays. Glancing down, not a square inch of space seemed unused. Even the area between his calves was occupied by a solid panel containing additional gauges, in sharp contrast to a Raptor's superior "glass cockpit", at where a few digital screens more efficiently displayed all the same data. Ryson frequently found himself tugging at the left and right control HOTAS situated on the cockpit's sides. The sensation of piloting a fighter craft again after so many years away felt both strange and familiar.

As a flight test engineer, Ryson had never done real combat, but he knew most of the maneuvers by heart from test fights in other craft. He had never imagined that his first call to combat would be against the world's most superb pilot.

Since taking off from Tanaris, he had glanced down at the sides of his plane every now and then to spot the two Raptors. They always appeared at the same location relative to his F-16, hovering just above the barren landscape.

Ryson took a deep breath through his oxygen hose to calm his nerves, but his agitated state only worsened as more time passed. In a last-ditch attempt to calm himself, he gazed down from the canopy again. This time, however, he didn't find what he'd expected amongst the inanimate scenery. He desperately scanned the mountainous desert, hoping to prove himself wrong, but to no avail.

The Raptors had simply disappeared.

ABOARD THE SUPERCOIL

McDermott now had a clear visual on the Falcon. It had just popped up like a sparrow on the horizon. It must have seen him too, since the SuperCOIL's wingspan was more than ten times that of a single-seat fighter, yet it had done nothing to evade or attack. Oddly, even its search radar wasn't on, as if its pilot had fallen asleep at the controls.

Curious, McDermott kept his course but held off on firing until the craft had come within the SuperCOIL's minimal consumption range of laser fuel.

ABOARD THE F-16

Ryson suddenly saw it: a growing dark shape appearing so razor thin as though daemons had cut a slit in the very fabric of the sky. The beast was headed straight for him, leaving no doubts about his having been spotted on its LPI radar, though its search sweeps never registered on the Falcon's Threat Warning Receiver. He was well within its laser range and considering the catastrophic encounter with the F-18s, he knew the time had passed for any effective evasive maneuvers. A cold sweat covered his face and palms, turning his flight gloves damp. He thought of Kathleen, the woman he was hoping to marry, as his sole source of comfort now.

But then he saw something amazing. Directly behind the massive craft and only a few hundred feet higher in altitude appeared two smaller dark specks above the horizon, yet they maintained a respectable distance from the pursued airfoil.

ABOARD THE F-22

If the restricting oxygen mask had not fully covered his mouth, Kessler's face would have broken into an even bigger grin. Just a short while earlier, the wily major had instructed his wingman to break away from escorting the F-16 and head for the far perimeter of the kill zone.

Snaking a furtive path through the canyons at subsonic speeds, the duo had accomplished their task in minutes. It was at this point that he had caught sight of the SuperCOIL above. With a full 70,000 pounds of thrust pouring from the engines, Kessler and his wingman powered their Raptors in a near vertical climb to 10,000 feet in just under ten seconds and then doubled up the altitude in the next seven. It brought them virtually level with the target, but at three miles aft, they didn't dare creep any closer and risk being visually sighted and fired upon.

The stratagem had worked; the SuperCOIL held its steady flight pattern, unaware of the ominous aircraft that had risen over the horizon behind it. From the cockpit of the F-22, Kessler at last had his elusive target in sight without having been detected himself. He was still too far for any missile lock or gun discharge, but a direct engagement was not his plan.

Taking a quick read of the plane's speed and heading for the bait F-16, he calculated its estimated position approximately forty-five seconds into the future and then relayed the coordinates of his newfound prey to the waiting ABL. The two Raptors then cut off throttles and fell further behind, neither wishing to be accidentally locked onto by the Mother.

ABOARD THE SUPERCOIL

The lone F-16 was now within minimal laser range, but McDermott still hadn't fired. There was something peculiar about this approaching plane that had intrigued him from the start. It had no search radar on, despite a full complement of air-intercept missiles. In short, it had exhibited none of the attributes of a Black Squadron fighter on a search and destroy mission.

He scanned the desert below and the skies ahead with suspicion. He had always loved the serenity of the desert, but except for the lone F-16 today, it was quiet— *too* quiet for a combat zone, not unlike the Iraqi desert had seemed years ago after a well-accomplished mission. And just like they had back then, his instincts now warned him that something was terribly wrong.

Then he sensed it, with a kind of prescience, just as he had over Iraq. Even before the warning from sensors mounted all over his craft began to blare, he knew that he was locked onto by a heat source. He tried to veer the aircraft out of the way but had only milliseconds to react before a massive energy beam mercilessly plowed its way deep into the SuperCOIL's airframe.

ABOARD THE ABL

"Did we get him?" McCane asked feverishly.

"Absolutely," the laser operator replied in a cocksure tone. Since receiving the latest data from the F-22s, he'd set up a tracking-laser sweep of an area where the SuperCOIL was expected to enter. Accounting for various factors such as the plane's velocity, trajectory and airfoil design, he had continuously steered the narrow-sweep tracking beams until he had found his prey. Within an instant of the acquisition, the main COIL was fired in the direction of the last read. There was no way a B-2 bomber could have moved out of the way in time; even a supersonic fighter couldn't have done that. The SuperCOIL was hit. He was sure of it.

"Excellent!" McCane exclaimed. "We finally got the bastard!"

"I can only assure you that contact was made with the target," the operator cautioned. "But I would have its destruction visually confirmed, just in case."

The general mulled over the suggestion, then turned to the communication officer. "Signal Unit Two to obtain visual confirmation of the target's downing."

"Yes, sir," the officer replied before relaying the message.

The ABL was beyond visual range of its prey, so no one onboard was able to view what happened. Only the nearby Raptors had seen any of the details.

"Patch me through to Tanaris," McCane ordered, with excited anticipation.

ABOARD THE F-16

Ryson knew he was as good as dead.

It had all happened too fast. Suddenly, an enormous surge of energy had appeared on his infrared scope as a giant searing line that had sliced its way through a vast swath of the sky to the black bomber in front. He had never seen anything like it, and no amount of theoretical readings had prepared him for actually witnessing the sheer power and precision of such weapon. He then deduced he might be next, now that Gorik's greatest enemy had been destroyed.

Reaching for the control stick, he tried to slow his speed by pitching the Falcon's nose to a high upward angle of attack while initiating a roll to turn tail. But his timing was off: the nose pitched too high and the plane turned too fast. The aggregate effects created a disproportionate airflow over the wings, pushing the Falcon into such a tight turn that it begun a flat spin. It was like a sports car that had jammed its breaks hard on ice and was now whirling out of control.

As a seasoned flight-test engineer, Ryson knew such an outcome was to be expected. But his memory of the event, still focused on the sight of the COIL's firing, left him shaken. He realized the error of his ways, but it was too late: he was in the grasp of the nightmare, his limbs immobilized. Anguish gaped, and he readily descended, impotently viewing the rapid gyrations of land and sky performing a dance of death before him as the Falcon dropped like a rock from thirty thousand feet on a terminal flat-spin dive, *falling, falling, falling* . . .

TANARIS

Gorik pressed the headset firmly to his ears, trying to hear over static. His stance toggled between elation and caution. "You sure the target was hit?" he asked again.

"Certain," McCane replied. "All energy reads point to that."

"And the visual confirmation?"

"It's being ordered. We'll know shortly."

Gorik smiled and allowed himself a moment of jubilation. "And the F-16?"

"Unit Two reported seeing it in a flat-spin, headed for a crash."

"Good. Have it verified too."

"Understood."

Gorik euphorically threw his headset onto the console. Breathing heavily, his heart racing, he gazed out the windows at the blue sky. Everything had happened as it should have—maybe even beyond his highest hopes.

Considering the strength of the ABL's megawatt laser, he knew that McDermott's plane had mostly been destroyed—just like the Black Squadron fighters McDermott had decimated. Further, it was unlikely that the lieutenant could have negotiated a flat-spin under those circumstances. And even if the pesky lieutenant had succeeded, there were more than enough air-intercept missiles in the Raptors' bellies to guarantee that Ryson would not survive.

With a sense of enormous relief, Gorik exhaled deeply. He felt a great weight lifted from his shoulders, and new doors to ascendancy once again parting wide.

ABOARD THE F-22

"Two, split up and scour the area to the right again," Kessler directed.

"Copy, One," the wingman said, splitting from the lead.

Kessler swore under his mask. The SuperCOIL was engaged, but it somehow had withstood the laser beam without exploding into the giant fireball he'd so eagerly anticipated.

Instead a more localized blast had occurred, followed by a surge of grayish smoke. The beast then made a dizzying dive toward the desert and disappeared behind the horizon's edge. Almost immediately afterwards had arrived the visual verification order of the plane's downing.

The Raptor duo went supersonic and closed in on what should have been the crash site. But no crash could be found. None of the typical thick bellowing smoke rose over the desert to guide them. It took several minutes of low-level passes through the surrounding canyons to confirm that the B-2 had not belly-landed nearby without exploding.

The lack of a sighted parachute also added to the mystery. Any pilot would have surely ejected out of the doomed plane, though perhaps McDermott's suicidal tendencies could have accounted for his alternate course of action.

Within fifteen minutes, the duo had regrouped again at ten thousand feet.

"If it's down there, it must have belly landed somewhere further out," the wingman observed. "Somewhere really hidden. We might need a ground party."

"Keep your eyes open still," Kessler said, then relayed his findings to McCane.

ABOARD THE SUPERCOIL, MINUTES EARLIER

McDermott was deeply apprehensive.

For the first time since taking flight from Azores, he realized how truly vulnerable his craft now was, having suddenly become a primary target of the very weaponry that had mastered him the skies.

The shot could have come, he reasoned, from only one source: the ABL, the only other operational airborne COIL platform in existence. That laser had found its prey despite being fired from beyond the visual horizon. The impact was devastating, jarring the SuperCOIL as if it had been rammed by a freight train.

Only his quick steering had bought him a few precious milliseconds, enough to throw the laser off its sure-kill target, but it had still done more than just etch a deep groove on the craft's curved underbelly.

Toward the airfoil's convex centerline, the laser had penetrated sufficiently to hit one of the partly full laser fuel tanks. Its peroxide contents had exploded, taking out a chunk of the bomber's ventral hide as it practically jettisoned itself out, spewing smoke. The blast induced a power surge in one of the four engines, which overloaded and caught fire, forcing McDermott to shut it down. Fortunately, not much other internal machinery was affected, and the automatic extinguishers went into action and quickly put out the raging fires.

As soon has he regained control, McDermott rolled the still-shuddering bomber toward the nearest valley at high speed, attempting to ward off another laser shot. It was a dangerously tight-turn dive, and unlike a regular craft, the tail-less bomber could plunge into earth like a knife if the banked angle exceeded 60 degrees. Despite the flight control flaps and fly-by-wire systems remaining operational, he barely managed to level the bomber above the valley floor.

In the midst of these maneuvers, he caught a glimpse of the silhouette of two Raptors and realized how the ABL had spotted him without itself entering within visual range.

The sight of the F-22s proved especially unwelcome, however; he suddenly realized that escaping the ABL no longer guaranteed his safety. It was a different game now, one in which he no longer had the edge. For not only the laser shot had etched a deep vaporized groove in the bomber's ventral RAM hide, but the explosion site had left an exposed underbelly that would now return a sizeable radar signature for any aircraft or SAM site to track.

He had lost the stealth.

ABOARD THE F-22

"Head for the ABL," Kessler urged. "It will need our assistance."

"Our orders were to look for Ryson next," the wingman answered.

"Then look to your three o'clock," Kessler said, pointing far to the east. A thick plume of smoke rose from behind a ridge line where they had last marked the F-16's uncontrolled spin. He couldn't directly see the wreckage beyond the crest, but no other source could have caused such a morbid spectacle of burning jet fuel. And no parachute could be seen.

"The poor bastard finally did himself in," Kessler said, in stoic tone. "About time he was put out of his miserable existence."

The wingman, refocusing on his next task, asked. "Which way to the ABL?"

"Follow me."

The two Raptors rolled to the right on a tight turn and then set out for the western horizon, on maximum supercruise.

ABOARD THE SUPERCOIL

The whine of the engines rose in pitch. McDermott felt the SuperCOIL shudder at lower altitudes from strong gusts swirling about the canyons. It was far from the optimal flight path he would have chosen, but as long as he remained inside the canyons, he was almost safe from the ABL. Both its tracking and firing were based on lasers, which travel only in straight lines, so for it to track him inside the valleys, the ABL would now have to appear almost directly above.

Likewise, he couldn't track or fire at the ABL. But McDermott had an advantage in that the ABL was neither stealth nor low flying. That gave McDermott some precious time to reach his own range of firing at the ABL.

Referring to the satellite map, he plotted a sinuous route that lay almost entirely below the elevated horizons of the valleys, then briefly popping above any ridgelines only when absolutely necessary. The ground-hugging flight per se did not really concern McDermott. The B-2 had been designed for handling low-flight penetration missions to bypass the Soviet defenses during daylight sorties, when high-flying could result in visual spotting. In addition, to handle turbulence at low altitudes, a special feature had been incorporated into the bomber's tail section.

This triangle-shaped control surface, known as GLAS, or gust load alleviation system, was an up-down movable flap that helped smooth airflow, an aerodynamic function akin to that of a bird's tail feathers, though its broad, flat appearance had it affectionately nicknamed the "Beaver Tail." In conjunction with an elaborate flight control system, GLAS enabled the B-2 to fly as low as 200 ft above ground.

But even with GLAS in full drive, it took pinpoint piloting to navigate the damaged giant bomber within the valley's contours. The peroxide tank explosion had left a gaping hole into which entering air now swirled. It disturbed the smooth laminar airflow over the airframe, causing a left-ward drag. McDermott was being constantly forced to perform yaw adjustments so that the plane would not veer to the port and smash into a valley wall.

But a quick glance at the laser fuel gauge indicated a more alarming concern. One of the conduits supplying the gaseous fuel to the laser chamber had been ruptured and was now leaking profusely, causing a light contrail-like mist trailing the bomber. Already low on laser fuel due to firing many shots, McDermott knew that at the current leak rate he only had minutes left before the entire supply would be bled into the atmosphere. Bereft of both stealth and COIL, the defenseless bomber would be a sitting duck for the prowling ABL or its F-22 scouts.

Deftly maneuvering past another way-point on the digital map, he remained keenly aware that time was now a greater enemy to him than he'd expected.

He had to reach the ABL, and very soon.

ABOARD THE F-22

"Why are you still at 20,000ft?" Kessler admonished the ABL pilot as soon as the 747 came into view. Flying at maximum supercruise speed—roughly one thousand miles an hour— the F-22 duo had covered the 120-mile trek in less than 8 minutes.

"Orders to remain," the pilot replied. "Search and destroy."

"Put the General on the horn," Kessler said, unsnapping his oxygen mask in frustration. The pilot quickly switched the communication over.

"I'm here, Major," McCane said.

"General, until we spot our target again, I strongly recommend lowering your altitude to five thousand feet to avoid hostile radar."

"Agreed," McCane said, and instructed the pilot to do so.

As the ABL began its descent, McCane looked apprehensively out the cockpit.

ABOARD THE F-16,
MINUTES EARLIER

Ryson could feel the alarming effects of the g-forces mounting. His heart palpitated as the Falcon continued its death spiral, kneading his body to a slow crush. He realized inaction meant imminent demise, but his mind remained locked in the nightmare's throes, falling into the black hole, and riveted on a familiar memory: his failure to rescue his fiancée. He knew that if he didn't stop the fall, all would be lost: this mission, his honor, and, worst of all, his chance to wed Kathleen.

He didn't want to lose her. This new focus gave him all the needed incentive to fight, as his thoughts shifted to McDermott, who had also suffered the loss of a loved one, though for different reasons. His mind replayed the legendary captain's chidings: *"The next time it comes gaping, don't run, don't veer away . . . Harden yourself! Jump in, and take control, bring yourself out of it like you would do with a plane that has gone into a flat-spin . . ."*

The mental recitation struck his frail psyche in epiphany. Yes! The analogy finally made sense. Most pilots in a flat-spin end up accidentally killing themselves because in attempting to get out of the spin they frantically embark on actions that pushes them further into it, such as pulling on the lever in the wrong direction, while thinking they'd done the opposite, until the spin becomes unrecoverable. If they had only taken a few seconds to think about what they were doing...

Taking a deep breath, Ryson analyzed the situation. His first instinct, which he'd always followed almost robotically, had been to climb out the gaping black-hole. But what if the solution was to do the exact opposite? All along he had been too fearful to try. Now, facing certain death, he had nothing to lose, and so he let himself go to a complete free fall.

The gap seemed bottomless, but Ryson held his resolve and kept focus on Kathleen above all.

And then, suddenly, inexplicably, a glow of white light sparked in the far distance. At first as small as a night star, then rapidly widening in its diameter like an exploding nova. It took him a few seconds to realize that he was now floating through thick clouds. It faded to something fog like, then he saw sunlight peeking through, and suddenly the falling sensation had ceased. He now felt more in control of his limbs, which had stopped flailing, and then of solid ground forming beneath him, his boots having landed on a grass meadow, the sun's warm rays stroking his face. He realized momentarily that he was standing on the very same spot where he had been before he took his plunge, almost as if the fall had never happened.

The sinking feeling in his stomach, however, told him otherwise.

His eyes opened again, this time for real. The greenery gave way to the sight of cockpit consoles and the HUD's readout, and then the dials spinning haywire, especially the altimeter.

He shook his head, dispelling the last of the fugue as his mind regained its full clarity. He flexed his formerly frozen fingers, which now responded with perfect dexterity. He then gazed at the timer and was surprised that fewer than twenty seconds had lapsed since he had entered and exited the nightmare. He'd once heard that lengthy dreams are often actually played out in mere seconds, and now believed it. He had returned from the nightmare's grip and had one person to thank for it: McDermott. The legendary captain had shown him the way.

But this was no celebration time, as he was still whirling out of control. He grabbed the control stick but stopped the impulse to push the plane further in the same direction. He pulled the stick to the opposite setting, brought the nose down from the high angle of attack, reset the stabilizers, and increased power to the engine. The plummeting F-16 stopped its rotary motion below the elevation line of a nearby ridge and recovered from the spin just seconds before impact.

A sweat-soaked Ryson heaved an elated sigh of relief as the Falcon leveled over the ancient riverbed. Knowing that other potential dangers lay nearby, he kept his flight to below the ridge line, then jettisoned one of his partly full external fuel tanks. The 375-gallon metal pod bounced off the riverbed a few times before settling into the alluvial soil. He made a swift low-altitude roll turn, dropping the Falcon back into the valley, then activated the targeting system, put the crosshairs of the Vulcan Gun straight on the discarded tank, and sent a dozen rounds into its stationary metallic shell. The strafing ignited the pod's remaining one hundred gallons of high-octane jet fuel into a huge orange ball, a furious conflagration ensued that sent a black plume of smoke a mile high into the sky.

Pulling out of the valley but still maintaining a ground-hugging low-radar profile, he observed the Raptors duo reconvene above, then abruptly heading westward and disappearing behind the elevated horizon.

Ryson laughed euphorically. For the first time in years, he felt free—and not just of Gorik and this sordid mission but of the haunting nightmare. Finally, that long-dreaded obstacle to his happiness had been overcome. From now on, he would be in control of his own destiny.

With thoughts quickly shifting to Kathleen, he plotted a course opposite that of the Raptors or Tanaris, and eagerly guided his Falcon east, to the bright life that awaited him.

ABOARD THE SUPERCOIL

The intercept radar screen chirped loudly, indicating a distant target, which McDermott instantly took to be the ABL. The giant 747, with its four exposed turbo fan engines, had popped up conspicuously on radar, owing to its large RCS.

Gearing up for the encounter, McDermott checked the laser fuel read but found it dishearteningly low. The leak had squandered nearly all the peroxide supply. He would now have at most one sustained shot at the ABL before being discovered and destroyed by its return fire.

He needed to come within the optimal range and angle for an effective shot, and that meant flying up to 6,000 ft, above the ABL's cruising altitude. If he was spotted in the climb, he could be targeted at once, but it was a risk he had to take.

A thought crossed his mind, something he had read years earlier in a classified technical manual. After a brief deliberation, he veered the bomber to a different heading, based on the ABL's bearing. When the point of action was reached, he threw his three remaining engines in full thrust, set the rear flaps to a climb, and powered the SuperCOIL skyward.

ABOARD THE F-22

A red triangle suddenly flashed on Kessler's threat warning receiver. The CIP had picked up a faint radar trace from afar and had categorized the read hostile.

It was also unable to positively identify the aircraft's type.

Most warplanes had known RCSs, which were tabulated in the Raptor's comprehensive avionics memory banks, and the Common Integrated Processor provided the data to the pilot. The approaching craft had no known match, but judging by its diminutive RCS, the CIP had categorized it as a very small plane.

Kessler looked curiously out the canopy in the direction indicated by the radar but saw nothing. This didn't surprise him, because the bandit was barely within visual range and flying low. He relayed a command to the wingman over the IFDL. At once, the duo broke formation with the 747 and set for the mysterious craft.

ABOARD THE SUPERCOIL

The SuperCOIL had just passed three thousand feet above ground when McDermott saw the two F-22s heading his way. He must have been spotted on the Raptors' LPI radars, which were invisible to his craft, just as his own was to theirs. They were still too far away to be an immediate threat, but since he had ascended into open space, the ABL could now take a clear shot at him. Fortunately, it was still obliviously lumbering ahead, following its predictable loop.

With 2,800 more feet to climb, time seemed to be ticking by with painful slowness. McDermott wished he could shorten the period by bringing the destroyed fourth engine back online but knew better than to ask for the impossible.

ABOARD THE ABL

"SuperCOIL directly ahead!" Kessler's frantic call came through the headset, striking McCane like a jolt of electricity.

"Battle stations!" McCane reflexively barked at the control center below.

Galvanized, the general peered out the flight deck's panes and saw the silhouetted aircraft rapidly rising out of the distance like a black demon. For the moment it was below the ABL's nose, but not for long. McCane wondered why they hadn't already been fired upon.

Even more strangely, McDermott was matching the ABL's movement, attempting to maintain its position relative to the 747. It was like a bird going out of its way to remain *inside* the crosshairs of a hunter's roving scope.

"Lock and fire the laser at that son of a bitch at once!" McCane shouted.

"We can't, sir," came the controller's stunning reply.

"Why the hell not?" the general asked.

"The ABL can't shoot at him from this particular angle."

McCane's eyes widened at the terrifying realization. "Turn us around, fast!"

ABOARD THE SUPERCOIL

McDermott had barely reached five thousand feet when he caught sight of the 747 as it veered ponderously to the right. A magnified scope view showed that the nose portion was rotating to a firing position. It would soon be ready.

Inability to shoot from a narrow frontal angle was a blindspot for the rotating targeting mirror in the prototype aircraft, but not deemed concerning as no missile was fast enough to reach the ABL before it had turned to shoot its laser. Being fired upon by the airborne laser of a hostile nation was considered too remote a possibility by its designers to justify a total redesign of the optical mirror system.

The SuperCOIL's dual turrets, on the other hand, were not nose-mounted but deployed on its top and bottom surfaces to conform with the B-2's flattened airframe. Each turret thus had a "hemispheric" 360-degree sweeping range rather than the ABL's 180-degree side-frontal range.

What mattered for the moment, however, was which airborne platform could get to its optimal firing position first. There would be no second chances.

ABOARD THE F-22

"Radar lock on the target," the wingman reported.

"I see it, Two," Kessler agreed.

Going full afterburner to reach speeds past Mach 2, the Raptors had covered nearly half the distance to the bomber and then turned on their more powerful search attack radars, which at this close range had managed to lock onto the damage exposures in the B-2's underbelly.

The strongest radar reads came from jagged rips rimming the explosion site, which spewed a gaseous mist, and then the exposed innards. Kessler had no doubt about having been seen by McDermott, and he expected a lethal laser attack at any second, but his determination to bring his old nemesis down at all costs kept his fear of death at bay and his F-22 on course.

"Proceed," he ordered.

In near unison, each Raptor disgorged a pair of AMRAAMs from its ventral in the direction of the SuperCOIL. As the deadly, advanced medium-range air-to-air missiles streaked toward their target, Kessler looked at his scope and saw that the ABL was almost primed to unleash its own lethal shots at the renegade craft.

ABOARD THE SUPERCOIL

It was a mere second before the ABL would come into position to blast at the SuperCOIL, but McDermott had arrived at his position first, by barely a heartbeat. The SuperCOIL's above-ground readout was now at six thousand feet and, more importantly, the plane was precisely at the optimal angle relative to the ABL.

Ignoring the shrill missile warnings, McDermott grabbed for the trigger, and pressed a button which sent the last of his peroxide reserves into the laser chamber.

ABOARD THE ABL

The Target-Acquired button had just blinked to life, and McCane's index finger had nearly pressed the firing button when a scorching beam of focused light poured into the cockpit.

The general opened his mouth to scream in unbearable agony, but his vocal cords never made a sound; in an instant, five megawatts of searing energy coursed through him and everything around. In a fraction of a second, he was on flames. His skin broiled, then vaporized, all in an instant, along with his inner organs, as the hotter-than-inferno laser beam sliced its way through his flesh and bone. The lethal beam continued along a slanted path, piercing the aluminum floor like warm butter, to reach the control deck below and killing the occupants just as swiftly as it had those in the cockpit. It then reached the tanks below, igniting more than 35,000 gallons of jet fuel that blew their way out of the plane's ventral.

For the briefest of moments, it appeared as though the massive 747 was resting on an expanding cushion of roiling orange flames, and then the fire blasted upward, ripping the fuselage along several structural weak points and sending a meteor-like spectacle of chunks of blazing metal to rain down on the desert.

ABOARD THE SUPERCOIL

McDermott let out a short breath, his eyes riveted on the dazzling destruction of the ABL. The distraction proved brief, however, as the blaring warning systems forced his focus back to the details of combat. Four missiles were heading his way.

He coolly rolled to the port and initiated a dive to expose only the bomber's "cold" topside to the missiles. Less than 3 miles now separated him from the quad of projectiles closing at near Mach 4, but McDermott kept with the descent. The missiles moved at frightening speeds yet now seemed to have ceased their constant course adjustments and were flying straight as arrows along their last trajectories prior to his dive. Soon they passed high overhead, not turning tail to pursue.

With the earth rushing upward, McDermott headed for the nearest valley and leveled the SuperCOIL barely a hundred feet above the riverbanks before resuming his course toward Tanaris. Within minutes, however, he saw the two Raptors in the corner of his eye as they swept in from behind.

At their current velocity, they would soon have him within range of their weapons. One glance at the internal gauges showed he had no laser fuel left to penetrate even one of the Raptors' titanium hulls.

TANARIS

Speaking heatedly into the microphone, Gorik demanded, "where is he headed?"

"Directly for the base," came Kessler's reply.

The colonel closed his eyes. He had just been filled in on the fate of the ABL. He'd never been terribly fond of either the plane or his boss, so the ABL's fiery destruction had not bothered him much. If anything, it had ridded him of the man he'd considered his primary competition for future leadership of the Air Force and provided solid evidence of the ABL's shortcomings in combat, thus help make a strong case for the developing additional SuperCOILs.

"Can you bring him down?" Gorik asked.

An extended pause followed.

"I have a plan," Kessler said at last. "He's vulnerable without total stealth."

"How badly is the SuperCOIL damaged?"

"Enough to get a radar lock on him from certain angles. The plane was also oozing a mist from its ventral, but it stopped soon after he fired at the ABL."

Gorik put up the SuperCOIL schematics on his screen. He drew a line at where the laser had reportedly pierced through the airframe and internal components.

"Looks like one of the peroxide tanks was hit, then exploded," he suggested, then ran his fingers across the digitized blueprint to trace the laser's path. "One of his conduit lines must have ruptured too. That might account for the mist you saw."

"But why did it stop?"

Gorik went pensive, then exclaimed. "He must have run out of laser fuel!"

Another pause followed before Kessler said, "are you certain about this?" He knew that his life depended on whether Gorik's speculation held true.

"Reasonably sure," Gorik replied. "It would account for his not shooting at your missiles, or planes. He was saving it all for the ABL." After examining the ABL's schematic, he traced the laser path and angle through the doomed 747, then shook his head. "That smart son of a bitch."

"What?"

"He fired at the ABL's cockpit windows and inner surfaces, a path of least resistance for its laser to both kill the crew and reach the fuel tanks with minimal dwell time on the target."

"How should we proceed?"

"Shoot him down if you can. If not, at least keep him on course for Tanaris."

"And just how do I get him to stay on course?"

Gorik pondered a moment, then said, "tell him I'll be waiting for his arrival."

He set down the headsets and walked to the giant bay windows overlooking much of the base. McDermott was proving a bigger puzzle by the minute. What did the captain hope to achieve by coming to Tanaris? What irreparable damage could he possibly inflict, other than taking out a couple of buildings, with a crash?

Gorik had never partaken in gambles, when staging military operations. He firmly believed there was no military engagement that meticulous strategic planning, a trained crew, and the right weaponry couldn't propel to certain success.

But now, facing a superb strategist who piloted a radar invisible aircraft of staggering firepower, he felt a sudden knot in the pit of his gut. With half his fleet decimated by a single warplane, it seemed he was left with no alternative but a move that was riskier than he preferred. It was a gamble but a calculated one: to make himself a known target to McDermott.

He would present himself as irresistible bait to a predator for whom he was saving his last and most lethal trap.

IN THE CHASE,
OVER THE ARIZONA DESERT

Kessler kept the black bomber in visual crosshairs as both Raptors swooped down to the valley, in tight synchronous arcs. They held position just above and behind their prey. The massive bomber now nearly filled the entire front view, but Kessler's mind saw only the haunting replayed images of the ABL's destuction.

An enormous energy beam had flashed past the Raptors, causing the distant grayish sky to light up on his IR scope. Kessler had watched the firestorm with an odd mixture of amazement and impassivity as the pride of the Black Squadron burst into a rapidly expanding sphere of superheated gas and disintegrated metal that stretched across the sky.

The ABL's pilot was a longtime friend, just as most of the other Black Squadron pilots under his command who had died at the hands of McDermott and his demonic machine, all in a matter of hours. A desire for sheer vengeance now coursed through him. He wanted to kill McDermott, just as badly he imagined the captain wanted to kill him.

With great effort, Kessler willed his mind back to the task at hand. Peering at various registers, he sought a read on the target, but to his ample frustration, he found none from his current range and angle.

McDermott was shrewdly flying low to the ground, keeping the B-2's damaged "hot side" facing away from the pursuers. The so-called "hot and cold" idioms were largely vestiges of the F-117's facetted approach, whose less sharply-angled top and back "hot" sides had far greater radar returns than its more-angled front and flat ventral "cold" sides, which returned almost no radar energy back to the source. The F-117 thus purposely wound its way through enemy territory so that only its cold sides faced the enemy ground radars.

The B-2, on the other hand, with its smoothly contoured airframe, lacked any vulnerable hot sides; since its continuous-curvature design reflected energy away from virtually all angles. Thus, like a warped amusement park mirror, it didn't provide a clear picture regardless of the viewer's relative angle. Of course, even without a clear picture, some form of reflection could be seen from near enough distances to alert the enemy ground radars that something was heading its way.

But missiles' onboard radars are far less powerful than ground ones, thus allowing the stealthy B-2 to break a tracking lock with a modicum of evasive maneuverings, as McDermott had done to the four AMRAAMs by exposing to the radar-guided projectiles only the SuperCOIL's still stealthy top-side.

Kessler flew above the bomber so that the Raptor's titanium hulled fuselage would shield its cockpit. He assumed that McDermott no longer possessed enough laser fuel for the prolonged burst required to pierce the Raptor's thick hull, but perhaps he still had just enough to incapacitate a human through the clear canopy.

So the three fliers flew on in their strange formation, with the trailing duo holding a respectable high distance from the black arrowhead. Kessler knew that the arrangement favored McDermott, who was getting closer to Tanaris with each passing minute. Kessler had to act soon, so he opted for the only weapon at his disposal that could definitely reach his adversary.

McDermott watched the chase Raptors holding position just out of range of his last reserve of laser fuel. He could still kill one, perhaps both pilots, if he could target their cockpits' canopies. For now, however, he had to content with keeping an eye out for such an opportunity. His focus remained on navigating the massive bomber within the confines of the narrowing valley; the SuperCOIL was an especially large craft, and he could not avoid obstructions as nimbly as his pursuers could.

Suddenly, the communication link blinked on the same frequency on which he'd been contacted before. But this time the transmission was coming from a nearby source. It had to be one of the Raptors. He switched on the radio.

"Captain McDermott," a familiar voice said. "It's Kessler."

"I know."

"I'm here to offer a truce, from the colonel. He's waiting for you at the base."

"And what does he propose?"

"Land the plane at Tanaris, and no one will get hurt. My word of honor."

"*Honor*?" McDermott chuckled. "Since when do murderers have honor?"

"C'mon now, Jack," Kessler said, feigning amiability, "you and I go back a long way. We're both ace pilots, a rare breed."

"You're an ace murderer who happens to know how to fly."

The caustic comment hit home. "You're an arrogant bastard," Kessler said. "We both know you have no laser fuel left, so quit bullshitting. Accept my offer!"

"And if I don't?"

"I'll blow you out of the sky."

"So do it."

Kessler was about to reply when the SuperCOIL's tracking laser locked onto his plane. It was too late for any maneuvers. Every muscle in his body tensed as he anticipated the lethal blast to follow.

It didn't come, however.

"That was just a warning," McDermott said sternly.

Kessler's body relaxed back into the ejection seat as a layer of sweat formed on his forehead. But he quickly regained his composure—and his audaciousness. "Now land your plane and I promise to not kill you like I did your wife."

The mention of her death struck McDermott as hard as any missile Kessler could have launched. Fresh waves of grief swept over him, and his throat tightened.

"There are worse ways to die than being crushed under a ton of rubble," Kessler said. "Who knows? Maybe I did her a favor."

Images of his wife now ran through McDermott's mind in an unstoppable deluge: his beloved dying under the debris, along with his unborn child. His eyes welling with tears, he was filled with an impotent rage, knowing he had no means of achieving vengeance against the man responsible for his grief. He reflexively targeted the F-22 again and prepared to fire his only remaining shot at the Raptor.

But his sense of logic stopped him at the last instant as he realized that firing a too weak laser would be a futile gesture that played right into Kessler's hand.

The lock signal flashed again, but this time Kessler remained unfazed. Instead, he grinned. The antagonizing ploy had worked, and now McDermott was certainly out of laser fuel. Otherwise Kessler would have been dead already. It was time to make the final move and finish off his nemesis once and for all.

He still needed an infrared lock, however, to shoot down the plane, which required creeping in much closer to the SuperCOIL's jet stream. The other weapon at his disposal was the Vulcan gun, but he considered this largely ineffective.

Downing a SuperCOIL-class B-2 by mere gunfire was not easy, since all vital mechanisms, engines, fuel tanks, and avionics were buried deep within the plane to maximize stealth. This made accurate targeting of them impossible; the plane's expansive curved airframe would deflect or soak up many of the bullets before they even reached its innards. Aerodynamics would also be far less affected. The integrated airfoil design eliminated the traditional dangers of a wing being torn from the fuselage because of enemy fire, which allowed the plane to endure far more punishment from hostile aircraft. Kessler doubted that the two Raptors carried enough rounds to bring the SuperCOIL down, especially from their aft firing position, which prevented direct shots at the cockpit.

Infrared was now the only real answer, he concluded—which meant that one Raptor had to get into the SuperCOIL's engine trail and lock an IR missile on the faint traces of heat coming from the cooled exhaust. Activating the IFDL, he ordered his wingman to obtain the necessary IR lock by creeping closer. Instantly, the wingman powered his Raptor past Kessler's toward the black bomber, now barely half a mile ahead.

A still reeling McDermott saw the approaching F-22 on his rear camera and knew immediately that his fake laser targeting ruse had failed. In seeking an IR read on his bomber, the advancing fighter had further dipped toward the valley floor but still not low enough for a laser shot at the cockpit.

Besides, there were two pursuers, and McDermott barely had one weak laser shot left. After taking a deep breath from his oxygen mask, he prepared for the pivotal decision he would soon have to make.

The wingman steadied the Raptor as it snuck closer. Its fly-by-wire-driven control surfaces were now constantly adjusting to compensate for low flight within the valley's confines, and a slip-stream of air formed behind the bomber.

Within all the turbulence gusts was a faint trace of heat from the bomber's three remaining engines, which the F-22's acute sensors essayed to detect like a snake's tongue. The wingman maneuvered in a bit further and before long had entered the B-2's so-called cone of vulnerability. The bomber's flattened exhaust baffles, however, had altered the expanding geometric profile created by the diffused hot gases so that it was less detectable—more like a narrow band than the typical cone. And the bomber's engine by-pass air conduits mixed-in cooler air into the exhaust stream to further reduce thermal imprints. But at this extremely close range such IR reduction efforts were inconsequential. Within seconds, the wingman's scope registered the seemingly impossible: a solid thermal lock on the SuperCOIL.

An IR LOCK warning popped up on McDermott's Threat Indicator defense screen, something he, too, never thought he'd see. With barely two hundred yards separating the planes, a launched IR missile would impact in less than three seconds, leaving no time for the bomber to resort to any countermeasures. He had no choice but to use his last laser shot in a desperate bid.

McDermott had reached for the firing trigger when the pursuing Raptor suddenly fulminated into a giant fiery ball, showering the valley floor with blazing shards of titanium.

Perplexed, McDermott quickly took his right hand off the trigger, as if the joystick had zapped him with electricity. A glance at his scope confirmed the SuperCOIL had not fired. He did not have to wonder long, however.

Looking to his aft left, he saw another plane emerging from aside the dissolving ball of fire, on a lateral ascent. But even before it fully cleared the inferno, McDermott saw to his disbelief that the craft was not the second F-22, as he had expected, but another familiar shape.

It was an F-16.

McDermott's eyes followed the mystery Falcon. For a brief moment the veteran captain was reminded of his former wingmen, with whom he had last banded over Iraq, and how they had come to one another's rescue just in the nick of time.

He imagined the unknown pilot to be another Lebrun or Franke and smiled grimly at the thought of his lost comrades. In a show of gratitude to the unknown pilot, he wagged the bomber's wing as best its massive frame allowed.

The Falcon replied nimbly in kind, then disappeared behind the canyon's wall.

An astounded Kessler was still taking in what had just happened in seemingly a blur: the mystery Falcon, approaching from high and aft at Kessler's seven o'clock, executed a long barrel-roll, crossing the valley's width inverted atop a wide arc, as if in a roller-coaster's giant horizontal corkscrew spiral.

The Falcon's pilot kept both Raptors in sight as his F-16 arced its way to the front right, tilting to sideways at Kessler's two o'clock and so close to the opposite ridge wall it looked as if the fighter's belly was to scrape it. But then it cleared past with an impossibly thin margin and continued to descend in a banked dive, sliding right-side up into the valley as if swung from a pendulum tether. Seconds later, it reached the trough barely above the riverbed, and for a moment the leveled F-16 lined up perfectly between the two Raptors, sufficiently close for an IR lock on the lead F-22. It then let loose an infrared missile. At such proximal range, the heat seeking Sidewinder had little trouble finding a home inside the lead Raptor's left nacelle. The explosion rent the loaded F-22 in a huge ball of fire.

The Falcon then sustained its natural spiral swing, swiftly ascending sideways back to above the left ramparts, ending at Kessler's two o'clock. It then dropped behind the opposite ridge and out of sight.

Kessler, however, had little time to further ponder the bizarre event. A giant wall of flames now appeared before him where his wingman had been just moments earlier. He banked the Raptor sharply, setting it on the right wingtip, then swerved around the hovering inferno to avoid intense heat and fragments from getting sucked into his plane's dual intakes. The ninety-degree roll had him flying parallel to the canyon's east wall and so perilously close he felt as if he could reach out of the canopy and rake his gloved fingers over the sun-drenched rocks.

As soon as he circumvented the conflagration, he rolled back to level and centered the Raptor on the riverbed. With the B-2 still hovering below, he searched the skies for the menacing Falcon. He was in for an even bigger shock when he discovered that the F-16 had reappeared—and at his six o'clock, directly behind.

A voice filtered through his helmet on the encrypted channel. "Major Kessler, you are under arrest for murder," the speaker boldly announced.

Stunned, Kessler raised an eyebrow in recognition of the speaker's voice. It was of the F-16's pilot, a man who, by Kessler's count, should have been dead already.

From the plexiglass canopy of his Falcon, Ian Ryson gazed down at the lone Raptor with a sense of vindication and empowerment. Soon after he had left the faked-crash site for a better life, he had realized to be merely on borrowed time. It would not be long before Gorik would discover of his survival and send Kessler's assassins after his beloved Kathleen.

He also felt indebted to McDermott for saving his life, most recently by indirectly helping him overcome his terrible nightmare during the extremely close call he had while in the flat-spin.

And he recalled his self-imposed final test intended to prove that he had truly broken free of the nightmare's grip: he had to save a loved one from death. Rushing to McDermott's aid and hence bringing Kessler to justice offered the opportunity to both repay his debt to the captain and to protect his beloved Kathleen. And if he could somehow dissuade McDermott from following through with his plan, he might just save the legendary aviator as well.

Invigorated by his noble intentions, Ryson had veered the F-16 back toward combat. He had taken a ground-hugging trek along the last known course of the F-22s and arrived on site shortly after the downing of the ABL. Spotting the SuperCOIL diving into the valley with the Raptors in tow, he'd flown the Falcon behind the ridge line to avoid radar detection and then picked up Kessler's communication on the Falcon's Black Squadron decryption channels.

As Kessler taunted McDermott by reminding him of his wife's murder, Ryson envisioned the same thing happening to Kathleen. A deep rage overtook him, and he blocked out all else. But this time, instead of paralysis he experienced a call to action. Drawing on all his formal training, he had executed the death-defying spiral loop in and out of the canyon.

Immediately after he emerged, he applied the airbrakes and pitched the Falcon's nose up to a high angle of attack, practically bringing the plane to a standstill. He counted the seconds for the Raptor to pass by on the other side of the ridge, then veered his fighter back into valley, this time directly behind the sole F-22 whose pilot, preoccupied with avoiding the wall of flame, had taken no notice of the Falcon's re-approach until it was too late.

For a brief second, Ryson felt he could power the Falcon forward enough to get a read on the lead Raptor's IR signature, just as he had done to the wingman, and kill Kessler. But he stopped himself short, and the moment passed.

He had found the feelings of exacting such vengeance strangely satisfying, but it had also offered a glimpse into McDermott's darkened world. He had briefly stood at its threshold by coming to the immediate defense of another, but he wished not to remain in that world lest it eventually would consume him, the way it had McDermott. Instead, he opted to ask Kessler to stand down.

"Ah, Lieutenant," Kessler mocked. "I thought you had done yourself a terminal favor by crashing."

"You are under arrest," Ryson repeated, ignoring the remark.

"On whose orders?" the major challenged, unfazed by Ryson's demands or his own precarious situation if a dogfight arose.

"The United States government. You are to follow me to the nearest airstrip away from Tanaris and surrender to the authorities upon landing."

"Why don't you arrest that madman instead?" he said, referring to McDermott. "Weren't *those* your orders?"

"They *were*. But the priority has now switched to you. Stand down!"

"And who is going to make me?"

"I am," Ryson said firmly. His tone included an uncharacteristically forceful conviction, which Kessler sensed. It was as if another man in Ryson's body were speaking on his behalf.

"You really think you're a match for me?"

"Just ask your wingman."

Kessler seethed at that reference, though he grudgingly admitted that Ryson deserved credit for his dare-devil shoot-down maneuver. But it all began to make more sense now. Only a veteran flight-test engineer like Ryson, hell bent on pushing a plane's envelope, would be both experienced and crazy enough to try something so unorthodox. Still, the element of surprise was now lost to the foolhardy engineer, and the F-22 was far superior to the Falcon.

"You should have left after that stroke of luck, when you had a chance, Lieutenant," Kessler said, quietly preparing for combat.

"And let you go after my loved one?" Ryson retorted. "No, *this* is my chance."

"And it's also your funeral. All that fancy flying isn't going to save you now."

"I'm at your six o'clock, Major. Even *you* should be apprehensive about that."

"Not anymore," Kessler said with finality, then clicked off.

Before Ryson could react to the message, the Raptor's twin nacelles suddenly glowed brightly, shooting out narrowed plumes of gas. The F-22 went on full-afterburner, peeling off the riverbed with incredible force and going from horizontal to nearly vertical flight in virtually an instant. Its 70,000 pounds of thrust, now directed at the alluvial soil by the vectored thrust nozzles, kicked off a huge obscuring cloud of dust behind which the Raptor vanished like a wraith.

A surprised Ryson kept his Falcon on course and was momentarily swallowed whole by the expanding earthly nebula before him. Fortunately, no major floating debris was sucked into the Falcon's large air-intake to damage the sole engine.

Once he had cleared the alluvial mist, he caught sight of the Raptor again, still on its power climb. He tugged at the throttle stick and sent the F-16 shooting out of the valley in pursuit, though without any vectored thrust the act took considerably longer. By this time, in performing an inverted inside turn, he had already overshot his opponent, which brought him under the F-22.

There was a faint trace of IR floating about, caused by the Raptor's uncharacteristic use of the afterburners. With no clear lock, he fired a Sidewinder almost vertically up, into the tenuous infrared trail.

Kessler immediately spotted the missile separation, its infrared tip pointed right at his tailpipe. Maintaining his composure, he cut off the blowers, then took the vectored thrust nozzle to its maximum angle, which sent the F-22 into an almost back-flip until its nose faced the desert. He now had a clear view of both the Falcon and the missile, which seemed to have lost its feeble lock on his turned tail.

Ignoring the threat as it swished past without consequence, he headed for the lone Falcon, swooping down like a bird of prey.

Ryson let out a whistle of astonishment at the Raptor's uncanny maneuvering capabilities and realized the chances of downing the craft and its ace pilot were now lost. He broke out of the engagement climb and set for a straight path opposite Tanaris, hoping to divert Kessler's attention from McDermott as long as possible.

Ryson was not a dogfighter, he knew. It was one thing to execute a precision sneak attack on an unsuspecting fighter within the confines of a valley but quite another to face the same enemy in the open. Here, the Raptor was by all counts a formidable menace. The best he could hope for was to buy time as he sent the Falcon into full afterburner, to flee supersonic at Mach 2. The Raptor accelerated at a frightful rate in its curved descent. Visible white contrails formed off its clipped delta wings, even in the dry desert air, as it aimed directly for him.

Kessler smiled at the Falcon's futile evasion attempt. The F-16 was a highly maneuverable plane, and perhaps in the hands of an experienced combat veteran could have served as a worthy competitor to the nimble Raptor. But this particular aviator had none of the skills of a seasoned fighter pilot and had chosen, instead, to flee at high speeds. Kessler sent the Raptor into full supercruise and then, with a few quick bursts of afterburner, prepared to overtake the Falcon.

Noticing the Raptor rapidly gaining from aft, Ryson cursed under his breath, half-angry with himself for not shooting at Kessler in the valley, when he had the chance. It was an internal moral debate he would have to leave to another day. For now, he needed to focus on survival.

His fuel status was getting critically low on sustained afterburners, with less than a minute of flight time left at that rate, so he cut them off and watched as the Raptor leapt forward even faster. He veered the Falcon out of the Raptor's path and dove into the nearest valley. The high walls blocked the sight of his assailant to provide a short-lived false sense of relief, which vanished when the twin canted tails of the F-22 abruptly broke over the ridge.

Ryson tried to turn the chase into a time-wasting hide-and-seek within the valleys, but Kessler brought the aspect angle down to near zero, moving directly behind the Falcon and quickly closing the distance for the kill.

A missile launch warning blared in Ryson's helmet, a radar-tracker AMRAAM was hot on his tail. With almost no fuel left for any evasive tactics, he spent his last precious drops for a climb, then used air-braking to slow down the craft and punched out at the minimum safe altitude for his velocity, barely two seconds before the chasing missile struck the starboard wing's base. The battered F-16 spun out of control and slammed into the mountain side in a violent blast.

Soon as the chute opened to stabilize his fall, Ryson spotted the chase Raptor as it veered clear of the wreckage and vectored out into the open. Taking advantage of the break in Kessler's pursuit, he steered himself down fast, to land on the soft soil. He had barely unbuckled the chute straps to run for cover behind the nearest boulder when the Raptor reappeared above the elevated horizon for another pass.

This time the F-22 dropped much lower, strafed Ryson's path with a dozen rounds—some missing him by mere inches—and then roared furiously back up to the sky and headed west, toward Tanaris.

TANARIS

The express elevator swiftly descended in its deep shaft, through yards of reinforced concrete and earth, to arrive at the Combat Center, the lowest accessible point in Tanaris. When its doors opened, a duo of heavily armed guards snapped to attention at the sight of their fierce base commander.

Colonel Gorik emerged from the elevator and headed swiftly for a platform of computer consoles that made up the heart of the combat center. Currently staffed by a crew of four, the deeply buried Cold War-era site, impervious to virtually all conventional attacks, was the wartime command and control center for the base. Gorik regarded the venue as his own personal Situation Room but had never imagined for facing one of his own aircraft.

"Display the defenses," he ordered.

"Yes sir," replied an operator.

A detailed layout of the airbase was projected onto the screen, with red dots highlighting elements of its integrated air defenses. Over two dozen fully automated anti-aircraft guns and surface-to-air missiles were displayed, enough fire power to decimate entire squadrons of hostile fighters, or one large bomber.

For this task, however, Gorik could realistically rely only on the guns. The SAM's radar wouldn't detect the stealth bomber until it was closer than their missiles' minimal range, but the guns had no such restrictions for killing a prey.

"Focus the search radars on the two canyons' entrances to the base," he said, knowing that the captain would opt for those routes to slither his way in, over a typical ground approach that would make him more visible to chase fighters.

Gorik smiled smugly at sight of the lethal fire power at his disposal to unleash at McDermott should he escape Kessler's grasp. It'd be a pleasure to personally vanquish the legendary captain and erase all traces of his re-entry to Tanaris.

To this end, hours ago he had dispatched all non-combat personnel on emergency leave, including the entire research & development teams, so to severely reduce the number of potential witnesses on the base.

"Radar set as you requested," the operator announced.

Gorik eyed the displayed images. "Good, keep all systems on full alert."

APPROACHING TANARIS

The wide control flaps along the SuperCOIL's trailing wing edges gracefully moved in a predetermined maneuvering pattern as McDermott changed course. He had altered his trail soon as Kessler vacated the arena to chase the F-16. The bomber ascended from the riverbed, crested a ridge near its starboard, and flew on a northwesterly heading for 3 more minutes before dropping into another valley.

Mindful of Kessler's prompt return following his hunt of the Falcon, McDermott had opted for a less conspicuous backup route, though at the expense of a delayed arrival at Tanaris.

But the delay did not concern the anguished captain. He measured his life like he would an unleashed missile, not in time units, but of miles remaining to the target—his destiny. And those miles, which once numbered in the thousands, now were coming tantalizingly close to zero.

Kessler visually scanned the skies in frustration but found no sign of the elusive bomber. The bold intrusion by the F-16 had temporarily stymied his plans, depriving him of a wingman while allowing McDermott to once more slip from his grasp. At least this time Kessler had made sure the Falcon wouldn't unexpectedly reappear. Kessler had been tempted to cause Ryson's death via bomb runs in the valley, but this distraction had already cost him enough time in his hunt for McDermott. He would capture Ryson later with a helicopter extraction team to be dispatched before Ryson could make it far on foot. Kessler had already come up with a plan for the lieutenant's perfect "accidental" death by the team.

Now, first and foremost, he needed to stop McDermott. Kessler wasn't about to waste precious fuel and time scouring the same valley where he had last encountered the captain. Instead, he focused on the only two viable inroads into Tanaris, which all valleys would eventually lead to in their approach. Exhilarated by the prospect of another encounter, he sent the F-22 past Mach 1 on supercruise toward the choke points on McDermott's route.

The digital console displaying the terrain contours, on which McDermott had traced his progress, warned that the watershed vale the bomber had slithered through for the past twenty minutes would soon come to an end.

Beyond that lay one of the only two valley approaches into Tanaris, the final leg of his journey. Soon the SuperCOIL arrived at the juncture, and McDermott set the craft to a climb as it crested its last ridge.

A massive boomerang-shaped flying body suddenly popped up along the portside of the Raptor's canopy, and a surprised Kessler beheld its demonic rise from the depths. He'd anticipated the bomber's imminent arrival to the area but had not expected it to be so furtive that it would catch him completely off guard.

The rising black beast then quickly leveled itself momentarily at about the same altitude as the Raptor. From that vantage point, the bomber appeared impossibly thin and razor sharp, even when viewed along the trailing wing edges. Then, just as swiftly, the ominous craft lowered its aquiline beak toward the next ravine, as if swooping on a spotted prey, and disappeared from view, submerged below the elevated desert landscape.

Kessler immediately rolled the Raptor to a sharply banked tight turn and emerged above the ravine. Gazing down the narrow passage, he saw that the SuperCOIL had already completed its dive to the valley floor and was aiming for Tanaris, like an impenetrably dark arrowhead.

Despite the ravine's high walls towering on both sides, McDermott resisted the temptation to turn on the Terrain Following Radar. Any radar emission, however localized, could prove fatal if detected.

"Miss me?" A sudden, ghastly but familiar voice, filled his helmet

It had been wishful thinking to imagine that Kessler would never find him, but his course adjustments had delayed it until his final approach to the target. He looked out the canopy, but the confining cliffs blocked his lateral views, then glanced at the aft close-range camera images and spotted the F-22, flying at his five o'clock, slightly below the raised crest-line.

"You'll have to excuse the brief delay," Kessler continued. "I had to take care of your little helper friend, Ian Ryson."

"Ryson?" McDermott asked, feeling genuine camaraderie toward the man.

"Yes, *was*. His carcass is now roasting with the rest of his plane," Kessler lied.

"You murderous bastard!" McDermott shouted.

"Don't worry. You two are about to be reunited—and you with your wife."

"All in good time," McDermott said calmly before flicking off the receiver.

Kessler regarded the curious remark as McDermott genuinely welcoming the prospect of joining his wife, a wish he was more than happy to grant the captain.

McDermott saw the Raptor sweep lower into the valley, the craft gaining speed in the descent, jockeying to enter the massive bomber's slip-stream, to obtain an infrared lock. It was a dicey proposition, the pilot trying to keep its cockpit above the bomber in a shielding effort. The captain let all his anguish drip off of him like water and reverted to his cold pilot self. He studied the F-22's movements and prepared to spend his last laser shot if the opportunity arose.

No longer apprehensive about his laser-depleted adversary, Kessler deftly piloted the F-22 toward the riverbed to steadily close in on the prize. The sun had cast the SuperCOIL an aft shadow, and from above, it looked like a pair of B-2s flying in perfect tandem formation. Only the slight wavering in the aft "plane" as it swept over rutted land made it appear to be the mere shadow it was. Within seconds, the Raptor attained level flight, forming its own tandem with the bomber at the optimal six o'clock position. It would soon be within the elusive IR range, and Kessler switched on the heat-seeker air-intercept missiles systems for firing.

He opted for missiles in the main weapons bay, realizing the reduced explosive loads in the new smaller Sidewinders in the Raptor's side bays might not do the trick against such a massive bomber. In anticipation of that problem, he had a pair of traditional Sidewinders mounted within the ventral bay, alongside his already-spent two AMRAAMs. The larger explosive packs in these infrared missiles could efficiently take care of the SuperCOIL. All he needed was a solid IR lock.

McDermott watched as the menacing Raptor crept closer. In just a few moments, it would come within the infrared acquisition range of the bomber unless McDermott could put more distance between them. With the three functioning engines already in full throttle, only one option remained for attaining higher speed, so he gunned the afterburners, hurtling the bomber forward.

When Kessler saw the trio of fire plumes shoot out from the SuperCOIL's engines, he smiled with great satisfaction. McDermott had committed his first blunder—and, perhaps, his last. The subsonic bomber still had no actual chance of outrunning a Mach-capable Raptor, but in relying on the afterburners the captain had tremendously increased its IR signature. Kessler now had the lock he had sought, even as the bomber pulled away. He quickly lined up the crosshairs aim on one of the bomber's two right engine ports and fired.

On command, the Raptor's ventral bay doors parted, the Vertical Eject Launcher readily jettisoned an AIM-9 Sidewinder into the open, and the doors set to close. The entire sequence would last just under three seconds.

But it was not fast enough.

At that instant, the *lock onto* signal suddenly flashed on Kessler's display, then followed by a seemingly impossible actual laser discharge. To his horror, he noticed it wasn't directed at the Raptor but at the just-launched missile. The weak laser shot, which had virtually no chance of penetrating the Raptor's titanium hull, easily struck the much lighter shielded Sidewinder.

The energy beam instantly pierced through the missile's outer shell, detonating the nearly 21 pounds of explosives in its Annular Blast Fragmentation warhead. In turn, the blast imparted immense momentum to the AIM-9's main destructive mechanism: a series of long metal rods laid around the missile's tubular core, like bullets in a revolver, hurtling them out synchronously in a pattern resembling a cylinder expanding in radius, which swiftly intersected the Raptor's ventral.

At such close proximity, the detonation was akin to the F-22 taking a direct hit from its own missile. Shards and rod fragments flew into the Raptor's innards from the open bay, tearing all in their path, and slicing through the airframe like razors.

The underbelly blow came like an uppercut punch. The F-22 involuntarily rolled to the right, veering out of control. Kessler, his face still harboring the frozen vestiges of a prematurely victorious grin, tried in vain to avert the inevitable.

In an instant, the Raptor smashed topside against one of the large protruding boulders in the canyon's walls. The force from nearly 70,000 lbs. of thrust tore out the fighter's titanium trapezoidal wings and large canted fins like cardboard and split the structurally compromised airframe in two in a burst of splintered metal.

The nose section bearing Kessler cart-wheeled forward at half a football field's length before glancing off an enormous rock. The impact shattered the gold-tinted canopy and sent the nose section tumbling hundreds of feet into the dried riverbed.

It wasn't until the SuperCOIL had flown clear of the propelled debris from the exploding F-22 that McDermott let out a sigh of relief. His risky stratagem in keeping the Raptor above the SuperCOIL had paid off.

Only from that angle, could the F-22's sole weakness—its parting bomb bay doors and briefly exposed innards—be targeted, and by flying at ground level, McDermott had ensured that Kessler could not fire a missile from any other angle.

The designers of the F-22 had known of this Achilles' heel, but they had minimized its importance because the portal's parting sequence would last less than three seconds. Even if a radar acquired it, no conventional launched projectile could reach the F-22 before losing track of it once the portals had shut. This had not taken into account the light-speed swiftness of an airborne laser-beam weapon, which had not existed during most of the Raptor's decades-long development.

Having disposed of the last of his aerial hurdles, McDermott disengaged the afterburners, which he had intentionally used to provide Kessler with the needed IR lock to launch his missile. He now turned his full attention toward his ultimate destination, the Tanaris airbase.

Inside the crumpled mass of twisted metal and instruments that had been the Raptor's cockpit, Kessler lay immobilized. Despite narrowly avoiding instant death, he was unable to move a limb, and his head rested listlessly on his left shoulder, his skull fractured. His right leg and arm had been smashed against the side-panels by the violent impact. Half his rib cage had caved in, puncturing his lungs, and he was coughing up blood spurts.

The severe pain that shot through his torso manifested the extent of his internal injuries; he winced taking even the shallowest of breaths. And copious blood was draining in numerous warm rivulets, pooling into his flight suit and helmet.

His life was rapidly ebbing, and he knew it would not be long before terminal darkness shrouded him, yet it all seemed to transpire excruciatingly slow, giving him ample time to anguish on McDermott's having bested him again, one last time.

NEAR THE F-16 CRASH SITE

Ian Ryson emerged from behind the protection of the large rock soon after the sky had cleared from the aerial menace. He dusted off his flight suit, then walked toward the riverbed, as he took in the scenery.

In the distant foothills, the Falcon's aflame carcass billowed a thick plume of smoke, which he feared served as a mile-high beacon to a Tanaris search team.

Following years of flight work around Tanaris, Ryson had come to know these locales fairly well. He recalled flying over a road in the final leg of the chase, and reckoned he was just few miles northeast of the motorway. Before long, he arrived at the valley's mouth and into a barren steppe stretching in the distance, still some hours walk from the road. That gave him time to think through recent events.

Somehow it did not all add up.

Both McDermott and Gorik had acted suspiciously. While captive in the Azores, McDermott had been violently erratic, causing Ryson to take seriously his threat to shoot down civilian airliners. Later, during his flight to Tanaris, Gorik had openly allowed him to read on the grisly details of the F-18's encounter fight with the SuperCOIL over the Atlantic, an account Ryson found horrifying.

It seemed that both deeds were intended to persuade him to recommend Operation Gold to the president, as if a main goal shared by both McDermott and Gorik in virtually collusive efforts to sway Ryson. It was also clear now that McDermott had never intended to attack NORAD or down civilian airliners, but instead having Tanaris and Gorik in his crosshairs the entire time.

All these details coalesced to one burning question in his mind: why would two men with such opposing views both choose to activate Gold, especially when one was sure to die as a result, and before having exacted his revenge on the other?

TANARIS

In a flight course far from any civilian airliners or airports he was accused of so wantonly threatening, Captain McDermott deftly piloted his stealthy plane on its final leg of a journey toward Gorik's black base. As he glanced at his wife's photograph on the clipboard strapped to his right leg, McDermott could almost sense the conclusion of his terminal trek, the fruition of years of agony and patient planning. He caressed her with his gaze, knowing soon he could be with her again.

In front, the towering canyon walls abruptly parted, giving way to the relative openness of the Tanaris crater. He had arrived.

Gorik keenly watched the large display screen fed with outside images as the massive dark frame of the SuperCOIL came into full view, emerging from the winding canyon entrance like a thing infernal. When he spotted no chase F-22, he knew McDermott had expectedly dispensed with Kessler. Over time, Gorik had grown increasingly weary of his ruthlessly ambitious second-in-command, in whom he apprehensively saw too much of himself in ascending through the ranks.

All things considered, McDermott had unwittingly spared the colonel a few tough decisions by disposing of both McCane and Kessler. The SuperCOIL was a juggernaut in front of which Gorik had tossed all his problems while holding the key to its destruction for the very end. That the plane and the vengefulness of its pilot were both his own creations was not lost on him. It was simply time to dispose of his creations, towards realization of his grand ascendancy plans.

With that thought, he switched on the IADs, setting into motion the over two-dozen fully automated anti-aircraft guns of the airbase's integrated air defense system. At such close range, one of IAD's powerful radar sweeps managed to track faint returns from the ABL-inflicted blast cavity beneath the bomber. The system then automatically directed all other guns to zero in on the general coordinates locked onto by the radar.

The locked-on signal flashed, and Gorik grinned. Looking at the main view screen, he beheld the avenging craft, piloted over five thousand miles to this base. He placed his right index finger on the trigger. "Welcome home, brother," he said, then fired. Instantly, a dozen gun encampments burst to life, sending hundreds of rounds of ammunition skyward toward the black flying apparition.

McDermott beheld the formidable spectacle as the sky erupted in a hailstorm of bullets. The bomber absorbed a series of salvos, followed by a brief silence before it was locked onto again. Taking full advantage of the airfoil's resistance to anti-aircraft fire, he succeeded in deftly maneuvering out of continuous radar lock by exposing the plane's stealthier sides to each tracking radar, a strategy that intermittently paused their gunfire as the bomber approached its target.

Nonetheless, the inflicted damage was punishing, and the plane's systems were in danger of failing. He could feel the drumming of AAA shells pounding into his craft, tearing away at the stealth coating, enabling radars to relock more quickly.

But they were too late.

As the headquarters' main building came into view, McDermott knew that Gorik would be hiding in its subterranean bunker.

The expansive bomber needed to reach a point precisely above the bunker, though the surrounding buildings prevented any traditional target-run approaches at low angles. In a flash of inspiration, and a sudden surge of exhilaration coursing through his body, McDermott utilized the full power of his three remaining engines and set the bomber to a tight curved near upright climb. The kneading g-force mounted as the bomber shot skyward. It then passed to the top of the arch, flying inverted for a split second at its zenith, like a roller coaster in a sharp loop, before hurtling straight down in a vertical swoop, toward the crater.

He now faced the roof of the headquarters building. The gun placements atop the edifice swiveled upward, obtained their lock with ease, and began vertically firing their barrage of bullets. A salvo of 40mm bullets tore through the cockpit panes. One hit McDermott on the right shoulder, shattering his collar bone. Others tore into his rib cage and pierced his stomach and right lung. Blood gushed from his punctured pressure suit. But it no longer mattered to him.

Even before he had prepared for his final descent, his thoughts had shifted elsewhere, as if dissolved into the past. And so he failed to fully experience the pain from his wounds. Only the final button secured beneath his finger still mattered. In his semi-conscious state, he pressed it. The computer calculated impact at five seconds. It was done.

He gazed out a last time, the massive headquarters building had now simply vanished, replaced in his mind by the image of his beautiful wife. She stood before him in all her glory, with outstretched arms, ready for an eternal embrace.

The bomber sliced down from the heavens like a fifty-ton scimitar. Its slim width had little trouble passing between the edifices on its precise pre-calculated route, all the way to base of the headquarters' building, and zeroing in right atop the bunker. The instant the bomber's muzzle made contact with the unforgiving pavement, a tremendous explosion ensued: first a bright flash, then an abundant outpouring of X-rays, followed by an enormous billowing mushroom cloud of white smoke, all uncharacteristic aftermaths to the crash of an out of fuel plane. The flames rose high to above the crater's rim, but not before the massive nuclear blast leveled every structure of consequence on the base.

Tanaris's natural crater walls amplified the blast's effect by bouncing its shockwaves and confining much of the thermal radiation. The crater's depression, a feature meant to protect the base from a weapon landing outside its rim, was now intensifying the effects of the one that had fallen within it. In mere seconds, the nuclear fireball expanded throughout the crater, reducing to cinders everything in its path. Buried beneath the conflagration lay the glowing rubble of a destroyed bunker and the vaporized remains of its murderous base commander.

SITUATION ROOM

"We're all ears, Lieutenant," the president said to start the meeting with Ryson, Norton and Fleisler, who had arrived just a few minutes earlier.

Ryson appeared justifiably exhausted, after his long desert trek. He had hitched a ride to a civilian airport and arranged for eventual transport to the capital for this meeting. He took his seat at the large table, pulled one of his own reports marked Top Secret from his briefcase, and read it aloud at the president's request.

"In the explosion's aftermath, the all-encompassing fireball obliterated Tanaris and vaporized the SuperCOIL, but with negligible damage to the surrounding area as the bomb was designed for a highly localized blast. With no vestiges to offer us clues, the cause of the nuclear detonation at the moment of the SuperCOIL's impact remains unknown. But McDermott's hand in it appears extremely likely."

"We know all that already," Norton said impatiently. "Get to the point."

Ryson cleared his throat, then continued. "One question, however, remains unanswered: how did McDermott manage to detonate the WT-100 self-destruct nuclear device onboard the SuperCOIL? It strikes me as implausible that it was just a coincidence. Without an explosion of such magnitude, his plan would have been useless, as neither the plane's airframe nor its laser weaponry could have so completely destroyed the bunker's virtually impenetrable concrete shielding."

"How do we know he was actually targeting the bunker?" Fleisler asked.

"Due to the WT-100's limited yield, only a precise delivery would have done the job. But what triggered the nuclear explosion at that precise moment? The force of the impact could not have caused it. A proper arming sequence was needed."

"The self-destruct code," Norton surmised.

"No," Fleisler said emphatically. "There had been no satellite transmissions of the self-destruct code since the plane was somewhere desolate over the Atlantic."

"McDermott re-wired the bomb to bypass the code sequence?" Norton guessed.

"That's impossible!" Fleisler interjected. "The WT-100 circuitry is tamper-proof. And the captain had virtually no training on nuclear weaponry."

"McDermott didn't need to go those routes," Ryson said calmly. "His success lay entirely with his timing."

"What are you getting at?" the president said. "Enough with the riddles."

"There is only one logical explanation: McDermott succeeded in disengaging the bomb's code-receptor module from its detonation mechanism, in the Azores."

Norton raised a skeptical eyebrow, "so the self-destruct code we sent didn't make it to the detonator to destroy the plane over the Atlantic?"

"Yes," Ryson replied. "But he must have used one of the plane's data-gathering instruments to record that code. Then at the precise moment over Tanaris, he released the recorded code into the self-destruct circuitry to detonate."

"Good God! And it worked!" exclaimed Norton. "The resourceful bastard!"

Fleisler shook his head in amazement. "That's why he revealed his intentions to Ryson and, later, his general whereabouts. He prompted us to rashly call for the SuperCOIL's destruction at a location that wouldn't hurt anyone else."

"We gave him the code," Norton concluded. "That's what he was really after."

"I was used," Ryson remarked sheepishly. "McDermott was superb, not just as a pilot, but also in making everyone play into his hand. Colonel Gorik proved no exception." Looking around, he saw that no one was inclined to dispute his claim.

"But why would he do such a vengeful thing?" Fleisler said, turning to Ryson.

"Out of a sense of duty," the lieutenant replied.

"Sense of *duty*?" Norton said.

"Yes sir. He believed that no one else could have brought Gorik to true justice or interfere with his insatiable ambitions."

The president's shoulders slumped noticeably. He silently agreed with Ryson's assessment, and regretted having given in to the colonel's thinly-veiled political blackmail threats, and was profoundly grateful that this evil influence was no more.

"Deceitful Gorik took us all for a ride," Norton said, seething. In his hand he held the testimony of the lone surviving F-15 pilot, now recovering in the hospital, which verified that F-22s, not a laser, had downed his F-15 squadron over the Gulf.

"And what you saw was just the tip of the iceberg," Ryson added. He produced a memory stick from his pocket. It contained duplicate backups of data in the one Gorik had destroyed in Tanaris.

Ryson displayed the materials on the view screen as others watched. With each page, their faces exhibited more consternation, especially as to ones that described other incidents staged by Gorik, including the killing of McDermott's wife.

"We can find additional corroborating evidence in our databases in time," Fleisler said. "And your displayed information can serve as our guide."

"Very well, proceed then," the president said. "Anything else?"

"How do we ensure that nothing like this happens again?" Ryson boldly asked.

The president looked at Norton. "The General will lead the Black Squadron till further notice. He'll be tasked to find it a new home, weed out unsavory elements, and recruit new members. Whatever it takes to restore the squadron's integrity."

Ryson nodded, then turned to the president. "Permission to speak freely, sir."

"Granted. What's on your mind, son?"

"Be as honest as you can," Fleisler added. "We're going to need it."

"What troubles me is how this whole situation got started," Ryson said. "Makes me wonder are there other black projects that could fall into the wrong hands."

"We've thought of exactly that possibility, Lieutenant," the president said. "We've created a new post: Inspector of Black-Classified Programs, tasked to visit all such sites, unfettered access and report his findings directly to the president."

"Sounds like a hell of job, sir."

"Sure is," Norton added, "and it requisites a person of utmost integrity."

"Looks like you'll have a long interview process ahead of you," Ryson replied.

"Typically, yes," the president said. "But in this case, we've made our choice."

"Who sir?"

The president smiled warmly. "You, Lieutenant."

Ryson's jaw dropped slightly. Normally, such an offer would have thrilled anyone—and him, especially. But these weren't normal circumstances. A storm was coming, with severe political fallout. For now, the events were under wraps. Tanaris's remoteness and restricted access had shielded the devastation from outside observers. The small nuclear detonation was registered only as low-energy ground rumblings on distant seismographs, and most of the radiation dissipated by the winds. The loss of such facility, however, would soon be discovered. And though via elaborate cover-ups, no outsider might come to know of McDermott's deed, or the extent of the president's political short-sightedness regarding Gorik's conduct, a general picture of the events would emerge, drawing considerable media coverage. It would, at the very least, be seen as gross military oversight that would ultimately befall on the shoulders of the commander in chief.

While confident in his own ability to carry out the responsibilities of the post, Ryson suspected that such a position was, at least in part, a political attempt by the president to mitigate the Tanaris disaster by presenting preventive measures. It would be woefully insufficient, however, and he doubted that this president would be granted a second term the following year.

Yet that wasn't Ryson's primary concern. "I am humbled by your offer, sir," he replied, "but I will have to respectfully decline."

"Come again?" the president said, rather unbelieving.

"I cannot accept the position," Ryson repeated.

"Why in the world not, son?" Fleisler asked, looking as puzzled as the others.

"I have my reasons," Ryson replied boldly, his thoughts shifting to Kathleen, a life for which he had waited over a decade. He wasn't about to let anything keep him from that life now, not even an offer from the President of the United States.

"That is all I can say," he concluded, and with such conviction that no questions ensued. What followed was an understanding expression from the commander in chief, who turned with disappointment to his advisors. In that moment, the lieutenant found himself pitying the world's most powerful man.

Ryson shut his briefcase and stood. Encountering no objections, he nodded a collective salute to all, and with a sense of great relief, exited the Situation Room.

EPILOGUE

The gentle breeze off the Pacific Ocean made the palm trees' fronds sway lazily, as the open-top convertible cruised down the coastal highway. Ian Ryson checked the rearview mirror before shifting the sports car to higher gear, briefly rattling the scuba equipment drying in the back seat.

"What a great day!" Kathleen remarked, leaning against the headrest as the warm wind caressed her hair. "I wish every day was like this."

"Count on many more such trips," Ryson said, smiling at her.

She nodded with a slight chin movement, then placed her left hand on his thigh. Through his shaded glasses, Ryson caught the glint off the diamond on her finger. He had proposed to her the night before, on the second day of their vacation.

"I should have done this a long a time ago," he said, placing his large hand over her delicate one.

"You did it when the time was right. That's what matters in the end."

His proposal had caught her pleasantly off guard, enhancing its thrill. Ryson was overjoyed to have done what he had yearned to for seemingly an eternity.

"It might sound paradoxical, but it was because of my love for you that I waited so long. I care about your safety more than anything else in the world," he told her.

"I know. I didn't understand that earlier, but I do now."

"I should have been stronger," he said.

She glanced at him. "You're plenty strong now."

Ryson did not reply.

"Will those nightmares ever get the better of my future husband again?" she playfully asked, gently squeezing his hand.

The question evoked many grim, anguished memories, but most of all, those of McDermott. It was tragic how the legendary aviator's life had turned out, but Ryson would always cherish what had once been the good in the departed captain. He owed it to the man who had saved his life to not let his advice on facing adversity with fortitude to fall on the wayside. All the fear and despair exited his mind, as if they now belonged to another man.

"No," he smiled, feeling a supreme confidence wash over him, "they're gone, forever."

He pressed on the accelerator, the sleek vehicle moving even faster along the strip of asphalt that seemed to vanish into the glorious evening sky—the most breathtakingly beautiful sunset he had ever seen.

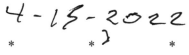

* * *

Dear Reader:

Thank you for reading my novel. If you enjoyed it, would you be so kind as to leave a review or a star rating for it on Amazon? It would be greatly appreciated!

Sincerely,
Robert Ari